ANGEL
LOVES
NOBODY

·

·

RICHARD MILES

·

PRENTICE-HALL, INC.
ENGLEWOOD CLIFFS, N. J.

c. 2

Angel Loves Nobody by Richard Miles
© 1967 by G. R. Perreau-Saussine

Library of Congress Catalog Card Number: 67-16379

Printed in the United States of America

T   03682

PRENTICE-HALL INTERNATIONAL, INC., *London*
PRENTICE-HALL OF AUSTRALIA, PTY. LTD., *Sydney*
PRENTICE-HALL OF CANADA, LTD., *Toronto*
PRENTICE-HALL OF INDIA PRIVATE LTD., *New Delhi*
PRENTICE-HALL OF JAPAN, INC., *Tokyo*

Author's Note: Despite certain street and place names
used in this book, Betsy Ross Junior High is entirely
imaginary, as is its staff, teachers, and student body. No
reference is intended to any living or dead person ever
encountered, or any school named after the little uphol-
sterer of Arch Street.

To Errol Jacobs, Teacher, *sine qua non*

Acknowledgments:

ANGEL LOVES NOBODY was the recipient of the
First Prize in the 1966 Samuel Goldwyn Awards, pre-
sented at the University of California, Los Angeles.
Judges were Robert E. Lee, Daniel Taradash, Colin
Young, and Bradford Booth. The author gratefully
acknowledges the suggestions that were incorporated
into the book, and the debt he owes Thomas Nielsen,
H. Maxwell Levy, George Savage, Sr., and the Ed
Leavitt Company.

A terrifying plot to execute school
officials at a slum school in California
is uncovered by Mr. Nielsen, the substitute art teacher.

• **ONE** •

The scraps of paper blew against the chain-link, rust-
proof fence and were trapped, vibrating in the wind angrily, struggling against the unbendable alloy mesh in
their efforts to break away. As he walked through the gate
marked TEMPORARY PARKING—FACULTY ONLY, Tim Nielsen was thinking, this is like a gauntlet. He did not own a
car, but for convenience he went through the auto gate
anyway. It shortened the distance to the administration
building by several hundred welcome yards, a whole half
minute less of being stared at by the students.

Avoiding the supplies truck parked half-in and half-out
of the gate, he nodded to the first face he recognized, the
senior head custodian, Jack something-or-other. The de-
ceptively young-looking Negro was supervising the un-
loading of the truck, as Tim picked his way through the
haphazard jumble of faculty and administration cars. It
was an irony that of all the schools, Betsy Ross Junior High
would have such a lot, however temporary, because of red
tape on the financing of a new building that had been
scheduled for construction on the cleared site. Although
the students were not permitted near the faculty cars, he

1

knew that he had been spotted by some of the stragglers
heading slowly for their classes in the administration
building. Word got around fast. He supposed he would be
a considerable curiosity for a while.

Taking a deep breath, Tim stepped off the safety island
of the dirt parking lot, and plunged in. As he walked along
the cement path, he tried to think of other things, of the
delicate grey color of the path, the loamy, recently turned
soil that was apparently being prepared for some kind of
new planting. He tried to preserve a neutrally agreeable
expression on his face as he passed groups of kids, clustered
in various social pyramids of status and intelligence, race
and sex. Girls with other girls, boys with boys of the same
or similar dark color.

A very small Mexican boy and a slightly larger, similar-
looking boy that Tim thought he remembered from one of
his classes watched him pass without expression. Then the
older boy, whose name was John Valdes, whispered to his
little brother Tio. The boy nodded, and took off at a full
run as Tim continued to think of the dark, soggy February
skies, the slant of early morning sun on the rows of windows, anything at all except the faces that were watching
him like a succession of well-thumbed copper pennies.

As he walked past, unconsciously quickening his pace as
he approached the Ad building, the students interrupted
their own conversations and studied him, their faces as
neutral as his own.

" 'morning, Mr. Nielsen," said a tall thin girl with a
birthmark covering one side of her face.

"Good morning." Tim tried to remember the girl's
name. He had her in fourth period Art Service, and had

not heard two words out of her until that moment. After only four full teaching days, this was some kind of breakthrough: an unsolicited good morning, his first. According to a pipesmoking, wheyfaced English teacher named Janis, it would probably be several weeks before certain unpopular students would try to make points by greeting him without being greeted first. Tim smiled. So much for that tall pipesmoker.

Starting up the steps of Administration, Tim noticed the engraved cornerstone for the first time: *In Beauty and Pride—Hon. N. B. Poulson 1949.* It was barely ten minutes past eight by his watch. It was a sturdy, suitably conventional American-made watch given to him by equally sturdy and conventional parents. They were sorry he was not going into the family dry-cleaning business, but relieved that he was going to work, instead of just painting and living on what his dad called "the dole." Teaching, even on the Junior High School level, and even a subject as useless as art, seemed to have solidity to it. If they only knew, thought Tim as he went into the building.

He hesitated in front of the principal's office. The lettering on the opaque glass door read "William J. Conrad," with the "D" in the principal's last name scratched out and replaced with a pale pink nail-polish "T." Tim's appointment with Mr. "Conrat" was at 8:00 A.M. He was exactly a minute early, which seemed to strike a nice balance between seeming eager and being late.

"Go on, man, Rat don't bite."

Startled, Tim turned and saw a slender boy with a solemn, handsome Mexican face. Tim frowned.

"My name is *Mr. Nielsen.*"

"I know. I got you first period," said the boy. "My name is Angel."

Angel. Tim remembered several students in his first period class with that name. There were a handful of Juans and Jesuses, and two Angels, neither of which he could recall marking absent, even though he had never seen this particular boy before. Looking into the long-lashed, intelligent eyes, Tim had the sensation that he was being judged and found wanting. He did not like the way insolence in this boy had somehow subsided into an unwary self-confidence.

"Don't worry none about Rat," said Angel. "He ain't bad. He just thinks he is."

Tim chose to ignore this. "If you're in my first period then, Angel, I'll see you in a few minutes." Tim tried a smile, but in the face of that stony appraisal it did not quite come off.

Angel nodded. "I guess you will. I got you sixth period too."

"Better start coming to class, Angel," said Tim.

"Wouldn't miss it," said the boy. He gave Tim one last look, and turned to join several others who had appeared as if from nowhere at the end of the hall. They were plainly waiting for Angel; as he walked right past they fell into step behind.

A dark-skinned boy with oriental eyes in his otherwise Spanish face bounced his fist lightly off Angel's shoulder as they rounded the corner, out of sight of the new, unexpected teacher. With an impatient gesture Angel signaled him quiet as two girls walked past, books under their slender arms, swinging their hips together in their cotton dresses. Angel ignored them, although they aimed their smiles at him. A stocky, eagerfaced boy looked back at them over his shoulder, giving a jump to fall into step with Angel.

"They know, Angel," he said. "Jennifer's name starts with a B, and Concha's . . ."

"Shut up," said Angel, making Jesus-Maria's eager face fall. Although he had turned fourteen, Jesus-Maria Ortiz seemed several years younger than the other A-9s because of his size.

"I don't want to talk in the hall," said Angel, more kindly. He knew how personal Jesus-Maria took everything. The oriental-looking boy, whose name was Ismael, cuffed him again lightly, trying to get his attention.

"Hey, man, what do you think of him?" he said, meaning the new teacher. Angel shrugged, supremely unimpressed.

"He don't look bad to me. He won't make no difference at all."

• • •

William Jeffreys Conrad was a florid, pink-faced man in his middle fifties, whose comfortable, drawling manner of speech suggested he had recently come from the deep South. In fact, he had lived in Los Angeles for nearly thirty years, half of which time he had been principal of various city schools.

"Well, Nielsen, how do you like the school?" He smiled inwardly at the cautious expression that crossed Tim's face. "I do suppose," he went on, "that it's a mite early to say.

You've only been with us a few days, isn't it? Did you get your faculty handbook from Miss Peters?"

"Yes, sir. Uh, four days today, sir."

The principal frowned worriedly. "Four days? That long? I would have liked to have greeted you a little sooner, but there's been a Human Relations Conference downtown, and I guess I qualify as the man on the spot for certain kinds of non-English-speaking minority problems —you understand. Sometimes we get a little behind schedule." He smiled in a way to suggest that he could criticize himself, and his school, with no hard feelings. Then his face turned serious. "And of course we weren't expecting —well, we were all very sorry about Muggeridge." He tried to convey his regret over the sudden demise of Tim's predecessor.

"It's been all right, sir." Tim shifted uneasily on the hard wood seat. "I know how busy you are."

"Well, nice to see you and all that, Muggeridge notwithstanding. I'm not sorry to see good young blood come into the school, and I'm sure you'll do just fine. I don't need to tell a bright young fellow like you that there will be a lot of things around here that you won't like."

"No, sir."

"You'll take steps, and find activities that are both useful and interesting, depending on your ingenuity and energy. Sometimes, if you're lucky, they'll work, and if not, well, a sense of humor is your best friend around here, son."

"I'll remember, sir." There was something about this man that he disliked, but it was not necessarily because of the principal's personality. Tim was aware that there was a considerable part of himself that automatically distrusted authority. The irony of his undertaking to become an authority figure had not escaped him.

William Conrad had wearied of gazing into Tim's blue eyes, with so little return. Why were they all the same, these new teachers? Why should a handsome young man be so guarded, so unadventuresome. He sighed, and turned his attention to the drawer of his huge, scarred desk. "I see from your file that you've a class in a few minutes." Conrad tilted his head up to squint through the bottom of his bifocals. "I'll make it brief, for both our sakes. Betsy Ross Junior High, as you can't have failed to notice, is a school in what I would term a less than privileged area." He smiled. "That makes you a less than privileged art teacher, and me a less than privileged warden." He combined his merriment with a phlegmy cough that made him reach for his handkerchief.

Tim forced himself to show an amusement he did not feel. He had not wanted to be a long-term sub for the semester, but his indecisiveness at the beginning of the term had settled it. Did this pink-faced clown actually think that he would have come to Betsy Ross if he had had any real choice? Tim decided to try a mildly optimistic, "So far, sir, I've found my classes pretty quiet and willing."

"They're testing you, son. They may do nothing for a while, and then *blooey!*" He did not specify what might be involved in the blooey, but the gesture of his small, well-manicured hands suggested a mushroom cloud. "Your classes are ninety percent Mexican and Negro. They're bussing in a few Anglos, but they're mostly the kids of liberals who are all too painfully aware of the earthshaking significance of what they are doing." The sarcastic inflection on his last words was particularly galling.

"And of course," he went on vaguely, as though he had lost his train of thought, "there will be other little odds and ends. As a blue-eyed, blond Dane—I take it you're a Dane with a name like Nielsen—" He had a sudden thought. "You don't have anything to do with the TV ratings, do you?"

Tim assured him that he did not.

"Good enough. If there's anything I can't stand it's a rich teacher. We had one once, and he thought he was the principal." He stopped for his joke to be appreciated, and when it was not, went on without hard feelings. "As a blue-eyed blond you will find most of your students stand-offish at first, except for certain young girls who'll be just too friendly for comfort"—he smiled confidentially—"unless you go for that sort of thing." He laughed crooningly to show he was only kidding. Tim nodded, determined not to look away from that open mouth.

"I've been warned about that, sir."

"You'll find that the faculty sticks pretty much together, son. For protection, I do believe. Seriously, you'll find them a pretty fine bunch. They keep their best friends right by their sides at all times."

"Their senses of humor," said Tim.

"That is right. I think you are going to do just fine yourself, son, if you keep in mind, 'Ever faithful, in Black and Gold . . .'"

"I beg your pardon, sir?"

"That's the beginning of the school song."

Tim heard the bell ring, and felt a sudden panic at the thought that he would be late. He could picture the class in an uproar, unsupervised, and a resultant black mark against himself. He shifted uneasily in the chair, but Conrad riveted him with a stare over the top of his round reading spectacles, which he had produced after a time-consuming, muttering search. Getting desperate, Tim cleared his throat, wondering if he should just stand up.

"I don't like to rush, sir, but I have a class."

"Just one more thing, son." William Conrad drawled, reaching into his desk drawer and producing a thick, battered loose-leaf binder which he put directly in front of Tim. "You can keep this as long as you need it—a week or so—Make any notes you need for yourself on your particular students. I'm not giving this to you to scare you, or fill you with any untidy compassions, just to help you out. If you are forewarned, son, you can avoid trouble with certain students."

"Trouble, sir?"

"Who to keep an eye on, in other words." Conrad extended his hand cordially, after wiping it surreptitiously on a clean section of his handkerchief. Interviews of this sort always made him a little nervous. Gladly, Tim got to his feet.

"Thank you very much, sir."

"You're welcome at Ross, son. If you need or want anything, try Miss Peters in my office, or Miss Twigg, and if they can't help, my door is always open."

As he walked past the Miss Peters in question, Tim was favored with one of her patented wintry smiles. He had been assured that under the exterior there was at the very least a heart of pewter, but it was quite an exterior. Miss Peters was in her late fifties, but she dyed her hair raven black, and kept it in an all-too-recent style. There was a faint mauve tinge to her pallor, reflecting in pastel, watery blue eyes. Or perhaps it was the other way around, Tim thought, and her eyes lent color to her skin, wrinkled like a carefully uncrumpled ball of ladylike violet air mail stationery.

"How did it go, Mr. Nielsen?" the secretary asked, smiling, her scarlet lipstick melting into the tiny wrinkles. Tim smiled back, not realizing that her friendliness was directed at the world in general. The following day she was to fly to New Orleans for the funeral of a much disliked older brother. She regarded it as an unexpected vacation.

In answer to her question, Tim held up the loose-leaf binder with a shrug. "I have a night's reading to do," he smiled, and the principal's secretary nodded her sympathetic understanding.

Once he was out the door, Tim knew that he was already more than a few minutes late, but he could not resist glancing into the folder as he walked quickly along the hall, toward the staircase. The folder seemed to be full of legal-sized reports on onionskin with headings like "Supplemental Petition" and "Probation Officer's Report."

Under the name, MARIA ESTRAGON, he saw something that caught his attention: " . . . two year old boy, Guadalupe, living at same address, born at Mother's age twelve, sired by own father currently at Atascadero (See Separate

Clinical on Father). Child currently being cared for by Stepmother."

Sired by own father. For a moment Tim did not understand, and then suddenly he did. Atascadero was the facility for sexual psychopaths, and convicted sex criminals ordered there by the court.

As he came to his classroom he was carrying the loose-leaf binder as though it were an injured animal. The room, as he entered, was ominously quiet, but Tim was so caught up in his thougths of Maria Estragon that he noticed neither his students, nor the slender, unprepossessing man who was seated patiently at his desk, chewing on a pale mustache. Until the man stood up with a relieved smile, Tim did not realize that he had been sent to supervise the class until he, Tim, arrived.

"I'm Will Willson." The earnestly blinking eyes and somehow foreign-looking hair were exactly the same burnt toast color as his tweed suit. Tim thought he could detect a trace of English accent as the man continued, "Conrad told me to take your class. Conference period, you know, for me. Got a bit of work done."

"Well thank you, that was very nice," said Tim, thinking that the principal had tried on purpose to make him sweat about being late, even as he was arranging cover.

Willson was collecting his papers from the top of the desk as Tim looked over the class. The students were watching the two teachers closely as Tim became aware of the bulky folder under his arm. Hastily, he stuffed it with difficulty into his shamefully new briefcase.

"Thanks again," said Tim, pulling out his roll book as

Willson waved away his gratitude and left. Tim could not bring himself to say *Good morning, class,* so he simply cleared his throat self-consciously and started reading the roll.

"Maria Valdes, Jesus Contreras, Concha Douvan, Rico Moreno, Angel Martine . . ." Tim read the names off quickly, without looking at the class. Each name called was duly followed by a *Here!* or *Present,* and he marked 100% at the bottom of the page, for his own edification. There were twenty-six names on the roll, and a glance told him that twenty-six were not present.

New teacher, lame teacher; until he gets wise, a good time to cut. What had his predecessor, the famous and lamented Muggeridge, done in such a case? Until they knew the students by name most new teachers might not do anything at all. It was too much trouble, even though attendance was compulsory, affecting the number of assigned teachers, affecting everything in an imposing spiral of local school funds, state funds, salaries for personnel, counselors, God knows who else, supplemental national funds for poverty areas, perhaps even the congressional budget for education and the Dodgers' batting averages. He had been told, in great detail, but he had forgotten the exact reason Here was such an important word.

" . . . Ismael Sato, Provencia Perez . . ."

The ones who had consented to attend were studying Tim. He told himself that he was as unfamiliar to them as they were to him. He tried to put Maria Estragon and her baby out of his mind so he could concentrate on which name went with which face.

"Billy Wilson."

"Here."

"Tommy Ishi."

"Here."

At least the ones present were paying attention. "Here." "Here." "Here." The art supplies had to be distributed, and Tim was uncertain whom he should single out for the honor, or, as it might be, the disgrace. It brought him an all too vivid memory of his first days as a student teacher, when he had not even known how to pass out papers. Seventy pitiless eyes were watching, relishing every wrong move.

His glance around the class stopped more than briefly on Angel Martine, the boy who had talked to him outside the principal's office. There was something in the boy's face that Tim did not like, although Angel put up a good front of paying respectful attention, and even smiled, as if at some private joke. Tim was aware of an unnatural amount of silence as he went to the table to unlock the supply cabinet. He picked out twenty-six large sheets of paper and twenty-six carbon pencils.

Starting at the first of the seven large drafting tables that served as community easels, Tim began to distribute the paper and pencils himself, talking at the same time.

"I'm damned if I remember any of your names, so anytime you answer one of my questions, or ask me one, start by saying, 'I am,' and tell who you are. At the moment you all look alike." There was absolutely no reaction to what he had intended as a little joke. Tim cleared his throat uncomfortably, and had trouble swallowing. "I guess nobody will report me for saying damn in class, unless he or she wants to flunk."

Tim handed a pencil and sheet of paper to the boy called Angel, and was preparing to move on.

"I am Angel Martine. Thanks." Angel's voice was like a thunderclap in the silent room. For a moment Tim was surprised; then he grinned, inspiring Jennifer Baily in the rear of the class to whisper, "He's cute," too audibly. Tim ignored it as he addressed Angel.

"You are welcome, Angel, I'm sure."

"I should be. I pay your salary."

Tim was stunned, but the insult had been delivered without inflection, with no suggestion of anything more than a simple declaration of fact. Most of the rest of the period Tim spent talking more rapidly than was natural, about the use of supplies, about the ceramic plates they would design, about the care of wet clay. While he was talking, he was considering Angel, wondering if he had been wrong not to have thrown him out of the room immediately.

"Today I'm going to let you draw anything you want on this big piece of paper. That means some of you will sit and stare, and others will make a lot of lines that don't look like anything, and some of you will mess around because it's so stupid, and some of you"—He directed this last at Angel—"some of you will try to make a picture."

Tim finished distributing the papers and pencils, and looked at the leftovers wryly.

"Just for the record, according to the roll there are twenty-six of you here, and only seventeen pieces of paper are being used."

There was a thin smile on Angel's face. Ismael, the cheerful, half-oriental with eyes like watermelon seeds,

seemed to be sharing secret merriment with him, and with
any of the other boys who would catch his eye.

"In a way it's a good thing there are so few of you here,"
Tim was saying, "since we've only got seven drafting
tables. You can let your buddies know they are doing us a
favor, and it won't show up until I mark report cards."

There was no stir, so Tim talked and talked and talked
until he heard the bell. As one of the brighter students, the
boy called Ismael knew that the new teacher did not know
what he was talking about with the report cards.

Angel just smiled, thinking how it was just the new
teacher's bad luck that Mr. Muggeridge had died of a heart
attack.

● ● ●

His throat dry, Tim went straight to the faculty room
after class, with the uncomfortable feeling that he was
running away. The first few days had involved demonstrating what materials would be used, and how to use them so
as to avoid waste as much as possible. The whole idea of
waste was a little ridiculous—he had seen thousands of
those yellow sheets—but he had decided that it did not
matter so much that the students learn anything about art,
as that they discover in their hands a dexterity and in their
eyes a selectivity that could provide a sense of achievement.

The first time they had actually tried to use the materials, most seemed to enjoy the chaotic results, the dabs, the
dribbles, the splashes, the lines, however secretly their en-
joyment might be contained. Most satisfied themselves
with constricted graffiti in the center of the huge sheets, or
laborious representation of humans. One boy, a short,

shiny-faced question mark of a boy named Jesus-Maria Ortiz, had proved more than competent at reproducing his favorite subject, female anatomy from the neck to the knees. Provencia Perez, a scrawny baby madonna carved of walnut, had covered her sheet with wonderful candle-people, faces burning. Her own face colored with pleasure and the efforts of concentration while holding her breath.

Tim did not fool himself that he would discover an otherwise lost genius in his classes, but he did hope to impart an awareness of the possibility of order and design in disorganized lives. As he walked along the institutional green hallway, past the broken lockers, the warped doors that closed with difficulty, the vents that led nowhere because of bad planning, he wondered how much worse must be the houses of most of his students. To give them an awareness of color and design would be an achievement, and if he could achieve something by teaching, some of them would, for the first time, achieve some learning. For a heady moment Tim had a picture of everyone in the world busily achieving. He had to smile. "Block that jargon," he told himself severely.

In his shirt pocket he had a single Lipton tea bag. When placed into empathetic conjunction with the plastic cup in the bottom drawer of the desk in the faculty lounge, and guided into a suitable interpersonal peer relationship with three-quarters of a cup of thermally maximated tap water, it would make a pretty decent and welcome cup of tea.

His second day at school he had observed one of the two elder lady teachers making tea from the hot water tap in the faculty lounge. When he had been offered sloppy seconds on the tea bag, he had decided henceforth to bring his own personal small jar of instant coffee; it would have the merit of being darker, thereby not showing the unmistakable rainbow film that sparkled on the unsteady surface of old Miss Jensen's beverage. However, in practice it had not worked out, for so many teachers borrowed just a little that it was gone in an afternoon. Not so dumb the blue-haired old ladies with their unsharable and portable tea bags.

Tim had furthermore discovered that there were certain rituals to be observed in the use of the administration building's three faculty rooms. Since Mr. Conrad and Miss Peters would appear with fair regularity in Room One, and since Miss Peters had a pathological horror of cigarette smoke, and since as the principal's secretary she was a most powerful lady, virtually no one used the room, despite its hot plate and supply of Arrowhead Spring water in a cooler.

For some reason still obscure to Tim, Room Two had come to be used primarily by the Mexican-American teachers, and the few Negro teachers who did not opt for uncrowded Number One, where their athletic natures were unhampered by the *no smoking* convention so odious to the others. It had not gone unnoticed that when Sarah Vardis, a handsome Negro scholarship girl recently graduated from U.C.L.A., had innocently used the Ladies Room in Number Three, Evelyn Raintree and Mariette Jensen had avoided it ostentatiously for a week.

Tim stopped in front of Number Three and listened for conversation. He had hoped that the lounge would be empty, but when he opened the door Jimmy Janis, he of the wheyface, and a shiny woman whose name he could not recall were sitting cozily by the only window in a thin haze of smoke from his pipe and her cigarette.

"Hello," said Janis, with a hale-fellow wave of the pipe. "How did the meeting go this morning?"

For a moment Tim was puzzled at being so addressed, and then he remembered telling Janis about the scheduled "pep talk" with Conrad several days before. The man had a memory.

"All right, I guess," said Tim, "Mr. Conrad gave me a folder to read over the weekend." Tim looked at the smiling woman, who was brightly moon-faced, average in every way except for her glowing auburn hair, perfectly arranged in a hanging garden of unlikely curls, each in its appointed place. "I'm sorry, I don't remember—"

The woman displayed an enviable set of white teeth, as she gave the English teacher a coy sidelong look.

"I'm Cleaire Devereaux." She spelled it. "Jimmy always neglects to introduce me to good-looking new teachers."

"Tim Nielsen, Miss Devereaux, glad to meet you." Tim extended his hand, still sweaty from carrying the briefcase. Although she reacted at once, Cleaire held his hand extra long to show she was not offended.

"So," said Janis, "the old boy gave you the scare folder, did he? You must have some beauties in your classes. That's the only advantage of the teaching program I have this semester; most of the bad ones can't get in." He puffed on his pipe with a touch of pride.

"You must be replacing poor Ralph," said Miss Devereaux, leaning closer to Tim. "I told him to watch out for fatty foods."

"I'll be teaching art," said Tim "and standing in for health this semester at least. I'm afraid I don't know the slightest thing about health."

"Just stay a page ahead," Miss Devereaux nodded, "and you'll be fine. Whatever you don't know, they don't know more of."

Janis chuckled as Tim nodded back at her, thinking that he detected a tell-tale clicking in her mouth as she talked. He had begun to speculate about that beautiful auburn hair, as an old woman with tight blue-white curls and patrician carriage came into the room. Evelyn Raintree sank into the only armchair in the lounge as though she owned it, catching the last part of the conversation.

"Pay attention to Cleaire, honey," was her advice to Tim, in an appealingly unlikely whiskey bass. "She's made a great career out of that advice for fifteen years."

"Oh Evelyn, you meanie, you know it's only been ten. Or maybe eleven."

Basso profundo and soubrette, they laughed together musically before Janis presented Tim to the old lady.

"We've met," she said, "at least four times, but good to see you anyway." She looked around with an air of help-lessness. "Does anyone here have a smoke?"

Cleaire Devereaux got up to give Evelyn Raintree a cigarette and the temporary use of her miniature gold lighter, wearing the whole time an expression that indicated there was no end to her trials. Evelyn Raintree nodded her thanks, inhaled, and coughed appreciatively.

"Have you seen Mariette? She borrowed my magazine." Tim supposed that the reference was to the tea bag lady, Evelyn's great friend, Miss Jensen. Cleaire Devereaux said she had not, but expected her any moment, as a pretty Negro girl looked in and asked about one of the teachers whose name Tim did not catch. Three more teachers were in and out, one talking about the violin and the other about computers and how they would ultimately replace teachers thank God.

"Smoke, Nielsen?" It was Janis, who took one of Cleaire Devereaux' cigarettes to offer to Tim. For a moment their eyes met and Tim glimpsed the possibility that this man might sympathize with him a little.

"I don't smoke, but thanks." Before Janis could turn away, Tim stopped him. "What exactly did you mean, I must have beauties in my classes? Bad ones?"

"Old boy, art is not exactly an academic subject, and they might very well feel that they can throw a lot of marginal boys and girls into your classes. Especially since you are new. Didn't you say this was your first teaching job?"

You know perfectly well I did, thought Tim. "Yes."

"I don't know why they do it, but they always do. The older teachers with better controls, the ones who are familiar, they give the easy schedules to."

"Easier," corrected Evelyn Raintree.

"Easier," agreed Mariette Jensen, who had come in and returned the magazine.

"There are no easy schedules," said Cleaire Devereaux, "I don't know what you could be thinking of." By this time Tim was pretty sure about her hair.

"Nonetheless, Nielsen, some of your kids will be on probation already, at one time or another, others will be. And I don't just mean academic probation. I mean trouble with the courts. Very rarely, there will be an assault on a teacher."

Cleaire Devereaux giggled, "A girl isn't safe in the halls sometimes—"

"Neither are the boys," grumbled Evelyn.

"Cleaire's kidding, Nielsen"—Janis was being solemn—"but you see what I mean."

"I suppose I do," said Tim, uncomfortably aware of Evelyn Raintree's glare—the old lady never seemed to blink—as Janis went on.

"Not to mention the obvious fact that in most cases the intelligence level is low. We can call them anything we like, under-achievers, special slows, or whatever—the fact is they are dumb kids, and they don't seem to be getting any smarter. They have trouble reading, and most are so afraid of failing that they won't even try."

"Some of them try and still are dumb kids, Jimmy. The school just isn't what it used to be." This was from Mariette Jensen, who had produced a copy of the semantics journal from her alligator purse and was reading the poetry. "It's amazing what they'll print nowadays. Listen to this," she said to no one in particular.

> "Cezanne would admire the tones
> Of the tanning bodies
> At Santa Monica beach.
> Old contraceptives surge
> And rearrange pointlessly
> In the sewage beneath the pier. . ."

She looked around as though she had proved her point. Even Evelyn Raintree looked unconvinced as Janis waved away her indignation. "You can't get past, 'How do I love

thee, let me count the ways,' Mariette. Not that what you
read is any good. Poetry is all political, these days."

"About the dumb kids," said Tim, and they all looked
at him. "In my kind of class they may do all right."

"They might," agreed Janis, "but Bill Conrad wouldn't
have given you the folder if he hadn't thought it might do
you some good. If you're smart you'll look at it."

Tim was about to make a comment about the quality of
the teaching having something to do with the dumbness of
the kids when a burly man burst into the faculty room like
a force of nature, a broad-shouldered, bristling red-head
some indeterminable way into his thirties. He looked right
at Tim and winked. "Hey, son," he stage whispered,
"you're coming undone."

Quickly checking his fly, Tim flushed as he saw that it
was securely closed. The newcomer bellowed with pleasure
as Tim blushed and Cleaire Devereaux gave him a pouty
but amused look of disapproval.

"Caught you," said Roger Post, fishing wildly through
the drawers of the desk. He chuckled. "It'll put you on
your guard when one of the kids does it. Sometimes they
just stare." He demonstrated comically. "Be funny if you
really were open."

"Roger, if you don't mind," said Miss Devereaux. Then,
to Tim, "Roger fancies himself quite a Red Skelton."

"Oh, come on, Cleaire." Post seemed larger than the
space he actually displaced as he hunched on the chair
Tim had been about to occupy, and hunted through a confusion of various personal belongings. "Pardon me, son.
Look out there . . ."

Tim backed off slightly, watching as Post paused to flick

his thatch of red hair back over his beefy shoulder. It seemed to be a regular tic, although the hair flopped right back. Tom cleared his throat. "Would you mind handing me the cup in the bottom drawer there? I was just about to get it."

"Sure thing, son," said Post.

Tim nodded his thanks.

As he waited for the water in the tap to get hot, Tim could hear them talking in the next-door faculty room. Roger Post's growly voice lowered confidentially, and Tim could not keep from straining to listen. "—do you know how you can tell a Polish airliner?" There was a respectful silence. *"It's the one with hair under its wings!"*

There was a pause, as Tim filled the white dime-store coffee mug, and lowered the tea bag. Carefully, with his forefinger, he pushed the bag against the side of the cup, as the burst of appreciative laughter grew in the next room, mingled with a disapproving but delighted, "Oh, Roger!"

As he came back in the room, Tim saw that Roger Post had finished appreciating himself, but was still searching for whatever it was he wanted in the desk. Cleaire Devereaux' eyes were wet with helpless, silent laughter, and even Janis was smiling tolerantly with Evelyn Raintree.

"Hair under the armpits," Janis shook his head mirthfully. "Imagine that."

Post frowned in exasperation. "Not under the armpits, Jim, under the *wings*. That's what's funny. Nielsen, by any chance did you see my medieval civilization book anywhere?"

"What did it look like?" Tim asked, reflecting that when he wanted something from you, Roger Post remembered your name just fine.

"Sweet Jesus, Nielsen, it's square and has numbered pages. It says, 'Civilization in the Middle Ages' on it in several places."

"Haven't seen it," said Tim, deciding to spend the rest of his conference period somewhere else. Something of his annoyance must have shown in his voice, for Post interrupted his rummaging and looked up with a disarming, ah-hey-now grin.

"Don't get your back up, son. I always shout. It doesn't mean a thing."

"Sorry," said Tim, although he was not.

"Oh, here it is. I put it in a cover," said Roger Post, holding up his book like a war trophy. In some ways, thought Tim, for him it was a war trophy.

"You see! All that fuss!" Miss Devereaux was looking in the mirror of her gold compact, studying her front teeth. "All that fuss and hollering. Whatever will Mr. Nielsen think of us."

• • •

As the church bell of Angelus Baptist rang, answered almost at once by St. Vibriana's competitive carillon, Angel was methodically putting his books into his locker. Although he had little interest in the books, he had respect for replacement charges if he lost one, and something went wrong with the Plan. He believed in covering himself. Glancing around to make certain no one was watching, he brought out a small black notebook and stuffed it into his jacket pocket so it would not show.

"Come on, man. We gonna be late." It was Ismael, tugging at his sleeve. Angel was unperturbed.

"If I'm late, it's OK. How many report today'"

Ismael thought. "Seven. Five each. Contacted and tight, that make thirty-five more."

Angel nodded. "Plus the hundred and sixty yesterday'"— He took a deep breath, and calculated in his head—"Makes six hundert and eighty-two."

"You think that new dude's gonna make any trouble for the Plan?"

With more confidence than he felt, Angel shook his head as they started up the stairs to the third floor. Jesus-Maria Ortiz was carefully tacking a sign that said CLOSED to the third floor Boys Room.

• • •

When the bell from the church finished ringing twelve times, John Valdes knew he had best hustle or he would be flayed alive, if only by Angel's disapproving silence. He handed his lunch bag to his sister, Maria.

"You can have this. I gotta go."

"Where you goin'? You always off at a run. One lunch I want to eat with you."

Maria was angry as a poked hen, but Johnny knew he could not say anything to her. It would be several days yet before Angel got down to names beginning with V. He could not even tell his own sister.

"I just *can't*. I'll see you later."

She watched her brother run towards the administration building, his long thin legs rising and falling like pistons. Maria Valdes knew that he was cooking something up with that gang, just as she had known the last time there was trouble. Even though she was only a year older than he was, she was eldest in a family that had one for nearly every year, until her mother died when Maria was twelve and John eleven. As the eldest she had rights, and it made her mad for him to keep secrets from her. If he would not tell, she would get it out of Tio, their younger brother who was in the A-7.

"We'll just see, mister," she called, but Johnny was too far away to hear or care.

• • •

Rico Moreno was whispering to Angela Vallens in the shadow of the statue of Betsy Ross, who was offering her granite flag for the endless and eternal examination of some unknown person. The clock had struck an indisputable twelve, and he was expected at the meeting. For a moment, looking at Angie's hurt expression, he considered pretending he had not heard, but of course it was unthinkable.

"I gotta go, Angie. See you at Social Studies."

"Where you goin', Rico? I never see you no more." She pouted, but he had a distant look, a little glazey. It worried her.

"Sorry, honey. It's important. Angel." It explained everything to both of them. "See you."

Without bothering to check if anyone was looking, he kissed her lightly on the mole by her mouth and started for the administration building at a comfortable but ground-covering lope. A tall, well-made boy of nearly fifteen, Rico Moreno was humming as he brushed past a couple of admiring pigeons on their way to Mr. Janis' English. He did not bother to notice.

Less than two years before, when he had first started at Betsy Ross, Rico had been a skinny, long-necked boy with an inferiority complex a yard wide. Those same tough-tit little pigeons would not have given him a glance, two years before. Now they wanted to make excuses to talk to him when he was not with Angie, and the accidental brush against his shoulder would be the topic of giggling conversation for an hour.

He owed his success to Angel. When Angel had decreed that Rico Moreno was his top General, and therefore important, Rico became important. He stopped sniffing glue. Working out at the gym and forcing himself to eat to live up to his position, he had grown into one of the biggest boys in the A-9. He even had his girl because of Angel. It was as though Angel had gotten an inspiration from God, and smited a big hairy rock, producing a miracle, the best-looking, nicest girl in the whole school. For him. It was really like that.

● ● ●

The bell had stopped ringing, but its echo was ringing in seven hundred and twelve hearts as though it were tolling Judgment. So unobtrusively had the twenty-one Generals detached themselves from their respective groups that it had been scarcely noticed that they had skipped lunch to

go to the administration building. Only a few unenlight-
ened students, like Angie Vallens or John Valdes' sister
Maria even bothered to worry over it, and they were not
worrying or wondering aloud. If something was going on
—and something usually was—it was better to shut up
about it.

When Angel himself and Ismael got to the meeting, the
head was nearly full. The sign on the third floor Boys
Room said CLOSED, but master keys for each General had
been cut and most of the time the CLOSED sign was safely
hidden behind the books in Jesus-Maria Ortiz' locker, to
go on and off as needed.

No greetings were exchanged as Angel checked out the
single high window overlooking the lunch yard. It surprised him that so many could be in on the Plan, accepting
of it, and still able to stuff their faces with day-old rolls and
peanut butter as though nothing big were taking place.
Ismael took his allotted spot in the front row, next to Jesus-
Maria, who had been daydreaming during the wait for
Angel.

Jesus-Maria was the smallest fourteen year old in the
school, but his small, soft appearance belied the skill of his
hands, his uncanny ability to get past any door, pick any
lock without equipment, and hide in the smallest of cubi-
cles. He had been given the important assignment of breaking into Jack the Janitor's house to get the set of master
keys for the whole school. It had been his moment of glory,
hiding across the street from Jack's house, watching the old
yellow and black Studebaker make its way into the driveway
with its boattail in the air like an easily unnerved hornet.
Old Jack had grumbled and groaned his way out of the car,

one leg at a time, the keys jangling on his belt at the end of a much worn chain that went in and out, in and out.

This had been Angel's final test of Jesus-Maria, to see if such a small boy was worthy to be a full General. The others had passed their tests, or, like Rico, did not need a test. Rico was General in charge of Contact. He wore the small gold pin on his shirt with insolence, pretending he did not much care about being a General. Jesus Contreras, for all his size, had trouble convincing Angel that he was smart enough, but finally he made it and had been put in charge of Muscle. Clark Cooper was the only blood who was a full General, in charge of Weapons and Blood-sponges. He had no trouble because Angel wanted a blood to be General, and Clark was the smartest, although he tried to hide it. He also had a way of getting a lot of weapons, because his brother was a big Muslim. Clark's pin, which he wore in his collar, glittered against the dark shirt that was already too small for his body.

There had not been any doubt who would be General in charge of Executions. Juan Laurindo was lazy about anything that did not involve fighting or hurting somebody for fun. There was no question in anybody's mind that when it came right down to killing, and killing plenty, he would not hesitate.

Little Jesus-Maria Ortiz was not smart like Rico, Coop, or even Juan Laurindo, nor strong like Contreras or the Turner brothers, but couldn't he sneak into a house like a shadow, past dozing pigeons in rickety cages, over floors more creak than wood, through halls that he had never seen before? He could bark his knuckles without a cry, wait cramping hours in a closet full or half-filled paint cans, waiting for Old Jack to fall asleep, and emerge into the full moon carrying perfect wax molds of every key to every lock at school, ready to hand over to Angel. He had earned his place and his gold pin.

Angel squatted, his back supported by the cold metal of the stall, and looked around.

"Everybody here?" he wanted to know. There was a general murmur of assent. "Where's Rico?" Angel let just a suggestion of displeasure into his tone as Rico came ambling through the door. "You are late," he observed softly, as Rico lowered himself beside Ismael, back with the Lieutenants even though he was a General. With a sigh, he crossed his legs and sat. Then he looked at Angel, pretending to be surprised.

"I thought nothin' start till I get here, man." There was a suggestion of a smile that Rico disguised by picking at something between his lower teeth.

In spite of himself Angel smiled, and the others took their cue to forgive Rico his lateness. They all knew that there was something between Angel and Rico that made both of them more comfortable when the other was around. They had grown up together in the same neighborhood, and if anything should happen to Angel, Rico would be next leader. Sometimes the awareness of this made even Rico thoughtful.

"OK, then." Angel's face hardened with concentration as he produced his breast pocket notebook and the chewed pencil stub he had lifted from Miss Raintree's desk. "I want a full report, on the double." It was an expression he had picked up at Probation Camp. "Coop?"

The first boy to get up was Clark Cooper, a gangly, de-ceptively shy Negro with sparse, nappy hair, so close-cropped by his plump, militant mother that he seemed nearly bald. He cleared his throat, trying to remember the report perfectly, word for word, just as he had repeated it to himself in memorizing it. It was at Angel's insistence that none of the Generals write anything down that might be found accidentally. In his own notebook, in code, there was a special section for custodial staff, the school nurse, Miss Summers, the librarians and counselors, and Con-RAT himself, who was lumped in Angel's private book with the janitors.

"Come on, man, let's have it," said Contreras, poking Clark Cooper impatiently with his big foot. He hated sitting around.

"I contacted Juan Laurindo, Maria LeSanto—" Clark grinned. "Charley Lees, Sandra Lees—that's Sandy—and Gil Lieber. They all in, just fine."

Angel looked satisfied, so there was a grunt of approval from a couple of the Lieutenants. For a moment Clark permitted himself a flash of shy grin, with a note of pride, but he cut it short when he saw Angel's frown.

"Take em one by one, man. One fuckup and the whole booty go. What'd they say?"

Clark gulped, momentarily forgetting his prepared speech under Angel's glare. "Uh, Juan said 'Great.' He want to know if you—" He corrected himself, cautiously. "He want to know who's the boss, you or me."

"What'd you tell him?" Angel's interest was slightly amused. Clark grinned.

"I think he guess."

"Nodding, Angel made a special note in his book about

Juan Laurindo. With the bright ones it was sometimes a good idea to get right to them personally, with an explanation, and if necessary, a threat. "And Maria LeSanto?"

Clark Cooper's grin softened. "Well, she wasn't listening to nothin' I said, that sex-crazy little bitch . . ."

There was a hoarse laugh which Angel cut short with a frown. He stared at Jose Contreras, who was the loudest offender. The burly, muscular boy with sleepy eyes and a cynical upturn at one side of his mouth shifted position uneasily. "Another noise like that in here during a meeting, Contreras, and I'm gonna cut me a throat." There was perfect silence—a pool of silence. Angel cast his next words into the fresh quiet with the accuracy of a dry-fly fisherman, each air-soft syllable spreading in the chastened thoughts of his listeners, ring after ring of warning that stopped their throats, and made them afraid. Angel shook his head.

"Man! I don't get it. You lames don't know what you doing, hootin' and laughin' like monkeys. You ain't so bad if you get busted though, I don't guess. No, you ain't so bad at Y.A." They kept silent, afraid and respecting his superior knowledge. Angel knew. The rest of his speech was a harsh whisper, directly at Clark Cooper. "We know all about Maria and your big cock, man. Now you tell me what that girl say."

Clark shrugged amiably, a little intimidated. "She said anything I wanted was OK."

Angel nodded, and put a small X next to Maria LeSanto's name in the book. "Next." He was feeling hot and more than usually impatient. Without knowing why, Rico was pleased. Feeling his foot about to go to sleep, he gave his attention to shifting to a more comfortable position.

"Charley and Sandy didn't want to hear nothin' about no Plan," Clark continued. "They was scared, kinda. I told'm what you say about no outsiders, and Charley he say they keep shut like a nun's pussy. But . . ." He hesitated.

"But what?"

"Sandy tell him straight out she wanta be sick that day. Finely she say OK though, after a while."

Angel circled the names in his book. *Charley Lees. Sandra Lees.* He looked up, expecting more. "Come on, Coop, next. We ain't got all day."

"Um, Gil Lieber OK, he say he want to cut Mr. Post's balls off personal and stuff'm in his mouth. He in, but I told 'm we didn't need no more Lieutenants."

"OK, Coop, good," said Angel, checking Gil Lieber off. "Who's next? Let's go."

"Hey, man. C'n I ask somethin'?"

Angel saw that Johnny Valdes, the youngest of his Lieutenants, was not about to be put off. He was practically going in his pants, he was so eager to get Angel's attention, jumping around like a baby. Angel briefly thought of changing Lieutenants, but if he did it now, he would be admitting he had made a mistake.

"What's the question, Johnny?" asked Angel, pretending to study his book.

"Why can't we tell our own sisters, man? I mean, it's dumb. Maria bugs me every day. She know somethin' goin' on, and she on Tio all the time, too." Back against the wall, his little brother nodded in agreement, pleased to be mentioned. He was the only seventh grader allowed at the meeting, so he could run messages.

Angel took a deep, patient breath. He knew that you had to repeat things over and over, always the same way. They would remember for a little while, then they would forget the reasons for things.

"We goin' alphabetical, Johnny, even for sisters. Don't worry about Maria; she'll know in three days. We check 'em off, Johnny, one by one. We do it any other way and somebody gets left out by mistake. OK?" John Valdes nodded, looking at the floor. "Who's got the next report?" said Angel.

• TWO •

Five minutes before school was to let out, the police squad car arrived at the Elm Street gate of Betsy Ross, and parked in a prominent place. Several of the jalopies filled with high school boys crept away circumspectly, without the customary laying of rubber that crisscrossed the street like lash marks on a convict's back. Half the apartment and bungalow courtyards that faced the school had Vacancy signs. Two bored cops sat in the squad car, their presence discouraging high school boys who would circle the school endlessly if they were not there, hoping to find a girl who wanted to ride with them. From time to time the police car itself would start up, and drive slowly around the school as kids poured out the gates, on their way home or across the street to the hot dog stand.

Old Jack was standing at one of the side gates, which he had opened for a supply truck carrying cement blocks and lumber. He pulled his thumb out of his belt and waved at the police car, whose driver waved back in a casual, familiar salute. On the sidewalk nearby, two B-7s were getting into a noisy verbal battle that stopped at once when Jack hollered at them. The boys looked relieved and ran off in opposite directions.

The young policeman at the wheel watched with a smile. "That Jack," he said to his partner, "if they were all like him there wouldn't be so much trouble."

As he walked past the hot dog stand on his way to the bus stop, Tim Nielsen had no idea he was being followed. The stand was full of students, pushing to get service, plus a few motorcyclists and their windblown riders congregating self-importantly at one end of the counter. There was a big, hand-painted sign, CYCLISTS NOT ALLOWED, but the busy old man behind the counter was not about to try to enforce it. He looked at the adults half as though he expected them to try to hold him up. Each time they ordered a hamburger, or a chili dog, there was a new reprieve in his harried, wet-rimmed eyes. Tim had eaten there once, on a lunch break when everything was quiet. He was hungry, but decided he could wait until he got home to make himself a sandwich.

Tim's two afternoon classes had been fuller than he had expected, but not unpleasant. He had even gotten through Health without too much trouble, and in his B-8 Arts class, several kids showed so much ability that it almost frightened him. What would he do with them? There were a very few lower-middle class Jewish boys that might have a chance, with scholarships, but it seemed inevitable that they would do pretty much as their fathers did, regardless of their promise in a field as normally irregular as fine art, or even commercial design. After all, Tim had to teach to live, and he regarded himself as being considerably above average.

As he got on the bus, followed by a small, nondescript but somehow familiar-looking Mexican boy carrying much-marked schoolbooks, Tim reminded himself that he would rather be Picasso, or a professor at a fine university than a Junior High School Arts, Crafts, Health substitute teacher. What the hell am I *really?* he wondered, thinking of his newly scheduled Nutrition supervision. Surprise, surprise, Mr. Nielsen. What could watching kids eat refined sugar and carbohydrates have to do with the price of tomatoes, or seeing to it that litter hits the trash-cans, contribute to the pursuit of Truth? He dropped his two tokens into the slot, and took his transfer from the bus driver.

As he sat down, he pulled the folder that the principal had given him from his briefcase and opened it awkwardly on his lap, being careful not to poke the sleeping, swaying black lady beside him. Tio Valdes sat down opposite him with a determined look, and pulled out a comic book. His firm instructions were to spend the next twelve hours observing Mr. Nielsen, the new art teacher. He was to find out as much about him as Angel might need to know, even though there was less than a week left before Zero Hour.

The boy was pleasant-faced, and slightly sleepy-eyed, but he would not be allowed to sleep until the following night. He would give his report directly to Angel, going over the head of his brother John for the first time. The days were running short on the Lieutenants now. Tio was fully aware of the dreadful importance of his job as he pretended to read the *Creepy Comic Book,* and accidentally got interested.

"Alvarado Street," said the bus driver.

Tim Nielsen rode to Western Avenue, studying the faces of his fellow passengers, relishing the wrinkles, admiring the drapery of a skirt. He noticed everything except the fact that he was being closely and grimly followed as he transferred South to Melrose Avenue, and started walking. Five minutes of trees, bushes, trash-cans awaiting pick-up, three dogs on leashes and one trotting free, and he was at the courtyard bungalow that was serving him as a long-term temporary home until he was no longer a longterm substitute, at which time he would find something closer to school.

Each available inch of space on the plaster-spackled walls were covered with large, tightly stretched oil paintings, mostly his own, ranging from the early, dark, moodily realistic studies of lonely figures in shadowy parks, to his newest work, starkly simple, childishly direct squares and dots struggling toward the light from thick rust and brown backgrounds. No one liked his new paintings as well as the old, but then no one had liked the old ones either, he remembered, until they became old.

Tim had converted the only bedroom into a studio, and slept on a pull-out couch beside the radiator. The bungalow, objectively, was a mess, and the bathroom floor was always so damp that Tim had thought of planting rice. A crooked second-hand easel from St. Vincent de Paul stood in the middle of the studio, with a half-finished canvas on it. The only furniture was an old hutch from the Salvation Army with room for his pallet and paints, turpentine, linseed oil, and a toothbrush glass filled with scotch. The bottom drawer served as a dirty clothes hamper, the overflow of which landed on the floor. The glass of scotch, Tim noticed, had a half-drowned but contented bug floating in it, conserving its strength, a relative of which had gotten stuck to the fresh paint on the canvas. He studied the effect for a moment, and decided to leave the bug where it was.

Tossing the other onto the bare floorboards with the ruined scotch he went into the front room to telephone Marge. He balanced on the lovingly carved but uncomfortable arm of the Victorian sofa he had rescued from his parent's garage, simultaneously reaching for the telephone and the crystal decanter of whisky that was on the end table. He stopped, one arm short of the necessary number, and looked at his glass. Hmm. Balancing as best he could, he poured himself half a glass neat from the decanter while doing his best to follow the lightweight phone around his lap. He was uttering a mild curse as he heard Marge's voice.

"Hello? Tim? Is that you?" There was disappoval in her melodious gargle of a voice, which always sounded as if she was about to clear her throat. Tim was enchanted, and let her go on for several more hellos. He could always tell just when she was about to hang up in disgust, a fact that gave him inexplicable, melancholy joy.

"Don't hang up!" he said, just in the nick of time, "It is I. Apparently I cannot juggle my glass and dial and balance gracefully on the arm of the sofa all at the same time."

"So sit," she said reasonably. "You sound faintly unhappy."

"I'm not unhappy."

"How was school?"

"It was all right. I don't think it's going to be so bad, but I'm not too crazy about some of my colleagues. And I can't stand the principal."

"The one who signs your Eval. That's fine."

"It's not that. I don't know. How would you like to have dinner with me tonight and pay for your half. I don't get paid for a month."

"I'd love to. I'll even pay for your half. Dad gave me a birthday check for one hundred dollars."

Tim's heart sank. "Oh, God, Marge."

"I did not mention it to punish you, or make you feel guilty. If I had wanted you not to forget I would have dropped hints for the last month."

"I swear to you, I adjure, that I marked in my appointment book birthday of Margery Clement, buy unique and expensive gift. I really did, in hand lettering. My appointment book looks like an illuminated manuscript. I just forgot to look in it."

"I'll come over and pick you up at seven and you can agonize in person, all right?"

"OK." As usual, Tim hung up without saying good-bye. He could tell by her voice that she was not mad.

Outside the small window of the small livingroom, obscured in a large, bushy and dusty camellia bush was Tio Valdes, listening to Tim's telephone conversation as best he could, bent over like a hunchback. There was a serious, thinking frown on his round brown face. "Margery." He repeated the curious name to himself, committing it to memory. "Margery Clement." It might turn out to be important, and so far Tio could not think of too much else to report to Angel.

Since it would be an hour before Marge got there, too much time to dress and not enough to get any work done on the new painting, Tim decided he would take Jimmy

Janis' advice and spend a while familiarizing himself with
the beauts at Ross Junior High. He started with the first
page:

N.B. Some of the following data has been
gathered by graduate research students and
social workers, and represents conjecture
rather than indisputable fact. Use of the
material should be handled with discretion,
and may be regarded as confidential as the
Probation Officer's reports, and the Petitions
to the Juvenile Court which are a matter
of official record.
MIGUEL ALANIZ - #765562-0074380 S.E.L.A.
Area Date of Birth 4/8/52 M-A. Address:
1833 West Fifth Street. Father Unknown.
Whereabouts Unknown. Mother: Maria Alaniz.
Stepfather: Raymond Alaniz. Brothers: Gilberto
(1948) Richard (1950) Robert (1953) Benio
(1954) Sisters: Julia (1949) Benita (1958)
Entered Betsy Ross as a B-8, flunked all but
one class first year, returned for a second
until described Vandalism. Mother works as
waitress, and most family duties evolve on
Julia, a phlegmatic girl with average
intelligence but a willingness to supervise...

Tim read on, without a great deal of interest, until he
saw that it was nearly six o'clock. He held off the beginning pangs of hunger with a soft graham cracker, and put
another ice cube in his drink. The case histories in the
folder were depressingly alike, with overcrowding, father-
less families, alcoholism, prostitution and probation camps
the norm rather than the exception. There was something
distinctly unreal about most of the prose, an elliptical,

bald-faced, translated English that seemed not to have been written, but instead copied from an earlier standard report, which in turn had been copied from still another standard report, in a series of increasingly faded duplicated tintypes of misery.

Tim yawned. Good God, he thought, it would never do to fall asleep at Marge's birthday dinner. She would be fascinated with every desertion, every child molesting, every wife-beating. While staying together for the sake of appearances, Marge's parents had detested each other for years. The simple but direct pleasures of assault and even uxoricide might be all too headily attractive. Tim was of the opinion, kept strictly to himself, that people raised between electric poles of domestic unhappiness were the most likely to appreciate blood sports, and there was nothing Marge liked better than a good bullfight or a World's Championship boxing match. Tim finished his drink and went into the soggy bathroom to start getting ready, the remains of the ice cube numbing his mouth.

• • •

As she slammed on her newly tightened brakes to keep from hitting the battered MG in front of her, Marge cursed impatiently under her Dentyne-flavored breath. She was her usual twenty minutes late, and it made her feel worse that Tim would be expecting it, and not care. He might even, God forbid, be expecting her to be wearing the red knit dress that she was wearing, and for sure he would be expecting her usual dab of Joy behind each ear.

She was straight from a long soak in the bubblebath which, along with the miserable god-awful traffic was why she was twenty minutes late. There were tiny, pristine, drinkable drops of perspiration on her forehead, a delectable dark brow of purest clover honey, the smoothest, most poreless, most lineless forehead that ever disguised a mind crawling with anxieties, neuroses, and, she had no doubt, the incipient seeds of premature menopause madness.

Glancing at her disgustingly regular face in the rear-view mirror, Marge wondered what dark thing her parents had done that she should deserve a face like that, even at twenty-one. It was too unworried, unwholesomely classic. There was even a velvety soft mole. She would have given half her allowance to see some trace of what she really felt in the large, untroubled coffee eyes that moo'd back at her, cow eyes, whelping bitch's eyes, foaling broodmare eyes, melted chocolate chips beneath the unplucked eyebrows. They were fuller than was fashionable, but better for the short oval of her face and the glossy black mane that thank God needed only a comb and a gentle shake of—

An old lady propelling her three-wheel cart ignored the boulevard stop blithely and crossed directly in front of Marge's car without a glance to left or right. Gritting her teeth, Marge swerved dangerously to the right and missed the old lady by an inch. Her one-year-old Pontiac rocked giddily as Marge squealed to a halt inches away from a parked car, and seemed to expel a great sigh as the motor stalled. Furious, Marge turned around to see the old lady driving silently away, unaware that she had nearly been killed while nearly causing a dangerous three car crack-up.

"You senile stupid old idiot!" said Marge between clenched teeth that squeaked with fury. Her heart had dropped into the pit of her stomach as she reached out to restart her car, and felt the motor turn over sluggishly. The crooks had just fixed her brakes, and now the battery was low.

"No, no, NO!" she insisted, trying again fiercely, pumping the gas as she knew she was not supposed to. This time, with the feeblest suggestion of a cough, the car started. Marge looked at the temperature gauge and saw that on top of everything she must need water. It did no good anymore to depend on the factory service people. They did not even check the water when they charged you eightynine ninety for brakes.

As Marge looked in the rear-view mirror to see if it was safe to pull out into traffic, the eyes that looked back at her were still maddeningly serene, unmarked by what had nearly happened. Yet, as she drove into the first gas station for water, she knew her heart was beating beneath the red wool of her hand-made dress as though she had just run a race.

Turning the corner at last onto Serrano Street, Marge was pleased to see a good-sized parking space almost in front of the bungalow courtyard. After three tries she slid into the space with only a foot and a half to spare. She pulled the handbrake meaningfully, enjoying its new tightness, as though it would somehow bring the Pontiac closer to the curb.

Getting out of the car, she stepped over a chewed-up dead bird and saw Mrs. Cleener coming toward her from her own parakeet-infested bungalow. She was pushing a rickety, empty, wood shopping cart.

"Hello," she called, with unwarranted gaiety.

Mrs. Cleener was extremely old, and had lived in the bungalow across from Tim so many years that she was paying only twenty-five dollars a month rent. She waved again, and Marge returned the wave like a long-time friend, even though she had seen the old lady only a few times. Once, since Tim had moved into the courtyard, Marge had shared tea in a dirty cup with her, admiring her sickly parakeets, none of which did much more than look morose and half-undressed.

"Hello, dear," said Mrs. Cleener. "Going out with our boyfriend again tonight?"

"Yes, Mrs. Cleener, I am." Marge smiled her rare smile that made her friends with everyone. "Have you been keeping an eye on him for me? How many beautiful women have gone in and out of his bungalow since last night?" Ugh!, she thought.

"Only me," the old lady cackled, "but I'm not as beautiful as I used to be."

"Oh yes you are, Mrs. Cleener."

The old lady laughed with pleasure at this foolishness, and clicked away down the cracked pavement, pushing her cart and waving one last time. Marge knocked on Tim's front door, got no answer, and went on in, since the door had presumably been left ajar for her.

Tim was looking thoughtfully at his chin. Although he had not shaved that morning, his beard was so light he might get away with a little powder. He heard Marge's *yoo-hoo, where are you?* at the front door, and that settled the question. There was not time to shave. He wanted to spend every minute with her.

"Sit down," he called, "and fix us both a drink if you can find everything. I'll be right out."

A moment later her hand was curving around the side of the half-open bathroom door, holding a glass.

"You didn't have any mix, so I made bourbons and a dash of branch water." Tim looked at her hand, so small and perfect, ivory. "Your lovely little carving of a hand is an eighteenth century Japanese lady's prosthesis, with edible rubies in place of mere fingernails." He kissed the hand in question lightly, scaring her and making her spill a little of the bourbon. He laughed.

"You're so silly. It would have served you right if I had dropped it. There's no more."

"There's always more. I love you."

"Oh, Tim—"

"I'm practically stark-naked, so either take off your clothes and get in here, or go fetch my brown checkered pants which are over the armchair."

"They aren't brown checkered." Marge's voice grew dimmer as she went to get them. "You make them sound like a burlesque comic's costume. You have absolutely no sense of style."

"OK, you picked them out, you tell me what they are while I cover my nakedness with them." His mouth was full of blue toothpaste, which he spat into the washbasin with a grimace. "You are the future fashion arbiter."

"They have an understated pattern of rust squares on charcoal, sporty enough for the resort, and subtle enough to wear with unpatterned jackets on more formal occasions. Here."

The pants in question came around the door as Tim was

wiping the mirror with some toilet paper. "Thanks. Go in the front room and get high. I may want to take advantage of you."

"Promises." Marge went over to the sofa, put the telephone on the rug and sat down. Tim's apartment was really very convenient; no matter where you were in any of the three rooms, you could converse in a normal tone with all other parts. She took a cigarette out of her purse and looked around for an ashtray.

"How was school. *Your* school?" Tim came out of the bathroom, a white YMCA towel around his bare shoulders.

"Fine, I guess. How can school be?" Marge had picked up the black folder that was lying on the makeshift coffee table, just as Tim knew she would. He went into the studio to put on a clean T-shirt and find a long-sleeved dress shirt.

"That's good." He knew that there was a plain tie lying around somewhere. Marge started to raise her voice, and then recalled that it was unnecessary.

"Of course, in my heart of hearts I'm a stifled Mary Cassatt or Berthe Morisot, but I'm doomed to end up buying Junior Fashions or Stylish Stouts for Bullocks, I'm sure."

"Never give up," said Tim. "There's a place for women, even talented ones. It just takes longer, if you have talent." There was the scrape of drawers being opened, and Marge pictured Tim running around looking for a nonexistent clean shirt.

"Damn, they're all dirty," said Tim with wonder. "I guess I'll have to take everything in tomorrow."

"Better put them right in the middle of the doorway or

you'll forget." She turned a page of the folder, reading, and frowned. "Good heavens."

"I guess this one will have to do. It's only been worn once, and I folded it so it wouldn't get wrinkled." So saying, Tim emerged with his shirt-tails out, tying his good black wool tie. He saw that Marge was reading the folder, and smiled. "I left that out for you to amuse yourself with while I conducted my fruitless search for clothing."

"Amuse! What in the world is this?"

"It's a poop sheet on all the bad and dangerous little ones at Betsy Ross Junior High."

"My God, it's so thick."

"They aren't all still there. Probably most of them aren't." Tim tucked in his shirt and started brushing his brown sports jacket rather dispiritedly. It needed to go to the cleaners, too. Marge paged quickly through the folder with growing indignation, trying several sections in an effort to be fair. It did not help.

"Horrible," she proclaimed.

"Yes, isn't it," Tim agreed. "But actually, I haven't found any of my kids to be different from what I expected. Some of them are even—"

Marge shook her head vehemently. "I don't mean the kids. I mean the people who made the book. Look at the way they write about them, as if they were lemmings. How do they find out these things? Listen." She read him a section describing the father of one of the boys. "Twice arrested for stealing ladies' undergarments and shoes. Why, he even made the poor kid parade around in the stuff he stole!" She was outraged. "And look here! This boy has a tested I.Q. of 148—"

"Oh?" Tim looked where she was pointing. "Well, what do you know? I have him first and sixth periods. He may be bright, but he's a hostile little bastard." Tim went over to look at as much of himself as he could in the mirror. "As a matter of fact he did a curious drawing this morning in class. After he consented to do anything at all besides sit like a sphinx and test the new teacher's self-control." He was going to mention the crack about paying his salary, but decided not to. "Angel Martine. I've got him twice, so he must be an operator."

"What was the drawing like?"

"Oh," Tim thought a moment. "It was loose, but fairly controlled at the same time. Organized, but really—grim."

"How grim?"

"Like a lynching, or a mob scene, but not very clear cut, or focussed. Big shapes, like this"—he showed her on a piece of scratch paper—"pulling together into a violent middle."

"You've got some charcoal on your sleeve." She wiped it off, and went back to reading about Angel.

"You know how Vieira da Silva paints those big blurry almost-cities, that look like abstractions until you look at them a while?" Marge nodded. "Well, Angel drew me an almost-lynching. I didn't shave. I hope you don't mind."

"You look fine," said Marge, a little wistfully. She put the folder down and looked him over. "Just dandy." He did look fine, a little unput together when it came to matching, but still . . . It occurred to Marge that she would probably decide at some time soon that she could not do any better than this particular boy. It should not

have been a sad thought, so she was unable to account for
the momentary melancholy that she felt.

"Where, pray tell, are we going for dinner that you are
paying for because you got your birthday check?"

"I know a good Mexican restaurant," she said kidding
him. Tim laughed.

"If I see one more Mexican—How about Scandia's, as
long as you are paying?"

"Come on. I want to have something left over."

"La Rue's? Delicious. Italiano."

"Still too expensive, and too close to a lot of tempting
little shops that create sudden undreamed of needs."

"OK, let's go for a little drive to Westwood and go to
the Center Club. Very nice view, very good food. OK?"

"OK."

He kissed her on the tip of her nose, inhaling that familiar, delicious scent. "Finish your drink and we're off."

• • •

If every word in every part of Tim's apartment could be
heard clearly in every other part, so too could it be heard
outside the livingroom window, where Tio Valdes had settled in the streetlamp shadows of a camellia bush. He had
tried several locations, and decided on the bush because of
its nearness to the only large open window in the bungalow. It occurred to the little boy that what might be shade
in the sunlight became shadow in the moonlight, a concept
that busied his thoughts during some boring minutes that
seemed like hours.

Tio tried to concentrate on what the teacher and the
woman were saying, but from time to time his interest

would droop noticeably, and he would catch himself tearing up a leaf or poking a bug into the soft dirt with the end of a stick. His ears pricked up as he heard the words, *If I see another Mexican* . . . The implied distaste was not lost on him, and he made a note to tell Angel: the new teacher hated Mexicans.

Then they had started talking about Angel himself. Tio had not realized it until the teacher said it out loud, unmistakably, *Angel Martine. I've got him twice.* At the mention of the leader's name, Tio had bumped his head painfully on a branch of the camellia bush. Tio was not sure about a silva, but he knew what a lynching was, and he thought the whole discussion would be interesting to Angel if he could only get it right. As they started to get ready to leave, Tio frowned. His instructions were to follow Mr. Nielsen everywhere tonight, but he was not sure how. Since the teacher did not have a car, it was an easy matter to keep up with him on the bus. Angel, having prepared everything, gave Tio plenty of tokens so he could not spend bus fare by mistake on something else, but he had not said anything about a woman. She had a car. It was a problem to follow a car.

Checking to make sure no one was watching, Tio raced across the grass to the woman's car. He looked in fast, and saw that she had left her keys in the ignition, attached to a lucky rabbit's foot. That meant the car was unlocked, even though the windows were rolled up. For a moment he considered trying the trunk, but a friend of his had died doing that, and nobody found him until he started to stink. Then he saw the brown blanket in the back seat, and made up his mind. He opened the back door and curled up on the floor, pulling the blanket over him so that he made only the smallest of mounds. He was uncomfortable, and the hump pressed into his stomach, but if he kept quiet he was sure they would not discover him. A leaf from the camellia bush had fallen down the back of his neck, and there it would have to stay.

"Well," said Marge as Tim remembered and stepped back to motion her grandly out the door before him. "I must say we both look wonderful tonight. Regular whited sepulchres."

"Speak for yourself," said Tim, "This is my regular color. I get red when I lie in the sun."

He opened the door on the passenger's side for her and went around to the driver's seat as though the car were his. He always drove, ever since a serious discussion they had when she had been given the car. He closed the door behind him with a thump and sat a moment admiring Marge's profile. She knew he was looking, and did not turn. Her coloring, so much the opposite of his with her dark hair and complexion, reminded him of some Egyptian carving, with raincloud light skin.

"You are a fairly beautiful girl." She smiled.

"And that," she allowed, "was a fairly nice thing to say." From all signs, she thought, it would be a good birthday.

● ● ●

Jack the Janitor's house was small but neat, and he was always glad to get home to it. Although he had been a widower for twenty-six years, at fifty-one, he looked forty; sometimes he thought there might be some sort of connection. As he walked across his front lawn, green as a craps table, and up onto his freshly painted porch, he took his usual critical look at his house and decided he would be not one whit happier in the bigger house he would have if he did not lose so steadily at his only vice, playing the Numbers. Like most people with only one vice, he had moulded it, perfected it, and spent a lot of time worrying about it.

From time to time he would see a re-run of a gangster show on the television, and there would be references to the racket, the Numbers. An unpleasant, unnecessary reminder, like ashtrays to a smoker who has quit. As a God-fearing Baptist with a fine bass voice who went to church twice a week, he could not even think of his weakness in those terms. A racket, a way of putting the lining in the jackets of the syndicate. Damn those Numbers, he said sometimes, and Thank the Lord for those Numbers, at other times. Damn the mob and Praise the mob, depending on the way your stomach felt.

Jack had been going to church twice a week for more than twenty years: on Sunday for the fine music and once a week to light a candle for his wife. He never missed lighting that candle, even though he did have to go to a Catholic church to light it, and even though he could not for the life of him recall what the good woman had looked like. They had no money for photographs in Baltimore in 1939, when she had been young, and it was too late now.

Officially, Jack was the Senior Head Custodian of Betsy Ross Junior High School, an eighteen-year man who was at the top of his pay scale, with four assistants under him to do the physical work that was getting harder by the year.

Somehow, "Jack the Senior Head Custodian" did not have the true silver ring to it, said aloud. "Jack the Janitor" suited him better, or "Old Jack," as some called him. He decided to have a can of beer before going to feed his pigeons.

In eighteen years of service with the City Schools Jack had learned to equate deliberation with dignity. If you rushed yourself in a foolish attempt to seem more hard-working, you just ended up doing the things all over that should have been done right the first time. Jack moved steadily, slowly, and always took time to talk to anybody who needed it. He knew that the whole world floats along on a sea of talk, and he was not about to grudge his time to a kid who was in trouble, or a teacher who needed some-thing done that would take too long through regular channels. Why, he himself was a valuable irregular chan-nel and everybody knew it, from the principal on down.

Jack opened a can of good cold Hamm's draft, in prepa-ration for feeding the pigeons and looking at the evening paper before dinner. He found himself thinking about a skinny little white boy named Harold who had taken to hanging around Jack after school, in violation of regula-tions. He had watched Jack studying the Numbers for many weeks before he had gathered his courage to ask the question that had been bothering him ever since he and Jack had started discussing the art of gambling, and why it was something that you shouldn't do at any age, unlike drinking.

If it's illegal, Jack, how come you do it? That had been the question, and Old Jack admitted right off that it was a good one. He'd have to think on it, he told the skinny white boy, so as not to give an easy answer that wouldn't hold water when you needed it for a long trip.

The boy had looked at him distrustfully, like he was stalling, but it couldn't be helped. He did need to think on it. Tomorrow, or the next day he would try to give a good honest answer, as soon as he could find it for himself. Until then he was going to feed his pigeons, drink his beer, and see what terrible things had happened in the world.

• THREE •

As far as Angel was concerned, the Plan was right on schedule. It was Friday afternoon, and by the end of next week everything would be ready for Zero Hour. Everything was in the planning, and as a planner he had no rival. He had even found a stamping machine that would put the date and hour on the stolen hall passes. Till then they had to count on the teacher's not looking too closely, a caution that had prevented too frequent use. Now, with the electric stamp, he would be able to summon the Generals in the middle of class if necessary.

Angel stopped at the liquor store where the owner would sell him cigarettes. When he came out, he turned down Alameda Street to go by the gym where he knew he would find Rico. Every day after school Rico went to the Spring Street Gym, and Angel would go by to watch him work out, and talk afterward as just friends. The strain of being leader at school got to him sometimes. In the gym he could just blend in, and watch other people doing the scoring and worrying.

Because of their respective positions, it was hard to talk to Rico freely at school, where the others would be watching. Angel was the leader, after a fight with Rico that had been as bloody as any in the memory of the oldest gang kids on the block. It was the kind of fight that would have left one boy dead if they had not been friends.

Angel had not even been the biggest or strongest boy in September, but he had a way of making other boys want to follow him, and support him. He had more experience, and could tell them things he had learned at Juvenile Hall. Most particularly, he knew how to handle adults, and lessen their power by making them feel guilty about using it.

It had not been a long step from having the strongest Mexican kids on his side, especially Rico, to making a deal with the blood group led by Clark Cooper, with the help of the Turner boys. There were useful rivalries all through the school. For instance, Contreras had the hots for Candy Kramer, at the same time as Billy Wilson. In turn Candy was interested in nothing but painting little ashtrays and dreaming of Charley Lees, who would not give her or any other girl a second look. Charley hated Wilson. Wilson was mad at Contreras for beating him out, in his fantasies, with Candy. Sooner or later they would all turn to Angel for his opinion of what to do, and how to do it. Angel had finally developed a knack for staying out of trouble, and everyone hoped some of that knack might rub off on them.

But being an oracle was not enough, and when Jose Badran got busted for stealing a car during Angel's B-9 semester, it suddenly became necessary to have a new leader. Jose was sent to Youth Authority for a year, and interest naturally centered on Angel. He was more than willing. Still, tradition demanded a fight for leadership, and nobody wanted to fight Angel. Without being certain why they felt as they did, the other B-9 boys were suddenly afraid of Angel. Not of his physical strength, even though he had used a broken bottle to send one boy to the hospital for a month in a fight with the Clover gang. What they were afraid of in fighting Angel was that if one of them beat him, he would have to be leader, and Angel would still be around.

The only B-9 who was not afraid, not counting the ignorant and preoccupied and plain indifferent, was Rico, and he would no more have thought of fighting Angel than he would have thought of hitting his father. Rico loved Angel like family, had grown up with him, and helped him gather collections of rocks, and coins, and melted bottles. They had rolled drunks together in the alley outside the Fiesta Cafe near Olvera Street, and one summer when they were twelve they had hitchhiked all the way to Las Vegas before they got caught and sent back. Rico would give anything he had to Angel, and he knew Angel would share anything with him. It was the one thing he could depend on as long as he could remember; perhaps the only thing.

When everybody started telling him he had to fight Angel for leader he could only scoff, but it soon became clear that Angel could not be leader as long as nobody fought him. Angel wanted to be Number One more than anything in the world. So, reluctantly, evenly matched in weight, and weaponless but for what they had learned in the streets of bareknuckle fighting, they fought. Both finished by getting what they wanted most, for after the fight Rico and Angel were better friends than ever, and everyone that counted was relieved and pleased.

It was also the same time that Angel talked Rico into giving up glue-sniffing. He had picked up the habit the summer before, by accident. He had been making model cars, and nearly choked to death one afternoon from a piece of fluffy fiberglas material that was intended for upholstery on a Model T. It ended up instead up his nose, and then in his throat. It had made him sick, and after everyone had finished laughing, some kid had taken him aside and shown him how to use the airplane glue to get a good buzz. It tasted better than cigarettes, and made him forget about everything while he sailed away through noises and blurring lights, and slow spinning that was like a friendly hand on his body, or a carousel. He loved it, until he started to notice that he could not move as fast anymore, or protect himself when a big kid picked on him. It made him nervous all the time, and he believed Angel when Angel told him that he would go crazy if he kept on sniffing.

So he quit, and when he saw some kid getting stupider and easier to clobber, he felt a pang of gratitude to Angel for telling him something true. It was a refreshing change. And then, a few months after the great fight with Angel, he discovered the gym, and in that smelly, noisy, busy place, full and ringing even when empty, he found a new way to sail away, and spin and dart, no longer toward hands that wanted to caress him to sleep, but knock him out. It was all the same.

• • •

As he ran up the dingy stair that led to the gym on the second floor—the first was some huge, perpetually available storefront—Angel could hear someone cussing loudly, and someone else laughing. Propped up against the spittle-streaked wall was a green blackboard scrawled with WORK-ING OUT TODAY and some chicano and jap names that were unfamiliar to him.

"Hey there, Abe." Angel brushed past the owner, a short man with elegant gold half-spectacles and an impeccable unlit cigar that never left his mouth. "Rico in there, Abe?" The question was academic.

"Yeah, yeah." Abe had long since given up trying to get money from either boy. Sob stories he did not need. He nodded cordially as he accepted a shiny Kennedy half-dollar from a tall man who smoked nervously as he followed Angel through the swinging door that led to the gym.

The room stank, of greased and sweaty bodies, of old leather, cheap after-shave, adhesive tape, cigar butts, sweet pipe tobacco and medicine soap, disinfectant, liniment—to Angel it was thick and rich, familiar. At the far end of the room, near the two training rings, he spotted Rico. He was skipping rope with dreamy concentration, wearing his new headguard. There was a pressure on Angel's bladder, so after a frown at the tall spectator who was watching him hopefully, Angel went into the can to take a leak. When he came back out, Rico was climbing into one of the training rings.

"Hey, man, how's it hangin'?" A young black boy who had just finished denting the body bag nodded at Angel cordially, his muscular arms around the bag to hold himself up. His face was running sweat, glittering like a piece of liver as somebody in a sweatshirt told him to move aside if he was through with the bag.

"It's hangin' good, Ray," said Angel, heading for the ring where Rico was jumping up and down, pumping his wiry arms, snorting and huffing impressively through the headguard. The bell rang, and Rico moved cautiously towards a caramel-colored Negro with spider-like arms and thick legs. Angel stood and watched as the trainer, Andy, partially blind in one eye, sauntered over and stood beside him, tilting his head to see better.

"Good boy," said Andy, and Angel nodded, not wanting to talk. The Negro was a little heavier than Rico, but it was soon obvious that Rico was too fast for him. He moved in and out, with good left jabs, while the tall boy seemed to have trouble getting his weight off the heels of his big feet.

"Keep your right up!" Andy called to Rico, having lost interest almost immediately in the big, slow boy. "Damn!"

The two boys moved around, and backed off, hitting each other glancingly for the rest of the minute. Rico held his right higher, too high now, but he moved well. He was fast. Once he hit the Negro hard with a left, connecting solidly. Seeing his opening, he bounced him back with a short, looping right. The boy blinked and back-pedalled.

After a few more seconds of stalking, the bell rang, and the tall boy came over and leaned wearily on the rope near Andy, who turned his blind eye to him in reproach.

"Man," he said, "I'm tired." Forgive me, his face seemed to say.

Andy nodded with resignation and motioned to a squat Negro with the beginnings of a middle-aged paunch, signalling him into the ring. It seemed to take him a long time to climb through the ropes as Rico continued to jump up and down lightly, skipping imaginary, dreamy rope without even looking at Angel. The first opponent, glad to leave the ring, cleared his nostrils arrogantly before surrendering his place. Without emotion, the Paunch looked at Rico jumping around. He was not about to waste any energy.

The bell rang, and although Rico could not get much solid leather on the older man, he didn't get hit either. Andy nodded right along, and said, "Right up! Right up!" only a couple of times. When Rico climbed out of the ring after three rounds, his opponent was visibly winded and sweating. Andy motioned Rico over to the sit-up table and occupied himself with the boy's gloves and bandages.

"Hey, Rico," said Angel slowly, as though his trip to the sit-up table was an accident, incidental, part of his ordinary tour of the gym. "You good today."

"Hold my legs, will you, man?" Rico pretended he did not hear the praise, and Angel was not sure he did. Rico climbed onto the table, unwinded, and Angel held his legs while he did sit-ups. Angel knew better than to break the concentration Rico put into his training routine.

Clasping his hands behind his neck, Rico moved up and down to a silent count, unconsciously adjusting his movements to the slap of skiprope nearby. He expelled his breath with an angry snort at the top of each sit-up. He was covered with sweat, the knots of his stomach muscles beginning to quiver during his fourth set of twenty-five.

"Hey, man," said Angel, "take it easy."

Rico fell back and lay on the table a moment. Then he swung his legs over the side and grinned at Angel.

"It's OK, man, I'm through. Come on while I shower."

Angel sat on a greasy, oil-cloth covered bench near the locker that held Rico's street clothes. He watched the fighters going in and out, as Rico showered. He knew many of them by sight, including the old ballet dancer from Russia who still trained daily although he was past eighty. The steam poured from the showers like a fog, and the mirrors over the wash basins were always clouded.

"You tryin' to burn us up?" came a good-natured voice from behind the steam. "Hey, cut it!" Then a hoarse laugh. "This for you, man." Rico's cocky adolescent voice rasped in answer. There was some profanity that Angel did not catch, several more fighters went in and others came out, including a balding heavyweight who smiled and greeted Angel. He had been a contender, against Floyd Patterson.

Angel returned the nod, with dignity, and kept watching the billows of steam coming from the shower. He felt like shouting, Hurry up, dammit I want to talk, but he would never have done it. He waited patiently. Since there was no bathroom where Rico lived, he always took a long shower. After about twenty minutes, he came out looking rosy through his dark skin, his short straight hair plastered wetly against his forehead. With affection, Angel handed him the towel. "How you feel?"

"I feel good. How's it goin', man?"

"Pretty good."

"That's good." They said nothing else as Rico dried himself carefully, then slipped into his best black chinos and a white shirt. This was a signal to Angel that Rico was going out with Angie tonight, and would not want to talk very long.

"All set?" Rico had come back from combing his wet hair. Angel nodded, noticing again that Rico had grown. Together they walked out past the main gym, and Abe with his still perfect cigar, and down the stairs to the five o'clock street with its rush hour traffic.

"Where do you want to go?" Rico was anxious to get over to Angie's, but he would never have said so. Angel shrugged.

"Any place we can talk. How about Maxies? We can get ourselves some bread." Rico looked worried.

"No, man, not for me. I gotta date and I don't want to get messed over."

"Who says we get messed over?" Angel looked at his friend shrewdly. "We'll get ourselves a drunk and see what he's got. Come on. Special Funds gettin' low."

Rico shook his head, with a touch of stubbornness. "We might get messed up. Maybe tomorrow. I never get to see Angie no more since the Plan start." There was a pause while Angel considered this.

"OK, check out. Maybe tomorrow." Angel did not want to push Rico. He indicated the Thrifty drugstore. "Let's get a booth. I want to go over somethin' with you, man. It won't take long."

Rico looked at his friend, curiosity tempered with caution. Angie was expecting him in an hour, and he would have to hitchhike. It was a bitch, but he could guess what his friend wanted. "Who you worried about?"

Angel smiled at the intuition. "John Valdes."

Rico shrugged. No big deal. "OK, man, let's get coffee."

They went past the drugstore window, Angel stopping briefly to inspect some war games that were simulating a battlefield across a strip of phony cellophane grass. Between the signs TOOTH-PASTE REGULAR 69¢ TODAY ONLY 59¢ and GOOD FOOD, there was an impressive display of submachine guns, toy soldiers, and doctor kits next to a single display-sized bazooka. PLAY VIETNAM, said a hand-lettered sign.

"This is it, man," said Angel, leaning close to Rico so the long-haired dudes in the next booth would not hear. "For the last two meetings Valdes has been peein' in his pants to tell somebody about the Plan. Yesterday it was Jack the Janitor . . . 'Gee, Angel, Old Jack's a good head . . .' " Angel did an accurate imitation of John Valdes' piping voice.

Rico shrugged. "So?" He knew what Angel was driving at, but he did not want to worry about it just then.

"You heard him today, Rico. 'Why can't I tell Maria? She's my sister—' Man . . ." he spat. . . . "like that makes a difference." Rico nodded, waiting for him to go on. He was thinking of Angie, thinking of being late. Angel read the look in his face, and took a deep breath. "So, Rico, get with Valdes and find out if anything's been slipped to Old Jack, or Maria, or anybody. Maria's not bad—she's hot for Laurindo, but Old Jack . . ." He shook his head. "You might get with him, too."

"OK." Rico stood up, without hurry. "I'm tight with both of 'em. Johnny likes me, man, so I let you know."

Angel nodded, seeing how anxious Rico was to leave. Distractedly, he was tearing up the paper tent that said MINIMUM SERVICE 25¢ PER PERSON. There was one last

thing bothering him, and he knew that if he made it completely clear to Rico it would sift down to the others.

"Rico?"

"Yeah, Angel?"

"The thing that scares me bad is that some lame 'll try to
let somebody go, like Old Jack, maybe, or Miss Summers
even." He chose his words extra carefully. "But if we let
one go, we all gonna go to Y.A. for three years sure."

"Hell, man, I know that." Rico looked at the full cup of
coffee he had left, as the waitress glared at them. "I gotta
go. See you later. OK?"

Angel nodded, and watched Rico go with a feeling that
he had at least one General he would be able to trust completely on Zero Day.

Rico had discovered his passion for killing at the age of
six. It did not matter what; a mouse would do, better than
anything, for which his unsmiling mother would give him
a penny. Or, for his own pleasure, a bee. Or a cockroach,
which would earn him a cherished disgusted look from his
sisters and a plea from his mother to throw it away, for
God's sake. By the time he had reached the age of seven
however, and then eight, other interests began to occupy
most of his time, even though in the back of his head there
always lurked memories of the day he killed forty-seven
living things, all different, when he was seven.

It was a record, for him, but even Angel was not told
about it. Angel thought anything was stupid unless he
thought it up himself first, so Rico's secret remained a
secret. He was exactly the same height and weight as
Angel, but his friend had the early advantage of good

coordination, and liked to play ball and organize things. Angel despised things that you did alone, like going slightly out of your way on a path to step on an ant or snail, or make a fast grab at a fly on the wing and feel the momentary terrified buzzing. Rico learned to kill without seeming as though it were anything more than a casual sideline to his real main purpose of the moment, whether it was looking through the glove compartments of open cars, or tightropewalking on the railroad tracks, or going inside empty freight cars to pretend that he was going to Albuquerque. There seemed to be so many opportunities for death. There were rock-throwing contests—sometimes he could throw farther than Angel—and heartjumping boat races in the gutter drains when it had just rained. For a while he and Angel had gotten an after-school job cleaning the pits underneath the trampolines at Jump Center, so they could use the place for free when it was not busy. Rico had gotten fairly good, and could spin terrifyingly in the air once he had built up enough altitude, twisting his feet just as he hit, swiveling his knees and hips on the way down so he could uncoil on the upthrust like a top, his skinny arms clutched tight around his red striped T-shirt, cutting down wind resistance. Up in the air, spinning, he had often thought that it could be him that would die, and the feeling would make him hunt for something later, with his BB gun—a cat, or a stray dog.

Angel was more scientific about his jumping. He stole one of the instruction booklets from the trampoline office and taught himself all the tricks in the first fifteen pages before the cops came one day and put an official chain lock on the gate, along with a little sign that said the place was out of business. Nobody had bothered to tell them. For the next two years he and Rico walked past the place every day on the way to school, and watched it become a hot dog stand, then a hot dog stand with Pitch 'n' Putt, and finally get torn down altogether for a new office building with sparkling stuff all over it and a small spotlight on its only palm tree.

Even though Angel never said a thing about it, Rico knew that he was mad. He had just been getting good when they had closed the gate on him. Rico would have suggested that they try a different trampoline center, but Angel had thrown away his booklet, and would never again bounce, now on his stocking feet, now on his knees, his arms outstretched joyously as though he could close them around the whole world. Angel was not like Rico, with his second wind for forgiveness. When Angel gave something or someone up, he gave them up for good.

● ● ●

Provencia Perez was one of the Unholy Three, and most of the school day she was inseparable from Maria LeSanto and Maria Estragon. They formed a triumvirate ranging in size and weight from Maria LeSanto's five-foot-five and one hundred and forty pounds to Provencia herself, who could get to five foot on her toes and weighed eighty pounds by drinking a lot of water and wearing her clothes on the scale. Maria Estragon was in between, but like the other Maria she was not a virgin, and even had two children that she had been allowed to keep. Provencia, the virgin of the Unholy Three, had as much shape as a peanut and was about the same color. She was good at only one thing, making signs and ashtrays, and little clay figurines.

Some people claimed that she was just in love with the new blond teacher, but Provencia knew she was good in art. Before Mr. Muggeridge had dropped dead he had arranged for her Walt Disney figures to be put on display in the first floor cabinet, and in the last two weeks she had been encouraged to try a bigger piece, almost two feet high. She had certainly not been in love with Mr. Muggeridge, no matter what they said behind her back.

Her new piece was a statue of the Blessed Mother, and everyone said it was good. The new teacher had said it was good, and even the two Marias admitted that they had seen worse in church. It had dried nice, with only one small crack that made no difference because it was right around the serpent at the foot of the robes.

"Whooo!" said one of a cluster of silly B-7s as Provencia walked past, her head held high, her statue of the Blessed Mother carefully wrapped in an old newspaper someone had thrown in the trash. "Whooo!" again. Provencia knew that they called her the Owl, and she didn't care. They could not do a statue, and nobody had given them a display, even if they hadn't started to develop as yet.

Oh! How her mind had jumped from the Blessed Mother to her lack of breasts she could not imagine. She quickly put her mind back to decency and waited for the green light. She had gone ten blocks before she became alert enough to her surroundings to realize that five of the B-7 boys were following her, like a line of silly soldiers. She had daydreamed past the vacant lot and the used car lot, Nothing Over $599, and the foundations for the new shopping center and the dominoes of little stores that usually engrossed her on her walk after school. There was the somber hobby stamp store, the antique and junk shop, the stationer with adding machines, and Italian typewriters, the print shop with a wedding invitation that always made her feel teary, dozens of little stores in a row, with dusty windows that seemed even dustier if the merchandise in them was new.

She did not stop to look in the windows, and did not realize the boys were following, because she was thinking so hard about what her father would say when he saw her statue. He was not very religious, she realized, and never went to church at all except to please her mother, but he had loved the ashtray she made him for Father's Day. The Little Owl had turned the corner to start obliviously up Weatherford Road when she heard the boys muffling their laughter behind her. It was a bad sign.

When she turned to frown at them, she saw that they were the same boys who had kidnapped some of Old Jack's pigeons and put them in the motors of rich people's parked cars to be slaughtered bloodily and expensively by the fans. She frowned deeper, warningly, and clutched her package closer. She was in the B-9, so she should have power over them, but she did not have a boy friend, and in fact they were all bigger than she was except for Tio Valdes, who hung back with a look that might mean shame, or boredom with the chase. "Whooo!" said the leader, cockily.

"Go away or I'll tell my father on you," replied Provencia, holding her statue tight.

"What's in the package, Owl?" one of the boys wanted to know, skipping closer.

"Leave me be."

"Leave me be," mimicked another, motioning the others to follow as he crowded in closer.

"We don't want to hurt you, Owl," said the first boy, as his friend punched him on the shoulder with indignation.

"Yes, we do," said the boy, but their ranks were shattered. Provencia turned away with her nose in the air and started up the hill to her house. There was nobody much out on the front stoop as she stepped around a bike lying on its side and went in, hoping her father was home.

● ● ●

Roger Post sat at his desk thinking of the new replacement's expression when he had told him he was coming undone. It cracked him up. He chortled to himself and swallowed beer simultaneously, with a gurgle. Roger was sitting in the dining room, his melancholy place of exile that he had transformed into a combination office and library. His doctorate was above his head, like a halo, along with a letter of dismissal from the university faculty that had been torn in half and then pasted back together. They both glowed together under reflecting glass, like fragments of the Dead Sea Scrolls. The beer he was drinking at a great rate was very expensive, to annoy his wife. He had altogether run out of things to do to keep from writing. All he could think of was his wife.

In the next room, seemingly next to his ear, Ellie Post was giving a piano lesson to the Clydesdale girl, an untalented, aptly named dumpling if ever there was one. If he had to listen to her drag through "Red, Gold, Brown" one more time—*Red, gold, brown, Red, Gold, Brown, Leaves are Tumbling—* Why, he would go in that makeshift, de-mure, totally foreign livingroom and tumble her himself. Haw! Red—that was for the blood. Gold? Her hair was sort of dirty gold—and Brown, the probable color of that downy fringe between her plump little legs. Red, Gold, Brown, pause, Red, Gold, Brown, pause, Ginger Clydes-dale, pause, Goes Tumbling Down.

"Ellie!" he shouted through the unlined drapery mate-rial that separated his "office" from the "music studio" that once had been a livingroom. There was no answer, but the piano stopped, in surprise, and he heard his wife mutter-ing something in that soothing way of hers. "Ellie!" he bawled again, determined to interrupt her, and this time she came at a trot, after telling the little girl to keep going, *one two three, one two three,* and she would be right back. A cloud of smoke preceded her.

"What *is* it, Roger?" Despite her annoyance, she kept her voice low, perfectly in control. "I'm giving a lesson."

"Oh. I'm sorry. I couldn't tell. Is there any more beer in the ice-box?"

Ellie Post sighed. "Refrigerator, Roger. I'll go look. You might get it yourself when you know I'm working."

Working? Roger Post snorted, and then decided to for-get the book for the moment and get on to the uncorrected tests that were piling up on his desk. He was satisfied to have interrupted his wife while she was "working" and make her perform a wifely duty for him, the only wifely duty that was of any interest to him anyhow. Roger was de-termined that her "job" as she insisted on calling it, be taken less seriously than his own, despite the two hundred

badly needed dollars a month that she never let him forget.

A moment later she reappeared with a freshly-opened
half quart of the expensive beer, and poured it carefully,
disapprovingly into his monogrammed stein. She remembered too well the time she had made the mistake of buying the cheapest brand in the market, and had been
obliged to sit and watch while he poured it, bottle by bottle, all over her living room rug. Just thinking of it made
her heart beat faster. She had been afraid that he had gone
crazy, and might hurt her, or himself, or hit her with one
of the empty beer bottles that crashed instead against the
floral wallpaper, leaving stains that would never come out.

"Thank you, Ellie honey." He did not look at her as she
poured him the beer. His mind was now on the inch and a
half of tests, his horn-rimmed reading glasses precarious on
the tip of his nose.

"You're welcome, Roger," she replied. The labored
piano sounds in the next room had spun to a halt like a
Victrola running down, leaving a ringing, eloquently helpless silence. She sighed audibly to make him guilty as she
turned to go, leaving the empty beer bottle on the desk as
a further irritation, a token of her neglect.

Roger Post was in the middle of writing a book that was
temporarily titled, *A History of Morality in the Middle
Ages*. It had been temporarily titled that for more than
two years. He had finished five chapters, and hoped that a
hard, uninterrupted summer's work would complete it.
Roger liked to think of his job at Betsy Ross as his personal
Elba, a colossal mistake that would soon be rectified and

recognized as the patent absurdity it was. When his book came out he would be back at a major university, and the prejudice of the fossilized administrators that had cost him his assistant professorship would become a celebrated underground joke in the academic community.

Two years earlier, Roger had been abruptly fired for teaching his legitimately held beliefs, and he could never forget it. With his unusual approach to Freud, his conviction that a Freudian analysis of the social life of earlier periods was the best historical method, equipped him to be what in fact he had become, the oddity of a campus that did not cherish oddities.

His doctorate, achieved by concealing his true opinions for six years, was from a good midwestern graduate school, which accepted his thesis only after considerable jockeying and revision. *Demonology in the Middle Ages* was the subject, with emphasis finally on the role of religious courts. What he liked to call Freudian Analytics played little or no part.

With the title Doctor ineradicably in front of his name, Dr. Post became a different, humbler, more confidently direct, approachable man. His growing student popularity was, he darkly suspected, a part of the real reason for his dismissal. His infamous lecture had been forthrightly called "A Kiss on the Devil's Behind," and although his published insights had won an admiring comment socially from the department chairman, his choice of words proved unfortunate in summary on the pages of the college newspaper. Perhaps, with the wisdom of hindsight, he should have repudiated the article, but Dr. Post had decided to defend his larger thesis in the glare of controversial publicity. He could remember to this day the bitter satisfaction of ripping up his letter of dismissal in front of the press photographer. It had not been his fault that the nervous imbecile had missed the shot, blowing the bulb, forcing him to start again with waning gusto on a substitute.

A brief campaign, "Bring back Post and Academic Freedom" had fizzled miserably. Roger was surprised at the fickleness of students, but he departed with a light heart and a mortified Ellie for California, thoroughly enjoying the role of free speech hero, carrying his clippings in a copy of *Don Quixote*. One of the longer accounts gave a tempting precis of his book, and he had framed it under non-reflecting glass as soon as he arrived in Los Angeles.

Unexpected success came to him almost at once, in the form of several much forwarded letters from publishers and a persistent agent. After some heady dickering, he accepted an offer from the house with the best textbook department, and got an advance of fifteen hundred dollars. From the moment the advance arrived in the mail, Roger found it next to impossible to get on with the book, even after he discovered that the advance was small. He kept asking himself, is this paragraph worth fifteen hundred dollars? The money lasted three months, Ellie began to teach piano, and he had to accept an offer.

The instructorship at Pasadena City College ended abruptly after a disagreement with the chairman of the History department, and two months later Roger was the head of the Social Studies department at Betsy Ross, thanks to his degree and a cursory investigation into his background. His salvation, as it turned out, had also been his death knell. Now, unless he could get away, it was only a matter of time before he died all over and altogether.

He picked up a letter from his desk, and opened it for the twentieth time.

Dear Dr. Post, it began, *We do not wish to seem unreasonable, but the first releases on your book were sent out more than six months ago, with the understanding that you would have a first draft completed by May, and a revised . . .*

Roger permitted himself the smallest suggestion of a sigh before he caught himself and put the letter back in its neatly slit envelope, and then into the drawer of unpaid bills. Embarrassment. What did a publisher know about embarrassment? He heard his wife obsequiously bidding goodbye to young Miss Clydesdale. After the front door closed, there was a momentary silence, as though Ellie Post were still standing by the front door, without knowing where to turn, or why, or perhaps even hoping that he would not have realized that she was through with the lesson. Kindly, Roger called out to her.

"Ellie honey, come in here. I want to tell you a joke I heard today."

● ● ●

To look at James Anthony Janis you might not think anything at all. Awful to say. There was nothing evocative about him. Because of a total lack of distinctiveness, he did not manage to be mistaken for anybody else. His protective coloration was perfect, dark brown tweeds, burl pipe, pre-smoked by Dr. Grabow, horn-colored glasses, a way of moving his hands slowly, meaningfully, as though he might be afraid of startling some small and nervous animal. There were red, almost pink hairs on the backs of his hands, fine hands, well-manicured with short nails, a single manly school ring on his wedding finger. Janis cultivated the look of a teacher, or perhaps a writer-in-residence, at a small college. His forehead was high and intelligent, lightly freckled above the squinting, blue-grey eyes. His hair was of such a texture that it stood up and out in various uncombed directions, and yet did not, would not, move, even in a high wind.

Jimmy had bought a sports car, a second-hand Austin-Healy with a fiber glass front end that looked strongly Italian, with a tragicomic mouth of a silvered grill. He had then discovered that the front end was fiber glass not because the previous owner had wished to customize and beautify an already graceful car, but because he had raced it and wrecked it. At speeds above fifty it pulled to the left, and no amount of sending it back to the dealer could change what seemed to be not a mechanical deficiency, but a willful predilection for swerving into the path of oncoming cars.

As he was dressing for the weekly card game, Janis stole occasional unbelieving looks at himself in the full length mirror that covered the inside of his closet door. He was thirty-nine years old, and according to *Time* magazine's article on the "Command Generation," he would be entering middle-age in less than thirty days. He looked younger, in the way of people who have already become more than thirtyish at twenty. He had been fully mature in college, with the beginnings of grizzled pink hair in his ears, and a virile bushiness of the eyebrows. He had capitalized on this quality for a while by dating very young girls, freshmen, and even an occasional high school girl when he was a last semester senior. They loved him and thrilled to being seen with him, and he loved them back, more than they knew. When he had come to hanging around high schools, waiting to pick up his afternoon date, he started going to a psychiatrist. It was the least he could do.

His four years of analysis gave him many insights, into himself, into his mother, his father, and his psychiatrist. He had discovered that he would never have any fun, and that was why he got so angry when other people did. Learning to live with this made it easier to accept other unpleasant truths. Because his father had killed himself by drowning in the ocean (he was drunk), Jimmy had the fantasy that the old man's mania was hereditary, despite everything, that he himself would one day decide to stop coping and let go of the polished walnut steering wheel while driving on the freeway at eighty miles an hour. Although he discovered for himself that his fantasy was nonsense, that madness was acquired, he also knew of the power of suggestion, and understood what his mother's great black silences were meant to suggest, when questioned on this topic.

All her life his mother had been much given to lying in bed surrounded by pastel pillows, but especially so after her husband's drowning accident. It had left her financially independent for longer than she was likely to live, even with all her energy conserved. An accident the death had been, officially, although she was careful to plant in her young son's mind that his father was much given to self-destructive depressions.

Awareness of this made it difficult for Jimmy not to do what she wished him to do, namely, hate her, relieving her of further responsibility for a late-coming and unwanted child. She made much of sending him without her to places full of what she called merry things to do, often with the apology (never made directly to him but always within earshot), that she had been blessed so late in life that she felt more a grandmother than a mother. The constant going to fairs and carnivals and circuses with young relatives had given Jimmy Janis the permanent melancholy expression that was now his only recognizable characteristic.

At the age of seventy-nine, his mother was still surrounded by pillows, but now they were in Montevideo, from which distant spot she had disowned him five years before when she had found out about his trouble with Carole. Jimmy Janis opened his closet and selected a tie, dark conservative brown, with a series of thin black bars running horizontally from just below the knot to three inches from the bottom. Like a whiff of cooking odor from a kitchen, it reminded him how dangerously close he had come to prison, when Carole's father had found out about them and complained to the police.

Carole had looked older than her fourteen years, much older. He could remember that even now, sixteen years later, but it had made no difference to the old man, Carole's father, nor did it move him that Jimmy wanted to get married as soon as Carole graduated. Her father was thirty-nine that year. As he finished putting on his sport coat, and fished around for his tobacco pouch, Janis further reflected that the lovely little lost Carole would be thirty years old two days after his own birthday, a doubly solemn occasion. She would be married, probably to a Lockheed engineer or a dentist, and she would have a houseful of beautiful kids.

As he gave a last, dissatisfied look in the mirror, Jimmy Janis realized that nothing really interesting had ever happened to him in his life, and nothing was likely to start up now. It might have been better if he had gone to prison, if he had had something to go to prison for. He might have had to fight for his own honor. The sad, indisputable fact was that even with Carole, the love of his life, nothing interesting had ever happened.

• • •

"I pass." "Up a dime." "Heavens!" said Cleaire Devereaux, "I pass, too." She smiled breathlessly across the green felt of the card table at Jimmy Janis, who had put his cards in front of him, face down, in a neat pile.

"Billy wins," said Dolores Conrad, "I've got nothing." Like many people who play cards, she seemed almost delighted to have nothing, as her husband raked in the eighty-two cent pot.

It was the weekly poker game, hosted as always by William Conrad and his wife in their comfortable, warm apartment. From time to time various other faculty members and their wives were invited, but in recent months it had settled predictably into the same five or six people. Conrad enjoyed Janis for his acid conversation, and tolerated Cleaire Devereaux because his wife shared an interest in antiques with her, and she was connected in his mind with Janis. Usually Evelyn Raintree was there, but she had begged off with a toothache and a cough, which, to Dolores Conrad, seemed to be one excuse too many. As usual, Dave Melnick, the math teacher, and his pop-eyed little French wife Dany could not get a baby-sitter. It made everyone sad, for they were genuinely nice.

"Your deal, dear." William Conrad's wife Dolores was a thin, finely arranged woman with very small hands and feet and a long white swan neck that she massaged nightly in slightly turned yoghurt. She was born in Atlanta forty-nine years earlier, but unlike her husband she had misplaced all suggestion of an accent. Her southern background showed only in the antebellum way she decorated the apartment, with fine old furniture and a cabinet of good French and renaissance bibelots inherited over the collective dead body of her family. She was inordinately proud of her small hands as she put out her standard fare of cashews and watercress sandwiches with sherry and espresso coffee. Hands could be blemishless, her mother told her, only if they were totally unnecessary.

As Cleaire was dealing, clumsily, Dolores Conrad remembered something urgent she had to do in the kitchen. She rose gracefully, motioning the men to stay seated. "I'll put up an extra pot of coffee in case we get sleepy. Have we set a limit yet, dear?" She was addressing her husband, who was watching Cleaire with ill-concealed impatience. He liked a speedy deal himself, and in his boyhood had fancied himself a future riverboat gambler. "Billy, dear?"

He looked up. "Hm? Yes, of course. We'll quit at one, if that's all right with Cleaire and Jimmy . . . oops!" He leaned over to pick up his last card, which Cleaire had dealt right off the edge of the table onto the blue and beige Aubusson rug.

"Fine with me," said Janis, looking at his hand with displeasure.

Cleaire looked at her own cards at last, and then blinked studiously at Jimmy. "I'll fold now. When you have that sad look it means at least a full house."

Janis could have strangled her. He really did not know why he let himself be dragged into these Friday night sessions, although he suspected they might be helpful when and if Roger Post left next year as head of the Social Studies department. He hated to think of Roger and his damned book.

"It's a pity Evelyn couldn't come." Dolores Conrad returned from the kitchen with a delicate silver tray of extra cashews and crackers. "It's really more fun with five or six."

"Sit down and play," said her husband. "Look at your cards, love, we're waiting for you." She obeyed.

"Poor Evelyn," said Cleaire, "I do hope her tooth feels better by Monday. She's been missing a lot these last few months. And it might turn grey."

"Her tooth?" asked Jimmy Janis.

"No ante?" Conrad asked his wife.

"I'm in," said Dolores, feeling rushed. "I thought Evelyn had a cough, too. It's not just her tooth."

"Oh dear, a nickel." Cleaire dropped one of her red chips into the middle of the table. Janis stayed, and Conrad put in a red and a pair of white.

"Up you two cents."

"When you're that confident, you're bluffing."

"We'll see. We'll see."

"See you and raise you a penny," said Jimmy Janis, feeling like the most foolish of human beings as Cleaire Devereaux reached out under the table for all to see and gave his hand a squeeze.

• • •

Jack the Janitor had told Harold Craner that he, Jack, would be gone for the day to make sure his order for the cement blocks would be delivered on time. Therefore Harold felt comparatively safe in telling Charley Lees that they could meet in the maintenance shack that night, especially now that he had been given a key. From time to time the two of them would fool around in the shack, tentatively, in the interests of science, but tonight Harold was anxious to talk. He hoped that Charley Lees would be in the mood for talking as well.

Most of the custodial supplies were kept in the basement maintenance room, an all-around storage and supplies area underneath the new auditorium next to the Administration building, the newest building on campus. The old shack, out near the handball courts, was nothing any more, just a limbo with a few worthless dried-out brooms and a single obsolete and broken power saw, a few cans of compound and institutional tile wax, and a rack on the wall that had held real janitor's supplies many years before the new auditorium was built. Now there were butts all over the floor. Jack himself rarely went near the place, and his assistants avoided it unless they had specific orders to clean it up.

Harold peeked in, making sure nobody had beat him to the place. He was perspiring heavily, and his thick glasses were constantly slipping down his nose, giving an unwanted owlishness to his naturally thin face. He was undersized for his age, which was approaching fifteen, and much given to breaking out in rashes when he was nervous. Since this was most of the time, he had a reputation of being pimply and rashy when in reality he had skin like snow. When he was calm, the blue veins shone through his thin pale skin, and his curly black hair tumbled to the single dark eyebrow that roller-coasted over owl eyes that seemed to reflect constant astonishment.

Since he was mortifyingly hairless when undressed, he tried whenever possible to avoid that state. The first small tufts under his arms had not been achieved until he was well into the A-9, and the situation between his legs kept him near breakdown for close to two years. Then, in the merciful summer of the B-9, he had suddenly matured. Although he could not be certain, despite books he had snuck out of the library, he credited part of his welcome new manhood to singleminded Charley Lees, who had been pestering him without success for three semesters. When Charley finally had given up in sheer fatigue, less than three weeks later Harold had turned astonishingly into a man. In his mind there seemed to be a connection, and as a result he found his first friend at Ross, and, when they were safely alone, even consented to call him Chuck.

Harold Craner looked around itchily, and sat on a can of sweeping compound to wait for Charley Lees. At second period he had flagged his friend down in the midst of danger from spies, and told him to meet him at the shack that night at eight. It was now ten minutes past, at least. Harold was about to start rashing when he heard footsteps outside the shack, and in spite of himself felt a jolt of relief.

"*Craner?*" Charley always called him that.

"In here, Chuck." Harold tried to make his cracking voice very small, although there was not much chance of anybody hearing. A second later a slender, sharp face peered around the corner, and was followed by an equally slender, angular body in blue denims and a red-checkered farm shirt with long sleeves and vaguely western, steer-horn buttons.

"I thought you wasn't gonna come." Accusation.

"I *always* come." Charley Lees looked annoyed at being doubted. He pulled up an empty can, and sat, less than a foot away from his friend.

"I know you do, but this time I thought maybe you wouldn't." They sat still a moment, while Charley looked around the shack with his usual expression of worried contempt. He was really fond of Harold, and appreciated his friendship, but he was a great expecter of the worst, a trait he had picked up from his father. In the last weeks there had seemed to be a great deal of the worst to expect. Harold Craner cleared his throat.

"I want to talk about the Plan."

Charley looked at him sharply. "I told you I don't want to have nothin' to do with that. Nothin'."

Harold Craner looked sorrowful, and for a minute Charley regretted talking to him so sharply. It was not his fault if those crazy Mexicans and Negroes wanted to get themselves into big trouble, but it would be his fault if he wasn't clear about it to his only best friend. "Craner, I just don't believe in any of it."

Harold looked at him severely. "You *should* believe." The way he said it, it was so simple, for him so secure, that for a moment Charley Lees felt shaken, as though a big bully's hand had grabbed him by the scruff of his skinny neck and given him a real shake. He tried to scoff.

"No, really, you *should* believe. It is gonna happen and I'm in on it." He paused to let this sink in. "In fact, I'm a Lieutenant, that's why I've got this pin, and these keys." He showed him, briefly, and then looked worried. "You shouldn't tell I told you or I might lose being Lieutenant. I know you can keep a secret."

The pin looked exactly like all the other pins in the world, but this reference to their ongoing secret made Charley Lees thoughtful. From personal experience he knew plenty enough of Harold Craner's pig-headedness, but he never knew him to be a liar.

"You wanta know why?" said Harold, eager to tell.

"Of course I do, Craner." Charley's voice softened, and he reached out to take Harold's perspiring hand. He held it without knowing quite what to do with it, but Harold did not mind. His hand was just a token for him, whatever it might be for Charley. He tried to explain.

"You don't pay no attention to Angel and his gang, Chuck. You got an unbeliever's mind, on everything. Whatever it is, you just don't believe it. But these guys aren't no dreamers. This gonna be something big. They couldn't do it if they didn't have Angel, but they do have Angel." Charley had been stroking his hand, but Harold preserved his distant look. "Don't laugh, but it's a good feeling to be included in for a change."

"What does it mean, Craner," said Charley, humbly, after a long pause, "to be a Lieutenant, I mean?"

"I can't tell you that," said Harold, without a single rash anywhere on his body. "But I'm included in, and I get treated equal just like everybody else."

• FOUR •

After admiring the fancy cover, Marge found herself checking the right hand column of the menu. It was a splendid affair, the menu, once inside. According to a small notation, the crest on its front belonged to the former royal family of Hungary, whose head chef was now the restaurant's. There was a fog toward the beach, but the view was magnificent, and sparkled competitively with the brass studs on the real leather armchairs. The cuisine, once Marge left the view and the red velvet walls, was mostly French: Tournedos Austerlitz $6.95. Langouste d'Hiver Petit Trianon $6.50. At the bottom, she was amused to see café au lait directly above buttermilk. Was there such a thing as lait du beurre, she wondered? When she looked up, to get her money's worth of the view, Tim was looking worried.

"Are you absolutely sure you have enough money?" Tim kept his voice low, so the people at the next tables and the sleek, cat-footed gigolo of a waiter would not hear. "It makes me nervous. Why don't you check and make absolutely sure?"

Marge was immovable. "I told you I have one hundred dollars in cold American cash right inside this lovely red plastic purse. We can even go dancing afterwards at the

Whisk a Go Go, if you can still walk after the Huitres
Chablis and the Escaloppes de Veau," she added lightly,
"sur le pont d'Avignon. On y danse, on y danse. . . ."

"Stop showing off," muttered Tim, studying the menu
irritably. "I don't like the Whisk a Go Go. Who's there?"

"How should I know? I've never been." She took a
thoughtful, superior nibble of the long, sesame-covered
breadstick.

"Unless it's somebody awfully good it isn't worth it."
Tim was concentrating on the right side of the menu. "I
don't know which is worse; to look at the prices wondering
what your date will order that you can't afford, or to look
at prices wondering what you shouldn't order because your
date can't afford it."

"Regard the money that is paying for this as coming
straight from heaven."

Tim made a wry face. "Your father is not my idea of
heaven."

Marge laughed happily. "I like you when you are
irreverent. Order us a good wine."

"You know more about that than I do. You're the one
who's been on a student ship."

"Bordeaux 1959, if we're having meat, of course."

"Bordeaux—what Bordeaux 1959?," said Tim, looking
at the wine list. "There's three kinds. You just said the first
thing that came into your head. It's a plot."

"How much does a 1959 Bordeaux cost? The best?"

"$8.50."

"How can we go wrong?"

Tim smiled. "You know, I had a brilliant idea today in
class."

"Oh, Tim, let's not talk about school tonight—"

"Just this one thing. It's important and I might forget it if I don't tell someone." Marge tilted her head at being called "someone."

"If you must, of course you must."

"No, seriously, it came like a flash today, in the middle of third period. I figured out a way to end juvenile delinquency once and for all."

Marge put down her butter knife. "Well hooray for you! You'll get a raise sure."

"Come on, Marge, don't be like that. I don't mean end it once and for all, I mean make a dent. I mean do something about it instead of just studying it. We spend all our time studying it, and no time doing anything about it."

The waiter came just as Marge was framing a retort, so they sat in silence, both eager to speak as he put fresh bread on the table, filled the water goblets and removed the two extra table settings. The waiter was young, exotically dark and sideburned, and Marge did not help Tim's mood by watching the skillful brown hands with interest. Tim purposely curbed himself, knowing that this was one of those excited nights when they might quarrel. When he spoke, the waiter's voice was low, faintly perfumed with an accent. Wisely, he addressed Tim.

"Will there be cocktails before dinner, M'sieur?"

Before Tim could say No, Marge answered, "Yes, thank you, a martini for me. Tim? What would you like?" To the best of his knowledge she had never had a martini in her life. He cleared his throat.

"A bourbon on the rocks for me, and a vodka martini on the rocks for the young lady."

"Very good, M'sieur." Before the waiter went away, Tim could have sworn that he looked at Marge's breasts in her red knit, admittedly revealing dress. Marge noticed that he was jealous, and blushed with pleasure. It was fun watching someone be big about something.

"A martini yet," said Tim a little nastily. "You planning on getting . . . shall we say swacked?" Marge watched his natural color go up three degrees. She decided to conciliate.

"Don't be mad at me, Tim."

"I'm not. All right, yes I am."

"And on my birthday."

"Will you go to bed with me tonight, at my place?"

"Probably not."

"I didn't think so. Do you want to hear my other great idea anyway?" Marge nodded, and looked so beautiful that Tim forgot his jealousy, and also forgot what he was going to say. He had been so concerned with the prices and the parking fee and the placement of their table near the view windows that he had forgotten to appreciate how tenderly her skin took the hushed light of the candles. She thought that he was looking through her, and tried to catch his attention by bobbing her head. "You were saying?"

"Oh. Well. Today when we were doing charcoal drawings, one of my boys, a clever little rascal named Jesus was drawing a picture of the NBC peacock."

"The what?"

"The NBC peacock, the color symbol that they have at the beginning of the programs, you know."

"I never watch TV."

"Neither do I, but that's just the point. They do."

"Who they?"

"Everybody. All the ones on relief, the mothers with ten kids, the houses with five families, the new shacks, the apartment developments, they all have that one thing, TV."

The waiter brought the two drinks, and placed one first in front of Marge, then the other, fastidiously, in front of Tim. This time Tim ignored him, as Marge leaned forward. Tim cleared his throat.

"The idea is this: use the only means that exists in the whole world to get at people when they are young enough, babies even . . ." He paused dramatically. "Don't you get it?"

Marge took a sip of the drink and made a face. "In a way," she said.

"Television is practically everywhere. In a few more years there won't be a house anywhere that doesn't have a set. If necessary, you could even give sets away to people below a certain income. Then, when the kids are home from school, till the time they're supposed to be in bed, you have nothing on any of the channels except things that are educational, but well-done."

"That's ridiculous."

"Why is it ridiculous?"

"It just is."

"If they can make interesting, amusing, well-written pitches for stomach pills, they can make *anything* interesting. Isn't it worth it?"

"You're talking about nationalizing. You're talking about 1984."

"I am not!" Tim's voice grew loud before he caught

himself, and repeated, more quietly, "I am not. I just realized it suddenly when I saw those kids in class, looking at each other's drawings. They're already too old, already ossified, but they can still tell when something is better than something else, even if they can't explain why in our lovely middleclass American English. They won't read books. You can't take great paintings around from house to house. But you can fix it so that when they turn on their TV set at certain hours, they will look at something that will enrich them. I hate that word, but you have to enrich little kids despite their homes, despite their families. Or lack of families. If you don't, they grow up bitter and aimless."

"You are a dreamer, poor old Tim." Marge was looking at him very gently, fond of him for his intensity. "You can't force people to be cultured."

"You force them to be *un*cultured. Everything they see is their culture. You take advantage of a child's natural selfishness, his natural cruelty, and prolong it by pandering to it until he becomes a cruel, selfish adult, proud of his cruelty and selfishness because it conforms to the national ideal."

"You're raising your voice again."

"Marge, it costs more to keep a criminal in jail than it does to send someone through college."

"What does that have to do with television?"

"It's a weapon against viciousness and crime that is not being used. There are standards that throw you in jail if you sell tainted meat, or dangerous drugs. The air is supposed to belong to the people, and the programs are supposed to serve the public interest."

"They are also supposed to sell things, beloved. And a lot of people don't want to be improved."

"There are plenty of places for advertisers to sell things, including TV when half the little kids in the country aren't staring at it. There's newspapers and magazines and bill-boards and mailers and radio—"

"You're still talking about giving a small group tremendous power over the minds of kids." Marge was determined not to give in. "Who knows what could happen with that kind of control?"

"How can you have more control than those big advertisers have now? They tell the stations what they want on the air, nothing to disturb the lowest level of interest in the audience, nothing, in other words, except sheeplike escapism."

"What's wrong with escapism?" said Marge a little ruefully. "This dinner was supposed to be escapism of a sort. I escaped from age twenty-one."

"Are you ready to order, M'sieur?" The waiter had padded up so silently that neither had noticed. The place was really candlelit. They looked at him now in surprise.

"Are we?" asked Tim, turning to her.

"In a minute," said Marge, picking up the menu again. The waiter disappeared, leaving the two of them in a hazy halo of candleglow, looking at the prices.

The rest of the meal went very well, as though the dispute had served to clear their tongues. The food was even better than the service. They were pleasantly surprised to receive personally printed matches with the name Tim Nielsen, gold matches that arrived with the dessert. Even though he did not smoke, Tim tucked the matches in his pocket as a souvenir. They went dancing at the Whisk a Go Go after all, then on to a frilly after-hours coffee shop in Beverly Hills, where they had soft ice cream and talked about painting and painters until Marge was practically nodding with sleep. Several times during the course of her best birthday Marge wanted to apologize to Tim for being such an all-around cop out, but she did not quite know how without raising the spectre that he might ask again. She satisfied herself with telling him several times, apropos of nothing, that she loved him, silly ideas and all.

• • •

Tio was curled in the back of Marge's Pontiac, fast asleep. First one attendant with a young voice had parked the car, and then another, and there were various half-heard conversations, and one interesting period, just before he fell asleep for the last time, when he heard them kissing. They talked a lot, none of it very engrossing.

When he woke the next day, he was in a scary dark room that turned out to be Marge's cluttered garage. It was seven o'clock in the morning by the disc jockey on the radio, which startled him by coming on the minute he turned the knob. He looked half-heartedly through the glove-compartment, against Angel's instructions, but he was very hungry, and his side hurt. It was best to go see if there was anything left to eat at home before giving his report on the new teacher to Angel.

• • •

David Melnick married his wife because at a party somewhere someone had watched them swaying together, breathless after a dance, and proclaimed them a perfect pair of Hummel figures. Of such simple beginnings come great things. The concept had delighted Dany, whom he had met and fallen in love with while on duty in that perennial trouble-spot of the world, Paris. His feelings were reciprocated, and they had gone on a rampage of happy rule-breaking—the rules, that is, of their respective families and religions. David, whose mother kept a kosher house and started him at three on the violin, gave his music up with a vengeance by throwing his D'Espinne into the Seine. He had written Dany a long poem to break the boredom of his duty at the Embassy, calling it *"Living in Sin by the Seine."* She, in turn, had taken to wearing a small gold star of David and sleeping late in the morning rather than attending her classes.

They continued to break the rules, laughing and dancing and going to the theatre without dressing, eating unhealthy foods or none at all for days on end, finally finding a small perfect two room apartment that David could use in exchange for certain favors at the Embassy. For a while, he had even considered becoming a double agent for Russia and the United States, but nobody made him an offer. He was totally caught up in the search with delicious little Dany for new rules that they could break together.

Finally discharged on his twentieth birthday, David thought he would have to marry Dany to get her into the United States, but sure enough, somewhere along the line one of his kindly commanding officers bent a rule and made a phone call and two months later Dany was on the plane for New York. So petite and wide-eyed and childish did she look that she actually made it on a half fare, despite her entry permit which unmistakably gave her age as eighteen.

In Paris, her family was under the impression that she was going to America for the summer to tour the grand spaces by bus, and would write long letters that they could show around to their friends. They received one letter the first month, informing them not to try to contact her. She was about to disappear into the frontier country of the wild west, and would spare them the pain of receiving her letters. The effect was not quite what she intended, for she never heard from them again, except for a letter from a favorite aunt describing the towering rage in which her father proclaimed her dead, for as long as she lived.

When she arrived in New York, her funny blue hat knocked crooked over her long, half-combed dandelion hair, she found a surprising new David that she had never seen during their blissful months of rulebreaking in Paris. He was morose. He had a new habit of looking up and muttering vehemently without sound through his irregular yellow bottom teeth. This bewildering action was normally the result of a trivial frustration. Then David informed her that he had found her a lovely little room quite near his family's apartment on the West Side. He had found *her* a room. Umhmm. She nodded her head wisely, further disarranging her little blue chapeau, and decided to use her ignorance of the subtleties of language as an excuse to keep her mouth shut.

Two months later she understood that her parents had abandoned her, and worse, David was being as dutiful as if they were unhappily married. She gathered her wits. David was constantly doing a thousand considerate little things.

His efforts to do business only with cash, in case his parents should find out, were agonizing to both of them. Then came the last straw. She discovered that the violin had been insured in New York, and he had gone back to practicing on the sly. After a tearful, kiss-filled confrontation damp with renewed ardor and apology, together they went to the parents' house, and announced that not only were they madly in love, but that they would never marry, as it spoiled things. David further suggested that his father sell the new violin for whatever he could get and turn the money over to them. Mr. Melnick promptly went into a rage, and called Dany a number of things that he would never be able to take back. You, he told David, henceforth are invisible, and to punctuate his words he jumped up and down on the violin himself, remembering in midjump that this time it was not insured.

The following day, with one small blue suitcase containing Dany's "essentials," invisible David and dead Dany Melnick started their motel tour to the west coast that ended in Los Angeles. David now remembered that great month of traveling with a tear in his eye as he picked up little Michelle, his one-year-old, flipped her over onto her back, and lifted her little sausage-like legs to undo the safety pins. He nearly threw up.

That first year in California had been too wonderful to last, with his G.I. Bill and savings to get him through his last year of college and a teacher's credential. It had been a year of agreeable classes, uneventful student teaching, and weekends in the sun with confident Dany, who could wear a bikini at a state beach and get admiring glances from even the ugliest women. It was something about her Frenchness, and her accent.

More parties, more fun, deeper sunburn and the fun of soothing it away, and fewer rules to break, which did not bother them, or even occur to them, until an accursed party at Seal Beach where none of the couples were married, and a half-tanked idiot had made the comment about Hummel figures. *Hum*mel figures. Dany had looked at him, bubbling. David had of course looked at her (he always did), and suddenly the two of them were looking around at all the other couples, every size and shape and color and weight, Republicans and Communists, all mashed to each other with the fervor of illicit, fleeting love, swaying to the music, so obviously mismatched, all of them; so obviously not Hummel figures, any of them.

A day later they were married, and a month later, as though the gods had fingered her for a little sport, Dany was pregnant. Well, thought David, not exactly as though the gods had fingered her. She did her best. She went horseback riding at Griffith Park, over the worst trails, seeking out the rocks, while David's wonderful grades dipped from the worry. She galloped, and did cartwheels around the beach, and flipflops, and drank a lot of wine so she would bump into things by accident. When David had the strength, they danced late and hard into the night when he should have been studying, but then—he sighed— he probably would not have been able to study anyway. Life was hell, and they nearly separated.

Seven months later they had a robust baby boy, who did not get a name for three months, as though that might somehow help them to believe that he was not there. But there he definitely was, finally called Etienne, wallowing at that moment in his excrement in the next room where Dany was watching the movie on TV. Michelle gurgled up at him with her pinkly wet little lips and slippery, precious fingers, a miniature marketplace of a perfect little body. David smiled slightly. Michelle, God help her, would look just like Dany when she got a little older. Whatever happened, she would not be allowed to go to Paris until she was twenty-one.

• FIVE •

Monday

As Angel watched the new teacher showing Jesus-Maria how to draw perspective guidelines, he thought of what Tio Valdes had told him and it did not make good sense. Nielsen had a rich woman who took him to dinner, according to their conversations, stayed in the room while he dressed, although they did not sleep together, and used big words. There had also been some static about Mexicans, but Angel suspected Mr. Nielsen was no racist, and Tio had just misunderstood. Angel could understand the new teacher, because he himself did not feel personal hatred, not for bloods, not for Anglos. Angel's plan had become much bigger in his mind than that.

The teacher went from table to table, making an occasional comment. Angel pretended to be drawing a large freeswinging bird on his piece of paper, and without thinking, produced a large simple outline that featured supersonic jet plane wings, and the beak of a bent, mournful seagull. He decided to put a wash of dark blue streaks all around it, so it would take up time and visible effort without interrupting his thoughts about the final stages of the Plan.

At lunch Rico would corner John Valdes and talk to him. At one-forty-five, there would be a top level meeting of the Contact Committee, and he would put a good scare into the Generals and Lieutenants. He understood that in several areas serious resistance was developing; sloppy, unorganized, but still, resistance. Charley Lees had even dared to come directly to him after first period and ask to talk.

—Hey, Angel, will you come over to the handball court a minute?—What do you want, Charley?—I just want to ask something. It wouldn't take a minute even, Angel.—Why can't you say it right here, Charley?

Charley Lees hated being called Charley, but no one called him Chuck except a couple of teachers and sometimes, for pity, Harold Craner. Angel suspected what Charley Lees wanted of him, but he looked at him as though expecting a revelation.

—Come on. Charley, I only got five minutes till Shop.— Uh . . . Charley was having a hard time picking his words; he did not want to involve Harold.*—Uh . . . Clark Cooper came to Sandy and me, and, uh . . . — What is it, Charley?—Well, uh, he said that you were going to . . . uh, well, he scared Sandy bad with what he said.*

Angel stared at Charley Lees' worried face. He was not going to give him the satisfaction of showing him anything, one way or the other.

—I mean, Angel, he was kidding wasn't he?

—Kidding?

There was a long thoughtful silence while Charley Lees realized that Angel was not going to be bothered with him. *Answer me, you bastard.* he was thinking, but his voice was a thin wheedle, a prayer.—*Angel, listen, he scared Sandy bad. He said that you were gonna shut the whole place up and grab every teacher and kill them.*

Angel shook his head, with a small smile.—*We ain't gonna kill 'em, Charley.—Jeez, Angel* . . . Charley's mouth managed a small recovery on one side until Angel leaned forward and transfixed him. His words dropped out of his mouth hard, and bounced at Charley's feet.—*We . . . ain't . . . gonna . . . kill . . .* Ready to run, the feet—*We gonna kill 'em each one in a special, poetic, proper, diff'rent way like they deserve. It wouldn't be fair to kill 'em all the same way, Charley, would it?*

Charley Lees' mouth moved without saying anything.

—*Some people deserve to die, don't they, Charley, if they don't fight back? Or if they fight so good but not quite good enough? I can't hear you, Charley, what're you saying?*

The bell rang for second period as Charley stared at Angel in disbelief, thinking what Harold Craner had said about him. Angel turned away.

—*I'll have Rico talk to you some more, Charley, if you have any problems, OK?* Charley Lees nodded.—*But don't have no more problems, Charley.* Those were the last words Angel had said to him. Now he was still nodding over his drawing paper, sharing a drafting table with Gil Lieber and Jennifer Baily. He never looked at Angel, never met his eyes, not since they had come into the room for ceramics. Jennifer was noticing a funny smell from Charley, and cursed her luck at being stuck with a couple of duds.

Mr. Nielsen had moved to Angel, and was studying his

drawing. Angel did not look up at him, but continued laying the dashes of dark blue over and around the out-lines of his former bird, now transformed into a flying machine.

"What are you doing, Angel? I thought your drawing was finished ten minutes ago?"

"I'm puttin' blue on."

"Prussian blue. Why that particular blue?," Tim asked, seeing the chance to slip in a point he had been waiting to make. Angel looked at the drawing sourly, his brush in the air. He shrugged. "I don't know. I just like it."

The teacher addressed the class in general, without moving from Angel's side. "The color Angel is using has been called one of the royal colors, like deep purple. It's been used for the military uniforms of many countries. Can anyone name me one?"

"Yeah," said Juan Laurindo. "The Fuzz in L.A."

Tim looked at the big, hostile boy, thinking that he must know what he was talking about. "That wasn't what I had in mind, but it makes the point. When Angel uses this particular color to surround"—He looked more closely —"what started out to be a dove . . . What does a dove usually mean?"

"Dove shit," suggested Juan Laurindo again, to general laughter.

"The dove is the bird of peace," said Tim, "and putting that blue together with that dove shows what I mean about how color and shape can say two different things apart, and say something else again when they are put together." It had gone over their heads, except for Angel, who watched him with interest. Tim examined the drawing more closely.

"What difference would it make, Angel, if instead of the Prussian you used a light blue, a very light blue?" He demonstrated what he meant.

"I don't know."

"The shape here"—Tim pointed at the body of the bird with his middle finger, as lightly as though he were afraid to hurt it—"would stand out more. It wouldn't seem so crushed."

"Maybe I want him crushed."

Tim looked at Angel, reacting to the quickness of his answer. "If you do, then you are on the right track, and you used the right color blue. I wasn't telling you what to do, Angel. No one can tell you what to do in Art. I just showed you what would happen if you came at the same problem a different way, trying to get a different effect."

"No problem, Mr. Nielsen," said Angel, without mockery. "I read you. I'll try it again with another sheet." He was one of the few boys who did not slip and call the teachers, "man."

Tim moved to a position several feet away from Maria Estragon, who was working at the same table as Maria Le-Santo and Provencia Perez, a talented little girl who was patiently finishing a portrait of an amply endowed girl, modeled after her two best friends. She was not their best friend in return, but they tolerated her presence in the belief that her awkwardness and lack of shape made them look better. The previous semester a boy had dubbed them the Unholy Three, after being unable to get up any gen-

eral enthusiasm for the Three Weird Sisters; the misunderstood name had stuck even after the boy's parents
had moved back to Woodland Hills and transferred their
son to Taft.

Maria Estragon was working feverishly on a drawing of a
round bush-like tree, covered with bright pure circles of
yellow, light orange, and red. Unsatisfied with fruit, she
started turning them laboriously into flowers. Suddenly a
nudge from Provencia told her she was being watched, and
she looked up hopefully at Mr. Nielsen.

"That's just fine, Maria," he said, remembering that
these two Marias and the little Provencia always stuck together. He was beginning to remember names, principally
of the kids that gave trouble. Maria gave a despairing,
three-tiered sigh.

"There ain't no spaces in it," she complained. "I wanted
to make some air between the branches, but it's too late. I
can't get the blue in now."

Tim smiled, charming the three girls. "Next time start
with the blue, very very light, then build your"—he looked
more closely—"flower tree on top. Keep letting the sky
come in from the back . . . see, like this . . ."

Maria Estragon nodded, looking at Mr. Nielsen's blue
eyes with fascination. She was a stocky, smooth girl, with
untapered legs and large breasts swollen still further with
milk for her second child. Two days earlier the little boy
had died, and Maria stopped being late for school. Not
knowing the reason for her sudden improvement, the
school authorities were pleased.

Tim had gotten accustomed to the way Maria Estragon
looked at him. Obviously she would not have a child

nearly two years old if she was the average American teen-ager. He did not know about the second baby. Still, he could not talk to her any way except as to a young child, and a sweet one at that, who was trying very hard in class.

Angel observed the Unholy Three's adoring eyes, never leaving the new teacher as he moved to the next table with Ismael Sato, Clark Cooper, and Juan Laurindo working to-gether. Actually, the three Generals were messing around, but as Mr. Nielsen came closer, they pretended to be mix-ing colors, barely able to control their laughter as they started colliding with their brushes and nearly overturn-ing their paints in a game of war.

"All right, that's enough," said the teacher, and they stopped, making a slow ballet of politely rearranging their supplies, Angel weighing the expressions in the various girls' faces as the new teacher spoke to them. It was a good thing Zero Hour was not far off, he realized.

As Tim leaned over to study the mess in front of Ismael, Maria Estragon stopped working on her flower tree and watched his thighs and buttocks almost thoughtfully.

"When we are through with our designs"—the new teacher was saying—

• • •

The way Rico kept his face straight forward, unwilling to look at him as they went someplace quiet, made John Valdes very nervous. He was afraid to talk, for fear that his voice would come out more of a piping squeak than usual, but he could not stand the silence.

"What do you want, Rico?"

"Just to talk, man."

Then why are you so quiet, the smaller boy thought as
he tried to watch Rico out of the corner of his eye, without
giving himself away. He brushed his bitten fingernails
along the chain-link wire fence as they walked toward the
maintenance shack at the far end of the volleyball court.
Unconsciously, he tried to imitate the older boy's butter-
smooth walk.

"Hey, Rico, please, what's the matter?"

"Maybe nothin', maybe somethin'."

"Is it about the Plan?"

"Shut up, man, can't you?" Johnny felt Rico's eyes turn
on him briefly in anger. He lowered his head.

"Sorry, Rico."

Rico Moreno was not mad at John Valdes. Angel had
ordered him to check out, warn him if necessary, but
Angel was not mad either. It had been made plain over
and over that no individuals were mixed up in the Plan. It
had nothing to do with the gangs; they were separate from
the Plan. Most would go along, and those that would not
could be forced to.

The lock on the maintenance shack was opened by
Rico's master key with difficulty. The freshly cut key did
not want to turn. There was nothing much inside to protect. In one corner stood a few dented buckets, some of old
Jack's dusty cans of floor stripper, solvent, and a paint can
shaker that had been imbedded in the cement floor when
the shack was new. Old Jack was one of the ones who could
remember the old school, the one replaced by Betsy Ross,
in the forties. That school had been on the same ground,
but the neighborhood then was made up of big private

residences, owned by well-to-do professional and business families with roots downtown. The old school had been for their children, and locked up somewhere in the cafeteria's kitchen was the set of Royal Dux china that had been used by the faculty, tea cups, gravyboats, centerpiece and all. Forty years before, the Administration building had been where the disused maintenance shed now stood, intimidating Johnny Valdes.

"Go on in, man," said Rico, not unkindly, and Johnny did as he was told. He was a Lieutenant, but he was still afraid of Rico, although he had never seen Rico kick anybody's ass without cause, or even get mad. He had heard all about the great fight with Angel of course, but even more than reputation, there was something behind Rico's velvety black eyes that made him afraid.

"Sit down."

Although he was going to be late for fourth period, John sat down on the keg that stood empty in the corner, a circle of old carpeting fitted into its top to make a seat. John waited humbly for Rico to begin.

"Seems you say somethin' to Maria that you shouldn'ta done." Rico reached in his shirt pocket for his last half-cigarette, wondering if Johnny had any he could lift.

"What kind of something?"

Rico shook his head, in faint disgust at Johnny's guilelessness. "Shit, man, whyn't you just say, 'No, I didn't say nothing'?" He looked put upon. "OK, what'd you say to her?" Rico couldn't get too shook. He didn't see Johnny's sister as being anything bad.

"I didn't tell her nothing, Rico. She thinks we gonna rumble. I say maybe yes, maybe no."

"Angel told you to say nothin' to nobody who wasn't next on the list." John Valdes hung his head, unable to think of an answer. Rico took a long, severe drag on his cigarette and offered it to Johnny. "Go ahead, man, we already cut the class. It don't matter. Nobody gonna get no grades this semester nohow." John took a timid hit and handed it back. "Now, what about your talk with Jack?"

At the janitor's name John bounced from the keg as if he'd been goosed. He fell back immediately, stammering, "I didn't tell him nothin', Rico."

"Bull shit. You told him to get sick next week cause there's gonna be trouble. He laughed and told you he couldn't afford to take no time off, cause they might find out he don't really do nothin'." John looked at Rico, wide-eyed. Rico went on. "Hell, man, old Jack's a buddy of mine, too. I'd liketa tell him, but we just can't. Angel told us why. If you can't cut it, baby, you gonna have an accident prob'ly." Rico lowered his voice. "Jack told me what you said a week ago but I didn't say nothin' to Angel. No sense both of you getting killed. You in with us, baby Lieutenant."

The cigarette suddenly burned John Valdes, but he did not let out a yell.

• SIX •

Tuesday

"This is the way it's gonna be." Angel held his notebook up, briefly, so the others could see it. "We down to the Rs, and that's good, but there's something else going on that gonna stop now."

Rico was kneeling in the front row, next to the chastened Johnny Valdes, and Jesus-Maria, with Ismael, Cooper, Laurindo and Contreras lounging uncomfortably, warily against the tile wall, keeping an uneasy eye on the door. The others watched Angel as he opened the notebook and pretended to be checking the names in it. Although he had long since committed its contents to memory, he knew the importance of symbol to his followers. Their black handkerchiefs, the small star tattoo'd in the crook of their thumb and forefinger, and the notebook he was holding. They were physical things that steadied their own uncertain emotions.

"It look like some lames wanta go along, but they don't want their hands on no weapons at Zero Hour. They want to watch the Executioners doing the work."

There was an uneasy shifting of position as a short, moon-faced boy with butter-colored skin and popping,

111

heavily-lidded eyes came through the door, looked over the congregation blankly, and crossed to the trough to take a leak. Angel nodded and said, "Hello, Lizard." Lizard, who was nearly mongoloid, did not nod back, but instead watched the boys out of the corner of his eye as the loud stream of urine splashed against the cake of disinfectant. The Generals and Lieutenants took Angel's signal to allow Lizard to finish in silence, following him with their eyes as he shuffled out.

"Why'n't you tell Ismael to guard the door right, man, instead of sittin' in here with us?" said Rico, with a trace of amusement. Angel seemed as cautious about an idiot as he would have been if the boy's vice-principal had come in to take a leak. Angel met his look evenly.

"This a public john, man, and we don't got the sign out," said Angel. "We don't want no complaints. Anybody sees us in here figures we catchin' a quick hit and that's all. OK?"

"Go on, man." Rico admired Angel's answer. "Tell us what we gotta stop—now."

Into Angel's eyes came the look of utter concentration that had buffalo'd many a stronger boy, and made more than one teacher uneasy. When he was recalling facts and figures, you could almost hear the programmed tape feeding into the computer. Rico loved to watch him thinking, so much that he missed the first of what Angel was saying.

"—so of the twelve hundred we count on seven hundred and fifty definite, three hundred keep quiet no matter what, and one hundred fifty in the close-out this week." He paused, knowing that his next statement would bring a dead halt to the shuffling feet and scratching of noses. "Two o'clock this Friday will be Zero Hour."

Friday. Two o'clock. Only two days away.

The boys looked at one another with a sudden solemnity as they realized that two months of painstaking work had finally brought them to Zero Hour. They thought about Friday, two o'clock, as Angel continued. "I put five new Deputies out this week, with ten contacts each. With the old Deputies working, that means Thursday noon everybody in."

"Jesus, man." Ismael looked serious, like a baby-faced Buddha, his hands glumly pushing up and distorting his soft cheeks. "You want to give'm a whole day to fink?"

"That's why the change of Plan," said Angel, although it was not a change of plan at all. He had known for a week that it would be necessary.

"You didn't say nothin' about no change," said Rico, feeling his heart beating strongly beneath its sheath of young muscle. In his mind, he added, You didn't say nothin' to me. When he was nervous, as he was now, he would knead his chest in an endless pattern of circles. "What change, man?"

Angel's brown knuckles tightened on the spiral wire of his notebook, with its blackpainted cover, and recently added dove design. He spoke slowly, and had their full attention. "Just to make sure that any fink-out knows just what'll happen to him, we gonna make us an example. They're four kids shining us on. They ain't with us."

Rico watched Angel, saw the tension in his hands, and knew what was expected of him. At moments like this, without exchanging words, Rico understood how much Angel depended on him to ask the right questions. He kept his voice quiet. "Who, Angel?"

"Lou Margadonna, Larry Staples, Charley Lees, and Bart Arthur."

"What we gonna do?"

"One of them's gonna have a bad accident. Then the Generals hit the Lieutenants, the Lieutenants hit the Deputies, and the Deputies hit the contacts with the word: he finked, he got hurt. Comes Zero Hour, some kids gonna get hurt with the teachers"—he hesitated, driving the point home,—"if we got any doubt about them. Any doubt at all."

Even Rico felt a chill as he watched Angel leaf thoughtfully through the much decorated notebook, looking at the notations on the more than seven hundred kids who had already been contacted. He felt pride in the fact that some had known for as long as three weeks without a single leak. It confirmed his belief that nobody would take a chance on saying anything that would be ridiculed by the authorities as unbelievable. Mrs. Del Valle in French class had indignantly read the class a newspaper clipping about a bunch of high school kids in the suburbs who had not finked even though they knew that one of their classmates had raped a girl, killed her, and hid her body in a cabbage field across from the new Panorama Medical Center. At the time it had not registered on him as anything but a stupid story, but as the Plan had begun to take shape in his mind, he remembered the story. Looking up from his notebook, he saw that they were all watching him expectantly.

"That's what the contacts will be told," he went on,

"and as long as it keeps them quiet until Zero we won't have to hurt any of them. After Zero we all in it together, including the contacts. Then it won't make no difference what nobody say."

Rico saw that Angel was finished, and shifted his weight uncomfortably onto his other ankle. "OK, man, but what about the examples? What we gonna do to them?"

Before Angel could reply, the swinging door opened and Tio Valdes rushed in from standing Assistant Guard, his eyes wide. "Mister Post coming! Right now!"

In a moment they were all dispersed around the rest room, cigarettes flushed down toilets, windows swung open while fanning out the fetid air. The boys were locking themselves into the stalls, or washing their hands, or standing at the urinals as the door swung again, and in came Roger Post, a wry, you-can't-fool-me look on his broad face. He looked around the room, lifting his head higher to sniff ostentatiously with his flaring nostrils.

The boys watched him noncommitally; no hostility, a few indifferent greetings. Several sauntered from the urinals to the wash-basins, without bothering with the pretense of conversation. Anyway, the teachers knew that nobody talked when they were around. Angel was leaning against the wall, as though waiting for a friend to finish his leak, the notebook tucked casually under his arm. Post's nailfile of a voice broke the loud silence.

"Just who do you guys think you're fooling? I could see the smoke pouring out of the transom halfway down the hall."

Rico stood casually, listening politely, his cupped hand fanning slightly to dissipate the smoke from his concealed cigarette. Post looked right past him, as Rico blew gently on his fingers.

"The reason for the rule against smoking is because this rat's nest might go up any time, dammit. If you have to smoke, go behind the volleyball court where you can't do as much damage. I don't care if you all die of lung cancer, but I like to get my paycheck."

Angel had done some careful research on Post, and come to the conclusion that he was doing him a favor by ending his misery on Friday. Anybody who hated his students that much must be miserable. Post looked around the head again, pugnaciously, then pushed out the door as rapidly as he had come in. For several seconds nobody said anything, and then Angel motioned them back to their places, without comment on the interruption.

"OK, we gonna vote on the finks," he went on. "We gotta make sure we get a lame who does us some good, so don't vote against nobody just 'cause he beat you out with some pigeon. It gotta be an accident, and it gotta happen blackass fast so we can get the holy word out to everybody in this book." Like an evangelist, Angel held up the black notebook, straight up, dove out, his elbow locked in place. "This afternoon the Contact Committee finishes the S through V, and I want all of them in on the accident, too. OK? OK." Angel looked around, for confirmation, and was surprised to see a bony hand in the air from the back level of Lieutenants.

"Charley Lees is just a fag." A thin, dark boy with pale skin and owlish glasses had piped up with determination. "He wouldn't hurt any of us." The others looked at Harold Craner pityingly, understanding that he was Charley Lees only friend. They looked at Angel, to see what he was going to do to Harold. He surprised them by replying in a soft voice.

"I just said he could cop out, Lieutenant."

At the word Lieutenant Harold Craner shut his face and leaned against one of the stalls. On the second try, he managed to accept a nervous hit off one of Juan Laurindo's cigarettes. He should have known better than to question Angel's decision, even though he correctly suspected that even his mild protest had made its impression. Each of the proposed victims might have his own champion now without inviting Angel's wrath. He looked around with a sliver of pride in his accomplishment as Jesus-Maria Ortiz put up his hand.

"Lou Margadonna's gonna be a priest, man." Jesus-Maria had decided to come to Louis' defense. "He said he wouldn't do nothin' because killing's wrong, but he ain't gonna do nothin' to nobody to stop us."

Angel looked at Jesus-Maria steadily, trying to make him look away. When he would not, Angel knew that Margadonna would get clued in that same night, which was what he was after. Once warned, he would not be dangerous.

"Maybe you right, man," Angel agreed affably.

"How come Larry Staples?" Gil Lieber cleared his throat. He looked personally affronted as he fingered his star of David under his T-shirt. "He's my contact, and he said very clearly that he was in."

"He's Bart Arthur's buddy," said Angel, getting to the point he was waiting to make. He looked at Gil Lieber sternly, "And we all know Bart's got something on his

mind, don't we, Lieber?" Anxious to disassociate himself
from Bart, Gil nodded his sandy head among general
murmurs of agreement.

Clark Cooper, in the slow drawl that covered a quick
mind, took advantage of the momentary silence to speak
up. "Charley Lees was droppin' around that he was high
on the idea of gettin' sick this week, but I dis-highed that
boy fast. Man, I thought he would never shut up about his
poor nervous sister, but I told him he better make sure she
keep her mouth just as tight as that sweet pussy."

"You want to put Sandy on the list?" asked Rico, bored
with all the talk. It was his cue to Angel to put the silver
bullet in the heart of the one he had been wanting all
along. Rico sensed the right moment to interrupt without
having to give it a thought. "What d'y' say, Angel?"

Angel pretended to think a moment. "No," he said, "I
don't think so. Sandy Lees is scared enough, and so will ol'
Charley be when I'm through." He paused for effect, his
heartbeat ticking in his throat like a timebomb. "Let's us
talk about Bart Arthur."

• • •

"Eat, Bart." His mother pushed the contents of a can of
artichoke hearts at him as though they were chips, and he
had just broken the bank at Monte Carlo.

"If the boy don't want to eat, don't force," said Mr.
Arthur. "Can't you see he is not with us?"

The last comment was delivered with tremendous sarcasm, and referred to the fact (indisputable) that Bart
Arthur's fork had hovered like a hummingbird over the
same piece of stew meat for a full minute, while his black
eyes stared deep into some private dream.

"For the stomach, thinking is not enough," Mrs. Arthur affirmed placidly, the suffering of six thousand years supporting her every statement. "We buy special treats he should enjoy them without doing us a favor. Artichoke hearts are a great delicacy."

Automatically, with his reflex to please, Bart Arthur took an artichoke heart. He began to dismember it with his fork, thinking that inside it looked like seafood, which he hated. His mother was satisfied, but not silenced.

"Filling out." She made the observation without pleasure, much as she might have said It's raining, and why shouldn't it. It's been threatening for days, and we've just been lucky. "And doing so well in school," she remembered. "We should be proud, and not pick at him so much over trifles."

His father snorted. "Don't talk about him like he isn't here. On second thought, he isn't here. Talk about him any way you like."

"All A plusses and a B, which he's allowed. If that doesn't call for an artichoke heart, what could?"

Bart Arthur was a slender boy with a pearly, opalescent skin that bruised easily, and stretch marks at various parts of his body where he had grown too rapidly. He ate his food slowly, mechanically, keeping in mind that a hundred chews had the effect of increasing the nutritional value of his food by nearly twenty percent. He had his father's thick, curly black hair, grown too low along his forehead, and a straight, handsome nose, but his mother had contributed the flaccid, big-lipped mouth that would never go away, which he studied nightly in the mirror with despair. His fingernails were long and smoothly manicured, countering a constant temptation to tear at them with his teeth.

After a decade of childhood nailbiting, all at once he had decided he would stop, and stop he had. It had been one of a rapid series of self-inflicted mortifications, none of which had made him feel more deserving, of whatever it was that one ought to deserve. His father stared at the hand holding the empty fork.

"Aren't your fingernails getting too long?"

That was easy. "No, they're not."

"First he chews them until they are bloody stumps, then he wouldn't give up a millimeter."

His father, a grocer with two small struggling groceries in run-down neighborhoods, privately felt that there must be something unmanly about the fingernails and the taking of baths all the time, scrubbing at the skin with Boraxo on the body. Nonetheless, he solaced himself by knowing, and repeating to anyone that would listen, that his son was the center on the best intramural basketball team at Ross, which was not bad at all, and might get him a scholarship in college if he pursued it.

For Bart the basketball was a way of selling out, of getting some unwanted semi-friends and keeping Mr. Williams, the coach, who also taught his worst subject, relatively content. He knew he was pretty good, and so he played, hating every minute of it and feeling strange in the locker room afterwards with all those shiny black bodies and their endless "mans" and "cats" and "check out." When he was alone in front of the mirror he could do a pretty fair imitation of the way his black teammates talked, and the jumpy, ass-up-and-out way they walked and flicked towels. He knew there had to be something wrong with him, because they obviously did not feel the same way about him as he felt about them. Worse, some of them seemed to like him for real, treating his sourness as a joke that they could see through easy enough.

Being liked was simultaneously the dream and the terror of Bart Arthur. He got along with Mr. Melnick, the math teacher, because he was naturally good at math. He suspected that Melnick did not really like him for himself, but for his ability at math, and the fruitless expectation that he might take a first at the upcoming science fair in Pomona with his genetics model. As well as being the best mathematics student in the school, Bart was good at design, and with the help of the shop teacher his model was beautiful. It was ironic to Bart that Mr. Brown, a plump and grizzled Negro, should help him build a science fair model that proved that Negroes were inferior. For this, in a subtle round about way, was what Bart Arthur truly believed, from careful personal study.

If he had to look at that hairy artichoke heart for another second he was going to vomit. "Excuse me, please," he mumbled, "I've got to study." It was the acceptable, unchallengeable excuse. His parents watched him escape them with a sense of accomplishment.

Bart Arthur was an only child, so he had his own bedroom, down the hall where he could be quiet. The apartment was old and uncertainly heated, with worn-out plumbing fixtures disguised with new brass, but it was a high-ceilinged place that had at one time been luxurious. As his father's business had improved falteringly, so too had the wallpaper, and the nylon carpeting, put in the previous year at great expense. Bart had lived there ever since he could remember, and only once, when his mother was pregnant, was there any real talk of moving. The pregnancy had been a false alarm. She had lost the child, and secretly Bart had been glad.

As he lay on his bed thinking, he had a temporary sense of privacy that made his toes curl. His parents never bothered him when they thought he was studying, and whenever he did not play his records or listen to the radio, that was what they thought. In reality, he was worrying over the Plan.

At first he had been flattered, since he was practically the first to know. Angel himself had come up to him, and invited him to listen to some ideas he was cooking up. The more he heard, the more fantastic it had seemed, until he remembered how Angel had organized the rumble in his first year at Ross. More than five hundred kids had known about that, and nobody said a word until it was on, and too late. Angel had pulled it off, with his gang that was almost all from school.

Bart had been younger, impressionable, and the way it went off gave him the willies. One day, right after fifth period, suddenly the chicanos all seemed to melt out of their classes, silently, without good-byes or comments. The girls watched the boys go, and everyone knew what was about to happen. An hour later eighteen of the gang were in county hospital, the police had shut down the school temporarily, and the rivals from the Clover Street gang had one boy dead of knife wounds, and thirty more injured. Since the boy died, it had even gotten into the papers, and Bart could not forget that Angel had not been scratched, or got into trouble with the school or police.

As Angel described the Plan to him, Bart saw that it had a chance. Everything depended ultimately on the fact that no one would believe it even if someone told. He could just picture himself saying to his father that some kids at school were planning to kill the teachers. His father would laugh.

Furthermore, the Plan as a concept intrigued him. As Angel started reeling off the echelons, Generals, Executioners, Lieutenants, Deputies, Assistant Deputies, Gatemen, Muscle, he had started to consider what he would do is he was in charge instead of Angel, if it had been his idea.

Bart had even drawn him a chart, demonstrating mathematically how all contacts could be completed in three weeks if he added two more Deputies. Angel had taken his chart and his advice, and thanked him kindly. A week later Bart realized that he was not going to be a Lieutenant, much less a General, in the carrying out of the Plan. It burned him. There was no way to avoid the conclusion that it had been because he was not one of them. Of Charley Lees, Larry Staples, the Wilson twins and Gil Lieber, only Gil had been picked as a Lieutenant, and that was because he wanted to be Mr. Post's Executioner.

In the weeks following, Bart heard nothing more from Angel, or Rico, or anybody. When they passed in the hallways there would be a nod of sorts, but he felt excluded. Even here it was prejudice, a monstrous race prejudice in reverse. They took the chicanos, and bloods like Cooper and the Turners, but they left him out. He had the school paper, and the science fair, and the basketball team and the school chorus, and he would not have wanted to be in at all, except that he was not asked. That he could never forgive.

• • •

Rico had been working out all afternoon, and touching him was like touching a piece of hard rubber. She loved to feel the line of muscle under his chest, the tiny teardrop-shaped muscles, firm like drumsticks along his ribs.

"Don't, Rico honey." Angela Vallens made a show of pulling his tense brown hand away as he put it between her legs and skootched up her nice cotton skirt. "Rico."

"I gotta." He felt her pushing against the weight of his hand with a gesture of desperation as he reached around with the other to pull her against him. He kissed her.

"You don't gotta, honey. You know how I am." Angie scooted her rear end around so there was more room in the car for his long legs. She was always afraid when her father loaned them the car that they would leave spots on the upholstery. For several minutes they did not move, except to press tighter together. Rico's clean white shirt was unbuttoned at the collar, the tieknot slipped down to free his neck. A trickle of sweat slipped over the edge of his chin, about to drop onto the V of his shirt onto his smooth chest. With the swiftness of an iguana going after a sleepy fly, Angie's tongue picked it off before it could fall.

"You're so salty, honey," she said softly. "You always get so sweaty. Sit still a minute."

"It's different for me, Angie," said Rico, moving his hand around so it was under her dress, feeling for the edge of her panties. He kissed her, and she kissed him back when he tried to pull away to concentrate on finding the panties.

"Not so different," she allowed, as Rico's hand touched skin, hesitated, and then moved farther, running over the mound of her buttocks without pressure, stopping a moment as his finger found her mole. They kissed again, still lightly, while Rico's fingers explored the crevices of her astonishingly cool body. Her slim hand rested lightly over the throbbing bulge in his pants. Her clear brown eyes showed no surprise as he groaned, "Angie, I want to—"

"Mmmm," she pulled away from his mouth, "Rico—"

"If you don't let me—"

"I know," she said, sighing.

Without knowing why, Angela Vallens realized that Rico had done something wrong again. She could always tell by the way he acted when he came to get her, the way he said hello to the family as they sat around the TV, the way he would accept the key to the old Plymouth from her father. He was practically one of the family, but for the last month he had not said ten words to her parents, or picked up the baby to launch him into the air convulsed with pleasurable fear. Rico seemed now to want to get in and out as fast as he could, to get away from the family, to get away from everybody but her.

Even his lovemaking had become different. He would not take no for an answer, not even when she told him it was dangerous. He felt her and touched her all the time like he was afraid she might disappear. At first she had been afraid that he was sniffing glue again. For the first time, he kissed her with his eyes open, looking right at her with a funny look. She always kissed with her eyes closed, and had only opened them in surprise when he suddenly kissed her so hard he hurt her. There was a trickle of blood where she had bit the inside of her lip, and Rico could not seem to take his eyes off it.

"I'm sorry, honey," he said. "Jesus."

"It's OK, Rico." She touched the bloody spot, and looked at her finger. Very gently, Rico took the hand, and

for a terrible moment Angie thought he was going to suck
the blood from her finger. He saw the look in her face, and
let go of her hand as though it had burned him.

● ● ●

"Stop it, Charley! You're hurting me."

"Don't talk so loud. They'll hear you. Come in my room
a second, will you?"

"What's going on there?"

"Nothing, Papa, nothing!" A whisper, "Are you coming
or not?"

For several moments Charley Lees didn't say a word to
his sister as she sat on the bed, her hands folded stubbornly
in her lap. He didn't know how to begin. "Sandy."

"What?"

He licked his lips. "You can't say anything."

"What makes you think I'd say anything?"

"I can tell. You were."

"That shows how much you know."

"You swear it?" There was a silence, as Charley studied
his sister and saw that she would never swear it.

"You know what's happening, and you don't care!" said
Sandy suddenly, the hard line of her mouth seeming to
come apart.

"I do care. I just don't want you to say anything."

"Charles! Sandra?" Their mother's voice. *"Dinner is
ready. Wash your hands."*

● ● ●

Louis Margadonna was standing in the back of the dark,
empty church. He had served six o'clock Mass for Father

LaFollette before going to school, just as he had for three years. A dark, intense boy with curly hair that grew low along his forehead, Louis was trying to make up his mind what he should say to Father. He had talked the matter over with Jesus-Maria and he was really afraid to learn that Angel thought that he was not to be trusted, even after he had given his word. Jesus-Marie had tried to laugh it off, out of friendship, but Louis knew it had been serious. He had been warned, and he did not know what to do, unless he could talk to Father LaFollette about it. But then again, what could he say without breaking his promise to Angel?

Louis moved along the center aisle, and slipped into the front pew to kneel and think. He could not continue to serve Mass with a huge mortal sin on his conscience either. He would have to tell Father that he would not be there any more at five-thirty, or . . . or, he might confess what he was doing. But what could he confess, except that he was afraid? He was not going to kill anyone.

Louis was still in the same position, an hour later when the ladies from the Altar Society came in to put flowers around for the wedding at nine.

· · ·

NATURE'S PARADISE said the marquee, and, in smaller letters, THREE WHO CARED. As Bart Arthur crossed the street against the light to get a look at the display photos, he saw an old man fumbling with his pants trying to take a leak against a storage mailbox.

"Hey, man, you shouldn't do that," he said. "That's government property." He pointed helpfully to a couple of cops on the opposite corner, but the old man obviously did not give a damn. It was Tuesday night on the corner of Third and Main, and as the man looked up at Bart, the multicolored reflections from the pawnshop made a pair of bloody tiaras of his eyes. "Gotta pee," he explained at random, a look of relief lighting his face as his only immediate problem splashed against the freshly painted blue and scarlet of the mailbox.

As Bart studied the movie posters with care, he was disappointed to see that the women's imposing breasts were covered with black stars, added by an unsteady hand that made some of them closer to asterisks. The advertisement said *Continuous all Night,* a piquant idea, and BINGO WEDNESDAY. Bart had half a mind to spend the whole night in the movie house, listening to the snoring and inhaling the smells, knowing that the worn velvet a few inches from his knees would be stiff with sperm.

Occasionally, very occasionally, thank God, he felt he just had to leave the apartment and start walking, hitching, anything to get downtown. When he had been leered at and groped, given several eventful rides to the wrong places—he went hoping that there were no wrong places—only to be released like a sneeze into the night life of Main Street, he was always disappointed. It was like poking a needle into a shiny, swollen balloon, only to discover it was styrofoam.

The bars were filled at the one o'clock peak, mostly with Orientals and Mexicans, with a smattering of young, shaved and stunned servicemen. It was a wonder to Bart that they did not seem to have any trouble getting served, when a lot of them looked just as young as he did, with bad

skins and youth written all over them. It was a further part
of the great conspiracy. Bart spat on the cement in disgust
as some stubbly man standing on the corner said something to him that he did not quite catch. For the next ten
minutes he was haunted by the possibility that it had been
something really important to him, aimed at him, for his
ears only, at last the meaningful statement about mankind
and love and how to find it.

"Aren't you scared of this place, a young fellow like
you?" asked a fat redhead, leaning over at him as though
she wanted to look down his loose collar. "You a service-
man?" she said, making conversation.

"No. I'm a . . ." Bart wondered what she might believe, and then despised himself for caring. "I'm a student
from U.C.L.A."

"What d'y' know," said the woman. "I shoulda guessed.
My name's Maidie and you're pretty cute." She wanted to
get to the point as quickly as possible.

Bart had missed her name, but he nodded anyway, wondering when someone was going to come along and ask for
his I.D. The busy bartender brought him his drink and
disappeared so fast that he did not even have time to look
guilty, fishing in his pocket for some change. All of a sudden people were standing at the bar three deep so he felt
lucky to have a seat. He produced his only five dollar bill,
which Maidie examined with diminished interest. "I've
done very well tonight," she said absently, looking around
the bar.

"How come you asked me if I was scared of this place?"
Bart paid for his drink, his heart pounding, and counted

his change hopefully. If it had been wrong, he would not have dared dispute it.

"Hm?"

He saw that Maidie was watching a confused grey-haired customer who had stumbled in and found himself in front of the huge mirror that ran the length of the bar. He had ordered a drink from himself very diffidently, before someone turned him around and pushed him toward the bar near Maidie.

"I asked you why you wanted to know if I was scared."

Maidie looked at Bart Arthur unsteadily, and for a brief instant her eyes seemed to clear. "Oh, I don't know, you look young, I guess— You might be my kid if I hadn't flushed 'em all down the toilet. Excuse me."

"Maidie!" said somebody at the far end of the bar, and Bart never saw her again.

SEVEN

Wednesday

Coming into the faculty room, a roll of charcoal drawings under his arm, Tim had an elated look until he saw Roger Post sitting by himself. His first instinct was to hide the drawings, so he would not have to talk about them, but he saw it was too late. An unwelcome look of camaraderie crossed the history teacher's oversized face.

"Tim boy!"—a nickname he had taken to calling Tim, "Where have you been? You've been mighty scarce the last two days." He closed his History Quarterly, and Tim felt done for.

"I've been running some special projects for Miss Twigg, some extra work. We'll be putting in a new display cabinet on the second floor." Tim put the drawings on the desk, and bent over to try to pull the stuck drawer open without pulling it out altogether. Roger nodded, and came over to look at the drawings, as Tim had feared he would.

"Cleaire was asking about you, so was Evelyn and Will Willson." He looked over Tim's shoulder. "Those for your special project, Tim boy?"

"In a way." Tim rolled the oversized sheets of paper tighter, slipping a thick rubber band over the end to hold them.

"We've got to get the audio-visual equipment in some kind of order, and nobody has volunteered except Sarah Vardis."

"Um-hm." Tim's look of disinterest was complete.

For a moment Roger stood helpless, his head shifting from side to side like a bull whose heart has been missed by the sword. Tim struck him as being one of the more intelligent faculty members, but he was damned if he would court him just to get a conversation. Suddenly Roger Post was lonesome, but he was not sure for what. He returned to his magazine with a big smile. "That's good, Tim boy," he said. "Don't ever lose your enthusiasm. Make those displays just as good as you can make them. If you ever think that your job isn't worth your very best, you're a lost soul, m' boy."

Tim nodded, preoccupied, and went to his next class.

Angel was sitting in front of a large sheet of paper. In one hand he held a new square edged piece of charcoal, while his other hand stood guard over the three big bottles of basic poster paint that he was to share with Ismael and Rico. When he was certain the teacher was not watching, Ismael leaned closer to Angel.

"Meetin' at break, man?" Angel nodded.

"Depending on the period," Mr. Nielsen was saying, "that is, the time in history, artists had different ideas about what they were for. In the earliest times, the artist

had a religious purpose, and his work had value only inso-
far as it made you think about God."

Rico whispered, *"Did you make up your mind about
Bart?"* Angel nodded. *"When?"*

"This afternoon at P.E. Falcons are playing Vikings."

"In the nineteenth century, most art had to tell a story
or it wasn't thought of as art at all. It didn't have to make
you think about God necessarily, but about heroes, or history, or things that happened in everyday life at home. It
had to look like something happening. Some of you might
be able to think of an example, maybe from your own
homes. Maria, can you give me an example of a story-
telling, or anecdote painting?"

Maria Estragon looked uncertain, while Provencia and
Maria LeSanto ate their hearts out with jealousy, and
Jennifer Baily sneered. Tim prodded gently.

"Can you think of a picture that tells a story?"

"Like Jesus praying at the rock?"

"Very good, Maria."

"What we gonna do to him, man?" Angel put his finger
to his lips.

"What story does that picture tell, Maria?"

She thought hard. "It tells that Jesus was praying that he
wouldn't have to die." There was silence in the room, and
even Ismael and Juan Laurindo turned their attention
from Angel to Tim.

"Could you tell that from the painting, Maria?" The
girl looked confused. "I mean, does it actually say that on
the painting somewhere or is that something you know
when you look at it?"

"You just know, I guess."

"So the painting doesn't have Jesus' wish not to die, but we bring what we know of the rest of the story of Jesus to the painting on the wall. It's actually a combination of lines, colors, and shapes. Nowadays we have some artists who don't like stories, because they don't like you to bring things you have heard about to their paintings. They think that the important thing is the paint itself, and what it says directly to us. The painters who feel this way are called abstract expressionists. You don't have to remember unless you want, but I'll write it on the board."

There was a shuffle of uninterest, and Tim immediately went to the blackboard to write: A B S T R A C T I M P R E S S I O N I S M. The noise lessened as he continued with the words, R I T U A L, A N E C-D O T E (S T O R Y) and A C T I O N. "Today I want you to choose one of the three viewpoints we have discussed, and using the primary colors, do something that will show me you know what I've been saying. I don't care which one you choose, as long as it really shows one of these three ways of thinking."

Ritual, anecdote, action. Angel smiled to himself as he looked at the blank sheet, thinking of that afternoon's intramural game. If there was a mistake, if it did not work, he was ready to call off the whole Plan. If he could not get Rico and Juan to handle Bart, the Executioners would never make it on Friday. Without telling any of the Generals or Lieutenants, he was trying one final test.

"Let me just warn you," Tim was saying, "the one that might seem easiest, namely Action"— he pointed to the backboard—"could prove to be the hardest."

Charley Lees was suddenly aware that the room had gone quiet. He tried to reorient himself to the snatches of the lecture that he had heard through the fog of his confused thoughts. He looked over at Angel, and colored as he realized that in the same moment Angel had turned to look at him. He lowered his eyes, as Mr. Nielsen went on.

"There are only fifteen minutes left to the period, so you have the added pressure of time that didn't bother Fra Angelico, Bougereau, or Jackson Pollack. Do your best."

As they worked, Mr. Nielsen moved quietly around the room, saying nothing one way or the other as he looked at the sheets of paper with their predictable quota of families, Christs at rocks, animals, planes, and—he stopped to look—a large and rather beautiful blue abstract by the tall, thin, quietly bitter Bart Arthur in the far back corner.

• • •

As he dodged the sweating, eager faces in front of him, Bart was nearly overwhelmed by his awareness of skin color. I'm ten shades lighter than anyone else on the team, he thought as he faked to the left and moved effortlessly past Rico's outstretched hand and made his basket. The gym was silent except for the sound of rubber soles hitting wood as Bart pulled back into position. He was scarcely breathing hard as he took the hand-off, and looked for an opening. It's because of my color that they won't let me in, he thought, passing the ball to a tall Negro named Zardis. Even my own side won't let me in. Half Jewish and half Black Irish—inherited a bad skin from one and a small cock from the other, he thought wryly as he faked out Tommy Ishi and made two more easy points. Easy, easy, he thought, it's easy for me with these yo-yos, and not—he made his basket—just because I'm tall.

The whistle blew and Bart reached out for the towel that Tio Valdes handed him. The Falcons were ahead by sixteen, no sweat, but there was an anxious look to the little chicano that stopped Bart for a moment. He followed the boy's look and saw that Angel Martine was standing all by himself near the door, watching an intramural game for the first time he could remember.

The whistle blew again, and Bart moved onto the court, more slowly. It irritated him that Angel was there, but he was not sure why. It occurred to him that Angel might have changed his mind about cutting him out of the Plan. If so, he had another think coming. Bart tried not to look over at Angel, not to break his concentration as he worked around little Jesus-Maria without difficulty, dribbled rapidly towards the basket until he was fouled by the muscle-bound oaf, Jesus Contreras. He managed to tip the ball in anyway, as Mr. Williams clapped his black hands and mumbled something that Bart did not get. He made his two points easily, and added four more before Mr. Williams blew the whistle ending the game with an eleven point win for his side, despite a last minute rally by the Vikings.

In the locker room, Bart felt self-conscious as he dropped his gym shorts and peeled off his sweat drenched protector. Everybody was quieter than usual, it seemed to him, but he chalked that up to the approach of Zero hour. As more and more came in, the atmosphere in school seemed to be dipping steadily. He figured that Angel would be nearly through the alphabet if he had stuck to his chart.

"Here, man," said the big Negro, Willis Zardis, tossing a green sliver of soap to Bart on his way into the steaming shower room. Automatically, Bart caught the soap, which was cracked and dry as a buffalo chip. It vaguely offended him that the only person to speak to him in the locker room was a Negro, and a Viking at that. After he had won the game practically singlehanded. Angel had disappeared as mysteriously as he had materialized—Bart still could not figure that out—but the others were there, Rico, Contreras, Clark, Johnny Valdes, and even the towel boy Tio who was sitting balefully by the lockers, waiting for his big brother to finish showering. Mr. Watson, who was supposed to be supervising the tournament, stuck his head in the door just as Bart was carefully hanging up his shirt and pants. He checked them over. Not a wrinkle.

"Everybody OK here?" he wanted to know.

"Good, man," said Ismael cheerfully. "Falcons win thirty-nine to twenty-eight."

"Good, good," said Mr. Watson, withdrawing his head. Ismael watched Bart Arthur pad into the shower room, and he remembered that the score did not make a bit of difference. The grin left his face, as he picked up his towel and followed Bart into the blinding steam.

Bart stepped under the shower-head, which gave him the choice of a feeble spritz or blasting hot needles. He selected the needles, and closed his eyes to escape the sting of chlorine fumes. His chest and shoulders immediately grew pink, but he stood still, letting the needles scald him until he got used to it. Although he looked skinny in his street clothes, Bart was actually a well-built boy, with sturdy legs covered with a fine down of black hair, and broad shoulders that tapered already into a V. He had a beginning nest of dark hair in the very center of his chest, the envy of the smoothskinned Mexicans, and a pigmentless appendicitis scar that pointed annoyingly at what he regarded as his weakest feature. He massaged the chip of medicinal soap into his privates, hoping to stimulate them into a respectable appearance.

Next to him, Clark Cooper was arching backwards into the spray, gargling a song, his ribs like a feathering of fish-flesh, lacquered black. They splayed out under his membrane of wet-suit colored skin, and stretched tight over every bulge of his stomach muscles slippery with soap. Clark's tool was an insult, swinging in front of him like the trunk of an elephant, long and lax and smooth. Clark had been in half the cunts in school, and Bart resented him bitterly for it.

Rico entered the shower room, Tommy Ishi was horse-playing with Contreras and Ismael, who did not want to play. Willis Zardas flicked a rat-tail expertly at the goose-pimpled ass of Harold Craner. Harold let out a yip, and jiggled around indignantly, but without his glasses he could not see who had hit him. He complained in general, while Rico neatly rolled his towel and tossed it over the top of the communal shower stall. He could not take his eyes off Bart Arthur, who was now soaping his underarms with the furious concentration of one who was feeling ignored. Tommy Ishi and John Valdes took what seemed to be two-second showers and got out of there fast, closely fol-

lowed by Ismael Sato. The others were watching full of
curiosity as Bart lifted up his face, turned around, and let
the full force of the suddenly thunderous shower-spray explode in his face.

Rico watched him, stalking with his eyes. He looked at
the sharp handles that stuck out of the tile near Bart's
head. Methodically, Rico was massaging soap into his own
skin, so much extra soap that he looked like a snowman,
made of froth. He watched Bart, intensely thinking of what
Angel had said to him. Get Bart Arthur, your own way,
but hurt him bad enough that he'll never forget it. Rico's
heart was pounding directly under his fingers, as though it
might escape.

A billow of steam made his eyes sting briefly shut, and
when he opened them he saw Bart, his eyes closed against
the soapy spray, the splatter. Rico saw helplessness. Bart's
thin but wiry body was washing clear of soap. He was
glistening like a freshly caught tuna, his legs and arms
shiningly white, the ripple of his rib cage and the strain of
his muscles as he made the effort of reaching blindly for his
towel. He was blinking, his head close to that jagged shape,
that looming fixture of lead and chrome and sharpness—

"Oh man, that's a lot of blood."

"Don't touch him—"

"There's water goin' in his face—it'll choke him."

"No it don't— Go get Watson. Go on!"

"What happen? *Jesus*—"

"Nothin', Willis, he slip and hit his head on the wall."
Rico was looking at Bart's face with cool amazement. It
had been easy.

"Hit his head! Man, it open!"

"Where's Watson?"

"Bart? Bart? You OK? Shit, I think he's dead."

The naked black form of Willis Zardas knelt in the shower water that shot from the hot shower head, spreading and beading over the still face of Bart Arthur as he sprawled on the grey-green tiles of the shower room.

"Turn off that goddam water, Rico, will you?"

"Sure, Willis," said Rico, reaching to turn the water off as Mr. Watson's voice could be made out echoing in the locker room, getting rapidly closer. Rico could not take his eyes off the drained white face of the injured boy as the gym supervisor burst in, nearly slipping on the wet tile.

"God damn it," he said, righting himself. Then his voice dropped to a whisper. "Good God, what happened?" Mr. Watson's voice, normally as loud as a stabbed bull's, was barely audible above the thin hissing of the one shower that had been left half-running. He was so shocked that he did not even pay attention to the fact that only Rico Moreno and Willis Zardas had stayed with the wounded, bleeding boy. The others had hightailed it out in the confusion and headed for their lockers, where they quickly dried off and started dressing.

"Jesus, you see that?" A whisper.

"Not exact, it was fast—"

"That Rico he *move*, man; it almost an accident for sure."

"Shut up, man. Here come Watson."

A bellow now from the partially recovered, red-faced man: "Ishi, get Miss Summers. Tell the office to call an ambulance, Miss Peters will . . . oh, Christ, she's not there today."

The Oriental boy looked stricken. "Mr. Watson, I got no pants on . . . I . . ."

"I'm dressed," said Jesus-Maria promply, a light in his eyes at the prospect of being the first to spread the news. The others looked from Watson, to Jesus-Maria, and back, as he tried to make up his mind.

"Go on, then, dammit. What's the matter with all of you? Why'd you let him lie there bleeding?"

"Bleed, man?" Jesus Contreras shook his head. "That cat, he bleed fast."

• • •

Tim Nielson spread the two drawings in front of him on the desk and looked at them. The very things that pleased him would plunge Marge into depression if he showed them to her that night. She would go into her "but they don't have any opportunity to use their talent" spiel. Still, he wanted her to see them. She would like them in and of themselves.

Bart Arthur's drawing was all in blues, with just an undertow of yellow to give an ocean feeling to the strong shapes. He had selected *Action,* and the paint moved on the paper as though it had a will of its own. The emotions in Bart Arthur's drawing were all swimming under the surface like a school of very large and very dangerous fish. It made an interesting contrast to Angel Martine's near-primitive *Story-telling* picture. He would have guessed that Angel would choose *Anecdote,* but the boy had surprised him. In its own way Angel's drawing was remarkable.

The bearded man riding a donkey was not Christ entering Jerusalem (although they had discussed that painting). The background was not Jerusalem but downtown Los Angeles, with the Central Market, Solly's Used Men's Wear, the Union Mission, the Main Street Gym, and the Buddhist Temple in the crazy juxtaposition of a Bemelmans' dream. The bloody butcher shop or the Buddhist Temple with its decorous wedding party did not have to exist outside of the colorful drawing, where the shirts of the men and the plain blue of the cloudless sky and all the other bright colors were indicated by the slightest dash of primary red, yellow, blue, and outlines of flat, soft black.

Figures—what were they?—moved toward the man on the donkey, to attack with a single-minded agression that seemed to have its answer in Bart Arthur's stabs of dark, transfigured color.

● ● ●

"This is a tragedy I find very hard to understand." In this excitement William Conrad had increased his southern accent noticeably. Although he tried to cover his fear by raising his voice, in fact Conrad had expected a possible accident in the boy's gym, where the walls and floors as much as the equipment took a terrific beating. "I find it impossible to understand, Watson. I don't like this report at all."

Herschel Watson, who taught mathematics and supervised the Wednesday intramural basketball tournament, found it impossible to understand either. He shook his head from side to side, shaken by the possibility that the principal would not sign the Pupil Accident Report that he had filled out so nervously.

"It was not my fault," he said faintly, remembering that he had not asked for the duty.

"I didn't say it was your fault," said the principal, furious at this little man for even suggesting such a thing. His eye fell on the section of the report, #20. Nature of Injury (CHECK ONE ONLY).The idiot had checked "other." He sighed.

"I'll have to have the secretary do this again, Hersch. After your last class this afternoon come in and we'll go over the whole thing. My God, Miss Peters was supposed to be out of here right after school—you don't know what has to be filled out, Hersch, for something like this. And worst of all, of course, is notifying the parents. He was one of our best boys."

There was an uncomfortable silence, while Conrad tried to be careful in the selection of words. He did not want to create any situation if one did not already exist, but he suspected that one did. "Tell me the truth, Hersch. What exactly happened in the showers?"

"Mr. Conrad, I wrote it up for the report. You've got it in front of you." Herschel Watson did not know how outraged he was allowed to be.

"Slipped and fell against the fixture, striking his head." William Conrad frowned.

"I wasn't there, of course. I was in the locker room, supervising uniform exchange—"

"You're absolutely sure no one pushed him? You know we've had such accidents before, and it's generally come out later that there was a little disagreement— It could be very embarrassing, Hersch. You know we'll back you to the wall, regardless, but if something should turn up—"

"He was the team center for the Falcons, Mr. Conrad, and a good one. I can't watch them every second, in the shower, but I'm sure nobody was mad at him during the game."

"Bart Arthur was a Muir transfer, Hersch. Did you notice any other resentment against him?"

"No, sir, I didn't. Mr. Conrad, I was given the assignment of supervising the game. I didn't ask for it. Mr. Williams put in priority forms for fixing the tile, but maintenance hasn't been near the gym. We can't keep putting in requests every day. I have five classes to teach."

Herschel Watson had been in the supply room smoking when the accident occurred. He was not supposed to be there. There was a brief silence as William Conrad studied the Pupil Accident Report, and then the tense, confused face in front of him. He tried to be gentle. "Well, then, pray, Hersch. Just pray that we don't get a hell of a lawsuit thrown against the city schools by the poor boy's parents. I'll see you after your last class and we'll go over this report with Miss Peters."

After Watson had left his office, Conrad had Miss Peters bring his folder in. It was already on her desk when he asked for it, and the grimness of her jaw as she handed it to him made it clear how she felt about the matter. Conrad looked at the old evaluations on the man, and a few scribbled memos loose in the folder waiting to be typed for the permanent record.

Inspected classrooms, said one, in Conrad's own precise, flowering hand. *Found windows in incorrect position, sunshades improperly drawn.* It was dated several months before. *Missed Mtg 1/15, Missed Mtg 2/8.* There was a note from Miss Peters, on her personalized memo pad: *Mr. C, Herschel Watson made two personal phone calls without putting them on the sheet. Also signs of nipping. Conference with him indicated.*

There were several other items, mostly of little importance. The evaluations themselves were not bad, he was relieved to see. In case of an investigation, he decided to take the bad notes out of the folder and dispose of them. Thank heaven they had not yet been typed up in permanent form for the man's performance file.

● ● ●

There was something wrong with Rico's timing as he sparred with a short white boy named Tiger for the tattoos on both his forearms. Even though they were just fooling around, waiting for the big ring, the white boy was the more serious, peppering Rico lightly on the stomach and headguard, trying to get him to take an interest. "Come 'n, man, defend yourself," said Tiger, landing two weightless lefts on Rico's chin. Suddenly Rico shook him off.

"Forget it today, man," he said, and jumped out of the small ring. "Friday," he promised.

"What about tomorrow?" said Tiger, but nobody was listening.

When Rico got out of the showers, Angel was waiting for him, sitting quietly on the bench by the lockers. He

was toying with a keychain with only one key on it, and
that to the front door of his apartment building.

"Rico." Angel nodded.

"I'll be out in a minute," said Rico, avoiding Angel's
eyes by pretending to study his face briefly in the mirror.

"No rush, man." Angel looked at the row of muscle
clearly defined across his friend's back. It occurred to
Angel that Rico had grown another inch and put on ten
pounds in the last few months. Part of it was from working
out at the gym every day, but mostly it was because Rico
had given up sniffing when he decided to start training.
Angel could remember nights going out with Rico to pick
up some money, cutting out drunks at the bar with Rico so
dazed from the glue that he could barely walk. Things had
changed.

"You know, man . . ." Angel hesitated, then: "I think
you could win me now."

Rico turned to look at Angel, a strange look in his eye
that seemed briefly to be fear. He said nothing.

"You bigger now, Rico. I think you could be leader if
you want. Do you want to be the leader?"

Rico shook his head.

"Hell no, Angel. You the leader."

When he was in the shower, Rico studied his body and
thought about what Angel had said. The day in September
when they had fought he remembered that his chest had
been smaller. His arms had been skinny, brown beef-jerky
arms, tight with buds of muscle not yet bloomed into manhood. Rico had been a tough, stringy kid, the best opponent for Angel, who was slightly shorter but fearless.

Angel knew how to use leverage to make the most of his weight. He seemed able to shut his mind to physical pain, to turn it aside until you wondered if you were moving him at all. You could hit him until you felt teeth break under your knuckles; it did not affect the calculating expression of his eyes as he studied you, waiting for you to relax for a second, or make a mistake and drop your guard long enough for him to come in and blind you.

Angel had learned to fight in the alley, and he was good. Although he had looked at the books in the library, he did not need to study karate to know that there were places on the body where you could do fast, bad damage. He had learned first hand, watching the older boys in the laboratory of the street. Angel had studied the science of death with the single-mindedness of a drill sergeant, from the not-so-accidental death of the skid row bum with his pension check to the purposely neglected baby, accidental victim of smothering in the bedding on the floor. In the course of learning how to defend himself, Angel had become expert in the use of his bony knee, and the toughened side of his hand to snap a wrist. He knew how to gouge, and cut the eyebrow with his signet ring, gaining in that instant of blood the necessary advantage.

When Rico finally realized that he was being maneuvered into a fight with Angel for leadership, he was afraid, not because Angel had ever whipped him other than in play, but because Rico was not sure about himself if he was fighting his friend for real. Still, there had been the insurmountable and ultimately final persuader. Until somebody challenged him and lost, Angel could not be the real leader.

In a way, Rico reflected, rubbing the cheap soap into his chest and muscles, kneading the abdominals that contracted lurchingly under his fingers as though he had just finished a thousand sit-ups, in some odd, half-understood way he had finally given in because Angel wanted him to, because Angel needed his help and let him know it.

Even though they weighed about the same, Rico figured to lose. Still, he would put up a good fight, the sort Angel could be proud to win. It would establish his authority for the next year without question, allowing him to pursue his dream of binding the bloods and the chicanos together against the whites.

Not all the kids had come to the warehouse at 8:30 on the twenty-third of September, but Angel made sure that the top bloods were there, Clark Cooper with his buddy Bill Turner, who was the biggest boy in the school, Bill's brother Booker, who was almost as big and twice as stupid. Cooper had wisely decided not to challenge for leadership, mainly because he was always getting into trouble, and Angel led a charmed life. The chicano had been busted once, for Grand Theft Auto, taken his nine months at camp and came out smelling like a petunia. Clark Cooper had never taken a car, not even a tape recorder out of one, nor a camera from a broken store window during the riots, but he was constantly getting stopped, shook down, put on suspension, near kicked out of school, and every other damn thing in the world. He wanted to graduate, and maybe get a job. He decided to play it cool.

Besides, there was sure as hell no guarantee he could kick Angel's ass. If he did fight, and come out on the bottom, he would lose his position with the other bloods for no good reason at all. As he never tired of boasting, he was a lover, not a fighter unless you mess with him.

With the Mexicans outnumbering them two to one anyway, he could just sit tight, guest of honor, and watch them kick each other's asses with good pleasure.

There were no pigeons allowed, for the very fine reason that tales of the fight would for sure be bloodier and more awe-inspiring than the reality. The one exception to the rule was Angela Vallens, the best-looking girl in school, who was Angel's. She was there because in theory she would belong to the winner, an academic question in the minds of most of the excited kids who kept their voices low as they waited for the action to begin.

The warehouse was three blocks from the school, and both the neighborhood gangs had keys. No need to break in, or make any hassle. There was a standing rule that nothing in the warehouse was to be touched, and nothing had ever been stolen from it. It served as a meeting place, a honeycomb of bedrooms—some of the big machine tools were wrapped in comfortable stuffed canvas wrappers—and a place to shoot craps, and fight with nobody to break it up.

The warehouse had a big flat floor that served as the ring. Even though more than two hundred kids were squatting, sitting, standing around, some on crates set up as grandstands, others up in the dirt-jockey's seats of earth-moving equipment that stood frozen like mechanical prehistoric monsters, everybody had a place, and the atmosphere was very formal, even solemn as Rico and Angel, stripped to their shorts, entered the open place and looked at each other. A squad of little boys was assigned clean-up; when a nine-tenths smoked butt would hit the floor, someone would be on it in less than two seconds. It would be dropped into a handkerchief, and at the end of the fight the clean-up crew could use the collection to make themselves rollies.

Ismael was the referee, timekeeper, and holder of Angel's wristwatch, which he would be using to time the fight. It was understood without words that the two boys would go to the middle of the cleared space, touch their bare knuckles together, and then the fight would begin. Ismael glanced over at Angie, who was standing in Angel's corner, and he was momentarily surprised to see that she was staring, not at Angel, but at Rico.

As he washed himself, and turned slowly around to let the soapy water flood down his body in a scummy avalanche, Rico remembered that he had been embarrassed standing in front of Angie in his underpants, waiting for the fight to begin. His heart had been pounding. He had not been able to read the look in Angel's eye—the warehouse was lit from one big skylight, for they dared not use the electricity in case someone from the street should notice and call the cops. The spectators were making whispered bets, smoking tensely, and as Rico looked around he felt surrounded by a witch's circle of haze, hanging in the stuffy, unmoving air. He felt self-conscious in his underpants, which had a hole in the right side. Rico was aware that Angela Vallens was looking at him. He could not conceive of any other reason but the shameful hole why she might be staring so.

The fight had begun, cautiously at first, amid occasional harsh whispers of "shhh!" when someone would forget that they were to keep absolutely silent. It was an important part of the game with the supervisors of the warehouse, who certainly must have suspected what was going on there at night. No mess, no noise, and nothing was to be touched or tinkered with. A fingerburner was passed to Ismael, who took a fast hit while trying to keep his inexperienced eye on the dizzying sweep second hand of the watch.

Then, suddenly in silence, there had been first blood, a small cut that had brought the beginning of a collective sigh halted by the perpetrator, Angel himself, as he stepped quickly back in an amazing lapse of concentration. "Shut up," he said, while Rico shook his eyes clear and smeared the unbelievable blood with the back of his fist. Once again there was perfect silence, and in that moment Angel had seen Angela Vallens' face, just as her eyes shut and her slender hand fluttered past her mouth in protest. Angel turned away at once and started chopping hard at Rico's face, taking advantage of the blood that was bothering Rico's vision, moving him relentlessly back onto an uneven section of the floor where twice Rico caught his heels and stumbled. Angel stunned him with a solid right cross that popped his cheek out on the other side. It surprised and pleased him.

The rest, for Angel, had been so easy that he could not believe it himself. Rico had felt Angel hitting him, and kept swinging without connecting as his arms grew too tired to hold off the fight that was becoming a slaughter.

The spectacle of no contest was deepening the eerie silence of the spectators as they watched with unblinking fascination.

Then, for no apparent reason, Angel's blows had lost their force. He pushed Rico around the open area at will, with slow, cuffing movements of hands that were no longer even tightly clenched. Angel's own cheeks were smeared with blood from the back of Rico's knuckles. He carried his friend carefully, putting no real weight into the attack that Rico had become helpless to divert. Even Clark Cooper looked impressed.

"Fall down, Rico, fall down!" Angie had screamed suddenly, with a loudness doubly shattering among the quiet of the others. Ismael had grabbed her arm with a frown, ready to pull her back, but when he understood that Angel was not mad he hesitated, long enough for Angie to pull away and start crying, her hands over her face. Rico's arms had dropped in exhaustion. He was standing in the hazy light from the skylight as Angel stepped closer, cocking his right hand for the knock out. He looked at the sobbing Angie for what seemed a full minute, his smeared fist ready less than a foot away from Rico's helpless chin. In that instant, Angel realized that she did not want him anymore, and he accepted her decision. Later that night, after Rico had come to and been cleaned up so he looked fairly decent, Angel had given him Angela Vallens, not without a touch of pride that had an edge of loss.

• • •

Angie looked at the strangely untidy Rico under the porch light, wondering why he had not gotten into his good clothes to come to her. It was plain from the hard set of his mouth that he was upset.

"Come in, honey. What's the matter?"

"Anybody home?" He looked around suspiciously, as though someone might be hiding behind her. She frowned.

"Naw, just Grampa and the kids. Mom went out to a show with the others. It's bingo night."

"Can we go somewhere alone?" He suddenly seemed aware that he had not changed his clothes.

"Sure, honey," she said, "we can just go upstairs on the roof. It's a nice night." She looked into his eyes anxiously. "Is there something wrong, Rico?"

"I'll tell you about it on the roof." He shivered.

"Shall I bring a blanket?"

"Yeah, bring a blanket."

"Rico, you want to kiss me?"

"No." Rico was lying on his back, looking up at the sky that was not so much black as dark grey, covered with smog and dirt so that not the slightest prick of starlight or moon got through the fat smokiness of that nice night. "Jesus, I wisht I'd brought a cigarette," he said.

"You want one? I'll go downstairs—" She wanted to show him that she had not blamed him when she found out about the Plan. It had almost been a relief. It explained a lot of things. "Grampa hides some in the dresser."

"I don't really want one. I was just talking." Rico reached for Angie's hand gently, feeling its cold against his own surface fever.

"You all sweaty, Rico," said Angie, almost pulling her hand away. In his mood that would have been a big mistake.

"I talked to Angel today. Everything all set. As of now everybody in. We just got tomorrow to wait."

There was resignation in her voice. "Why wait till Friday? Why not tomorrow?"

Rico turned his head slightly to look at Angie, who avoided his eyes. They? Why didn't she want to include him?

"It's been set for Friday at two for a month."

"Ain't"—Her voice was a whisper as she unconsciously looked around the tarpaper roof to see that they were alone—"ain't Angel scared somebody cop out tomorrow morning?"

Rico smiled, but he did not seem happy. "Not after what I did to Bart Arthur this afternoon."

For a moment Angie did not trust herself to speak. Like everyone else in school, she had been contacted after the accident. The way Rico said it, half-smiling, she could not believe that his words meant what they said.

"I killed Bart Arthur, Angie," said Rico, too loud, as though trying out an idea in front of a mirror, turning it this way and that. His eyes were wide open, studying his image in the sky. "He died before he got to County."

"You didn't kill him, Rico."

"I sure as hell did, pigeon. You want me to tell you all about it? You want some *de*-tails?"

"Don't be angry, Rico." Angie, scared, turned her head away from him. She thought of his beautiful face covered with blood, warehouse dirt and blood rolling past the

throbbing pulse in his throat as Angel stood over the two
of them, holding her by the hand firmly, and looking at
the unconscious, beaten Rico. She could still feel the pressure of Angel's hand, questioning her. "You did it because
he told you to, didn't you?"

Rico nodded.

"Well? There!" Her voice trembled.

"I liked killing him, Angie."

"Rico—"

"I like this whole thing. I don't know if I can wait till
Friday. I want to take every one of those—" He turned his
head away, not wanting her to see him cry.

"Rico, I love you."

"Every time I get in the practice ring, I used to think
about killing the guy I'm fighting. Every time. I think I
want to know if I hit him one more time he don't get up
and hit me back. But I can't know it! The bell rings, the
big gloves get in the way, somebody gets in the way, something—"

"Rico, don't talk no more about it. I'm scared."

"You're scared! That's a joke."

"No, it ain't, Rico."

"You still want to kiss me, Angie honey?"

• • •

Angel put his key in the front door lock and turned it.
By lifting the heavy oak door slightly on its hinge, he
could push it open easier, across the worn but still too
thick carpeting. Closing the front door locked it automatically behind him. They had lived in the apartment more

than two years, ever since Antonia's husband left her with
so many back bills they had to move. After two years, he
still noticed the grotesque yellow-edged red and green
leaves all over the rain forest of carpeting that looked as
though it had come from some old downtown movie palace
that had been demolished.

It was past eleven—the front door was locked at ten
thirty sharp—but Angel did not have the energy to go anywhere, or do anything. He hated to come home, but with
luck everybody would be asleep but Antonia and he could
be alone with his thoughts. He passed the elderly apartment manager's door, with its pretentious little brass
plaque, and started wearily up the three flights of stairs.
The carpet changed abruptly half way up to a well-worn
green.

Angel did not really feel tired, and he knew that he
would not sleep. In his shirt pocket he had his black book.
It could take several hours to read through it again, checking his memory, testing the territory set-up for the Executioners. He sighed. And then, go through the whole process again, of check and doublecheck.

The door to 308 was unlocked, and no lights were on as
he slipped into the front room, seeing in the shadows that
Antonia was snoring peacefully in the big arm chair. It
had always fascinated him how she could snore softly, but
not speak. Moving quietly across the area rugs in case the
children were asleep, he clicked on a small ruffled reading
lamp next to the shabby sofa. It sighed as he sank into it,
opening his black book. Before he had a chance to start
reading there was a loud snuffle from Antonia that made

him look up. The glitter from the wheelchair in the corner told him that she had moved it.

Her legs had slipped off the ottoman and hit the floor, her rabbit fur slippers making a funny soft noise. She was awake, her hand resting on the plastic arm-rest of the old wheelchair. By turning the light up a notch he could make out the frown of pain on her unmarked forehead, and the glitter from the edge of gold along her front teeth as she bared them in silent and temporary annoyance at him.

"Sorry, Antonia. Didn't mean to scare you."

She made a curt greedy gesture with her left hand, moving it rapidly to her lap from her mouth and back again as she bared her teeth in a display of hunger.

"I didn't get anything," said Angel, with fatigue in his hoarse young voice. "I thought there was still stuff in the icebox."

Antonia nodded eagerly, so Angel went to the kitchen and groped for the light switch. In place of curtains, the windows had been painted a dull grey to keep out the daylight sun as much as that of the new street lamp that preened its swan neck just outside the window. As he found the switch, he discovered that the bulb had burned out again. He cursed under his breath.

Antonia could hear the comforting noises of his cautious movements in the kitchen, feeling his way by the faint light of the refrigerator bulb. The cold was escaping into the stuffy room as he called to her. "There's a piece of cheese here. I'll cut off the edge and bring you a piece of cheese and a glass of water."

Although he could not see her, he knew she would be

nodding with satisfaction, always glad of the attention as much as the food. The cheese, and even a piece of bread, had been there all evening, but with the bulb burned out, Antonia would not have gone near it. She was afraid of the dark.

"I should've got something for breakfast," he called. "Maybe I should go to the all-night market so I can have a big breakfast tomorrow." The thought of going wore him out. "Jesus, I rather starve."

His aunt Antonia was a big woman, in her early forties, with large shapely breasts that rested comfortably on her high round belly. The legs that showed beneath the thin cotton of her nightgown were strong and young; her hands and plump arms were beautiful as they lifted periodically from her lap to make fluttering gestures, talking to herself with her fingers.

"Everything all set, Antonia." Angel's voice came from the kitchen with the sounds of cutting. "No mix-ups, everybody in. And tomorrow—" The ice-box closed, rocking on its four legs. Cautiously, Angel made his way back to the light.

As he came into the front room, there was a smile on his face as he handed a half-sandwich to Antonia. She took it and looked at it critically, on both sides.

"I found a piece of bread. It ain't too old. Eat it, go on. Where's the kids?" Antonia touched her breast with her forefinger, and made several gestures around her face, indicating that they were asleep. She began to eat the sandwich with fastidious little bites.

"Good," he sighed. "We got the place to ourself." Antonia stuffed the last of her sandwich into her mouth with one delicate finger. Her bright brown eyes looked up at Angel happily. She tilted her head and signaled with both hands, making a cup shape like a fine fat brown flower. She smiled.

"Do you have any money?" Angel knew without even looking that the answer was no. "Nobody come today, huh?" Antonia looked regretful, as she reached out to take Angel's hand. "Well, it's OK. I got plenty till the weekend. Did you get enough to eat?" Antonia nodded, and made the flower shape with her hands again, hopefully.

"Shit, Antonia, I've got a lot of stuff to do tonight. I got to go over it all again, to make double sure nothin' gonna go wrong tomorrow. I got forty-three Room Executioners to set up in one hour. One hour." Antonia crossed her hands at the wrist, and waggled her head back and forth. She made a tentative thrust with her hips, but Angel shook his head.

"I can't. I got to cut third period to check the absents and I sure don't want to miss Mr. Nielsen after lunch. He's telling us all about"—he smiled and closed his eyes with the delight of it—"all about artistic revolt."

Antonia cocked her head, and pulled Angel closer to her. Holding him firmly around his hips, she started to bite at the flap of his belt, leaving dents with her strong white teeth. He seemed scarcely to notice.

"Only one more day, Antonia. As soon as we hear that bell, they'll be clicks of lockin' up all over that school . . . the gates to the street gonna close shut, and the chains will wrap around them—" Her fingers loosened the prong of the frayed belt, as Angel's eyes looked past the top of Antonia's head, past the dimly lit lithograph on the wall of

Jesus praying at the rock, past the grey brown wall with mottled watermarked roses, past the thick stuffy air and heavy sky and crowded evening hour into a simple, good-smelling world where everything went exactly according to plan, and nobody made you do anything that you did not want to do.

• • •

The alarm clock ticked by his ear. In his dream, Old Jack was patching up some windows that had got accidentally broke. He was using a new kind of quick-dry caulking that had come in with the new budget. He could have had one of his men to fix the window, but it was the type of nice, relaxing job that he enjoyed, not much lifting or climbing, and no having to think on things every minute to keep from making a mistake. Putting in new windows was a job that he could do with his hands, leaving his mind free for more important things.

For much the same reason, he raised his prize pigeons, keeping them in large cages on his back patio. He had built the cages himself, tall and round, a crisscross of thin white wood that would cross-hatch his broad black face in the sun as he reached for the waterbowls that swung from real bark-peeled tree branches. Jack could spend hours watching his pigeons, feeding them and caring for their young. His mind would wander to pleasant memories of Baltimore, where he was born, or a ruckus at school that needed thinking about in peace and quiet. Or, no matter how he tried, the Numbers.

He could not forget that skinny white boy's question, "if it's illegal, why do you do it?" He had finally answered, after a week's thought, that he just could not think of it being wrong, as much as he considered it as plain stupid. There was just no way to pass laws about being stupid or smart. As he fixed windows, or fed his pigeons, or worried over his wood-shop saw in his garage, he often thought that he would never play the Numbers again. He would just pretend, and put the money away in the savings and loan and forget about it. He would think along this line sometimes, but then he would remember that he did not have anything big he wanted to buy, no place he wanted to go —well, maybe back to Baltimore every Christmas, but he could afford that well enough the way things were. And most of all, there was nobody to leave anything to. Jack snuffled in his sleep, disturbing a fly that had landed on the pillow beside his head. He had finished the last broken window, and looked at the clean new panes of glass with satisfaction.

• EIGHT •

Thursday

Maria Estragon was feeling the wall through the cloth. By putting her back right against the wall, she could feel the little lumps and valleys, and pretend that each valley had its small houses filled with small people, with children, and dogs. The people's eyes were mostly blue and their hair was like Mr. Nielsen's, light and fine, blown around by any little breath of wind. The little people played with their babies, and laughed, and ate from tables that were covered with white cloths with blue fringe. The people in the little valleys loved each other very much, and danced slow dances.

The beautiful dream lasted until her back warmed the wall and a drop of sweat ran down. She tried to turn the drop into a tear from one of the blue eyes, but the tear was too big, and the eyes too small, and the whole dream just ruined.

The hall was not empty, but nobody seemed to be talking as much as usual. They passed quietly, usually in pairs, on their way to class. Tim felt the solemnity in the air,

162

supposing it to be the result of the accident in the gym.
The boy's funeral had been set for the weekend, and it had
to be on most of their minds.

Tim sighed as he glanced at his watch. He did not want
to go into the faculty lounge for his conference period, but
he knew he should spend some time on his Art Week display at the Sports Arena, a duty he had inherited. Inde-
cisively, he stood outside the lounge, a moment too long to
escape Maria Estragon as she came toward him. "Hello,
Mr. Nielsen."

Tim turned and saw the serious round face looking up
at him. He was immediately on guard. "Yes, Maria?"

"I want to talk to you personal."

"There's nothing you can't say to me right here, is there,
Maria?" Several students hurried past, as Maria nodded.
Tim could see that she was searching for her words with
her control stretched to its utmost. "Are you all right,
Maria?"

"I love you, Mr. Nielsen."

For a moment Tim was speechless. Then, as calmly as he
could, he tried to put a friendly but neutral expression on
his face. "That's very nice, Maria, and I appreciate it very
much. Everybody needs to be loved, and maybe teachers
need it more than anybody." The solemn look on the girl's
face was unchanging. "I love all my students, Maria"—her
face darkened—"the way you love . . . your child. There,
Maria—"

His words had brought a gush of suppressed tears.

"Not as much as I love you, Mr. Nielsen," she finally
managed to say.

For a moment Tim felt helpless. He did not wish to discuss the varieties of human love in the hallway with the tardy bell about to ring, but he did not see how he could break off without hurting the girl's feelings, and worse perhaps, jarring her into doing or saying something that could embarrass him, or make him foolish. "Don't you have a class starting? I don't want to have to give you a tardy excuse." She shook her head, and Tim saw that she was not going to budge. He got a sudden idea. "Maria, tell me something. What are the kids saying about Bart Arthur?" If he had a chance of getting an honest answer from anyone, it would be from Maria.

"Bart?" She looked at him, puzzled. "Bart?"

"I mean, is there someone they blame? Is there anything at all, Maria?"

"What happen to him?" Maria had a secret look on her face. She had admired Bart Arthur on the basketball court, and knew that he had looked at her sometimes as she walked down the hall with her friends. She thought Mr. Nielsen was making reference to those intimate looks.

"Why, he's dead, Maria. He died on the way to the hospital—" He saw that she was not understanding him. "I thought everyone in school knew."

"He dead?" The word struck fear in the girl's heart, a defensive fear. Dead. She remembered shaking her baby when he refused to take the nipple, or open his eyes as she screamed. Dead. She had shook him and shook him, and started to cry furiously when she realized that he was not going to wake up. Dead. She did not understand. He was so small. Dead. It meant the Welfare would not give her any more money for the baby, and he did not even have a name yet. It meant that her father would hit her if he came home. The tears rolled down her cheeks.

"It happened this afternoon, Maria. I'm sorry—"

Maria Estragon's eyes seared him. "I didn't do nothin' to him. Nothin'."

Tim looked bewildered. "I didn't say you did anything, Maria."

"I didn't do nothin'. I just shook him when he wouldn't wake up. I thought he just sleepin' good."

Tim said nothing, as the tardy bell rang. He was simultaneously puzzled and transfixed by Maria's face as she stared at him, now close to hysteria. "Maria, why don't you come with me to Miss Gleason's office—" He reached out to urge her around and saw her suddenly stiffen. Neither moved, as his hand fell back uncertainly to his side and her eyes seemed to dry and crack as she looked at him. "You touched me."

Tim said nothing.

"You touched me!" As her voice started to rise, Tim's first instinct was to slap her, or tell her to shut up. He stood motionless, his own voice jammed as she started to scream.

"Help! Help! You tried to—" The last words were lost as several nearby doors opened, and curious teachers' faces looked out. Maria screamed the words again, louder, but still not distinguishable as Tim realized Janis and Willson had left their classrooms. He felt a strong hand on his arm pulling him away as there was a confused scuffle. The girl kicked at him.

"Come on, it's all right. Cleaire, grab the girl—"

Maria was now trying to fly at Mr. Nielsen, as Wil

Willson with difficulty tried to block her without physically grabbing her. Tim heard Cleaire's excited voice, "I
don't want to touch her . . . Stop that. Don't do that,
Maria! Stop it!"

• • •

In B-9 Science, Angel looked over at Ismael and
shrugged. With Miss Devereaux out of the room there was
a pause before the beginning of activity everywhere as
Angel mouthed the words: It's just Maria Estragon. A ball
bearing rolled along the aisle with a shuddery, rumbling
sound, as Miss Devereaux returned, clapping her hands.

"All right, enough! Back to your seats! Now!"

Cleaire Devereaux fixed her fiercest stare on Booker
Turner, who ducked in embarrassment as he bumped his
knee against the radiator in his haste to get back to his seat.
Miss Devereaux glared around the room as it settled fit-
fully into silence.

"It was nothing at all," she said, automatically arranging
her wig with a nervous gesture that set her bracelet of gold
astrological charms to rattling. Several girls made a pantomime of copying her characteristic gesture, taking advantage of her astigmatism and vanity. She kept her pearl-
studded glasses obscured in her hand unless they were absolutely necessary.

"And those of you who are most full of fun when my
back is turned," she added warningly, "had best know a
great deal about the human central nervous system when
the surprise quiz takes place sometime this week."

She waited for the groan of protest. It never came.

• • •

Clark Cooper had been coming out of the Boys' Room when the commotion had started up, and instead of continuing to his next class, he decided to dawdle behind the group, consisting of an hysterical Maria, Mr. Nielsen looking white as a ghost, Mr. Janis and Mr. Willson as they marched to Miss Gleason's office with blood in their eye for Maria. Cleaire Devereaux had rushed past him in her anxiety to get back to her class.

Clark concealed himself adequately as various people passed, and it was only moments before Janis and Willson returned to their rooms, leaving Maria with Nielsen and the girl's vice-principal. Five minutes passed, then ten, before Maria came sullenly out of the office and glared at the closed door, with its dirty old scratched lettering. Clark Cooper edged closer, lazily, and leaned against the wall, looking at Maria with her big tits.

Inside the office, Miss Gleason was exercising her facility for smoothing things over by talking all around the situation so rapidly that Tim could only nod at her various conflicting suggestions for minimizing embarrassment and annoyance. It seemed that she was all too familiar with Maria Estragon's problem, and thought she could handle it without involving Tim. It seemed there were certain problems at home—Tim nodded.

Clark whistled softly through his front teeth, but Maria was still too angry to pay him any mind. Inside, Miss Gleason and Mr. Nielsen were still jabbering about her as she stared sullenly at the grey-glass bubbly door, thinking grey thoughts about Mr. Nielsen. There were heavy footsteps coming toward the door, and she spit heavily right where he would step. The teacher opened the door, saw what she

had done, and just looked at her. Clark kept inconspicu-
ous, studying the pattern of splinters on the door-jamb as
he made nervous little circles on the floor with his black
pointy-toed spanish shoes.

"Mr. Nielsen!" Maria spat the words as though she had
not been able to swallow them for the disgust.

"Maria," Tim hesitated, trying to keep his voice from
betraying fear or reproach, "you are lucky that Miss Gleason decided not to punish you more severely for what you
did."

"You gonna be killed," she said, with much personal satisfaction. Clark Cooper's head came up, as he looked at
Maria in amazement. Maria continued to stare at the
teacher, at those eyes that looked more than ever hard and
cold like the stone in Miss Devereaux' ring. Tim shook his
head in dismay.

"Don't talk like that, Maria. Just don't." He started to
walk away, and for a moment he was surprised to find himself looking at Clark Cooper.

"You are!" said Maria. "You gonna be killed sure, and
so is she. She gonna die tomorrow!" Her finger pointed at
the door of the office. "We gonna lock up all the gates tomorrow and cut all your lying fuckin' throats!"

Suddenly her voice broke in half and her next words
were unintelligible. Tim could hear the sounds from the
hall, muffled, and in the distance a traffic sound like a
broom sweeping. Again he looked at the tall Negro boy
who looked spooked and ready to take instant flight. He
started to tell him to get to his class, but he was distracted
by Maria's grotesque whisper. "You don't love nobody,

Mr. Nielsen. Tomorrow you gonna be dead. Angel tell me so."

"I'll take her out, Mr. Nielsen," said Clark Cooper, taking the weeping girl's arm without her noticing. Her thoughts had now turned in on herself. She was crying for her failure to deserve the beautiful teacher's blond, blue-eyed love. If he did not love her, then she was not lovable.

"Come on, Maria," said the black boy. "It's OK. It's me, Coop."

She looked at Tim one last time, and spoke with sad conviction. "Angel, he tell me so."

Clark looked at the teacher and then at the door of the girl's vice-principal's office. He hoped that Maria's new outburst would not draw Miss Gleason's attention until he could get her away. "Mr. Nielsen?" He wanted permission.

"All right, Clark," said Tim, looking at the unwavering but no longer angry girl with fear. "Thank you, son."

"I loved you," he heard her say as he went into Faculty Lounge Number Three, his heart beating rapidly.

"Come on, honey," said Clark, in a low voice. He held Maria close to him with an unrelenting grip. "You been a mighty bad girl, honey."

Maria looked at him, suddenly aware of who he was. Testing, she tried to pull her arm from his painful grasp.

"You spilled the Plan to that dude, honey. Angel told you not to do that, you recall?" Afraid now, Maria shook her head and tried to pull away. "Well, he did. Lucky for you, nobody believe nothin' you say nohow." He was moving her toward the double swinging doors of the Boys'

Room, past the sing-song of someone reciting in B-8 English. Maria winced.

"Let me go, man," she said. "You just let me go."

"You spilled the Plan, honey. You recall what happen' to that big white boy when he just *think* of spilling the Plan?"

"*Let go!*" Without a word, Clark Cooper shoved the girl through the door, marked IN, at the same time closing his hand over her mouth as she started to cry out. The strength of his arm was terrible as he put his lips against her ear and kissed it very lightly, at the same time pushing his body up against her, forcing her legs apart against the concrete. He kissed her again, this time gently on the eyelid. Maria shut her eyes just in time and held them tight shut, furiously, as Clark reached under her dress and found that she was naked. He grinned. "Nothin' you say'll make nobody believe you, honey. Don't fight." He slipped his finger in and felt her stiffen, her eyes still closed, her thighs moving closer together. Clark knew he was no place unless she wanted to. "Easy, honey," he whispered. "Relax, come on. You told Mr. Nielsen"—her eyes opened and looked at him hard—"and what'd they tell you? Stop lyin', girl, that's what. You tell 'em about me and what you think they gonna say? Hm?"

For a moment his hand moved gently, deeper, then he had to pull it free to open his pants. He shifted his weight slightly backward with a crook of his hips to keep from catching himself on the zipper whose whisper was the only sound in the room. "I won't hurt you none, honey," he said. "You will like it . . ."

Clark's eyes swivelled sharply to the door as he heard

footsteps coming toward the Boys' Room. He froze in position, his left hand across the girl's mouth, his elbow braced against the cold wall, his chest pressing the fullness of her breasts. The throb in his right hand was keeping time with his heart as he knew that the footsteps had stopped outside the door. Here I go, he thought, always gettin' caught—

He did not move, nor did Maria as the door swung open, and Harold Craner saw them both. Quickly, he closed the door and started to sweat.

"What the hell is she doing in here?" he started, but Clark interrupted him.

"Hold her arms for me, man, will you?"

For a moment Harold hesitated, thinking that it would really be something to see. Clark felt Maria relax, and saw the look in her eye that made him drop his hand. She ran her tongue along her lips as Harold watched them staring at each other, unyielding. Finally, Maria reached out and took Clark. "Shit man," she said. "You don't need nobody to hold me. Least of all him." Harold felt affronted as Clark clasped his big hands around her waist so his fingers met at the small of her back. "It don't do no good to fight," she said, leaning back. "Not no more it sure don't."

• NINE •

Dinner had been a continuous battle, ending in furious chewing and avoidance of eyes. The waiter poured the last of the Chianti into Marge's glass, while Tim studied the checkered tablecloth rather bitterly.

"If this is a sample of what it would be like being married to you," he said, as soon as the waiter was out of earshot, "the sooner we have second thoughts the better."

Marge looked at him with mock surprise. "Who said anything about being married? I thought we were talking about extra-marital sex." Tim sighed.

"I don't know what you were talking about, but I certainly wasn't. There's no point in discussing anything with you once you've made up your mind."

"Why don't we have another bottle of wine, to help our digestions, of course. I know mine could use a little help."

"You could use something, that's for sure."

"Got any suggestions?" Tim sighed again. It was getting to be a habit, as much a part of dining with Marge as salt and pepper. He decided to try a conciliatory approach.

"Marge, this is getting us no place. I wouldn't have told you about that girl this afternoon if I wasn't afraid you would get it secondhand from somebody else and misunderstand my part in it. I see that you couldn't misunderstand more than you already have, and it makes me mad."

Marge smiled coldly. "Girl, huh? Two kids already at fourteen, and probably a third on the way for summer vacation. Some girl!"

"I told you, Maria Estragon is really disturbed. She doesn't belong in school, but they just don't know what to do with her. She's a baby-machine, and they probably ought to sterilize her." He stared at the near-black wine morosely. "She pulled this on a couple of teachers before, and according to the girl's vice-principal they were as innocent as I was."

There was a long silence while Marge contemplated the scarcely touched food on her plate.

"Probably. You know, the disgusting thing is I haven't got the slightest doubt that you're telling the truth. I don't know why I want to believe terrible things, sometimes."

"Marge, I don't understand you at all." Tim's hand reached across the tablecloth and closed over hers. This time she made no effort to pull it away. "I told you that the minute she pulled that stunt I took her straight to Miss Gleason. With that girl they don't take those charges seriously for a second. But I was really scared, Marge, and I thought what might happen to me, and then I thought, from whom? Maria hasn't got any parents to complain. Nobody else gives a damn except to feel sorry for the teacher. Good God, she's so confused she even accused Cleaire Devereaux of propositioning her once."

"Oh, I know—"

"No you don't, or you wouldn't have been on my throat all night." He tried to make her feel sorry for him, but she did not take the opportunity.

"I did know about that girl," she said, analyzing herself. "After all, I read all through that . . . that Baedeker for delinquents, which I'm sure is more than you did."

"It wasn't necessary. I see the ugly part first hand, not in reports. I listen to those kids, and sometimes I watch them actually learn something, even if its just how to handle a color problem in crafts. When they do it better than they did it the time before, I'm proud of them."

"I think that's rather nice," said Marge, feeling a little better in spite of herself. "Nicely put, too, a color problem."

"Margery, you are a classic American woman." She looked at him. "Of the sort that has a mystique."

She could not help laughing.

"Knowing how you mean that, I take it as an insult."

Tim smiled. "Just remember, classic American women can be too sharp for their own good. Unfortunately, I love you anyway."

"Unfortunately for both of us, maybe. Let's have a truce and try to enjoy our nice cold spaghetti and meat balls."

"Well—" Even though Tim was feeling somewhat better his stomach was still too jumpy from tension to enjoy the food. He poked at a meatball and it crumbled under his fork, as he let his mind consider the double tragedy of the day. If Marge could really handle the Estragon incident, then he would show her the beautiful thing the poor dead boy had done in class, a few hours before he died.

Roger Post had told him about the accident in the

faculty lounge that afternoon. His mind immediately had gone to the rolled up piece of drawing paper in the desk. He had not dared go over and look at it again, not while the others were in the room. It seemed too sentimental a gesture, or worse, a perversely curious one.

"That boy was one of the only good students in the school," Roger Post was saying, with more sorrow and heat than he could really bring himself to feel. He had once given Bart Arthur a B+ to his own amazement. Jimmy Janis sucked quietly on his pipe.

"Didn't have him this semester," he said, between puffs, "but he certainly wasn't a troublemaker."

David Melnick was sitting in the corner, an unread magazine on his lap. He was thinking of Herschel Watson, feeling sorry for him. Dave hated himself for the suspicion, but he could not help thinking that Hersch might have been some place he shouldn't when the accident had happened. God knows they were all vulnerable.

"Bill's scared the Board will hold him responsible," said Evelyn Raintree. "We've had too many accidents lately, it's true. I feel sorry for Herschel," she added complacently.

"Are we sure it was an accident?" Mrs. Del Valle, the French Teacher, looked from face to face darkly, looking for encouragement in her suspicions. She found none. "Bart Arthur didn't belong to any cliques," she offered. "Maybe he was being punished for his independence, and it went too far?"

"Oh, Lupa! He fell and cracked his skull. It could happen to any of us at home. Look at John Glenn."

"The showers are poorly designed, of course." Janis

puffed on his pipe, reading the English journal but still half-listening to the conversation around him. "And they were never properly fixed after the Medina boy fell down."

Cleaire Devereaux disapproved. "Jimmy, you don't know that for certain."

"Call it an educated guess."

"Someone pushed him. They probably didn't really want to hurt him." All attention turned to Dave Melnick, who seemed embarrassed by the sudden attention to his diffident suggestion. As a friend of Herschel Watson, perhaps they expected him to go further in defending him from the unspoken but still definite sense of accusation. He shrugged. "After all, Bart was Jewish, and wasn't so crazy about some of the others. That isn't so remarkable around here. Even the faculty isn't immune, I've noticed." He looked past Evelyn Raintree and Mariette Jensen, and then remembered that Sarah Vardis was in the room, sitting quietly. She smiled at him.

"It's all right, Dave. I don't mind."

There was a brief uncomfortable silence, and then Mariette Jensen broke her longstanding rule of never saying anything if she could possibly avoid it.

"It comes," she said clearly, "from bussing them in and out. It's our own fault." The others just looked at her. She had been choral teacher in the old school before it "changed," as she put it. She was marking time until she could retire, and everyone knew it.

"I don't think that's true, Mariette." Jimmy Janis returned the old lady's look steadily, but she did not give an inch. She nodded her head vehemently.

"It certainly is. This was a decent school once, but you wouldn't remember because you weren't here then. Evelyn remembers, don't you?" She turned to Evelyn Raintree, who looked unwilling to defend her.

"Well, Mariette—"

"This was a decent school, and we had respect and discipline. Then all the elements came in—forgive me, Miss Vardis, but I must be candid—and the school got progressively worse. I've lived within a half mile of this school since nineteen thirty-eight, and I'm not altogether blind."

"You could have moved, dear," said Janis.

"No, I could not." She turned on him, blazing. "I have always lived here, and taught here, and I am going to retire in two years. Do you really think I could sell my building and transfer to another school?"

Evelyn Raintree tried to interrupt gently. "I don't see what all that has to do with bussing, Mariette."

"We all make our own beds," observed Cleaire Devereaux.

"If you didn't bus in white students to make the others discontented you wouldn't have this constant turmoil. I have three boys in my class who come all the way from the valley, and they dress different. God knows, they act different, and who can blame them? I've never seen such miserable kids in my life, and never hope to again."

Tim had to interrupt. "Which children do you mean, Miss Jensen? Surely, you can't mean Harold Craner? He seems quite adjusted."

She turned her puckered, old lady eyes on him as though he were a personal traitor to her. "What about the Wilson boys, Mr. Nielsen, and Jennifer Baily. Or yes, Harold

Craner for that matter. He may be Jewish, Mr. Nielsen,
but he is white."

They were still arguing, mostly off the point, when Tim
quit the room in disgust.

• • •

"I wish you wouldn't," Tim said gently, as Marge
turned her head away. Her face was calm, and there were
no visible tears, but he could feel by the trembling of her
body that she was about to bawl. "It makes it hard for me
if you cry," he said, regretting his clumsiness at once. For-
tunately, she did not take it the wrong way.

"I'm not crying," she said determinedly. "People cry
when they are sad, and I'm happy."

"Funny, you don't look happy," he said comically.

She smiled, turning her face back to him, examining the
pigmentless lashes that surrounded his serious eyes. "Maybe you've never seen me this happy before." He put his
head down on her breast, lightly so it would not be uncomfortable for her.

Marge had made up her mind during the dessert, perhaps as much because of the incident with Maria Estragon
as anything else, but regardless, she had made up her
mind. By an instinct Tim did not know he had, he realized
that if he wished it that night they would sleep together.
The thought of it put him into a slight panic.

Since he had never slept with anyone he really knew,
much less cared about, he feared that he might be one of
those unfortunates who put "good" girls in a never-never
land of respect, while taking real pleasure only in pick-ups

or hookers. Marge was in a never-never land of a sort, being one of the intellectually liberated generation who could accept all the reasons for sexual freedom without being able to put them into practice. A lot of good that did.

His rustic bungalow looked somehow different tonight in the white light of the street lamp, which seemed not so much to illuminate as to blur the red tile roof with imaginary snow. As always, Marge looked at her tiny wrist-watch at the door, and whispered faintly that she did not see any reason why she might not come in for a short cup of coffee.

They looked as they always did to see if Mrs. Cleener was peering at them through her dirty front window. Tim's mock harsh whisper startled Marge, making her jump.

"Boo!"

"Oh!"

"Don't worry. She's asleep. Come on." Tim closed the door behind them.

"Who's worried? She's seen me come into your place dozens of times late at night. My reputation is in tatters." Tim started to laugh, until Marge put her hand severely over his mouth. She tried to make her husky voice sound angry, but she was about to join him in laughter. "You seem to find everything particularly hilarious. We mustn't laugh."

Tim stood in the middle of the room, suddenly serious as she dropped her hand. He felt as though he had a clumsy pendulum between his legs, caught up against his boxer shorts. Marge sensed his change of mood, and licked her lips as she went straight to the hutch, after an unsuccessful shake of the decanter beside the sofa.

"Scotch or scotch," she asked gaily, seeing that he had only one half-empty bottle. It gave her a momentary sinking sensation, then she decided, if we have to be drunk, it's no good anyway.

"Scotch," Tim decided, adding, "with a water chaser, if you please." It made her go into the kitchen to hunt for a clean glass. He was left feeling very much alone in the front room, which he now wished he had cleaned up a little. There was junk all over the place, while the fifteen-year-old vacuum stood mutely in the corner posing as pop art sculpture, about all it was used for.

"Here you go," Marge reappeared carrying two stingy drinks. She had put tap water in hers, and a single cloudy cube of ice.

"Thank you."

"Heavens, you're so polite. This is getting ridiculous. I don't know if I should go out and come back in again." There was a pause. "Do you mind if I ask you a question?"

Tim swallowed hard. She wanted to give herself an out by offering one to him. There could always be an excuse.

"No, Marge, don't. I think I know what you're going to ask, and it's one of those questions that have only wrong answers. If I say yes you'll be depressed and never forgive me; if I say no, I look like some kind of heel. Do you see what I mean?"

"All right," said Marge, although she did not see what he meant. She drank her drink casually, since it was mostly water. A question with only wrong answers? It was sinister.

She had forgotten what she was going to ask. They stood for a long time, studying each other.

"You know," Tim said at last, "I'm a little bit afraid of you." She said nothing, which turned out to be the right thing to do. Tim went on, gaining courage with every word. "It may turn you off, that is, assuming that there is something to turn off, but I have to take the chance. I look at you now, and I'm afraid. I've wanted to go to bed with you for nearly a year—"

"Eleven months."

"—but somehow or other we never have, mainly because you haven't wanted to."

She corrected him. "I have too wanted to, but I couldn't."

Dear God, thought Tim, don't let me talk it to death. She had grown tired of standing. As she sat there, balanced now precariously on the edge of a chair—why wouldn't she sit down all the way? Tim had never seen her look so beautiful.

"I'm afraid that you made up your mind for the wrong reason, and will end up regretting it. Then you'll hate me, or worse, you'll hang on like grim death through an engagement and maybe even a marriage hoping it will make everything all right." He took a deep breath. "I will not *necessarily* marry you."

"What's the right reason then?" Marge put her drink on the coffee table, and held her arms out toward him. "You'd better carry me off right now, and we'll blunder through as best we can. If we don't now, we never will."

After kissing her on her nose, Tim picked her up and was agreeably surprised at her light weight.

"I will trust you," she added, "to take it easy."

"I will," he promised.

"But not too easy," she said, resting her head with great relief on his nervous wet shoulder.

● ● ●

When Charley Lees turned his cheek away from his pillow, there was a wet sound as the grey nylon stuck to his face, pulling away without awakening him from his feverish, mumbling sleep. He rolled onto his stomach, splaying his spindly legs out on either side, leaving his calloused feet dangling over the splintery sides of the army surplus cot that was his bed. Charley Lees smiled in his sleep, for he was killing Roger Post.

Mr. Post was standing in front of the class, a look of the most exquisite surprise on his face. He had been caught flatfooted when Charley had stood, holding up a black handkerchief with dignity and accusing him of being a rotten teacher. There was a murmur of approval as Roger Post stood open-mouthed.

"Just what do you think you are doing?" said Mr. Post as Charley's assistant, Ismael, went to the door flourishing a key with which he locked the door from the inside. The sarcasm had drained from the teacher's face as Ismael turned and looked at him, inscrutably. Roger Post could not help but sense that something was out of the ordinary, but he produced his usual reaction, heavy-browed frown and deepening of the silly-ass voice as he clasped his hands behind his back.

"All right, Mr. Sato, you may unlock the door now"—

Charley knew just how he would say it—"and bring me that contraband key at once."

Ismael, with the most superb of toothy white smiles, a parody of the obsequious oriental grin, dropped the key into his shirt pocket. He winked in tribute to the leadership of Charley Lees, who was the honored black kerchief-carrying Head Executioner of 210. Charley acknowledged the wink with a careless salute. All was silence, the most beautiful of creepy, grey-green institutional silences.

"Take off your clothes, Mr. Post," said Charley. The red-haired man looked at him as though he had lost his mind. Charley Lees did not move. "You seem not to understand." Taking the black kerchief from his pocket, Charley tied it carefully around his neck, with the flaring knot in front where the class could see it. He was standing so close that he could hear Mr. Post's breathing, and imagine its heat prickling his neck. "This handkerchief," Charley was explaining, "means that I am your Room Executioner. I am in charge of your death."

Mr. Post blinked, the sweat rolling now from his bushy hairline into his thinning eyes. Despite the salty burn of the sweat, his eyes remained frozen on Charley as he tried to smile. "You're mad," he said. "Report to Mr. Sousa."

Charley laughed at him, mimicking the tone of his voice, "Report to Mr. Sousa! Do you think you have any control over me anymore, Mr. Post?"

"You bet your—" Post started, before he saw that every boy in the room had quietly produced a switchblade and placed it on the desk in front of him, point toward the teacher.

"Take off your clothes, Mr. Post," Charley Lees whispered, squirming on his stomach in pleasure. His mouth was open against the smooth nylon of the pillowcase as he shifted his head violently to the other side.

"You are utterly crazy," said Mr. Post, crossing to the window as fast as he could and looking at the deserted yard. Everything was frozen. There was no movement at all, not even at the ghost hamburger stand across the street.

"The yard," Charley explained, glowing with leadership, "is empty, because every other teacher is in the same boat as you, with an Executioner looking at him. Downstairs, a committee has put Mr. Conrad under arrest, and Miss Peters, and Miss Gleason, and special Grounds Committees have brought the janitors and gym teachers to the gym, which is now also locked."

Roger Post looked toward the temporary parking lot. The cars were like cattle in a pen, jammed so tight they could not move. There was no one entering or exiting.

"Gates, of course, are closed," said his Executioner. "The gatemen locked them all, five minutes ago, all at the same time. Nobody can get in or out."

"You're lying." Roger Post's voice was now a fearful croak. His legs had begun to shake visibly in his trousers. Charley was unperturbed.

"All Executions will take less than five minutes. When we are through, the police will be called. Now, will you take off your clothes, or will we have to strip you by force?"

"But what did I do?" Roger Post whimpered, now a child about to be punished for half-remembered crimes.

The other boys stood, switchblades in hand, to back up Chuck Lees, Head Executioner and Top General.

"You stayed in when you should have gone out three bets ago, that's what you did," said his wife, looking at Roger's two pair with disdain. She had held four jacks.

"Oh, that's all right," said William Conrad jovially. "Rog won that pot with an outrageous bluff, but a success all the same."

"Let's play up-and-down the river, pass three to the left," suggested Cleaire, since Jimmy was at her left.

"Pretty good bluff," admitted Janis, who had nothing anyway.

"Can't get away with it usually," laughed Roger, giving his wife a pinch on the chin, a little too hard. The line of her mouth grew thinner but she managed to smile, wanting to rub the pink spot left by his fingers.

"My deal," she said. "You'd never know it was all in the family the way Roger takes chances. You'd think it was all his to lose." She watched him rake in the pot.

"Now Ellie," smiled Dolores Conrad, sensing danger, "don't take it too seriously—"

"It's just a friendly game," said her husband. They all smiled at the cliché, except Roger.

"Atmosphere seems strained tonight." Jimmy Janis squinted past the smoke of his pipe as he examined the cards as they came. "What are we playing, Ellie, Up-and-Down?"

"Straight seven card stud," she said, dealing the last card to her husband with emphasis.

"Oh, all right. Any ante?" Cleaire wanted to know.

"Two cents." Obediently, Cleaire put her two cents in the pot, as Janis followed, with a wry shake of the head.

"Hit me with three," she said precisely.

"Another hand like this," said Roger Post, with a responsibility-pinning look at his wife, "and I'm dead."

Charley Lees lifted his head from the pillow with a moan, and looked around the small room desperately. For a moment he was not sure where he was, and then he saw the crack that ran up the wall to the edge of the hall door. He relaxed, his face falling back onto the pillow. It was soaking wet, and as he looked at the sleeve of his pajamas, he saw that it was wet too. "Jesus," he said softly, remembering his dream.

He thought of his sister, asleep in the next room, and was seized with a desire to talk to her. Very quietly, being careful not to make enough noise to awaken his parents, Charley Lees put his big bare feet on the wooden floor and got up very slowly, to keep the cot from creaking.

There was enough light from the streetlamp across the street that he could make his way easily to the door without bumping into anything, or making any inordinate noise. He opened the door to Sandy's room, gingerly, with a low creak, and poked his head in. "Sandy?," he whispered, "Sandy, are you awake?"

There was no answer, awake or not. His sister's bedroom was empty. Charley Lees looked at the rumpled bed in shocked surprise, and quickly checked the miniature pink alarm clock on the bedside table. He could not read it until it was practically against his nose, ticking like a timebomb. It was one-thirty in the morning, Friday morning, and the window leading to the backyard was open, and screenless. He felt a gust of cold air on his neck, and turned to look at the open window. It was then that he noticed the crumpled note on the floor beside the bed. When he held it up to the windowlight he could make out the neat, perfect handwriting. *Meet me tonight,* it said, *at V. LM.*

There was a full moon. Charley looked up at it, thinking about astronauts as he tucked in his shirt. The moon had been spoiled for him when he saw a real photo of it from close-up in Mr. Melnick's class. It was just a big pile of dirt and dust, just what nobody needed. The only thing he had liked about it was sitting right next to Rico, watching the photo so close to him that he could smell his breath that made Charley wonder if he brushed his teeth with some kind of soap. Rico had not thought much of the moon either.

Charley tiptoed past his parents' bedroom, doubly afraid that he would wake them up, and they would discover that Sandy was gone. Charley listened for a moment before he opened the front door, and then closed it behind him, home free. Once he was safely out, he was not completely sure that V had stood for Valdes, but it made the most sense. There was also no mistaking Louis Margadonna's handwriting, since he had gone to a Catholic grammar school, and made nice round loops. The thought of his sister meeting Margadonna the night before Zero gave Charley even more of a chill than the frosty air as he rolled his thin collar up and hunched his even thinner shoulders.

To save time, he decided to take a chance and cross the

old streetcar tracks and the vacant lot to the chicano block where the Valdes' lived, in a huge old house that was bursting at the rafters with children and grandparents, even one awesome great-grandfather, aunts, uncles, and cousins. He looked at the long shadows cast by the deserted streetcars and shuddered to think of stupid Sandy making the dangerous trip herself, past drunks and bums that slept in the cars, and the bunkers that had been the basements of nice houses before the streetcar tracks had come, to be obsoleted in their turn, by the unused lot.

As he stepped across a rusted line of pipe that led nowhere, he heard something or someone stir a few feet away, behind a clump of bushes. He froze, as there was a clicking sound he did not recognize, and a glittering object flew past his nose and dropped in a graceful arc into soft dirt a few feet away. It was a small green bottle still stinking of sweet wine. Charley moved on quickly, not wanting to seek its source, his eye hard on the big wooden house in the distance.

• TEN •

Antonia smiled in her sleep as she reached across the bed, her plump fingers brushing Angel's cheek as he stared into space, his mind full of weariness and problems. He had neatly figured out the answer to the final stumbling block, how to inform each Executioner that he had been chosen. He had been worried that he would have to pull them out of class with the forged summons. But he had figured out a simple system that he could handle with Rico, marking their desks first period in the morning. Another mark—he stirred uncomfortably—like the gold pin, the black handkerchief. Angel knew the importance of such things in preserving loyalty.

Since his own sixth period would be Mr. Nielsen's class, he decided to change his original intention of remaining aloof and be Executioner himself instead of Rico. Although he did not much like the idea, it might be necessary in terms of real leadership, to prove that he, Angel, was first of all.

Antonia's hand, now awake, felt his cheek, and he caught her looking at him. He did not return her smile. "Go to sleep, Antonia, or I won't let you stay here with me." She looked hurt, but he was unrelenting. "I have a lot of things to think about tonight. Big things." He phrased carefully, so she could read his words. Antonia nodded, and immediately closed her eyes in a pretense of sleep. Angel knew she was pretending, so he continued to talk to her, softly, trying out his ideas and even expressing his fears. She would not even understand them, much less reveal them. From the beginning when he had first conceived of the Plan with Rico, he had tested his ideas on dumb Antonia as well as all-too noisy Rico. More and more he had stopped talking to his old friend about his doubts. Mention of them seemed to bring an unhealthy color to Rico's eyes. His attention would wander. He would seem to be changing the subject without saying anything. There was no such problem with Antonia, who bore the weight of doubt without effort.

As the Plan progressed from talk to the first meetings about who should head up the Committees, Angel had profited from what he learned at probation camp. He made sure that each General had to worry about keeping fewer Lieutenants in line than he could actually handle. From the first, Rico had been like a full partner, able sometimes to guess what Angel meant when he was not sure himself. Even as children they used to have elliptical conversations.

—*Let's go to* . . . Rico might say.

—*Can't.* Angel would reply, his mouth full of bolts he had just removed from his bike. The reason was clear to Rico.

—*But she won't have it ready, man.*

—*Yes she will. Where'd you put it?*

—*Underneath.*

—*I looked there already and it ain't there.* It happened so much that sometimes they were a little embarrassed.

Increasingly, Angel was realizing that Rico liked what they were doing more than he himself did. At first it had been a lark, a faint whim, a bragging, mouthing game that refused to go away, like the sun when you had been staring at it too long. Then, like the sun, the idea was suddenly everywhere, for hours. Angel knew that they would likely not shoot you for thinking, so he thought. He saw the news on television, and saw all those dudes running through the burning streets, like a bunch of strangely calm animals, sometimes left alone, sometimes clobbered while they carried on their breaking and robbing. Meanwhile, all the nice safe people in the nice safe neighborhoods clucked and called their insurance companies.

"Sheeyit," Angel thought out loud, "that ain't no way to do it. Climb in those nice houses one night when it's dark and you bucks are all invisible but for your eyes and teeth. Do it quiet, and plan." Plan. Then it would not go away.

No matter how much he told himself that they couldn't get away with it, that they'd get busted sure, he began to wonder just how much he could do before he would have to quit and say, "Well, it was an idea, man, but it just can't be done." It was the chance that intrigued him at first, nothing more, but it would not go away.

And then there had been Rico, and afterward Clark Cooper, just as eager as molasses-slow could be with his disguise of stupidity; then Juan Laurindo, and Jesus-Maria, and before he knew it there was no simple succession of phony suns, too bright to blink away. There was a real, possible, honest-to-God plan of attack, with allowance for a margin of error.

Glee. *"Hell, man, we gonna be famous!"* Bitterness. *"I hate school, man, maybe they close it up."* *"Hey Angel, what we gonna do with the nurse?"* *"Angel, what we gonna do with cool heads like Old Jack?"* Angel, Angel, Angel . . . it made him tired, but every time a problem came up he could think of some kind of answer, and after a while he realized that some kind of an answer was enough for most people. He took to looking in the papers, for good pictures of good riots, and wondered what they would say about Betsy Ross Junior High. When there was even one killing in a school the unwritten law about school riots went out the window and it got in the paper.

And always—Angel yawned, beyond fatigue—always there was Rico, and decisions. He was sick of pretending to be sure about everything. The more he pretended to be sure, the more everybody believed everything he told them, to the point that he sometimes felt like telling a deliberate lie, right in their teeth, a lie so big and bald and hairy that nobody could believe it. But they would, and then he would have to make it come true. Somehow.

Rico did not have any of these concerns. He was not scared of anything but responsibility. He could kick the ass of anybody in the block now, and he probably knew he could be leader if he wanted. Why didn't he want? Angel yawned again.

Suddenly thirsty, Angel sat upright, and Antonia turned to look at him. Her eyes narrowed slightly as she saw that something was wrong. She immediately felt guilty that Angel was not happy. She tried to remember what he might have been saying to her. Plaintively, she lifted her hands in the gesture of a blooming flower. She looked hurt as he frowned and shook his head no, fiercely.

"I'm going to get some water, Antonia."

Her show of hurt made no impression on him, so she abandoned it at once. She knew that she was in danger of being carried back to the sofa if she was not a good girl.

• • •

Charley Lees looked up at the window that he knew to be Maria's. Of all the younger Valdes', only she had her own room, a cubicle in the corner that had been a grander lady's walk-in dressing room three decades earlier. Once, he had taken Maria Valdes to a dance, mostly at his sister's urging, and he still remembered the experience with shudders. In the process of meeting the whole family he had made an obligatory tour of the big house, in his uncomfortable dark suit, with new shoes pinching and his collar wearing a hole in his neck, all because of his stupid sister's stupid friendship with Maria. This is the livingroom and that's grampa's chair and that's the diningroom—yes, it's very old furniture—and that's the hall and that's the stairs and these are some of the bedrooms, this one's Wendy and Beatrice and Tessa's, and this one in the corner—very proudly—is mine. Big deal, he had thought at the time, but now the information was coming in handy, which just goes to show.

Mentally, Charley tried to follow his faintly remembered grand tour itinerary, trying to remember how far the stairs were from the front door, and whether he had turned left or right on the second floor. He wished now that he had looked out the window of Maria's room so he could be sure he was at the right corner. He estimated the considerable difficulty of scaling the brick wall along the drain pipe, and edging across to the window where he could pull himself up and look in. God forbid he should find himself looking into the parents' own bedroom. It would be bad enough to be caught looking into Maria's room, only to find out that Sandy was not there. It could happen. Maria might see a dark figure at the window, that shiny little round pile of dirt up in the sky, silhouetting him black as any coon. She'd set up a fine scream for sure, and they'd all come running or hobbling, Mamma and Pappa and Grampa and Great-Grampa and Johnny, and Tio, and Tessa and Wendy and then the cops and then his own folks, to kill him. As a compromise, he hunted around for a good-sized pebble to throw against the window. He would just hope Maria would hear it.

Upstairs, in her small bedroom, Maria Valdes was sitting on her neatly made bed, next to Sandy Lees, who was next to Louis Margadonna, who leaned over on his elbow so there was no room for anybody else on the bed. Larry Staples, a dishwater blond boy with a sallow complexion and a stammer, was astride the only chair in the room, while Johnny Valdes sat on the floor holding a small lamp, the only source of light in the room. He held it between his crossed legs, cautiously, where he could cover the top of the small lampshade with the palm of his hand.

They had to keep very quiet, for in the next room the bunk bed that held Tio and Beatricia Valdes was right up against the wall, mere inches from Johnny's back. None of them heard the pebble glance off the window-frame before falling back nearly to the feet of Charley Lees.

"I wouldn'ta come if I knew there was only five of us," said Sandy Lees. She looked accusingly at Louis Margadonna, who was studying his hand.

"We need a puh-puh-plan," said Larry Staples, his egg-white face even paler than usual.

"Sure, that's it, we need us a plan," said Johnny Valdes sarcastically, in his high voice. He was already sorry he came. He moved his hand from the lamp to gesture his disgust and for a moment looked like a devil, or a witch leaning over a fiery cauldron.

"Keep that covered, John," said Louis, his dark curly head bowed, his arms now crossed and held tightly in his armpits. He was disappointed too that only half the people he had given notes to had shown up.

"There ain't only five," Maria hissed. "How many you think we fit in this room, huh?"

"The point is," said Louis, "five or five hundred, if we don't try to do something we gonna be just as guilty as anybody else. There are sins of commission, and sins of omission. One's as bad as the other."

"We ain't talkin' about sins, man, we talkin' about our necks." Johnny's voice was scared, and a little contemptuous now of Louis as an opponent for Angel. "You were a buddy of Bart's—"

"Me ta-too . . ." said Larry, interrupting indignantly.

"Even if we do somethin', we guilty," said Maria impatiently. "I should've hollered bloody murder the minute I knew somethin' was up." She directed this last severely at

Johnny, whose hand was getting too hot from covering the lampshade. He whistled and pulled it away.

"Yeah, but you didn't, did you?" Johnny blew on his hand, quickly, resenting his sister's attitude, but deciding he was going to play it smarter from there on in. Since his talk with Rico in the maintenance shack, he had grown increasingly guilty and afraid. He had told Maria about the Plan too soon, and there was nothing to keep her from telling Angel if she wanted to get him into trouble.

"Everybody says the same stuff over and over." In her irritation, Sandy let her voice rise dangerously. "We all know what's gonna happen, and we don't want any part of it. But we're too scared of our shadows to say anything. And then when it happens, we all gonna be busted whether we had anything to do with it or not. I'm even scared to talk to my own brother about it. He might tell Angel—"

"*Your* brother," said Maria, "How about Tio? He's Angel's spy, sleeps right in the next room." Johnny Valdes nodded ruefully.

"He memorizes everything he hears from anybody even if it don't mean nothin'."

"They can't bust us all," said Louis, with a passion that suggested that he did not believe what he was saying. "How will they know who really did it, huh? That ain't the point."

Another pebble, larger, struck the glass of the window and cracked it. They all stared at the crack, their eyes wide, as Johnny Valdes quickly clicked off the light, leaving them all tensed in the darkness, not knowing what to expect.

In the next room, Tio Valdes lifted his head sleepily, interrupted in the middle of a dream about slot cars. His car had been just about to win. Blinking in annoyance, he heard another definite sound, and looked over to see if his sisters had heard. They had not, so he got out of bed, slipped down from the top bunk and landed lightly on his bare feet. He disturbed a film of dust on the wood floor as he went to the window and looked down at the gawky boy who was standing in the shadow, feeling more mysterious than he looked. Tio wondered what Charley was doing at that hour of the morning, interrupting the first race he'd won all night. It took all his strength to get the window open. His noisy exertions made Mikey roll over on his bed and mumble in sleepy protest. Tio leaned out the window, and called down. "Cut it out."

In the next room, Larry Staples had positioned himself at the window, crouched low, motioning the others to keep still. He opened the window with an unwelcome but unnoticed creak, and they all listened tensely.

"I wanta talk to Maria."

"She's asleep. Go away, man."

"Is Sandy there?" Charley immediately regretted the question, even though it earned a firm, "No."

Sandy looked at Maria and started to say something, but Louis Margadonna put his forefinger warningly to his lips.

"You sure? She told me she was going over there. Tell Maria to come to the window, Tio. Come on."

Maria leaned closer to Sandy, angrily. "Did you tell him you was comin' here?"

"No!"

"How'd he find out?"

"You don't have to tell nobody nothing, man," said Johnny Valdes, leaning back against the wall in resignation. "They just know." He clicked the lamp back on, and looked down at the little bulb. He wasn't gonna fool around with this counterplan shit no more.

"It don't matter now," said Louis Margadonna, with a shrug. There was an almost inaudible tap on the door. "Might just as well let him in."

● ● ●

"It's two o'clock in the morning, Roger," said Evelyn Post irritably, looking across the semi-darkened room where her husband was at her personal writing desk, still working under a small Tensor lamp, filling sheets of yellow-lined paper in longhand and dropping them on the floor. After the first few she could imagine a crash as each fell.

"Honeybunch I thought you were asleep," said Roger, his back to her.

"Obviously I'm not. Aren't you coming to bed? You have school tomorrow."

He scribbled something on a sheet.

"Not right away."

"I can't sleep until you turn that light off, dear. Aren't you tired from the game tonight?"

"No, not really. I thought I'd do something on my book while my thoughts are fresh. I got a new approach today that might help this sixth chapter along quite a bit."

Evelyn sat back against her pillow, biting her lip.

"Honeybunch, you know I have to get this finished or we're in trouble." Roger scratched his nose absently. "It's funny. While Janis was talking about the feeling some of the Mexicans might have against that Jewish boy, I got a sudden insight into the sexual possibilities of the Albigensians as a way out of my bind. You remember."

Evelyn said nothing. Her lids were so tired, her eyes were burning, but when she closed them her mind raced so fast that she might never sleep again. "Those poor Albigensians," she said bitterly.

"What did you say, dear?"

"What did they have to look forward to? A life of being hunted and persecuted, not being able to sleep for fear of the knock on the door, the clop clop of sandals on cobblestones in the middle of the night." That did it. He turned around to look at her.

"I believe you're dramatizing, dear," said Roger, amazed at his wife. "I hope you don't mind if I work clear through tonight." For a moment he thought she giggled.

"What about school tomorrow?"

"I'll take a pill, and go to bed early tomorrow."

"All right." There was a long silence, as Roger re-read what he had just written. "I hope you don't mind if I fall asleep?" said his wife, filled with an odd merriment.

"Of course not, dear," said Roger.

ELEVEN

Friday–early A.M.

The pounding of his heart had not subsided when Charley Lees finally squatted down beside John Valdes, his pimply face flushed with the recent anxieties of having to walk up the stairs and past the closed doors of the hallway. Tio claimed with some accuracy that he knew which part of the stairs and hallway creaked and which did not, so Charley was obliged to follow directly behind the disapproving little boy, and even wait for him while he went to the bathroom. Tio came out an eternity later and sneered, "Don't look so worried, Charley. I wasn't gonna flush it."

Once in the miniscule bedroom, all the silenced attention focussed on the unreadable Tio, who stood in his bare feet and looked at them, one by one, understanding everything at once. The memory of a thousand unrevenged indignities flooded over him as he thought how much Angel would like to know about this meeting. Maria read his face.

"Tio," she said, "if you don't wanta go to bed, you can stay." He weighed this offer a moment, and then noncommitally sat on the floor, a little away from the others. "And if you tell anybody, you in big trouble, understand?" His big sister tried to keep just the right balance of threat and pleading in her voice. The others looked at Tio anxiously.

"Not for me there ain't," said the boy at last.

"Tio, you listen good." All attention turned with surprise to Louis Margadonna, whose black eyes were angry star sapphires in the light from the lamp. "You better remember what happened to Bart Arthur because Angel thought he was a fink. You remember, Tio?" There was a shocked silence, and even Louis seemed surprised at the threat. Tio nodded, less certainly. "The same'll happen to you, only worse, if you say anything about tonight. You read me?"

"Aw come on, Louis—" Johnny Valdes started, outraged for his little brother. The dark boy turned on him savagely, only his oddly distorted mouth seeming out of place in his angelic round face with its crown of soft black curls. "You shut up, Johnny," said that mouth, "this is your fault, too. Always looking up to Angel, always doing everything he says. You the leader, Angel. What d'you want me to do, Angel? Grab that old lady's purse, break that gum machine? How about slittin' that convertible's top and checkin' out the glove compartment? Sure, Angel, anything for Special Funds for the Plan. You just great, Angel." Louis turned his head away from the surprise in John's face. He looked as if he could not find a clean spot to spit.

"You been doin' all that? For Angel?" Maria's voice was devoid of emotion. She had forgotten about Tio for the moment. The little boy continued to squat near the door, considering the threat. It amazed him, coming from Louis.

"Maria, it makes no difference now," said Sandy. "Everybody in here's in trouble one way or the other, and we can't start fighting now or we won't be able to figure anything out." Louis Margadonna ignored her.

"Tio?" He was staring at the boy, a sudden bitterness at what he was doing turning his normally bright eyes to sooty marbles. He was no better than any of them. "Tio?"

"Please!" Maria's voice broke, suddenly pleading in the face of stubbornness. "I'll give you my radio."

"Don't bribe him," said Louis Margadonna, disgusted now with everything.

"Yeah, don't bribe him," said Sandy, sarcastically. "Threaten him. Threaten to kill him." She took a deep breath. "Tio, I'll give you my watch. Look, it'll fit. Charley, give him something." She started fumbling with the leather watch band.

"Here," said Maria. The radio was small as a pack of cigarettes, edged with gold metal. It had a little strap that could hang around your wrist. Maria urged it on her little brother, knowing he had always wanted it. He looked at it.

"Well . . ." he said. Nobody had ever given him anything, least of all Maria. "OK." They all looked at him, so he repeated it. "OK."

"OK, wha-wha-what?" asked Larry Staples.

"OK I won't tell. But I'm still gonna be Angel's messenger." He looked at his radio, not wanting to try it out until he was alone.

"I think we better forget about this meeting," said Louis Margadonna. Larry Staples nodded his agreement, and stood.

"Don't everybody leave all at the same time," said Maria anxiously. "Go out one at a time."

As they were walking across the vacant lot, both lost in their thoughts, Sandy did not turn her head to address her brother. She supposed that he had come after her to try to save her from something. She had never felt about him quite the way she did at that moment. "What do *you* do tomorrow, Chuck?"

"Nothin'. I don't know. I go to school."

"Why don't you tell Dad?"

"Why don't you?"

Sandy lookd at her tall brother with a touch of bitterness, seeing the pink pimples on his chin, one freshly scratched. "Two weeks ago you lied to me. You said you didn't know what they were doing."

"I didn't. Not exactly."

They walked a little way farther, and Sandy found herself almost hoping that somebody would come jumping out of one of the cement basements, brandishing a broken bottle as a weapon. Maybe if they got a little bit hurt and went to the hospital . . . She looked around, but there was no one in the deserted lot, nothing but a bunch of paper and garbage, and buildings in the distance where everybody was sleeping. "You want to do it," she said at last. "That's the truth. You aren't against it at all."

"Sure I am," said Charley, wetting his lips so she would not see him. As they walked, close together, he seemed to catch all the wind in his throat, with the dust. He spat. "What do you mean, I want to do it?"

"You're scared, but you want to get back at Mr. Post. And worst of all, you think you can get away with it, and not even have to do the dirty work."

Charley shook his head. "That's a sick thing to say."

"Ever since he made you get up in front of the class and practice your walk, you've hated him. He said you walk like a girl, and you hate him."

"I won't do anything, Sandy. I won't touch him. I don't know about the others, but I won't do anything bad. There will be an Executioner."

"He'll have to murder!"

"Sandy, you heard Dad. People get murdered all the time. Thirty thousand people are killed every year with knives and bullets and they never find out who did it. Don't you see? Most of the time, they don't really care who did it."

"That's bums on skid row, Charley Lees. That's people who're better off dead probably." Her voice had begun to shake. "What happens if that Executioner won't do it? Then will you?" Charley looked straight ahead, without answering.

● ● ●

Angel had once thought of changing the color of the Executioner's handkerchiefs from black to the color that meant royalty, Prussian Blue. It would be a tribute to the new teacher, in a way, if they used blue handkerchiefs, but Angel knew he could not change anything at this stage. If he seemed the least bit uncertain about anything, the whole Plan would start to collapse. It gave him a weird, high, dizzy feeling to have so much power.

Nobody could be absent from school. A cold drop of sweat swung briefly on Angel's earlobe, and dropped silently to the coverless pillow's blue ticking. First period, a list of absentees would be assembled, so they could be dealt with later. He worried that perhaps he had not made it clear enough what the penalty would be for missing school on Friday. Everybody had to be on the grounds by lunch time, and after that, nobody would be allowed to leave.

But the Executioners. Angel knew it would be safer if there was uncertainty as to who actually killed each Target. If there were two in each room, not too crazy about each other, perhaps even two guys who hated each other— he was too tired to think about it any more. Everyone would be equally guilty, with fingerprints on all the weapons, blood everywhere. There could be no special guilt among the guilty, no individual responsibility, not even for himself. When his great Plan came to its end, he had decided that it would be his last act as the leader. Angel turned over onto his stomach, opening his eyes to look enviously at Antonia as she slept, one arm thrown across her chest. The weight of his lids forced them shut, closing out all but a last consideration: after Zero Hour, he would give the leadership to Rico, without a fight, without regret. It would not be quite the same as when he had given him Angie.

• • •

"Darling?"

"Yes?"

"What are you thinking about?"

"That's a question you should learn never to ask, at least until you learn to read minds so you can check my answer." Tim leaned over to Marge and kissed her on the cheek, as he might a sister. She smiled at his solemnity.

"What time is it?," she asked.

"Oh, about three-thirty, I guess. I don't have my watch on."

Marge giggled. "I know."

"Why do you want to know what time it is?"

"Because I have to get home before my parents wake up. God forbid Mom's waiting up." She looked dour.

"If she is, she'll know." Marge's head lifted from the pillow in the dark. Her eyes, the color of bitter chocolate, looked at Tim disapprovingly.

"What a horrible, dreadful thing to say."

"It's just the truth. She will."

"She won't."

"She will."

"How could she think such a thing?"

"They always do." Marge thought about that.

"You make my poor mother sound like Calpurnia."

"Nero's wife?"

"Caesar's, I think. You knew what I meant—" Marge started to laugh, and she laughed so hard that she had to put her face into the pillow to stifle the sound. Tim kissed her on the back of the neck, excited again. Suddenly Marge stopped laughing and turned her face to him.

"I wonder if I'll be able to face you in the morning."

"You won't get a chance to. I have to go to school and so do you. Such are the facts of practical existence."

"I mean, the next time we see each other. Tomorrow night."

"Pretty sure of yourself, aren't you? How do you know I liked it?"

"Don't even kid about that."

"OK."

There was a long silence. "Tim, did you like it?"

• • •

Cleaire Devereaux' apartment was tasteful. As her regency clock chimed three-thirty she turned her head, which was swaddled in a terrycloth bandanna, just far enough to peek over the top of her bifocals and check the hour against the mantel clock. She sighed, annoyed to be so restless that she could not sleep. She put it down to the fried oysters she had for dinner. Sometimes they upset her stomach, and sometimes they did not. The one bedroom apartment was roomy and L-shaped, arranged so that it seemed even bigger than it was, and at least twice as expensive. Cleaire had selected scaled-down reproduction antiques from a good shop on Robertson Boulevard, including a shapely divan that made into a comfortable bed in case she should ever have a visitor.

Cleaire had bought her furniture one piece at a time, with complimentary decorating advice from the store that sold her her first big purchase, a dining room set. They had sent a young man out to look at the walls that would receive their "personality influence." The young man, who never smiled, took one look at her inherited French clock and decided that her cultural heritage could be brought out to good advantage by doing the whole place in French. It meant starting practically from scratch, but the young man was persuasive.

Furthermore, Cleaire had to face the fact that she had no one to spend her salary on but herself, and since she was not one for going out much, she would indulge in periodic good accessories, or a fine expensive liqueur for her bar.

She thought of her apartment as an Ivory Tower, and indeed the colors, if they could be called colors at all, leaned toward the ivories and creams, beiges and eggshells that the decorator had decided was "her." Pale blue throw pillows, now neatly stacked on the immaculate white carpeting beside the sofa bed, were his sole concession to what he termed her businesslike self. In Cleaire Devereaux he had noticed nothing of unmuted passion, and the hot colors that she longed for were denied her.

Only her very small bathroom, which she did herself, with its wild scattering of bronze doré fixtures, violet, purple and red fluffy rugs, towels, toilet-seat covered with imitation zebra, a cornucopia of miniature perfumes in cut crystal, only these things gave any hint of the extravagant side of her nature. Whenever possible, Cleaire would buy something outrageous for "her" room, like a gold-plated powder puff holder, or a sparkling paper collage by Sister Mary Corita, or, maddest of all, the possession of possessions, the polished ebony and hand-chased silver holder for her wig.

At that moment Cleaire Devereaux' wig was resting at a slightly careless angle on its sumptuous holder, which had been shaped to the contours of her head by a cosmetic phrenologist. He had sent his model to Italy to be custom carved, and then delicately filigree'd with sterling silver. It had of course cost a fortune, but then so had the auburn wig, which replaced the ragtag affair she had scrimped to buy twelve years earlier when an unfortunate fever caused her to lose all her hair. The new wig was a sensible, well-made thing that had come to be as much a part of her as her teeth or fingernails. It took a styling well, and was only slightly better in texture than her own hair had been.

As she read her magazine, her lips moved silently, a habit she slipped into intermittently when she was not paying attention. She had gone through reading courses years before to break her habit, but they had not done the job. She looked again at the clock as it chimed four, several minutes too early. Insomnia was an ugly thing. She was glad she suffered from it rarely. Putting her magazine down on her lap, she thought about Jimmy Janis. He had seemed subdued at the poker game, and she supposed it was for the same reason they all felt so strange and quick-tempered, that awful accident. Coming as it had right on top of the rape charge against the young Art teacher, it made an ominous pair that seemed to be waiting for some third disaster to complete the cycle.

• • •

Rico was neither asleep nor awake, but was more asleep than otherwise despite the sounds of breathing—he held his breath—he knew came from someone other than himself. There was light and then dark, the sheets felt damp, he could not breathe because his nose was clogged. He made an effort to inhale deeply, during the moment of dark that seemed to follow whenever he opened his eyes. He felt as though something had broken in his chest. Stopping his breath utterly, he arched his spine with the effort to break through, to fill his starved lungs, as then as suddenly as he had clogged up, he burst open, breathing in and out with a high thin trill.

He was in a forest, which had broken the dark walls and let the air in for him to breathe, warm night air, providing at the same time a rustle, a whisper of leaves and branch-creaking that signalled him the world was breathing as well as he, now in, now out. It was a moonless forest, a dirtless forest, a birdless forest, smelling of nothing but warm night air as his hand trailed along the worn floor-boards and came to the soft braided edge of the rug. As though the softness had stung him, his hand leapt back, and froze in the air as his breathing caught again.

There was a rag on the floor of the bathroom, a gauze rag like the face masks worn in operating rooms. Next to it was the tube of airplane glue, curled like a scroll, turned on a hairpin around and around until its lead-colored tail was hard against the cone of tin whose top lay half a foot away.

It was a dark night, the moon behind a cloud that made it some blind Orphan Annie's eye, but Rico knew he had to get up and walk, and keep walking. He struck his side against the washbasin on the way to the door, and had to hold the pain in place with his left hand while his right reached out, palm down, steadying the path along the patterned rug. He would go to Angie's, but hardly a step had been taken when he found himself at a cemetery. It was a devious trip, for there was no cemetery between his place and Angie's, but he skated past the blinking traffic and past the chipper stopsignals thumb out as though he were on a moving sidewalk; spun past the loops of concrete turning into, into, and cannibalizing the freeway below him, tight-rope walker now, teetering and rolled and dove like some old fighter plane in Nazi movies on TV, slid in the car whose tipsy driver took his mumble for instruction, over hands that touched him, a mouth that pressed against his lap, futile, the narrow shoe that left a dustprint on his seat as he was ejected—*whoosh,* sweat drying on his face, wind from the window, and then into the sidling street with lights for crosses, stars for crosses, fire hydrants for the monument—a cemetery. He stopped a moment, lifted his leg and felt the spreading warmth along the inside of his pants. From far away, a long way off his eye separated small piles of dirt from the general forest, one of which, the farthest pile, seemed to grow as Rico approached at a stagger and saw fresh earth leaping from the shovels of people who he could not see for the spectators all around, surrounding them, their banners and flags and noises jumping up and down in front of the great mound of dirt.

He ran, the damp pant leg chafing him, until he saw that he had overrun his destination. There was nothing ahead of him except a vista of peaceful animals, cows and buffalo, grazing without a care, small deer lifting their heads, unafraid, their muzzles wet from some stream that he could not see. He knew it was there, for he could hear its cheerful bubbling.

Turning quickly, he saw two men, the diggers, leaning on their shovels near the open grave, their seamed face running with the sweat of their recent exertion. They looked up as he ran toward them, but he soon discovered that their look of expectation was for a young man who came from somewhere behind him, holding a pointer, a blackboard pointer, and carrying under his arm a tombstone remarkable for its apparent lightness.

The trees were in a row, with lights between them like

stars as Rico stumbled forward onto his face and looked up to see the teacher planting the tombstone at the head of the open grave. Rico watched as the pointer began to scratch on the tombstone.

R was the first letter, painstakingly slow, and then, with a casual slash, *I*—

Docilely Rico understood, and stepped into the grave. He found it so fresh that the bugs were still circling in confusion on the newly denuded roots protruding from the sides.

C went the pointer, above his head now, scarcely visible in the spreading fan of foliage that shook with the weight of a landing sparrow. The sparrow saw him and nearly toppled from the shock. He looked closer to the sparrow, wondering if it had been a sparrow he had known—*O* went the pointer—and he felt the first drops on his face that told him of the rain.

Brushing the droplets from his forehead, his hand came away bloody. *M* went the pointer, as Rico looked up to see a dog standing over him, a German shepherd with a black muzzle dripping blood directly onto his face. He murmured the dog's name, Rex, remembering the old neighborhood and his father's friend's dog. He had used a shovel to kill the dog, the dog was joined by a cat, the cat pretended to be a bat, a flying bat that sprang across the open grave to land on the smallest of the sparrows that were lining the edge where the grass was smeared downward like little green fingers of accusation. A buzz grew loud as singing telegraph wires, a loud sizzling rocking hum as he felt himself floating. Oh God! he tottered to his feet, kicking at the ground where insects, earthworms, burdened ants that never reached the hill were scurrying in confusion, suddenly in light, unburied—

Angie waited for him for two hours, and then decided to go looking for him. When she opened the front door she nearly stepped on him, lying on his face across the steps, his good shirt ruined, his damp right leg encrusted with fresh dirt. She was thanking God that her father had not opened the door first as she took him down the steps to the basement, half dragging him. She left him on his back, lying by the furnace with his eyes closed while she went upstairs to get the makings for an improvised bed. When she kissed him she had immediately noticed the odor of acetone, but he would be all right if he could take some coffee and rest. No matter what happened, she decided, she would sleep next to him once her family was safely asleep.

I don't know nothin' about this boy, Angie was thinking several hours later when Rico seemed finally to be sleeping on her shoulder. Her right arm was cramped. From time to time she would shiver with cold from the open window, but she didn't dare move, or even breath heavily, for fear of waking him. With her left arm, she tried to ease the edge of the blanket up so it would partially cover them.

She had never heard him talk so wild as he did between bursts of making love to her. She had not even expected him to wake up at all, but he had come three times, hurting her the first time as though he were doing it on purpose, squeezing her breasts hard and biting her on the neck so that she could not keep from crying out. He did not like her to make noises, and she tried to please him; she tried to lie still like he liked, but this time he had been different, mean, and yet tearful in a way that made her afraid. She was not sure anymore how he was when he had been sniffing as bad as that.

Even though she had been Angel's girl for a whole semester, she found out more about him in the two hours in the basement with Rico tonight than she had found out the whole rest of the time before. She had not understood it all; Rico had talked about Angel, and somebody called Rex, and Bart Arthur—that made her shudder—and the Plan having something to do with bugs, in snatches of nearly unintelligible murmuring and crying. The things he and Angel had done together in the streets; at first Angie had thought they made love, and then she understood that they had robbed together, and fought, and rolled old drunks and fairies off Main Street. She had always known it, but he had never talked about it before. She realized that he was not talking to her anymore; she was just listening in.

"I love you, Rico," she whispered. "All that other stuff ain't love. Angel don't love nobody."

He murmured and rolled harder onto her arm, which was already asleep. She took a chance on pulling it out, at the same time rolling up an edge of the blanket to rest her head on for what was left of the night. It made no difference now, she didn't suppose, but she was gonna be all kinds of hickeys in the morning.

The worst thing, the thing that scared her so bad, was the way Rico carry on about Bart Arthur, like he killed that boy for no reason but to have a good time. That wasn't the reason at all, but he didn't know it, so it might as well have been. Angel say kill, and Rico kill, like he

have everything in the world as a special present from
Angel. Even her, or maybe her especial. Angie's honey eyes
grew darker as she turned her head away from Rico, hating
that gratitude, hating Angel. Tonight Rico acted different
to her than he had ever acted before, as though he didn't
love her, like she was something to get a little dirtier on. It
was a funny feeling for Angie to have a crying boy on her,
mustering up a new strength that was near gone to come
once more before he pass out cold. She'd had them drunk
and sober, some real serious and gentle, and some just
plain mean, but nobody never cried on her when they was
coming, like Rico had done.

· · ·

"I hate to leave."

"I hate to have you leave, but you have to."

"I know." Marge hoped he would not think her next request was silly. "When I get out of bed, don't look at me."

"Why not? You're beautiful."

"I just don't want you to."

"OK, I'll close my eyes."

"That's silly, isn't it?" It was a statement.

"Sort of."

"But I would prefer that you don't watch me as if I'm
some sort of . . . I don't know what."

"You don't want to feel like a slave girl naked at the
slave market, with drooling eyes all over you."

"I guess that's one way of putting it."

"You don't want to feel that I'm the midget and you are
the Circus Fat Lady that he loved pretty wisely."

"Huuh? What midget was that?"

Tim smiled. "Well, there was this very greedy midget who married the circus fat lady, and every night he made her take off all her clothes, very slowly, and then run around him in very little circles while he slapped her on the rump and chortled, 'Tons and tons, and all mine!' "

Marge laughed. "Funny little man."

"Not really. It makes excellent sense if you think about it. That's more than most things do."

"I'm going to confess something to you."

"Oh, oh—"

"Despite war and taxes, misery and suffering in the world, and very little hope of my kind of afterlife, I am at this moment a happy and chastened woman. And all because of you." Tim said nothing. "Well, I really have to go."

"I'll turn my head," said Tim, pretending it was so he would not watch her dress. In reality, the sight of her lovely body, at just that moment, would have stopped his heart. She kissed him on the back of the head before slipping out of the bed and pattering like a child to the closet.

• TWELVE •

The alarm clock rang and Tim's hand reached out, felt for the button on top, and pressed it down at the second groping attempt. He felt pleasantly depleted, and toyed for a moment with calling in sick.

Antonia had awakened to find herself back on the sofa, and Angel gone. She didn't remember being carried back. She looked around the room bellowing with her eyes, hitting the side table with her powerful palm until one of the twins came out, rubbing sleep from his eyes, and shouted at her to shut up.

Tim looked at the clock through a cloudy squint, watching it say 6:20 when it was really 6:10. He rolled over onto his side to catch a few more seconds sleep, and then he saw the other pillow had slipped onto the floor. As he reached over to pick it up he saw the faintest smear of pale lipstick on the pillow case.

Antonia pounded on the table stubbornly, harder, until the twin came grumbling back out, and went to the kitchen to put on hot water for instant coffee. Antonia shook her head vehemently no, to an absent Angel, although there was no one to see her red-faced displeasure.

217

Automatically, ten minutes later, the reminder alarm on the clock began to drone and this time Tim swung his reluctant legs over the side of the bed as though they were made of wood, and stretched in a violent yawn. The reminder bell's hoarse stutter stopped as Tim shut it off with bumbling fingers and stood up, stretching out his arms. He had worn pajama bottoms in deference to Marge, but now he let them drop into the wicker laundry hamper as he opened the window wider and looked at the hazy sunshine glumly.

One-two, one-two, he did several knee bends, thinking of Marge, breathing deeply. He touched his toes twenty times, and ran in place for a minute, elbows pumping. Finishing this routine with gratitude, he pattered barefoot into the cold bathroom, and turned on the shower to warm it up before he got in. Standing on a hand-towel, he examined his teeth in the mirror, and then brushed them carefully with MacLeans while he speculated on the effect that it might have on Marge to see him go through his A.M. ritual, day after day for years. Were boredom and overfamiliarity inevitable, he wondered? And, equally important, what did Marge do in the morning that he might find repulsive?

The details of someone else's hygienic routine, even Marge's, he felt sure he could easily do without. She would surely do the normal things, the same things men did, brush her teeth, gargle, shower—or, more likely, she would take a warm, pine-scented bubblebath. There was something distinctly piney about Marge, who needed practically no make-up. He thought about that pale smear on the pillow.

Antonia allowed the girl-twin to pull off her nightdress, and help her with her clothes. She sat placidly naked in the front room while the yawning little girl brought her blue dress with the white flower design, and a clean slip. Cheerfully, the little girl ordered her to lift her arms, straight up. The little boy-twin, who was seven, loved to tickle her on the ginger-colored tufts of her armpits as the girl-twin pulled the bright dress over her head.

Tim stepped into the warm shower, letting the water flatten his hair down onto his forehead as he threw his head back and shut his eyes, groping toward the chrome soap-dish for what was left of the soap. It was little more than a chip of exhausted bubbles. He had forgotten to go to the market.

"Damn," muttered Tim, forced to drip and cuss his way over to the medicine cabinet to get a fresh bar. He was out of his regular soap, but he remembered the fancy little box on the back of the shelf that he kept for just such an emergency.

Antonia pretended to laugh as the little boy tickled. After the neck of her dress had been smoothed down, she opened her mouth wide and shook her head up and down in an uproarious pantomime of happy laughter that found its echo in the boy-twin. He stepped back satisfied, as Antonia lowered her arms and shifted her weight so he could pull the dress the rest of the way down around her hips.

Tim nearly slipped and broke his neck trying to get back in the shower. He looked wryly at the imitation lime, perfect in every lumpy detail, a gift from three Christmases before. At last, by necessity, he would reduce it to a smooth green egg. He started soaping himself with the fancy lime luxuriously, wastefully, washing his pink genitals with particular possessive pleasure, running the hot water on himself until he felt loose and strong, ready to go again.

There you go," said the girl-twin, shooing her brother away masterfully. *"Do you want some mush? I'll make you some hot mush."* Antonia shook her head and made a face.

Tim had not washed his hair in three days, and it was not too dry—he had not had dandruff since summer—so he reached for the plastic squeeze bottle and opened the cap, tilting his head back into the spray and wetting his hair with a side to side motion as he put a ball of clear shampoo on his hand.

Charley Lees and his sister looked at each other after their fight over the Wheat Chex with a bitter tenseness that their parents, as a fighting pair, found not at all out of the ordinary. It even made Mrs. Lees comfortable and secure.

"Eat your breakfast. It's getting cold," she said, with her characteristic lack of emphasis. It was as though she found it too tiring to use accents. She poured herself a second thick cup of coffee as she kept an eye on the door where she expected her husband to emerge any minute, grumbling.

"I feel sick," said Sandy, biting every word off short and keeping her mica bright eyes on her brother. He refused to waver.

"No, you don't, you feel fine," he said, pretending to eat his eggs. They dried on his tongue before he could swallow. There was a furious silent conversation with their eyes.

"I am not going to school," said Sandy.

"Oh yes you are, young lady," said her mother firmly. "You're healthier than a horse. Eat and get out before your father comes in to raise hell."

"Sandy," said her brother very low, without looking at her, "I warned you!"

After Tim had dried himself carefully and dressed in his coat and tie, he went into the kitchen and broke two eggs into his mixer, added milk, molasses, wheat germ, yoghurt, starlac, gelatin and natural honey, and pushed the lever to *medium*. He wondered what kind of cook Marge was. It had suddenly occurred to him that in all the months they had known each other, she had never mentioned being able to cook anything. The thick liquid in the blender bubbled and splattered, churned and twisted, as he toasted a piece of French bread for roughage.

When the phone rang, he looked at the clock over the stove, which said ten minutes to seven. He assumed it must be Marge, and wondered if she had gotten into some kind of trouble with her folks. No one else would telephone him so early in the morning, he thought, as he picked up the phone, keeping an eye on the whirring blender.

"Hello?" he said, after an empty moment, but there seemed to be no one there. Tim frowned. "Hello, Marge?" There was a click as the phone was put down at the other end. It annoyed him that wrong numbers did not have the courtesy to apologize rather than just hanging up. He poured his breakfast into a large mason jar, watching the gelatin globs rolling along the side of the jar to the bottom. He was about to drink, when the phone rang again. This time he knew it was not Marge, and he felt himself tightening up.

"Hello," he said sharply.

There was a silence, followed by a girl's voice saying, "Don't go to school today."

"What? Hello?" Tim clicked the phone a couple of times, but it was dead. He put it back in its cradle and drank his breakfast slowly, with discipline, chewing thoughtfully on the thick cud of gelatin on the bottom.

That morning as he waited for the bus, Tim was quiet to the point that a woman who always took the 91B with him on the way to work commented on it with concern.

"Do you feel all right? Tim?" Tim nodded brusquely, without answering. The old lady turned to her morning paper with a flush of humiliation.

Tim could not imagine who it could have been. Nobody had his phone number at home. It was unlisted, and only Marge, his parents, the school office and a few close friends had it. Certainly no students, and yet the voice seemed to be that of a young girl. His mind turned at once to Maria Estragon, and then, because of the accent, or tone of the voice, he had doubts. There was no way to be sure, since he had not been listening for anything in particular, and she had hung up so quickly. It could have been a young boy just as well, he realized. And why not go to school? There was no threat in the voice. None at all.

Tim tried to concentrate on his paperback of *The Pawnbroker,* which he read to and from school on the bus.

He had set himself the goal of two novels a week, after giving up on newspapers. If there was to be daily carnage in his life, he wished it at the first remove of art. Three times he read the same paragraph, understood nothing, and closed the book with a sigh that made several passengers look up at him.

Again, unwillingly, his mind returned to Maria Estragon. He considered their exchange in the hall, judging her words against the passion of the moment. He wondered if she might be trying to get even with him by frightening him. It seemed senseless, and, considering the way she had always acted toward him before, uncharacteristic. Besides, how could a student get his unlisted phone number? How?

● ● ●

From time to time the Unholy Three would feel that mystical oneness that made them indestructible, more important in their own minds than any individual in school, more distinctive, more . . . more *more*. That was the only term that fit them; they had even thought of forming a singing group called The Mores, until they discovered that Miss Jensen would have nothing to do with their rock and roll careers. But recently, it had become increasingly clear that they were breaking up.

Maria Estragon, the middle Maria, had shown unmistakable signs of weakness, and the Unholy Three had not known what to do about it. She had even contacted the good-looking new teacher, shamelessly, and when she admitted as much to Maria LeSanto and Provencia Perez, they were in a delirium of uncertainty. There had been no question of telling Angel, and Clark Cooper had gotten what he wanted in the boy's head. He would not tell. They resolved the problem by vowing never to speak to her again.

• • •

Angel sat alone in the third floor Boy's Room, looking at his loose-leaf folder. It was turned to the two hand-written pages on Timothy Leslie Nielsen, which outlined his date of birth, place of birth, residences, friends, background, everything in short that Angel had been able to gather in the few days he had, from the new teacher's personnel file and Tio Valdes' observations, however unreliable and scanty. It was gratingly unsatisfactory.

All the other teachers and staff had Dossiers—Angel used the impressive word from the dictionary to describe the detailed pages that he had begun many months before, when the Plan had first started to take form. He studied the methods used by investigators to gather information on suspected criminals. He went on a Teen Post tour of the Police Academy. It had been one of his much admired insights that the technique of the dossier could work both ways. If the F.B.I. could keep storehouses of fingerprints and unassorted information on everybody from the ten most wanted to a Civil Service clerk, why couldn't a smart criminal keep his own dossiers on the men most likely to investigate his crimes? Angel grew enchanted with the idea. He read every word on the police that he could, how they got information, what they did or did not do with it, and adapted the file to his uses with the teachers and staff at Betsy Ross. He knew everything the school office knew,

and much more. It was his observation that the easiest files
to get into were the ones marked confidential.

With the exception of Mr. Nielsen, all the teachers and
administration had many pages in their dossiers. There was
plenty on Post, on Devereaux, on Conrad, on almost anybody who had worked any length of time at the school. If
they were not waiting for raises based on Federal funds, or
moonlighting on Poverty Program jobs, or trying to transfer to other schools, then they were like Miss Jensen or
Miss Raintree, holding her breath every time she came
near a student, hanging in until they could retire and get
out. It disturbed Angel that the entries on Timothy Nielsen, his own Target, were the scantiest. Under Griev-
ances—a word Angel particularly admired—he had come
up with exactly nothing. It had been a stroke of terrible
luck that old Mr. Muggeridge had dropped dead of a
stroke just when everything was going right on schedule.

Thinking of schedules, Angel looked at sixth period
again, and foresaw no trouble except in Boy's P.E. He had
carefully picked Zero Hour to coincide with Social Dancing. He knew he could not trust any girl to be an Executioner, and the problem of Girl's P.E. had taken much
thought. He had to be very careful not to upset the delicate balance of disgrace and fear, competition and threat
that would control the Executioners and their Assistants.

He had given his promise that nobody would be an Executioner unless he wanted to be, but three good candidates
had been picked for each room, eliminating anyone who
would be physically or emotionally incapable. Then, with
the help of Rico and a seat chart for each room, he planted

the black handkerchief before First Period in the Executioner's desk before anyone had arrived at school. The whole job, by himself, had taken an hour, and now he had come back to the meeting room to wait for Rico. Angel was sure he would be the first General to show.

Opening the seating chart, Angel looked at it again with satisfaction. First period, less than an hour away, each room was marked twice, once with a star, for Assistant, and a large black X for Executioner. The X would find the handkerchief in his desk when he sat down, and know he was actually to do it. But no one else except the Assistant would know, for the rooms would be cleared at Zero, to make it word against word as to who really did it. Neither boy could rat on the other without seeming to be covering up for himself, and since the fingerprints of every kid in the school would be on the knives, the carefully calculated confusion should be total.

Once again Angel looked through the room charts, stopping when he came to sixth period, Mr. Nielsen. The seat next to his own, Rico's, had been marked weeks earlier with a neat black x. He hated to break the news that he had changed his mind.

At that moment the door from the hall opened and Rico's head poked in, wearing a tense but pleased grin. He let himself in, swinging the door shut behind him, and using his softest, most secret voice, even though there was nobody on the entire third floor to hear. "Me first?" Angel nodded. "Hey, man, how long you been here?"

"Since four-thirty." Angel looked at the dark circles under his friend's eyes. Rico knew he looked like hell, but he tried to brush it off. "Jesus, man didn't you sleep?"

"You kiddin'?"

"You gonna kill yourself. Gotta get your forty winks, baby." Rico squatted down beside Angel to look at the charts, so close that their shoulders were touching. Angel moved away from the other boy's body heat as Rico studied the seating charts, trying to concentrate. "Hey, that one's mine, huh? You get 'em all around already?" Angel nodded. "Any trouble getting into the rooms?"

"Keys worked, like always."

"What time's the meetin'?"

"No meeting. Just you and me and Coop and Contreras to set up Muscle and Gatemen. That's all we need, everything else set."

Rico shook his head, giving Angel a whiff of mint as he spoke. He had been chewing gum. "No meetin'? Maybe you should just talk to the Executioners, just once. Or I'll do it." Rico's voice was eager and clear, but he was speaking a little slower than usual, and there was something wrong with his eyes. Angel shook his head firmly.

"Nobody's talking to nobody. Not till the gates are locked tight." Rico noticed something in Angel's tone; maybe he was mad. He decided to play it cool. "OK, Angel, whatever you say, man."

"You ain't gonna be Executioner sixth period, Rico." Angel tried to keep his voice as unemotional as possible. "I'm gonna do it myself as an example. We need an example."

Rico was looking right into his eyes, about to protest. Then he realized it was not the moment. Despite the coffee, and the chewing gum, and all Angie's efforts, Angel knew that he had been sniffing again, and in Angel's place he would have done the same thing. It was an emergency decision.

"I decided last night, Rico." Angel patiently started marking random xs all over the now useless seating charts. "I thought it over and decided I better do it."

"Last night?" Angel nodded, not understanding the sorrow that shot across Rico's face like an explosion of fireworks. In an instant all was black again, velvety and not to be probed. Angel stood and stretched, feeling the lack of sleep in his bones.

"Let's take a look at Chains and Locks, and make sure Coop's blood-sponges are set. OK?"

"OK, Angel," said Rico.

● ● ●

By the time he got off the bus, a block away from Ross, Tim had succeeded in quieting most of his worries. He tried to think about the previous evening with Marge, to preserve a good thought, to try to think positively. If everything had not been solved—and it had not, he realized —at least it had been a step in the right direction. He was proud that he had managed to carry it off to the evident satisfaction of them both. From time to time Marge would sleep with him now, and the thought delighted him. Since they both knew he could not afford yet to get married, a love affair seemed the intelligent alternative to breaking off, or struggling with both of them working, going to school, and trying to raise a family all at the same time.

The worst barrier had been Marge's fear of sex, pills or no pills. If she was over that, his own anxieties about her were certainly gone after last night. She would not actually be living with him, so she could be spared most of the annoyances of marriage, and they would have many of the satisfactions. If, when she was through with school, their love had matured, they could get married and have children, when Tim would be at a Junior College, or even a university, with his M.A. in Fine Arts. He calculated that he could have his degree in two years, which no longer seemed such a very long time.

The brick and concrete buildings of Ross, criss-crossed by the wire fence, looked like a prison or a military installation to Tim as he passed the gate marked TEMPORARY PARKING—FACULTY ONLY. The word ONLY passed through his mind, along with the thought that his draft status was not totally safe. If they started taking deferred men over twenty-five . . . he tried not to think about it. He was one year past the limit.

Standing by the gate as he passed was Ismael Sato, the long-faced half-caste who, along with Jesus-Maria Ortiz, was the best student in Crafts. Ismael was standing by himself, and seemed rather forlorn as he greeted Tim with a half-smile. "Hello, Mr. Nielsen."

"Hello, Ismael." A moment after the new teacher had passed, Ismael checked his name off, he nodded cordially to Gil Lieber, who was taking his job of Gateman Observer so seriously that he did not achieve his supposed goal of being anonymous to Ismael. Gil frowned in annoyance, secretly hoping that Ismael would miss someone so he could report him.

Tim walked past a silent group of girls standing near the bicycle rack, and nodded to them. There was no response, not even from Jennifer Baily, who normally gave him her version of a seductive smile. He looked thoughtful as he started up the stairs of the Administration building, disturbed by the stoniness of the looks that were greeting him.

Even the first floor hallway was oddly empty, as Tim went to the Number Three Faculty room, passing Jesus-Maria Ortiz on the way. The boy refused to catch his eye, and seemed to quicken his step when he sensed the danger that Mr. Nielsen would stop him to talk to him. Tim watched the boy hurry away, and went into the lounge just as Jim Janis and Dave Melnick were coming out with their first period books and papers under their arms. David had his up-all-night-with-the-baby look.

"Hello, Tim," said Janis.

"Jim, Dave," nodded Tim, glancing at his watch. "Is it fifteen to eight, or is my watch slow?"

"We're on our way to the cafeteria for a quick cup of coffee. Want to join us?"

"Thanks, no," said Tim, going in the lounge. Cleaire Devereaux was sitting in Evelyn Raintree's armchair, having a heart-to-heart talk with Sarah Vardis, while Roger Post was stapling something, and Wil Willson struggled with a lapful of papers. Chewing his lip, Herschel Watson was studying the bulletin board for any notices that he might have missed. He was toeing the line pretty carefully, everybody knew, and Tim greeted him first.

Tim could not help noting that Roger Post looked as though he had slept in his own face. Even his normally brisk greeting to Tim was subdued, his mind far away as he went through the mechanics of stapling a textbook list.

"How do you feel, Roger?" said Tim, "Good poker game last night?"

"Not bad, Tim-boy," said Roger absently. Cleaire had been having a secret conversation with Sarah Vardis about certain Job Corps positions that she knew would take part-time, pregnant help. At the mention of the poker game, she turned to Tim, eagerly full of gossip that she was allowed to tell.

"Bill Conrad is climbing walls about yesterday," she said, "although he pretends to be very calm. We might get sued, our appropriations may get cut, the publicity, you know, on and on." Remembering that Watson was only a few feet away, she cut it short.

"Cleaire, you exaggerate," said Roger, right before he noticed that several of the price lists for his department had just been stapled together upside down. "Oh, damn," he said.

"He had me in a conference for an hour yesterday, for all the good it did." Herschel Watson was talking to everyone in general, clarifying. His eyes never left the bulletin board. "It's a miracle there aren't accidents every minute. If a window gets broken, and you let that glass sit there while you go get a broom, or call the custodian, and some kid comes along and cuts himself on it—"

"I've stapled half of these damn things the wrong way," Roger Post was fuming. Herschel Watson looked at him, and stopped speaking. No one encouraged him to continue. Cleaire turned quickly back to Sarah Vardis, looking for some sign in the colored girl's smooth face, some physical change. She knew the thing they were not talking about had a physical effect on a woman, but she had not noticed it. Of course, if she noticed it, then Sarah would have to admit it, and lose as much as a month's salary, or even more.

"Mark my word," said Willson, "in a few weeks the Arthur incident will be ancient history. Oh, everyone will be on edge for a while, but nothing will come of it."

"Well, I have to be going," said Sarah Vardis, getting to her feet with grace that Cleaire envied. Tim was stuffing his roll book in his binder.

"I'll see you at lunch, Sarah," said Cleaire, with a tender feeling for the young Negro girl that surprised her.

"On edge," said Tim, looking for a sharp pencil. "Maybe you're right, Wil. It might explain why the kids seem so funny this morning." He did not want to ask if anyone else had noticed it. Cleaire turned her interest to Tim now that Sarah Vardis had left the room, just ahead of a morose Herschel Watson. "What was that, Tim?" said Cleaire, "I'm sorry; I wasn't paying attention."

"The kids. They seem funny this morning."

"It's not surprising," said Cleaire, "After yesterday what can any of us expect?"

"They always seem funny to me," said Roger, "I won't get these finished in—" He looked at Tim, who was taking books out of his briefcase, poking around in the bottom. "What are you hunting for, Tim-boy? You make me nervous."

"A pencil."

"Here." Roger Post held out one of his own new, freshly sharpened pencils.

"I had the oddest dream last night," said Cleaire, "If you believe in dreams." No one said anything about believing or not, so she went on, turning her conversational focus to Wil Willson, who was grading tests as fast as he could, referring every few minutes to his wristwatch. "As I was telling Wil, some people think that you can tell a lot about dreams." Willson grunted, pretending to be listening. "Dreams, after all, are said to be the mirror of the soul, and this one was really something. I thought I would never get to sleep. I was awake, reading a book till all hours, when I finally dozed and it was only a matter of seconds before I saw this entire thing, a . . ." She searched for the word. ". . . a pageant!" She looked around hopefully, but Roger Post was removing staples with his fingernails, Wil Willson was adjusting a contact lens that was giving him a bad time, and Tim Nielsen was a million miles away.

"Don't laugh, please," she said, adjusting her hair, "But I dreamed I was Joan of Arc."

There was a long silence.

"Well, nobody laughed, honey," said Roger Post.

• • •

Ismael watched William Conrad's new black Chevy Six pull into his assigned parking place. He put a neat x beside the Principal's name. The boy's vice-principal Mr. Sousa was already marked, as was the nurse Miss Summers. There was only one place empty, where Miss Peters usually parked her Valiant. Good. Ismael knew she would not be in, and he thought, that's the luck of the draw for Miss Peters. Angel had selected him for the delicate job of checking off administration because he knew that Ismael had the deserved reputation of being well-behaved and pleasant, and had the best chance of not being chased off for being where he shouldn't be, namely near the cars.

Jack the Janitor had arrived several minutes before, with a puckered up expression that he attributed to gas pains when Ismael asked him why he looked so funny. "Gas pains, son," he had said striking himself gently in the appropriate place. Ismael had laughed, and was sorry as he saw Jack shuffling toward the auditorium. It was a solitary, dusty chuckle from Ismael.

Clear on the other side of school, at the big west gate, John Valdes was feeling conspicuous and jumpy with his list concealed at his side, under his arm. It was quarter to eight, and all but one of his names had been checked off, and sure enough it would have to be Larry Staples. That made him just twice as antsy. Johnny had taken a big chance since he had gotten Larry on his list, and offered to let him stay home, and check him off anyway before turning the list over to Angel. The dumb idiot was not able to stammer his refusal before Johnny understood that he was afraid of what might happen to him afterward. It did not make any difference if the Plan went perfectly, or partially failed. Neither boy could imagine it failing altogether, and Larry decided it was safer to show.

Every entrance to the school grounds had a dozen or more Gatemen, under the eye of a Gateman Observer who was responsible for his lists to a Lieutenant. Each Gateman was checking off his list, not entirely sure which of the others might be his Observer. It kept everybody in line, although most of the time the Gatemen could guess well enough who was watching him.

Clark Cooper, with his added status as General and boss

of the bloods, was whistling happily through a chip in his tooth for all the world as though he did not know what day it might be. He was an Observer, but he also had his own list, and it pleased him as he recognized an old Ford stopping by the east gate. It discharged Sandra Lees, and her brother Charley, two of his specialties. They exchanged some heated words, then noticed Clark at the same time. They stopped talking at once, those two proud white children. Keeping several feet away from each other, they went directly to the administration building as Clark looked again and saw his list was all checked off. His Gatemen were in, so Clark tucked his T-shirt into his jeans and spent a moment just feeling good about everything. This was Angel's gig, and if it didn't come off it wouldn't make him any blacker. If it did—he smiled in anticipation.

• • •

As Louis Margadonna came through the north gate, his face was pale, his eyes as dazed as if he were stoned, which was clearly an impossibility. The Gatemen watched him with particular interest. He was checked off, then he hesitated, and the boy who checked him off waited to see if he might not turn around and go right back out. He looked as if he had just been sick, and had no place to spit the taste in his mouth except onto a nice clean rug.

Louis had gone to St. Mary's that morning as usual, a half hour earlier than his regular 5:30 A.M., despite his intention never to go back. Father LaFollette was awake, but he had not yet shaved or put on his jacket when Louis knocked on the rectory door and asked whether he might go to confession before serving Mass that morning. Look-

ing strikingly like some winos Louis had once seen, Father
cheerfully agreed, scratched the network of fine veins on
his nose, and lumbered sleepily into the confessional tuck-
ing his yellowed undershirt into his suspenders.

It was an agony for Louis to begin, but once he started
he poured the whole story out, how he had been told
about the Plan, and prayed about what to do, what he had
done in trying to organize resistance, the terrible head-
aches and dreams that he had started to have about Sandra
Lees, who in a moment of passionate conviction had said
she would protect the teacher in the classroom with her
own body if necessary. He had been waking every night for
the last week in a sweat, his pajamas drenched, with half-
memories of the Jewish girl, yes, Father, Jewish, in the
front of the room, her dress cruelly ripped down the front
with a switchblade stuck directly between her breasts.
Even telling about it, Louis found himself trembling.
There had been a great silence on the other side of the
black mesh, so complete that for a moment Louis thought
that Father had gone to sleep, or left the confessional. In a
panic, he started to grab for the handle of the door to the
confessional when he heard Father LaFollette's reassuring
rumble, muffled as though he were speaking through his
fingers, or a handkerchief. There was an asthmatic snuffle.
"And these dreams, my son," the priest said finally, "Did
they get you aroused?"

"Father?" Louis could hardly breathe.

"These dreams of the half-nude girl, Louis, did they
make you pollute yourself?"

● ● ●

In the third floor Boy's Room, Angel was sitting with Rico beside him, and the Generals and Lieutenants who could report complete Observer check-offs. They were nearly all in, each boy wearing his gold pin, each boy nervous, watching Angel for the slightest sign that he felt as they did. He frowned, making a mental picture of the responsibility ladder, and holding it. He started to call assignments, his voice soft and very steady. "Contact."

"Yo," said Rico, without smiling.

"Target."

"Yo," said Jesus-Maria, proud that he had been called right after Rico. He had just found a long hair on the side of his face, and tugged gently, hoping it would seen become a beard.

"Muscle."

"Yo," said Contreras, squatting, his head hunched down into his bull neck and shoulders.

"Weapons."

"Yo, indeed," said Clark Cooper, scratching his balls with easy pleasure. "And if you pardon me, I go get ready."

Angel nodded. "Go ahead, Coop. Executions."

"Yo, I think," said Juan Laurindo wryly. He was the least nervous, and he had one of the toughest jobs. "All desks marked and doublechecked, but—" He shrugged, and grimaced.

Angel ignored his clowning. "Gates and Locks."

Harold Craner swallowed hard, as Angel looked at him, his eyes focussing off the Responsibility Ladder and onto the sweating Lieutenant. "Gates and Locks," repeated Angel.

"Not quite yo," Harold apologized. "Gil Lieber hasn't reported in—" He looked helpless, thinking that of all the ones who could not sing out *Yo!*, like a mensch, it would be him. And who would be the cause? Lieber.

Angel had turned away, and regained his mental chart of the Generals and Lieutenants. "Messenger."

Tio Valdes was startled. He had not expected to be called equally with the others, and for a speechless moment he thought that Angel had found out he was keeping back stuff.

"Yo?" said Tio, but he had misunderstood?

"Go get Lieber wherever he is and tell him to get his ass to me on the double. Go on."

Relief flooded Tio's face. "Sure, Angel," he said, stumbling in his hurry to get out the door.

Angel took a deep breath. Spread out in front of him were the room charts, and to his left a pile of twenty-nine sheets of blueprint paper, each with the names and addresses of fifty students. More than ninety percent were in, personally checked off from Observer sheets. So far not the slightest real trouble; it looked like all the kids would show up.

Out in the hall, Johnny Valdes got the OK sign from Bill Turner, who took turns with his brother guarding the door. Johnny pushed through the swinging door, his sheet safely under his shirt, touching his bare skin. Two other gatemen were right on his heels, awaiting the formality of a nod from Bill Turner to enter. Thank God Staples had finally showed, Johnny was thinking. Three more gatemen were hurrying up the stairs as the electric clock beside the door to the principal's office read three and a half minutes to eight.

Johnny unfolded his sheet with fingers whose shaking he was suddenly unable to control in his excitement. Part of the sheet was damp from bodysweat as Angel marked his own copy, and dropped the sheet on top of the others to his left. Johnny stood watching, until Angel said "OK," as a signal to step aside for the next. "Numbers twenty-four and -five," said Angel, for his own benefit and the impression of his Generals and future Executioners. He glanced at his watch, and turned to Rico, who was watching his efficiency with a kind of awed amusement. Angel addressed all of them as a group. "Get to class now," he said. "Rico, I'll be down in five minutes; no, four minutes. You get right back here after first period. We won't have more than a few minutes to see if anybody missing."

Rico nodded, and less than two minutes later the last of the upper echelon were quietly entering their first periods as Angel sorted all the sheets numerically, and saw that only two were missing, Gil Lieber, and Ismael, who was not expected until after second period anyway because he was handling the administration staff. Angel heard the eight o'clock tardy bell with pleasure as he put the sheets away in a three-hole binder that he would take to class.

• • •

Gil Lieber, totally ignorant of the excitement he had created in the uncertain heart of Harold Craner, was folding his sheet carefully and slipping it into his shirt pocket as he barely beat the tardy bell into Mr. Janis' classroom and sat. His last contact had come through the gate only moments before, so he had not time to turn in his sheet. It could wait. Gil Lieber was a reddish-haired, freckled boy who always wore his Star of David outside his shirt, although there was nothing semitic about him. It did not make any problem, but he would not have cared if it had. Mr. Janis' voice was droning—"Menendez." "Here." "Robson." "Here." "Carter." "Here." Every time someone said *here* he looked up from his rollbook to check their identity. "Wills." "Here." "Kramer." "Here." "Sanchez." "Here." "Bravo." "Here." "Balzarett." "Here."

As his eyes swept the classroom, Janis was aware that nearly every seat was filled. He was so accustomed to absentees that he stopped, and looked at his rollbook again. "Cangiano." "Here." "Lieber." There was a pause.

"Here, sir," said Gil. The exaggerated politeness escaped the teacher, although several girls smiled at Gil for his mockery. He had been trying not to think about being selected for real as Executioner, and put off until the last possible moment the probable disappointment. He started to slip his hand into the desk, over the carvings that he had learned to read like Braille.

"Lyons." "Here." "Sordelli." "Here." "Vallens." "Here." "Estragon." "Here."

Gil's nervous hand stopped on something soft in his desk, and for a moment he just sat there, without daring to move. Suddenly he realized that Angel might have been serious, and he might really be the one. He felt his pulse throbbing at the base of his throat as he pulled the soft material toward him, stopping it at the edge of his desk.

Looking with disbelief at the triangle of black handkerchief, he turned to find Juan Laurindo watching him. It might have been his imagination, but he thought Juan nodded brief encouragement as Mr. Janis finished reading roll.

• • •

"Angela Vallens." "Here." "Clark Cooper." "Here."

Tim finished marking the roll, and then looked around the room without disguising his curiosity. "Nobody absent," said Tim, closing the book. He looked at Angel, who was watching him with that veiled expression that Tim found so frustrating.

"Very good." Tim moved around the desk, and leaned back against it, crossing his arms. "Today, I want to give you a rough time, and talk about the real craft of crafts, or, how to make the things we do look like we want them to. So far, we've been drawing designs and modelling clay. Now we're going to find out what makes a ceramic, what its good and bad points are, and why we should bother at all."

Angel looked over at Rico, who was staring in front of him, oblivious. Angie was watching both of them, hoping nothing was wrong.

"Modelling clay isn't just making an ashtray," Tim was saying, noticing the abnormal lack of interplay between the boys. "There are porcelains from Capo di Monte, which is a place, and pots from the Aztecs, who are a people. As we can see from looking at these pictures, they are not the same."

Angel saw the wary look on Mr. Nielsen's face, and low-

ered his eyes to the scratched desk top in front of him. He
studied the name, *Gregorio* elaborately carved with em-
bellishments. In a heart the name *Serafina* had been
started, but the artist had grown tired, so only the *Sera* was
equally resplendent. Idly, wishing it was fourth period,
Angel traced his own name invisibly with his finger on the
heart.

"Part of the reason why the two ceramics are not the
same lies in how they were done, the *technique,* and that's
what we're going to work on. We'll try to find out why an
Aztec wanted a pot like this, and how he could make it so
that it would last. If you learn a little about the Aztec In-
dians at the same time, it won't hurt you. We'll concentrate on trying to make our own copies of this type of pot
on Monday morning." Tim saw the change of Angel's expression at the mention of Monday, and it made him wonder. Charley Lees was sitting tensely at his desk, hands
spread out in front of him, looking at Angel. His panic was
so evident that Tim lost his train of thought, and had to
grope for his next words. "In Greek, *keramos* means Pot-
ter's Clay, and no matter how fancy the porcelain, it's basi-
cally made of this simple earth, and is a close relative of the
most primitive caveman's pot, a Ceramic. Tim paused,
aware of an unnatural degree of attention that he could
not credit to his interesting lesson. Then he noticed Clark
Cooper playing with something in his desk. *"Mis*ter
Cooper."

The silence in the room was total, far more horrified
and horrifying than the mild tone of reproach would justify.

"What have you got there, Clark?" said Tim, almost
afraid suddenly what the answer might be.

"Nothin' much," said Clark Cooper, after a moment to catch his breath and look to Angel for a clue.

"Nothing?"

"Just a handkerchief, man," said Clark, sullenly holding the cloth up as he slipped his blade deeper into the front of his jeans. Tim looked at the handkerchief, which seemed to have been dipped in ink. He nodded.

"All right, Clark," he said, disquieted. "Put the handkerchief away while we talk about temperature and its relation to hardness." The boy did as he was told, after shooting an anxious look at Angel. It was impossible for him to tell if Angel was really smiling, or licking the back of his teeth. Tim turned his back to the class, and went to the blackboard. "Temperature, the secret to good pottery, as well as fine porcelain, is temp-er-a-ture—" He spelled it out on the board. "Angela, will you please give me your definition, in your own words, of a kiln?"

Angie stood up unsteadily, white-faced, mouthing the single word in a whisper, "Killing." She looked first at the new teacher's back, and then tried to look pleadingly at Rico. He was chewing the eraser on his pencil to shreds, staring straight into space. Angie found to her horror that she was suddenly unable to turn her neck, not even a quarter of an inch. "Killing," she whispered a second time. Then she moaned and pitched forward onto her face before anyone could catch her.

THIRTEEN

Laura Goetz was typing a letter and trying to ignore the fact that the principal was studying her. He had come to the conclusion that she had several imperfect features, including the overwhittled nose that her mother had picked for her seven years before, but the rest of the substitute secretary was so far above what William Conrad had expected that he had been reduced to a full ten seconds of surprised silence when she had introduced herself. It was obvious to William Conrad that her painful show of shyness was an act.

Miss Peters, who presumably was stretching her period of mourning as far as it would carry her, had not arranged to return until Wednesday. This meant that Laura Goetz would be his personal secretary for three more school days, while the actual business of the office would be run by a stick of a spinster named, appropriately, Melinda Twigg. The prospect delighted Conrad, even as the girl pretended to ignore him. Deprived of Miss Peter's regular office, occupied for the moment by the cadaverous Miss Twigg, Laura Goetz found herself working at a typewriter and desk too close to the principal's for comfort. In addition to concentrating on her shaky spelling and punctuation, she

244

had fleeting moments of concern over what to do if the man acted out his obvious impulses. For the tenth time since she had started on the correspondence he had gotten up from his desk, circled it like a fighter pilot and finished by breathing unwelcomely on her neck in a pretense of seeing how she was doing. He had been sucking on a mint.

Willaim Conrad loved looking at the back of her bare neck, snowy beneath the stylish helmet of bleached hair. He appreciated the Japanese feeling that the female back of the neck was the loveliest of human attractions, and felt sure that if he had the chance to try, it would taste of vanilla and lime. Desperately, the girl kept typing. She made an O for an I and felt like screaming. She took a sheet of Quick-erase, inserted it in front of the first, then the second carbon.

"That's fine," said Mr. Conrad absently, going back to his desk. A moment later he had returned, and she made another mistake. In momentary exasperation, her hands rested on the keyboard of the electric and there was an immediate and rapid sdfghihg in the middle of the letter to the Area Supervisor. Since he was looking directly at it, Miss Goetz waited for a snide comment. There was none. Instead, a paternal, well-manicured hand settled on her shoulder with the lightness of a butterfly. It patted her shoulder.

"Mr. Conrad, if you don't mind." She was holding herself quite stiff, but he was a long time in withdrawing the offending hand. She removed the ruined letter, and started the tiresome process of inserting carbons between fresh sheets. Her fingers shook a little at the annoyance of such an obvious pass.

"When you're through with that, I want you to bring a probationary file up to date, Miss." He put the Herschel Watson folder on her desk. "We might be needing it early in the week and I want it up to date."

"Yes, Mr. Conrad." She put the file right beside her so she could get on it. It seemed only a few seconds passed and he was back, looking over her shoulder.

"How are we doing, Miss Goetz?"

She turned to give a hard look to her molester, a look that was to convey polite loathing, total uninterest, and a warning. A line of tinted talcum ran from the ear of the round, foolish face to the upturned corner of his mouth. Conrad leaned closer, pretending to be inspecting the letter in progress, while flickering his eyes towards her ample breasts. He enjoyed a brief fantasy of her two proud, pink, erect nipples, tapping away on the typewriter while her milky hands caressed him unspeakably. Miss Goetz murdered the dream by leaning forward with determination, obscuring his vision with her shoulders. Then, she felt his hand again, and drew back by reflex with a small gasp. She coughed violently, rackingly, but the hand simply followed her violent motions.

"I'm sorry if I gave you a case of the starts, Miss," said the principal, now all unctuous confidence. She looked pointedly at the hand, noting the perfection of its half-moons, and the busy-carved class ring that had worn a little groove in the wedding band. She tried to think of something more diplomatic than what she would have liked to say.

"Mr. Conrad, I find it hard to get my work done if I am constantly drawn into personal conversation."

"Oh, nothing personal, Miss Goetz," said the principal,

with a comradely squeeze of the shoulder that left her feeling faintly insulted. Mr. Conrad returned to the folder on
his desk, leaving a trail of loud tuneful breathing that resembled whistling. He glanced at his watch several times
again, and inspected the view from the window once. After
fifteen heavy minutes the secretary was able to hand him
the letter for his signature. "How much do you make a
month, Miss Goetz?" he asked idly, as though they had just
been discussing it and he had forgotten. The question was
so outrageous that she could only stare. He signed the letter with a flourish. "Little enough, I'd guess, working as a
substitute. Have you ever thought about going on full
time?"

She said nothing. In the next room Miss Twigg was
putting her things in order for when she got back from her
coffee break. Conrad looked up from the letter, and saw
Miss Goetz' strange look. "Oh, I don't mean work at Ross,
Miss. I mean in the system. Oh, no, Miss Peters will always
be with us."

"I have thought about it," said the secretary.

Conrad nodded. "As it stands you couldn't make enough
to have a really good time and put some away unless you
have a lot of boyfriends. A pretty girl like you must have
to fight the boys off, right?"

A flush was tinting Laura Goetz' throat and cheeks as
she fumbled with the switch on her typewriter. "I generally manage to fight them off," she said, as Miss Twigg
opened the door and looked in, without a glance at the
substitute secretary.

"I'm going on my coffee break, Mr. Conrad. I'll be back
in fifteen minutes."

"Fine, Miss Twigg. Take your time."

There was a silence, as they both seemed to be waiting for the doors to close behind Miss Twigg. The first closed, then the second. The girl felt they were closing on her, as the principal came closer, and she switched on her typewriter. It sat and hummed protectively.

"You give me hope then, Miss, if you manage to fight them off—only generally." He smiled benignly, feeling safer now that Miss Twigg would be out of the way for a few minutes. "You are a lovely girl," he said, quite sincerely. "And if you are truly interested in becoming permanent, remember that I could put in a powerful word for you downtown. Irv Luckerman is a personal friend of mine."

The girl looked at William Conrad, without the faintest idea who Irv Luckerman was. Yet he looked so proud. She was seeing the chubby principal in a slightly different, rather pitiable light. It was pointless to pretend that she did not find the interest of any man flattering, and even reassuring. A girl's psychological big nose was not so easily whittled. She knew she could never permit him to touch her, but she did speak somewhat more gently.

"Mr. Conrad, I am engaged to marry a boy who is attending Stanford. He is studying to be a doctor."

"That's wonderful, Miss Goetz."

"And I could not help noticing the wedding band on your hand, since it was resting on my shoulder, only inches from my . . . nose." The word nearly threw her.

Conrad smiled wider, admiring her even more for her moxie. "Indeed I am married, Miss Goetz, and I do love my wife. She's a wonderful woman, generous and gracious, an excellent hostess, and damn goodlooking in the Mary

Astor style." The expression on her face showed unfamiliarity with Mary Astor. "Or like Grace Kelly. A lady."

Miss Goetz wondered if that was meant to suggest something. "You're a very lucky man to have such a wife, Mr. Conrad, and I'm very lucky to have Stephen. Shall I do that evaluation file for you now?"

"Dolores comes from one of the good Catholic families in Atlanta. There are some, believe it or not. And let me tell you, there were some long faces, on the part of both our families, when we decided that we would get married. Yes, Papa was dead set against my marrying a Catholic. He thought they ate babies, or something." He smiled, and for an unguarded instant Laura Goetz saw a chubby, rather sad, old Romeo instead of a powdery and ulcerous principal with high blood pressure.

"But she stood by you," said Miss Goetz.

"Dolly's family did have some money, not too much, but surely enough to make them wish she would marry a Yankee Romanist like her papa did. When she stood firm on a poor but honest Education major, and a Baptist at that, well"—He smiled, enjoying the memory even as he saw that he was getting to her—" I sure wished I was studying to be a doctor. The only doctors around were giving smelling salts to our mammies, and outrageous bills to our pappies. I don't think a body can be any happier than I was then."

Laura Goetz was touched in spite of herself. "Mr. Conrad, doesn't the memory of those days make you think about your wife now?"

"Can't say as it does," he answered truthfully. "I'm a wicked man now, and I wasn't then. Wicked, mind you, but gentle. I could arrange for Miss Twigg to move back into her regular office. Three days, Miss Goetz. You're only going to be here three days." He stared into some beautiful dream.

Laura Goetz looked at him closely, with the nutty feeling that she might miss something, she was not sure what. The old man had a nerve, she had to admit that. It was intriguing to see just how far a person could go with nothing at all but nerve.

• • •

Tim's first thought was that the girl was having a menstrual reaction, which he had been warned about; or, worse, that she was pregnant. The way Rico Moreno had jumped up when she had fainted made Tim suspect that the boy was thinking the same thing he was, possibly with more cause for concern. The two were inseparable, even in the halls.

"Harold," said Tim to Harold Craner. "Get the nurse."

"She's OK," said Rico, as the girl came to and looked at him. Harold Craner hesitated at the door.

"Are you sure you're all right?" Tim was addressing Angie, who had bruised the side of her forehead. Very gently, as though they were alone, Rico was touching the bruise.

"I'm OK," said Angie. "Don't send for no nurse."

Harold looked at Mr. Nielsen for instructions.

"Maybe the nurse should look at you, Angela," said Tim, leaving Harold Craner hanging at the door, his hand on the knob. Tim got a small piece of paper out of his drawer. "I'll give you a hall pass, Angela, and Harold can go with you—" He had decided that it would be better not to send Rico with the girl. He had completely forgotten Angel, who was watching impassively, thinking that all he needed was an outbreak of hysterical girls.

"There you go," said Tim, handing Angela the pass. She looked at it, and then at Rico, afraid.

"No! I said I'm OK. I'm not goin' nowhere." Tim watched her in surprise as reluctantly she pulled away from Rico and moved unsteadily to her seat, where she remained the center of class attention. Although there was good order, Tim had the feeling that things could break loose any second.

"The nurse might want to send you home, Angela."

"I don't want to see no nurse!" She threw the crumpled hall pass at the wall in a fury, surprising Tim, and electrifying Rico and Angel. The pass bounced against a photographic display of national monuments and rolled to a stop in front of Harold Craner, still waiting at the door patiently. "I don't want to see no nurse," she wailed, tears now streaming down her face. Tim felt as though he might lose control of the room if he tried to press her. Harold Craner picked up the crumpled pass and pretended to throw it into the waste basket. In the tension no one noticed him slip it in his pocket, a light rash developing immediately across his furrowed brow.

"All right, Angela, but if you feel funny, leave the room and report to Miss Summers, do you hear? The rest of you sit down. Angela, you have to promise me." He smiled at her, reassuringly. After a sharp look at Rico, who was frowning, and Angel, who was studying the graffiti on his desktop, Angie nodded with a touch of bitterness. "If I feel bad," she promised, "I'll go downstairs. I'm sorry I hollered."

Once class had settled down, Tim finished the introductory part of his lesson faster than he expected, and went on to what he hoped were interesting historical sidelights. Charley Lees was hearing nothing. He was sitting like a zombie halfway back on the end of the row near the window, trying to orient himself in a world that suddenly seemed entirely crazy to him. There was nothing in the whole room that was real, from the pinned pictures on the corkboard, to Angie fainting just as Clark Cooper was flicking his black handkerchief, to Angel doodling thoughtfully while they all waited for sixth period. He had not been selected; he had not really expected to be an Executioner—It was as though Angel knew more about him than he knew himself.

He sat frozen still in his seat, trying to listen to the teacher talking about kilns, and realizing at the same time that kilns, and clay, and Mr. Nielsen himself had become unimportant. The blond young man, probably not so long out of school himself, was pointing at the blackboard with his pointer, unaware that he was dead.

Charley looked around the room, hoping to catch one eye that might show by some sign that someone else in the world felt as he did. It was the awful quality of aloneness that made Charley feel as though the bottom had dropped out of his stomach. He tried to get Harold Craner to look at him, at least Harold, but the skinny boy was sitting tensely on the edge of his seat, his hands clenched in front of him. It was intolerable. Charley felt as if he had stopped breathing. All he could see was ears and necks and backs of heads, ugly necks, fleeting blurs instead of faces. At least two of the thirty-six in the room were Executioners, Cooper and Contreras, who had both flashed their handkerchiefs, and then tucked them arrogantly into their pockets. Contreras would have Melnick, and Clark Cooper would have—who? Charley Lees tried to think—Miss Devereaux. Jesus, he thought, Coop with that sex-starved old broad! It was not hard to imagine how that execution would go.

Charley had forgotten Rico, who would probably be Mr. Nielsen's Executioner, even though he had not shown any sign. Charley was glad he would not be there to see it, although it would not be easy to watch Gil Lieber take Mr. Post. How did Angel know that he, Charley Lees, would have not been able to do it, no matter what he said? And know with equal conviction that Gil Lieber would do it without hesitation.

Charley looked closely at Rico's eyes, and saw that he was not looking at Mr. Nielsen, his target. He wondered what Gil Lieber was thinking at that moment in Mr. Janis' room, what he was seeing with those greedy, bright eyes. Nobody really deserved to get away, he knew, and all the kids deserved whatever punishment they would get. There was never enough punishment in the world to make up for all the evil people did to each other, and still, when he watched Mr. Nielsen telling them about how crummy savages cooked food— He decided to take the first real chance he had ever taken in his life. Reaching into his desk, Charley Lees brought out a small piece of paper.

After a quick glance to make sure no one was watching

him, Charley took his charcoal stick and rubbed it on the rough bottom of his desk before he started scratching a note.

Dear Mr. Nielson—Tim squinted to make out the blurry, charcoal crumbled words. His eyes widened as he deciphered—*Don't read this around nobody.* For a moment he felt foolish, then, with scarcely a glance at the hastily retreating figure of Charles Lees, he folded the scrap with trembling fingers, and stuffed the result between two sheets of drawing paper in his briefcase. Charley managed to angle his way to being one of the last to leave the room after first period, but he had not escaped the attention of Angel, who also made it a practice to be one of the last to leave.

"What'd you give him?"

"I didn't give him nothing!" Charley Lees looked at Angel, and then at Contreras and Clark Cooper, who had been hastily called by Angel. "Nothing, I swear," he whispered.

"I saw you, man, stop shittin' me." Angel's face was very close to his, and Charley couldn't keep his eyes open. The salt from his sweat was making them burn. I won't beg, he told himself fervently.

Angel gestured, and Clark and Contreras took Charley by the arms and moved him unresisting toward the stairway.

● ● ●

Don't read this with nobody around. Tim read the rest of the message with utter disbelief. *Sixth period they close the school and kill you. Don't say nothing to me, call the cops. CL.*

"What do you have there, Tim-boy?" Roger Post took off his tweed jacket and draped it over the back of a chair. Tim shielded the note from him as though he had been caught doing something wrong.

"It's nothing," he stammered. "Just a—" He did not know what he could call it. His mind had begun to race, thinking of the telephone call that morning, of what the Estragon girl had said the day before, and most convincing of all, the expression of legitimate terror on Charles Lees' face when he had just now handed him the note. It seemed impossible to imagine that so many would conspire to play a practical joke on him, and yet if it was not a joke, what could he think? Cleaire Devereaux entered the faculty lounge, looking in her purse for her compact.

"Have you seen Jimmy this morning, Tim?" she asked solemnly.

"Hmm?"

"I said, have you seen Jimmy? Has he gone to his next period already?"

"I don't know." Tim studied the Lees note for some bogus quality that would cancel out the conviction in the boy's face. "I haven't seen him since seven-thirty."

"Did you hear the latest elephant joke, Cleaire?" Roger looked up from a stack of tests.

"I haven't time right now, Roger," said Cleaire, wondering if Jimmy would pop into the lounge before she had to leave for her second period class. Somehow, unintentionally, she had allowed a misunderstanding to develop, and she did not know what to do about it.

"It's a funny joke, Cleaire." Damn Roger and his jokes! He was undeterred by her lack of interest. "Do you know the difference between a bull elephant and a grape?" he inquired, eager to hear his own answer. Cleaire shook her head more vehemently than she intended, and started fixing her lipstick with nervous fingers. "A lady elephant does!" he said, and waited for the reaction.

"That just proves," said Cleaire, blotting her lips with a Kleenex, "that I am not a lady elephant, Roger."

Willson, Hersch Watson and Dave Melnick came and went, and Evelyn Raintree asked to borrow one of Cleaire's Kleenex tissues. Cleaire was about to ask her if she had noticed a certain coldness recently in Jimmy, but Evelyn was clearly in a rush. Even Sarah Vardis came and went with scarcely a greeting. Suddenly there was no one left in the room but Tim, who was sitting as though he was not going to class.

"Tim, if Jimmy talks to you, would you—Tim?"

"I'm sorry, Cleaire. I wasn't listening."

"Tim, you don't have a conference period, do you? No, of course not. You're going to be late."

Without explanation, Tim held Charley Lees' note out to her. "Read this, Cleaire, and tell me what you think."

Taking the note, she had to fumble in her purse for her glasses. She hoped it would not take long to read.

● ● ●

Angel had picked up Juan Laurindo in the hall and the three of them had escorted Charley Lees to a room that was closed for repairs. Loose wiring dangled from black rectangles in the ceiling, and a metal ladder stood in the corner where they pushed Charley. No matter how he tried, he could not understand the whispers, until Rico raised his voice indignantly.

"Hell no, man, I don't want to do that, not to Charley." Rico looked at Angel, and saw that he might as well have kept quiet. The two of them went over to the corner. There was a whimpering sound from Charley as Contreras and Juan Laurindo held his arms behind his back. He started to say something, and Angel smothered the sound with his hand.

"You say anything and you one sorry boy," said Angel. Slowly, he took his hand away from Charley's mouth, a few inches. A string of spittle stretched between Charley's lower lip and the brown palm of Angel's hand, swung briefly, and broke. Angel wiped his hand on his pants as he addressed Laurindo.

"OK, Juan, you do it." Juan nodded and left Contreras easily holding both of Charley's arms. "Stand back, Rico," said Angel and it was a moment before he was obeyed.

Charley could not take his eyes off Angel's mouth, curved only inches from his own as they enunciated his instructions clearly, syllable by syllable. "You say even one word except to answer questions and you dead, Charley. You understand good?" Charley nodded, his eyes flickering to the knife as it spun now in Juan Laurindo's nervous hand. "You gave that new dude a note, didn't you?"

There was no answer. "Juan—" Angel's voice was not angry; it was almost tired. He had not planned on any of this. Juan nodded to Contreras, who reached over and undid Charley's belt. Using one hand was awkward, and the position of Charley's legs further complicated matters, so

Juan helped. He reached out, pulled the boy's pants down to his bent knees, and stepped back fast out of Angel's way. Again Angel put his face close to Charley's.

"We only got a minute, Charley. We ain't gonna waste time." Charley shook his head, so afraid that he could not move his lips, or force out a sound. "Contreras?"

Again the beefy brown hand reached out, and grasped the shorts to pull them away. Then he hesitated, looking at Angel.

"Go on." The shorts ripped across the side and in a second jerk pulled free to dangle in the big Mexican boy's hand. He looked at Angel, pleased with himself, and then tossed them onto a pile of rags on the floor. Angel looked down at the pathetic sex, with its halo of curly black hair. He pointed. "You gonna be needing that, man?"

Charley closed his eyes, with a weird sense of power. He was delaying Angel, he was giving him a bad time, he was going to last. Suddenly he opened his eyes fast when he felt Juan Laurindo's hand seize him and tighten gently over his testicles. He was about to scream when he looked into those soft brown eyes of Angel's, so close to him.

"Angel . . . ask . . . you . . . if you need this, man."

As the change bell rang, Charley nodded, his eyes stinging, a trickle of sweat running cold down the inside of his bare thigh. He kept nodding, afraid to stop.

"Then you better tell Angel about that note."

A whisper. "I can't."

"Then we ain't gonna waste no more time with you, Charley." Rico's voice surprised them all, and even Angel stepped back as Rico took the knife from Juan and put the sharp edge right against the soft undercord of the boy's scrotum. Charley arched up, onto his toes, as Juan stepped back, his eyes fastened on the knife.

Angel looked at Rico, and realized at the same moment as Charley Lees, that he would really do it. The knowledge scared Charley shitless, but at the same time it gave him a free, big, weird high. He understood what Harold Craner had meant when he said he was in, and Charley wanted to be in, too. He wanted everything, everything, except for the knife in Rico's hand to move.

"All right," Charley whispered, starting to cry his first adult tears. "All right." Angel had to motion Rico away. The blade was tossed to Laurindo with a slightly contemptuous look that made him squirm. As for Charley, the cords of muscle in the thin boy's thighs were shaking as Angel lifted his pants, and started to buckle the oversize belt with his own unhurried hands. "Sorry about your shorts, Chuck," he said matter-of-factly, after motioning Juan Laurindo and Contreras to race the tardy bell. "We're listening." The *we* was Angel and Rico, as Charley Lees wiped his nose, and looked at them. Something that he knew was important to them.

"I gave Mr. Nielsen a note," said Charley, proud of what they had had to do to get him to give in. After a while he stopped shaking.

● ● ●

Cleaire Devereaux did not understand at all, and did not hesitate to say so. Even after Tim had described the phone call, and reminded her what she had heard the Estragon girl say about killing, she simply could not conceive of it, and she said that if she were Tim she would forget about it. She handed him back the note, just as the change bell had rung. She had to leave for class.

"But I want to do something," said Tim.

"I'm sure I'm at a loss what to suggest. Unless you just go and tell Bill Conrad what you think. I wouldn't like to do it myself, I'll admit." She thought a moment. "Maybe, Tim, you could have the Lees boy stay after school for a conference with you and Mr. Sousa. You might find out it's nothing."

Tim nodded. "Thanks, Cleaire. Sorry I made you late."

"Oh, I'm not late," she said, running out the door.

Tim made up his mind. He would ask Hayward Brown to supervise his class while he insisted on Conrad's attention. It would be better to have Charley Lees with him, but he did not want to waste the time tracking him down. The hall was deserted as he rushed to the stairs and took them three at a time to the second floor, where he knew he could collar Hayward. He found the teacher on his way to spend his conference period correcting tests.

"Sure, Tim," said Hayward. "I can correct these any-place." A few moments later he was back downstairs, heading directly for the Principal's office, checking to make sure the note was still in his shirt pocket. As he passed the display cabinet he made a sharp left, his footsteps clattering hollowly in the corridor leading to the administrative offices. He was mentally cursing his decision to put taps on his heels to make them wear better when he practically knocked over Harold Craner, coming rapidly around the corner.

"Sorry, Harold." Automatically.

"That's OK, Mr. Nielsen."

The boy gave him a strange look, expecting to be asked for his hall pass. He stepped back to let the teacher pass, and closed his eyes briefly with gratitude when he did.

Tim continued to the principal's office, noting wryly that the ConRAT was back to its normal spelling. That was done fast enough, he was thinking, as he reached for the door to the outer office without hesitation and tried it. Harold Craner had made it down the steps and out the door before Tim could register his shocked surprise. He tried the door to Miss Peter's office again, leaning his weight against the grey, opaque glass. Unbelievably, the door was locked.

As soon as he was out into the yard Harold was aware of how much his heart was pounding. He did not know how the teacher could have missed it. If he had asked to see a hall pass, he could not very well have shown him the one he had himself signed for Angie Vallens less than an hour before. The only worse person Harold could imagine bumping into was Angel himself, but he had made it. It gave him a lift, and now he could always claim that he was out checking the Gates. If anyone doubted his word, he could silence them by showing the thing he had found in his desk first period, a large, not very clean black handkerchief. Since he was in Miss Devereaux' class at Zero, and Cooper was the Executioner, he could only assume that he would be assigned one of the administration, or staff. He had done everything Angel wanted, with scrupulous care, but he had not expected this. The black handkerchief was folded as small and neat as he was able; still, it made a lump in his back pocket that was annoyingly present, like some boil inside your cheek that did not hurt, but would not go away. Harold was perfectly aware that he was taking a chance in leaving the building during second period, but he had to find Jack the Janitor, and if he waited until third period, he would not be sure where to find him. Second period was the hour for checking the results of the previous day's Numbers in the paper. Looking around supercarefully, to make sure no one was watching, Harold Craner made a beeline for the basement of the auditorium.

• • •

"Today we are going to discuss the hand, one of the most complicated and wondrous parts of our body." Cleaire Devereaux' nearsighted cat's eyes moved quickly across the rows of seats, noting with a pleased blink that only Harold Craner and Charley Lees were absent. She marked her roll while Jesus Contreras leaned over to Juan Laurindo and whispered, "A hand job, man, today we gonna get us a hand job from Miss Devereaux." They exchanged mock solemn nods, glad to forget the incident with Charley Lees.

Normally, Cleaire took perfunctory and scattered attendance. This Friday would have been no exception had she not been surprised to find her second class in a row nearly all present, not to mention the strain of her uncertainty about Jimmy Janis. He was ignoring her completely. She was vacillating between a desire to forget everything else and apologize for whatever she had been doing wrong, and a wish to tell him to go to hell for being so childishly petulant. It was unfair for her to have to be the strong one in their relationship. Why did she always have to conciliate? Why was she always the one expected to be clever and resourceful? Cleaire struggled to force her thoughts back to the lesson plan for the day. The first face that caught her eye was Sandra Lees, who sat in the front row practically under her nose. "Sandra," she said, "can you tell me how many bones there are in the human hand?"

"The hand?" Sandy Lees looked blank, her worries over her brother disagreeably interrupted. Charley had disappeared between first and second period, and she knew something was wrong. Miss Devereaux nodded.

"Yes, dear, the hand." There was a pause. "I didn't have you prepare this on purpose. I don't want anything more than a simple estimate—"

"I didn't read the chapter," said Sandy irrelevantly, pulling her attention away from the empty desk where he should have been. Removing her rimless distance glasses, which she needed for seeing the blackboard, Sandy started polishing them with a dirty Kleenex from her purse. There was some uncomfortable foot-shifting in the room, especially by those who had seen Charley Lees being hustled off by Angel, Rico, Juan and Contreras. Jesus-Maria Ortiz wanted to ask Juan what had happened, but he had not gotten the chance.

"You needn't have read the chapter, dear." Cleaire tried not to be provoked. She knew her temper this morning was not up to little games. "I want an estimate of how many bones are in your hand, your own guess, dear."

Sandy looked even more confused without her glasses, as Booker Turner cocked his oversized head to stare at her.

He was playing with his gold pin, stabbing it lightly into his powdery black forearm, in a little pattern of circles. Kindly, he mouthed the word, "Twenty."

"I—uh—" Had Booker said something about her brother? Sandy's panic increased. Cleaire Devereaux frowned in exasperation. It was beyond her how these children could fail to answer even those questions designed to have no right or wrong answer. Perhaps Jimmy had been right after all, and the job they were trying to do was pointless and self-deceiving.

"Sandra," she said firmly, "I want your answer, and only your answer. You won't find it in your glasses."

Everywhere Sandy looked she saw a boy smirking up at her, the tiny glisten of gold stuck in his shirt collar, until her eye landed on the black handkerchief that was being twisted in Juan Laurindo's thick, powerful fingers. Without her glasses on, it looked like a black furry animal being tortured. Sandy's unexpected scream made Cleaire Devereaux' be-ringed hand fly protectively to her auburn hair.

"Where is he?" she screamed. She was half out of her seat, the teacher's question totally forgotten as Sandy leaned towards Juan Laurindo's shiny black ducktail, crying, "Where is he? Where did you take him?" There was an ominous heavy stir in the room as Cleaire came quickly around her desk, and hesitated. Juan scowled, and muttered inaudibly.

"Here here, Sandra, stop that—" The girl's glasses were spinning in her hands, compulsively faster. Jesus-Maria was hypnotized with the speed of her fingers, and the dazzling reflections from the lenses as the teacher stepped forward to restrain her. The hand was jerked away from

Miss Devereaux' with such violent force that the glasses flew against the wall. In the same instant, Sandy's heavy-lidded, solemn black eyes swung on Cleaire like a double barrelled shotgun, and she fell back involuntarily from the force of their accusation.

"They did something to my brother," the girl said, "and you won't do anything."

"Who are you talking about?" said Miss Devereaux, as Jesus-Maria Ortiz returned the glasses miraculously un-broken. He wanted to see her spin them again.

"Please, sit down, Sandra." Cleaire had recalled what Tim Nielsen had said about the terror he had seen in Charles Lees' face, and the insane note he had written. She looked at the trembling girl as though for the first time, wondering about the whole family.

"You won't do anything," Sandy moaned, suddenly de-feated as she saw the resentment on Juan Laurindo's face, and the plain hatred in the ape Contreras. "Ape!" she said hopelessly.

"Who are you talking about, dear?" said Miss Devereaux more gently. She did not want to emphasize the ape thing, for the Contreras boy certainly did have a simian look, with his size and low forehead, and most of all the long, downy upper lip that he refused to shave. Juan Laurindo blew his nose with a loud, vulgar honk, then raised his hand, waving it directly in front of the teacher so she could not avoid seeing it. "There there, Sandra dear, please."

"You won't do anything, oh God," said Sandy, com-forted now by the repetition. "You won't do anything."

Miss Devereaux looked at Juan Laurindo. "Yes, Juan?"

He cleared his throat, drawing all attention to himself

even though Sandy remained standing, hunched now like an old lady. "There's twenty-five bones in a human hand, Miss Devereaux, give or take some. That's my guess."

Bill Turner exchanged a gleeful look with his brother, "That's jus' exactly right. Very good."

"Thank you, Juan," said Cleaire Devereaux, trying to remember her lesson plan for the day. She had thought of an original . . . a good way— They were all now watching Sandy, who was conspicuously swaying. *If I say I'm sick,* she was thinking, *will they do something to Charley?*

"All right, sit down, Sandra, we are going to cover some material," said Cleaire, to get away from the red-faced girl with hysterical eyes streaming into the tearbeds furrowed only moments before. That sallow skin seemed to cook tears, soak them in, sizzle them dry like cracked desert rock. Cleaire made her way back to the sanctuary of her desk, feeling a headache coming on. "You must sit down, Sandra," she said firmly, "until after class, and then I'd like you to wait and talk to me. Please."

Shaking, Sandy Lees sat, or rather sank down. Juan Laurindo looked at his handkerchief with satisfaction, then bunched it up and put it in his pocket. Behind Sandy, Maria Estragon ignored the warning looks of her former best friends, and leaned forward to whisper to Sandy.

"Better hush up, honey," she said. Then she stuck her chin in the air at Maria and Provencia to show them that she was glad they were not bothering her anymore.

● ● ●

William Conrad had removed his glasses, so when his impassioned eyes left the soft-focus sweet pink mouth and lime scented ear of the substitute secretary, he could only peer in the direction of the intruding sound, seeing a geometrical series of blurs, here table, there filing cabinet and door. "Who could that be?" he said in a fury, holding his wristwatch almost to his inflamed nose. Bristling at the offending door, he shoved his glasses sloppily onto the same nose. Miss Goetz tucked in her blouse unnecessarily. There was a second, clearly audible knock on the door to the outer office.

"I knew it was ridiculous," she said to no one in particular. "My God, I just can't imagine what—"

"Shut—be quiet." The principal's fleshy forefinger touched his upper lip warningly, the same blessed forefinger that moments earlier had been caressing a soft shoulder through the seductive crispness of her cotton blouse. With Miss Twigg out for only a few minutes he did not know what he had hoped for. A kiss perhaps, a nostalgic moment of filling a young girl, any crevice would do, a touch would do. It had been such a very small chance, for the opportunity of filling that softness even in imagination, gorging on her, touching the young skin that was so unlike the hormonal desert expanses of Dolores Conrad. How could he fill her now? He giggled. Where in that firm anatomy, that hanging garden of dimples and ripe honeydews, was Miss Goetz's now? A little hysterical, against all sanity, the principal giggled again and pushed her away, holding on as he pushed, a play-push, with his unserious lips saying, "Arrange yourself, arrange yourself."

"This is impossible." Laura Goetz picked up a pencil and dropped it immediately. "Someone wants to see you, and here I am, supposed to—" She was interrupted by a still more urgent knock and this time they heard a voice say, "Mr. Conrad? Miss Twigg?" The principal was frozen, with the expression of a man hoping for the impossible. The ruddiness seemed to blossom from beneath his chalky chin to the rout of sparse hair at his temples. He looked at the girl, expelling his breath with a furious volcanic bubbling that seemed to come from deep inside him. "Mr. Conrad" repeated the voice, suddenly all too recognizable to the principal. He gained strength by closing his eyes.

"*I am coming,*" he said, so loudly that the girl was momentarily startled, and then amused. Her lips curled into a girlish smile as she thought, but this is really too funny. The impossibility of the situation had returned, stronger than ever. Later, when she would tell Steve about it, it might not be exactly what happened, but the essence of honesty would be preserved. Miss Goetz firmly believed that honesty was the foundation of a happy marriage. The manicured hand, in the telling, would not have gotten a millimeter past the buttons on her blouse, the slight wet mark on her neck would dry and the clumsy pawing of her new skirt would transform itself again into an expertly parried, unimportant verbal proposition, of the sort as common to pretty girls as the air they breathed. Laura Goetz watched the principal check his pants and belt automatically as he went to unlock the door, muttering.

Whoever that is, Laura Goetz said to herself, I'd like to kiss him. No, on second thought, I'd like to shake his hand for saving me from my fate.

The substitute secretary had come to the conclusion that William J. Conrad was a little too much to handle. She would get sick at lunch time, and ask for a substitute substitute. She probably would not lose her job, and if she did, there were other jobs for a girl who could type and take shorthand.

● ● ●

Tim heard the heavy footsteps, and even before the door opened he knew he had come at an inopportune time. He had never known the door to Miss Peter's office to be locked, but then he was not familiar with all the folkways of Ross, and perhaps the head secretary's emergency had something to do with it. For a naive, hopeful instant when he had first knocked, he had an intuition that Conrad had believed him after all, that the locked door had to do with steps he was taking to secure the school. There was a click and the door opened to reveal a baleful and perspiring Conrad, his spectacles slipping infuriatingly down his reddened nose. "Yes?"

"I'm sorry to bother you, sir, but I have to tell you about something that's come up all of a sudden."

"If it's disciplinary, you should go to Sousa."

"It's not for him, sir."

"Can it wait till lunch time, Nelson?"

"No, sir, I don't think it can."

Tim looked directly at the principal, determined not to say more until he could sit with him privately. He heard some movement in the principal's own office, and surmised that something was going on, but he was damned if he would go away discreetly and return at lunch. He was not even sure he would be allowed to return, if he did not see Conrad at that moment.

"Nelson, I'd be very glad to have lunch with you and

talk over any problems you might have neglected to answer at the new teacher's assembly. My door is always open to problems, but right now Miss Peters is called away, and it's the middle of a period—" He had a sudden thought. "Who's covering your class for you, son?"

"Hayward Brown," said Tim, glad that he had remembered. "No, this could not wait until lunch."

Mr. Conrad opened his mouth, just as a noise behind him drew his attention. Holding the door protectively ajar, he addressed someone with an unmistakable note of dismay. "Yes, Miss Goetz?" "I'll take my coffee break now, Mr. Conrad," said a woman in a pleasant, no nonsense tone. Reluctantly, the principal opened the door wider. A pretty blond that Tim had never seen before passed between them, murmuring apologies and leaving a faint trail of perfume.

"Well, come in, Nelson," said Conrad harshly, closing the door quickly to spare himself the torture of watching the lost Miss Goetz walk away from him, down the hall, her high heels snapping along, her skirt tight with every young stride. He stalked into his office, Tim right behind him. Instead of sitting in his chair, he stood at the window with his hands clasped tightly behind his back.

"Close the door and sit down, son," he said. Tim did as he was told, lowering himself into the still slightly warm chair that Laura Goetz had just vacated.

• • •

Charley Lees had agreed to everything. Angel and Rico had been very good to him, and if he did exactly as he was told, he would avoid trouble. He understood that they could just as easily kill him as give him a chance to make amends for giving the note to Mr. Nielsen. But instead, he would be Special Executioner, and under the watchful eye of Juan Laurindo, he would take care of Mr. Watson in sixth period Boy's P.E.

The set up satisfied Juan. He would have the double pleasure of tormenting Watson who he despised, and finishing the job with Charley Lees that had begun in the unused classroom on the second floor. Juan liked the way Rico had stepped in less and less. He had just been waiting for a signal from Angel, and now he felt cheated.

As the three of them, Angel, Charley, and Rico emerged just ahead of Juan from the first floor stairway, they saw the substitute secretary Laura Goetz coming out of the cafeteria. She passed them briskly, conscious of their eyes on her. Her heels made a lot of noise as she strained her slim tweed skirt to its limit with every step. She was in a good mood.

"Oh man," said Rico, when she was barely out of earshot "I'd like to take care of that one myself."

"Too bad she ain't Miss Peters."

"You can't get 'em all, Angel," said Rico. Angel looked at him, and saw that he had not meant anything by it. Producing one of Jesus-Maria's forged hall passes, he checked to make sure the time was close enough. There were passes for every quarter hour of the school day, safe in Angel's locker. He handed the pass to Juan, who hesitated in front of Mr. Nielsen's room.

"If he's back, say you had to make an emergency head call," Angel told him. He motioned for Rico and Charley to follow him, as Juan waited until they were down the hall before he went into the room. Mr. Brown was at the desk, supervising a study period. The room was very quiet.

Angel, Charley and Rico turned the corner at the end of the hall, and waited in front of the door to the basement while Angel unlocked it with his master key. There was very little light on the dusty stairs, and Charley Lees, still too dazed to be wary, stumbled three times on the way to check out the inner recesses of the Arsenal.

• • •

His fingertips dancing together in impatience, William Conrad pursed his lips. If he understood what Nielsen was saying, he had never heard anything so foolish in his life. "And you think that's sufficient evidence to shut down an entire school, do you?"

"I think, sir, that the coincidences are a bit too strong. There is a definite desire *not* to do or say anything to alarm. That would defeat the purpose of an intimidation, it would seem to me."

"Mr. Nielsen, you've been at Ross less than a month, and yet you have become an expert in the psychology of our students."

"I didn't say I was an expert, sir."

"Let me finish, please. You claim that two children, two out of a student body of over eleven hundred, have come to you, to warn you that you were to be murdered." He emphasized the last words roundly, scornfully.

"No sir, not just me. I don't believe it's aimed at me personally." It occurred to Tim that the loss of this stubborn, pompous, idiotic man would not be much of a loss.

"I see." William Conrad had decided to enjoy himself, have a little fun. He stared hard at Tim over the top of his glasses, as though he were taking him very seriously.

"And the, uh, capper was an anonymous phone call telling you not to come to school today. I have a little voice inside that tells me the very same thing every morning when the alarm clock rings, and my wife wakes up to see if I'm awake." The mention of his wife seemed to take the fun out of his little joke.

Tim swallowed. "Sir, normally I would be as skeptical as you about a phone call like that, but when I think of the other things that have been happening, and the Lees' note—"

"Have you given many quizzes in the last week?"

"I beg your pardon, Mr. Conrad?"

Once again the manicured fingers pressed together.

"Did you have quizzes, or tests, or schedule any, or blow your stack and cuss the little monsters out? If so, it's forgivable. Most of the teachers around here blow their corks from time to time. The kids like it; it proves the teachers are human." Tim studied his hands, stained under the nails with oil paint, as Conrad continued. He could vary his voice like a full orchestra. Now, gentle, "Have you ever had some delinquent write I Hate Mr. So and So on the board, just before you came into the class?" Louder, "Or gotten good and mad hearing about some teacher getting hurt preventing a vandalism, or getting caught in the middle when a rival gang decides to invade our 'turf'? I think they still call it that. Boy culture is built on threat, son, only teachers are supposed to be too old to play games with the boys."

"I don't think we are talking about the same thing."

William Conrad made a church with his fingers, then a steeple. "Is it possible that you had an unpopular test scheduled for today, and since you are new and obviously inexperienced, you might be scared out of coming to school?" He turned the church over, and there were the people. He feigned delight.

"I am an art teacher, Mr. Conrad. I don't give 'tests.' If my students don't like what I'm doing, I haven't noticed it." Suddenly Tim wanted to get away from this man and this office as fast as possible. He could sit and argue with him for days and it would not make any difference. Mr. Conrad's puffy eyes flicked past the piece of scrap paper on his desk, with its note signed *CL*. He decided that this conference should be in this new teacher's evaluation file. He would see to it.

"Son, you put quite a bit of faith in the word of that Estragon girl, don't you? You say there were witnesses—"

"Several—" Tim began, before he realized what Conrad was driving at.

"And yet, you contend she was lying when she said you had tried to . . . tried to—" He held out his hand, for help. The immaculate fingers reached flutteringly for the word, until Tim supplied it. "Rape her, Mr. Conrad."

"Yes. Well. Don't you think that's farfetched?" The hand waved helplessly in the air, and then fell onto the desk top. The Principal exhaled as though he were suddenly exhausted. He lowered his eyes. "How old are you, son?"

Convicted, thought Tim with disgust, of the crime of

youth. He could barely contain himself. "Twenty-seven, sir."

"Twenty-seven." Conrad looked at him now with venom. "Then I strongly suggest, my boy, that you act it. What you have taken my time with is preposterous. That you would waste my time and your own in this manner indicates that your good judgment might be in considerable doubt when it comes to evaluating you. If you pursue it further, there would be no doubt. Do I make myself clear?"

Tim nodded, not trusting himself to speak.

"If it would serve any good purpose, which it would not, I would bring the Lees boy in and have this childish threat out with him. I've kicked out many a boy for less, and if he thought I would see this note, you can bet your bottom dollar he would not have given it to you." Conrad started to say something more, but heard the sound of high heels, long before Tim did. A moment later the door opened and a refreshed Laura Goetz looked in and smiled. She had put on darker lipstick. Forgetting about Tim, Conrad beckoned her in, but she just smiled at them both. "I'll be in the next office, Mr. Conrad, and after I'm through with the committee correspondence I'll bring you the file you wanted."

William Conrad nodded, his throat too dry to risk a reply in front of Tim. As the girl closed the door behind her, she was closing more than a door. Suddenly he felt quite old, and far too depleted to fight with anyone, least of all a paranoid young art teacher that he had not wanted to hire in the first place. No experience, no contacts. He looked at Tim wearily now, and took off his glasses so he could wipe his irritated eyes. And apparently no sense. The girl in the next office started to type, slowly but steadily, as the young teacher got to his feet, feeling as though he had been sitting in a puddle.

"I'm sorry then, Mr. Conrad," he was saying. "I see I shouldn't have bothered you about this." The principal's reply was automatic, with close to its regular quotient of cheer.

"That's all right, son. My door is always open."

Not always, thought Tim, as he turned to go. The principal listened carefully to the typing sounds, and he could have sworn that the girl stopped for several moments while the young teacher passed by the desk.

• • •

Sarah Vardis was teaching a class of indifferent girls how to bake an apple pie, but the apples were bad, two of the bake ovens were on the blink, and no amount of calling mechanical could seem to get anybody up to fix them before Monday. What did those people do downtown? Quit work in the middle of the day on Friday? Sarah felt like crying. As a Negro teacher she felt keenly that she had a certain position to keep up, and it just made her mad to be teaching how to make bad pies. She knew that some of the girls would talk to her when they would not talk to anybody, not their counselors, not their folks, no one. It was a big responsibility.

And yet, Sarah Vardis was pregnant, and beginning to look it, although nobody mentioned it. This would be her first and last semester of teaching. She looked at the burnt pies, and just could not give a damn.

Mariette Jensen was teaching choral singing, in the room directly next to the Negro girl's homemaking class. She did not really like being next to poor Sarah, but it was an improvement over the semester she was next to Mr. Brown's shop class, with his drills and buzz saws and what she swore had to be a fullsized jackhammer. The noise had been just too much. Miss Jensen had done the same things, made the same gestures, said the same words so often that she could think about anything she liked while she was conducting a class. Everything was done meticulously, in her gentle, patient, little old lady way. She was only sixty-three, but she cultivated old age the way some people cultivate orchids, as an excellent defense against many kinds of unpleasantness. She fed on her own withering, lingered lovingly over every wrinkle in her mirror. Evelyn Raintree, who was exactly the same age, looked ten years younger even though she smoked and drank and kept late hours on the weekends. Nothing could persuade Miss Jensen that if she ever grew frail and light enough to blow away, as everyone said, the wind would not take her straight to a very nice protestant heaven.

• • •

PROVENCIA LOVES MR. NIELSEN, said the sign on the auditorium wall, written in shocking pink nail polish. It stood out, because the auditorium was the newest building on the grounds, and was not much marked by the signs and tokens of love that were carved and drawn, scratched nearly everywhere else. Each semester's succession of hearts faded or were scrubbed away, or painted over, like some great baroque pearl.

In the basement, Jack the Janitor listened patiently to everything the white boy said, feeling that he owed it to him for not giving a good answer to his last big question. No, he would not be off the grounds during sixth period, he had work to do and not enough time to do it. Harold Craner showed him the black handkerchief, and explained what it meant. He looked for some sign of understanding, and received none. Jack was anxious to get back to the Numbers, and he only listened out of politeness, Harold could see that. Crushed, he asked Jack if he could stay there until just before the change bell. Jack looked at him real close, saw how he felt, and said he could.

• FOURTEEN •

For a moment Tim stood outside the principal's office, not sure what he should do. Perhaps the man had been right, and the whole thing was senseless, paranoid. It would be a good joke on a real idiot to make him kill himself off with stupidity, running to the office with stories. It would not be beyond a boy as smart as Angel to set him up and make him harm himself, perhaps even end his career with words out of his own mouth. That would be cruel enough, but murder? Tim could not conceive of such a risk being taken by so many. Still, massacres had been started by single incidents, and there was always Bart Arthur. If he had been injured on purpose, and died from his injuries, whoever had done it had gotten away with it.

Was it equally possible that someone barely fifteen years old would be able to convince himself that he could get away with murder? He recalled an uncomfortable jumble of truths and half truths; the gang killings that were virtually written off, the valley boy who had bragged for months that he had killed a schoolmate, and no one said a thing. He was not sure, except that the change bell had rung, and the faces of the students who walked past him in the hall were telling him something. They were grim, and no one was willing to meet his gaze, except for one. Maria Estragon saw him, and stopped in her tracks.

"Hello, Maria," he said. The girl shook her head, and hurried past, as she noticed that Ismael Sato was watching them.

• • •

SURFERS EAT IT, said the sign, so wobbly that it was close to illegible. It had been Lizard's contribution to the war between the Surfers and Greasers, and gained him no points with either side. He had been promised a chance to use a knife at Zero Hour, but nobody would tell him where the knife was. After listening to the explanation, the patient explanation, so often that he could almost repeat it, he understood that they would get the Surfers, but first they had to get the teachers.

Evelyn Raintree's hearty baritone was so loud that for a nervous moment Tim thought she was in trouble, and then he realized that she was reading Shakespeare to her A-9s. Tim had managed to get through his third period, and now had some extra time during nutrition to try to get a call through to Marge. The only public telephone was at the far end of the hall, past the water fountain—JESUS SAVES—and into the phone booth, where he was about to reach for some change. The sign hit him in the eye—SORRY OUT OF ORDER—because it had been done in his art service class, on his special good paper that he gave out only sparingly. It looked like the work of Jesus-Maria Ortiz.

Walking as fast as he could without actually running, Tim went to the faculty lounge and went in, shutting the door heavily behind him. He noticed something about the bolt handle, and looked at it more closely. It had been tampered with, skilfully, and would not lock properly. For the moment the lounge was empty, but in a couple of minutes it would be full. There was the sound of girl's volleyball coming in through the open window, and a slight breeze clicking the wooden part of the half-drawn shades against the sill. Some laughter, and the faint drone of an airplane joined the clicking as the only sound. The telephone, sitting on the desk, had a small sign taped to it that read: *Please Do Not Make Personal Calls.* Tim picked up the receiver, and it was dead. His eye followed the cord to where it had been neatly cut.

Immediately he thought of the telephone in the principal's office. As much as he dreaded another confrontation with Conrad, he knew he had to get ahold of Marge. Quickly, he scribbled a note to Cleaire Devereaux, and left it on the desk where she would be sure to see it. *Look at Phone,* it read, *Everything points to the truth of what I said. Tell Janis and Post.* Tim was not sure if it would do any good to tell the other teachers, but perhaps one of them would notice something during the period between nutrition and lunch that might help him convince Conrad to close the afternoon classes.

As he opened the door on his way back to the principal's office, Tim found himself staring into the brown eyes of Angel. Standing behind him was a boy named Contreras, and Larry Staples.

"Can we talk to you, Mr. Nielsen," said Angel politely,

and Tim nodded at once, anxious to see what Angel would say. Although it was against the rules, he motioned them to come in as he looked at his watch. In a few minutes the teachers would be in for nutrition period, including Hayward Brown, who had taken his class. There was not much time and he also wanted to call Marge, although he wasn't sure what he would say to her.

"Mr. Nielsen, Charley Lees said he gave you a note," said Angel. There seemed no point in denying it.

"Do you have something to add to it, Angel?" Larry Staples, who had been a great friend of the Arthur boy, was looking as though he might get suddenly sick.

"That note dumb, Mr. Nielsen. Charley scared you take it serious."

"I do." Tim tried to appear calmer than he felt, "It was no joking matter."

"No, sir," said Angel, his eye going to the note Tim had left on the desk. "Sorry if it made trouble—"

"There's been none yet— Angel, what are you doing? That's a personal note." Angel had picked up the scrawl and glanced over it. "Put it down, Angel. At once."

The outrage had made his voice crack, just as Jimmy Janis came in the lounge and looked at the boys in surprise, and then at Tim.

"Sorry, Mr. Nielsen." Angel's eye went to the disabled phone for a moment, and then met Contreras' questioning look with the suggestion of a shrug. "We'd better go. See you after lunch, Mr. Nielsen." He nodded cordially, "Mr. Janis."

"Wait, Angel," said Tim, ignoring the odd look from

Jim Janis. Angel was herding the other boys out the door.

"Come on," he said. "We don't want to get nobody in trouble."

"Angel!" The boy turned with a questioning look. Tim moved just outside the faculty lounge, feeling strangely alone with Angel despite the hallway activity, and the approach of the other teachers.

"Angel, I want to hear from you what you're doing."

Angel gave him a long, narrow look of reluctant admiration. "You one smart dude, Mr. Nielsen. You just keep working on it."

Tim watched the three boys walk away from him down the hall, mingling with the other students. He turned on his heel and started for the principal's office. If it was locked he was going to kick it down.

Checking over his shoulder, Contreras saw that it was safe to talk. "Hey, man," he said sullenly, "you ain't gonna let him go are you?" Angel looked at Contreras sharply.

"Let him go where? Where's he going?"

"Muh-muh-man, tuh-to Ca-Conrad!" said Larry Staples, his outrage overcoming his shyness and fear.

"He already talked to Rat. Didn't you see the note I was reading? He spilling his guts all over. Nobody buying."

"How can you be so sure?," Contreras frowned.

"Man, the onliest reason we gonna make it all the way is nobody'll buy till it's long gone." The hall was filling with students, all their faces hard and smooth, with no place to go to cry. Those that passed him on the way to the stairway paid tense but visible homage. He was making it. He motioned to Larry, "Staples, you go get some sun and then straight to third period, OK?" The question was rhetorical, and Larry quickly nodded his willing agreement.

• • •

"Sandra dear," said Cleaire Devereaux, stopping the girl in the hall, "I believe I told you to wait after class."

Sandy looked at Miss Devereaux blankly, wanting to go and look for Charley.

"Come here, dear," said Miss Devereaux, standing by the door as her class emptied. She did not mind missing some of nutrition period if she could be of some help. She entirely missed the strange looks that the last of the boys had given Sandy as they went out. Sandy missed the looks as well. "Now tell me what you meant about your brother, dear."

"Come on, Contreras," said Angel impatiently. The bigger boy was suspiciously watching Larry Staples go down the hall, past the faculty lounge. "Don't worry about Larry."

"I dunno, man—"

"Come on, we got a tight schedule."

Upstairs in the meeting room, the Generals were passing around a single cigarette, waiting for Angel.

"Jesus man," said Juan Laurindo nervously, "didn't nobody bring no cigarettes?"

"Meeting won't take long." Rico studied the finger-burner a wasteful moment before passing it to Clark Cooper.

"Yeah, man, it's almost over," said Jesus-Maria. "I near got caught cutting the faculty phone."

"I be kinda glad when this all over," said Ismael, refusing a drag on the cigarette. He passed it on to John Valdes.

"Two more phones to go," said Jesus-Maria, to no one in particular.

"Here comes somebody. Maybe it's Angel." Harold Craner ignored the cigarette. He was nearly wetting his pants, worried that someone knew that he had told Jack and not been believed. He would not do anything like that again as long as he lived. If nobody cared about a good deed when you did it to them, it was their own look-out.

• • •

"But dear," Miss Devereaux was saying, "you did say they had done something to your brother. Who are *they*, and what did they do?" Sandy's eyes narrowed as she looked at Miss Devereaux. She tried to imagine her without her false hair. The painted eyebrows arched quizzically as the woman leaned closer, a sickly gust of mint-breath driving Sandy back. She shook her head stubbornly, determined now to reveal nothing.

"Now you weren't just pretending, Sandra." Miss Devereaux was insistent, a note of annoyance creeping into her tone at the thought of missing all of nutrition, and not achieving anything. Sandra Lees bit her lip. Jennifer Baily had stopped by the open door in curiosity, watching her. Jennifer hated her and would be the first to fink if she told the teacher anything.

"I . . . didn't mean it." Sandy could not look the old

lady in the eye. "He's really sick today. Charley's sick with flu."

Without speaking, Cleaire stared at Sandra Lees for a long time. When she looked closely at these girls she saw the peaches beneath the make-up, the somehow heart-breaking softness that seemed to scream for pity, that they were young; little girls. The young had rights that could only be lost gradually. Cleaire sighed, and waved her hand vaguely. "All right, dear. I won't force you. How quickly you change your mind." Sandy's eye was caught again by the sapphire ring on the woman's hand, a ring that she had often noticed. Suddenly it occurred to her that someone in the room was going to make a grab for that ring in the confusion of sixth period. Her own desk was closest, if Clark Cooper didn't stand in the way. She could not take her eyes off that ring, wickedly blue like the glance of her dream prince.

"Run along, dear, I don't want you to miss all of nutrition." Cleaire sighed. She had done her duty.

• • •

William Conrad was looking at Tim absolutely without expression. It surpassed belief that this young man would dare return to his office after what had passed between them. For an irrational moment Conrad even felt threatened by such stubbornness. The request had been curt but acceptably polite; he was not sure what it was in the request to use his phone that seemed to him a naked, direct, contemptuous challenge. If he permitted himself to think about it too much, he knew he would find himself in a rage, controllable only at great personal loss. A backflush of acid was burning his throat and sizzling over the tender surfaces of his stomach. Acid was killing him. He had to swallow something unpleasant before he could get the words out. "Of course you may use the phone if the one in the faculty room is out of order. While you're at it Nelson, you might have Miss Twigg call the repairman when she gets off the line."

"It's not out of order. It's been cut. So has the public phone in the hall. I've told you twice, sir."

Conrad studied Tim. Mentally, he was puffing a cigar, pushing the forbidden smoke sadistically against the tender ulcers in his belly. Was it possible that this young man would cut telephone wires, just to try to prove his fantasies correct?

"I'll have the custodian look at it," was all he could manage to say. "The phone is right in front of you."

"Thank you." Tim was barely able to control his voice. Pushing the second button on the phone, he heard the dial tone, reassuring and nasal. Wishing the principal would not stand right over him, he dialled 113, and after a series of rings got the operator. "Information."

"I'd like the number for the University of Southern California School of Design, if there is such a—yes, in Los Angeles." He was informed that there was a number for Administration, Campus Police, School of International Relations, School of Medicine, School of Public Administration, Student Health Center, Tax Institute and Ticket Reservations. Which did he prefer?

"Administration, please," said Tim, exchanging a short look with Mr. Conrad, who was making no attempt to disguise his displeasure. The number was RI 4-5444. Tim dialled slowly, not wanting to make a mistake. The phone was immediately picked up, by someone with a husky but melodious voice. Nothing would perturb the owner of such a voice. "Good morning, University of Southern California."

"Hello, this is an emergency." The principal's mouth hardened as he turned away, conveying clearly his contempt for Tim's words. Tim continued, angry at having to speak in front of Conrad, "I must talk to Margery Clement, a T.A. in the school of fashion design. Do you, uh, can you please check her schedule and tell me where she can be located?"

The principal could tell from Tim's face what the answer to that had been.

"I said it's an emergency. All right, I'll explain the nature of the emergency to the director of Student Personnel's office. Yes, yes, I'll hold."

When he saw the expression on the principal's face, Tim felt like throwing the phone at him.

"I'll be out for coffee, Nelson," he said ironically. "You can make your call in privacy."

• • •

Angel squatted beside Rico, and waved the cigarette away without a glance. Contreras remained standing, very much aware that he was in charge of Muscle, and had just been on a special assignment with Angel. Flexing his chest as he pushed his calloused palms against each other, he breathed in, pressed, and breathed out, knowing he would not have to listen too much. Juan Laurindo reached over to hand the student folder to Angel, wrapped in paper, cradled in his blunt hands like a holy relic. Angel waved it away as contemptuously as he had the smoke, as part of the same gesture. "Never mind, man. We brought Staples in, no sweat. Everybody here. We can burn that now."

The others nodded solemnly, except Contreras, who was not listening. It was a powerful gesture, to burn the student folder, but it would have to be done later, after lunch. Still, the mention of it was enough, and showed Angel's perfect confidence. Only Rico smiled at the obvious impossibility of starting a fire in the boy's head without being immediately discovered.

Angel looked at the smooth faces of his Generals and tried to read them for some sign of criticism, some doubt. There was none. The original strongest objection had been that they could not get everybody to school on the same day. He had proved, secretly to his own surprise, that if you scared them enough, you could indeed. If he had been proved wrong, if more than a handful had stayed home, he would have cancelled. The Plan would have failed, and he along with it. Rico was looking at him, waiting, and Angel noticed that he had acquired an excited, glassy look. Angel leaned close, so that their noses were almost touching, and sniffed.

Rico did not back off, but returned Angel's grim smile tantalizingly, purposely breathing out so the faint acetone smell drifted to Angel. He wanted to see what the leader would say.

"Man, you been sniffin' just now?" Angel looked regretful, and there was an apprehensive shifting of position as Rico stood his ground. "I thought you was off that for good," Angel added, a little more gently.

"Some," Rico admitted. He held his hand out, to show how steady it was. "I can still cut with this, man." His fingers, stiff, touched Angel's throat, a sacrilege. "That's all I need, right? Right?" Angel saw that a part of Rico was not there. He nodded, resisting the impulse to pull away from those fingers.

"OK, Rico." Angel turned to the others, with a frown to make up for his lenience. "But nobody else, understand? Hang loose till after. Anything you want after; you can lick the blood off the floor if you want, but not till after!" He did not want to add that it would no longer be any business of his what they did, once Zero Hour was over.

"We got five minutes, Angel." Ismael was watching Angel with his black, unblinking time-keeper eyes. He was searching for some sign that maybe it would suddenly end, and all turn out to be just another initiation, a ritual, a proof of loyalty to Angel. There was no such sign anywhere, and even though it scared him it also made him high.

"We got time enough." Angel pulled his notebook out of his shirt pocket and held it like a talisman, just under their noses. "I want to check off, each teacher by home room sixth period, Room Executioner and Assistant. While I do"— He reached for his key to the arsenal— "Laurindo get ready to distribute the cutters for fingerprints. One to everybody in school. Coop, you get the blood-sponges ready, and the bucket—"

As he spoke, he could feel the excitement mount. Each General was practicing in his head what he would say to his Lieutenants in the lunch meetings. Contreras had stopped exercising, with the solemn realization that he would be assigning the Executioners for the faculty lounges. John Valdes' high piping voice broke the tension with a comic squeak. "Man, I can feel it in my balls. This gonna be better than Watts. We gonna be famous!"

There was the unexpected sound of footsteps outside the door and even Angel felt a chill. Then the door swung open, and Tio Valdes practically fell over himself in his hurry to get to Angel. "Hey, man—Margadonna tried to get out. They caught him at the gate."

"Where is he now?" Angel felt the skin tighten around his throat.

"They got him in the auditorium head."

Angel thought a moment. Since the classes were suspiciously full anyway, a few absentees would not hurt. He turned to Juan Laurindo. "Juan, you and Contreras get one of the Turners and take care of our little priest."

• • •

Marge had still not caught her breath as she listened with growing exasperation. Several times she tried to interrupt the flow of words, without success, until he finally took a breath.

"Tim, listen, you're not making any sense. Do you know how hard it was to—why if it hadn't been for Sally here—" She listened. "But I have classes until three. Why can't I see you tonight?"

The mousy girl who had tracked Marge down watched from a discreet distance, as Marge nodded her head, sighed, and then shook her head again. From the way Marge was reacting, it did not seem to Sally like much of an emergency after all. She was disappointed. Marge finally broke through again.

"I think you are being a trifle dramatic, but if you insist, I'll try. Of course, I promise. Goodbye, Tim." Marge hung up, and looked at the phone with disgust. "Oh really!"

"Is everything all right?" Sally, who was a Psych major, was dying to know. Marge looked doubtful.

"Oh, I don't know. He wants me to cut my classes and go all the way over to his school to pick him up. He says he's not staying there this afternoon."

"You mean just pick up and leave?" Sally made it sound like the most adventuresome thing she had ever heard. Then she sighed deeply, and frowned. "Oh oh—" Marge looked at her.

"What do you mean, oh oh?"

Sally added a nod to her frown. "I mean it's classic, this sudden irresistible desire to run away. It happens all the time, especially to the upper classes."

"Not what Tim said doesn't happen all the time, Sally. But it's ridiculous."

"What's ridiculous?"

"Oh, I don't even like to repeat it. You'll think I'm engaged to some kind of nut."

"Not a nut, Marge," said Sally piously, "a seriously disturbed young artist who is about to throw away a good safe career because of an impulse, and an inability to cope alone. I think it's worth a little drive to prevent it."

"Oh Sally, sometimes you make me sick. It's not like

Tim to get excited over nothing. It's hard to get him excited over anything, in fact, except art and politics. He says somebody is trying to kill him."

"Oh brother." Sally was wide-eyed. There was a silence.

"That's what he said."

"Well, are you going to go?"

"I promised I would, sort of."

"Well? Are you?"

Marge looked miserable.

"I'm going to flunk if I cut Dr. Jones very many more times. She hates me anyway."

"Everyone to her own delusions," said Sally, "But if I were you I'd go."

• • •

As he looked at his fourth period class, it briefly occurred to Roger Post that not only were all his classes strangely full, the students were alert. There was not anything in his lesson to warrant such attention, so he would not have been surprised if they were planning a trick. He would be alert.

For reasons he could not specify, things were looking up for him. Although he felt the lack of sleep of the night before, he was beginning to believe that he could complete the revisions on the Albigensian chapter of his book before Monday morning. If he sent a really fine chapter to the publisher they would surely realize that his book was worth the slight delay.

It had become urgently important to him that he finish the book, and not just because the publisher was screaming about the advance. There was something in the way Ellie

treated him now that suggested she was losing the one
quality in her that he most admired, her feeling for him,
her sensitivity to his moods. Last night she reminded him
that they had not made love in more than a month, and
then, when he had tried to kiss her, rolled over sobbing
and said she did not like to beg.

What could that mean, he wondered, as his mouth went
on about American government. He knew the rubbish so
well he did not even have to think what he was saying.
What could she mean, beg? And why had he felt relieved
when she rolled away from him? Even her heartbroken
sobs had not moved him in the least. He was just as strong,
just as virile as he had ever been, and yet he did not feel
like touching her the way he used to. It was not Ellie, God
knew. She had always been like a stick of driftwood in bed,
and it had never stopped him before. They had gone at it
every night and often in the morning before he would
leave for the university. Those were the days when she
could lie in bed until eleven, sipping delicately at the
tepid half-milk, half-coffee that had become a part of their
nuptial rituals.

Trying to remember Ellie as she had been then, he
found himself thinking of bread rinds left in plates on the
bedside table. His mouth paused and smiled, and he forced
himself to look at another ritual, the open text on the
desk. He became aware of the class, and realized they were
listening to him, waiting for him to go on. There was a
long silence, interrupted only by a nervous hacking cough
from Larry Staples. Larry lived in constant fear of being
called on to answer in class. Feeling something wrong in
the air, Roger Post surveyed the entire, tightly packed

room. He recognized this kind of silence too well. The little bastards were up to something. A ball-bearing would start rolling down the left aisle, then another, somewhere else in the room. He would not be able to watch two places at once, and if he tried, they would laugh. He felt himself coloring. It was bad enough that he had to pretend to teach them, the congenitally unteachable. The farce of his presence, day after endless day, in a room full of faces that understood nothing he was saying, was too much for a man to take without wanting to avenge himself for their bottomless, hopeless stupidity. He started pacing.

Gil Lieber watched him with a phlegmatic, nearly hangdog hunch to his bony shoulders as he recognized the angry walk. Gil recognized two distinctive walks in Mr. Post, the uncaring, and the angry. Two years of taking the same classes, and flunking them, had trained him to assume a protective stance when that particular walk was approaching.

Moving slowly, coming around from behind his refuge, the scarred shipwreck of a desk that he kept between him and them, he moved through the silent rows as legs stopped being scratched, scabs picked, desks gouged. Not every wound bleeds, thought Roger Post grimly. They looked at him. Guiltily. He stopped next to a likely troublemaker, Gilbert Lieber. He looked disdainfully at the bony freckled wrist sticking out of its cowboy sleeve, twisting, guilty. What luck to have him twice a day, this lovely creature, destined to pass just so Roger Post would not have him back a third hopeless time. "Lieber?" Here it came.

"Yes, Mr. Post?" Why am I still afraid of him, thought

Gil, terrified that he would disgrace himself. He would pull out his knife and stab himself before he would allow the stinging tears to show. He was the center of interest, as the others marvelled at the spectacle. The teacher badgering his Executioner! The thrill of it stood like points in the eyes of Tommy Ishi, and Jennifer Baily, who sat next to Gil.

"I'll let you answer for the class, Gilbert. How would you like a fifteen minute essay on religious minorities in America during colonial times. Could you handle that?"

Gil gulped, trying to keep his voice baritone. "No."

"No, what?" Hatred made Gil Lieber's eyes swim now, a hatred that seemed to press against his belt like a hunger. When would the signal come? How could he wait until after lunch?

"I said, No, *what*, Gilbert?" There was a competitive brightness now in Roger Post's eye, as he forgot Ellie, forgot his book, forgot the sickness in the morning as he left nothing to go nowhere in bumper-to-bumper traffic.

"No, Mr. Post." Gil swallowed again. "I could not."

"You do know enough to write such an essay, don't you, Lieber?"

"I suppose so, sir." Mr. Post's gaze swept the room, venomously. What did Ellie mean, she did not like to beg?

"In that case, I suppose you don't have any feelings about a surprise essay, one way or the other." Perhaps, he thought, he had misjudged the quiet in the classroom. Maybe they were not planning anything after all. It annoyed him to be wasting his energy with all this if there was no reason for it. He was not a vindictive man. "I will assume," he announced, "that there is nothing concealed in any desk, of whatever shape, intended for launching purposes along our admittedly noisy floor." They all looked at him idiotically. "Lieber?"

"No, Mr. Post. As far as I know."

"Fine. Then I can get back to my lesson with light heart." Why had he said that? Why that particular ridiculous phrase? It was the sort of thing you said to university students, not this bunch of monkeys. Once safely behind his desk, Roger looked dimly at his text, trying to remember what he had been talking about.

● ● ●

The change bell rang and Angel looked at his watch. Sixty-five minutes to Zero, a busy sixty-five minutes for him. He would personally check out each General for their sub-meetings during lunch, and then everything from Gate Locks to the Arsenal Distribution. As of that moment everyone who went in or out of the gates would be reported to him, and he would make individual decisions as to what should be done. Up to the instant of locking the gates, in an emergency he would still be able to call it off.

Obeying the bell, he got up with the others, mingling now, ready to blend into all the brown and chocolate and olive faces. During lunch, he would be one of eleven hundred, filing, straggling, horseplaying along the halls. Tio, who was waiting for him at the water fountain, got the signal to check the Gate Observers. He took off at a run, nearly colliding with Maria Estragon as she came out of homemaking. She glared at him, and then saw Mr. Nielsen nearly bowl Miss Devereaux over as she locked her classroom. Maria went to her locker to put away her sweater, and thought and thought about what she was going to do.

The fact that Tim was even paler than usual with anger would not have excused him if he had succeeded entirely in knocking off her wig. Cleaire giggled nervously, checking quickly and satisfying herself that everything was all right.

"I'm sorry, Cleaire, goddam it," he said through clenched teeth. "That stupid bastard." He had just come out of the principal's office, past Miss Twigg, who had butted in with a warning that Conrad had asked for his evaluation folder. Cleaire fell into step beside him on the way to the lounge.

"What's the matter now?" She wondered if she should feed the fires by telling him about the Lees' girl's spell at third period. His obvious bad temper decided her against it.

"Did you get my note at nutrition, Cleaire?"

"Why no. Did you leave me a note?"

Tim looked grim. "I don't know how I can be so dumb. He would have sent somebody to get it." He took her by the arm. "Come on, I want to talk to you."

"Are you still talking about that threat?," she wanted to know. As they went into the faculty lounge #3, Tio Valdes was slipping past Sarah Vardis on his way to check his brother, John, first, on the Twenty-second Street gate.

● ● ●

"Report," said Angel. Larry Staples licked his lips.

"Ja-Jack out the no-no-north gate." Angel thought a moment, and looked in his notebook. There was a cement pick-up—

"Was he driving the panel truck?" Larry nodded. "OK," said Angel. "He's gonna be back in twenty minutes."

Larry felt like he should be saluting as Angel moved off, on his way to the auditorium basement. The perspiration was standing out on his forehead, as he passed Angie Vallens, and neither acknowledged the existence on Earth of the other.

● ● ●

As they sat down in the lounge, Cleaire's feet were killing her. It was nice to be listening for a change, but it did seem to her that Tim was talking more for his own benefit than for hers. Sitting hunched down in the arm chair, Tim noticed that the cut phone was now missing altogether, and he could not feel a jolt. Whatever they were doing, they were certainly doing it thoroughly. Cleaire half-listened, wondering if she should mention that Evelyn Raintree would be in any minute with her lunch-box, and would want her seat. Or Jimmy might come in, and pull out his pipe to talk to her and eat with her like he used to.

Jimmy was standing at the window of his now empty classroom, dreading the walk to the lounge, and the walk to the cafeteria. Dreading, in fact, seeing anybody. He went to the open door and pushed it shut, wishing to spend a few more minutes in the empty room. He returned to the window, and looked through the blinds as the girl's P.E. class straggled from the volleyball court, led by their grizzled instructress. He smiled faintly at the baggy gym clothes on the girls, who plodded along as though they were on their way to the firing squad. Narrowing his eyes to see better, Jimmy became aware of his heart as he looked at one of the girls, and imagined her jumping in the air, her ill-fitting shorts moving to a different dance from her boy-slim but budding torso. Each girl glistened slightly from exertion, her hair resisting the efforts of damp hands to push it into place. What did they talk of as they went past the blinds, increasing Jimmy Janis' excitement by being totally unaware that they were being admired? How much better he liked them when they did not know that they were beautiful.

• • •

"Report." Tio was out of breath, and when he opened his mouth nothing came out for a second. "Every gate OK," he said, and Angel just nodded.

• • •

"Cleaire?"

"I'm sorry, Tim. Go on."

"I said that then I had a second visit from Angel, right before nutrition, after he found out about the note Charley Lees gave me. And now Charley is nowhere to be found."

"We all seem to be having difficulty with the Lees. He wasn't in my second period at all. I can't understand it."

"Somehow Angel seems to have the run of the school with those two big buddies of his. Doesn't anyone ask them for hall passes? Of course, they probably have them—"

Cleaire Devereaux had eaten only a little dry toast and coffee for breakfast, and she felt her stomach was about to grumble embarrassingly. It surely would not be rude to take out her lunch, and listen while she was eating. Or would it be? As Tim continued, she eyed the old refrigerator, where her spare diet lunch was wrapped in quilted aluminum foil.

"Angel went to great lengths to tell me that the note from Charles was nothing, but what I can't see is why he would bother if he was going to try to kill me in particular, *only* me."

Cleaire Devereaux' small round potbelly rumbled, as Evelyn Raintree came in, and glared at Tim sitting in her chair. Cleaire raised her voice, as the interior rumbling continued. "Hello, Evelyn. Tim, you're in Evelyn's chair. Come over here." She took him by the hand and they moved to the window seats, where their heads could be closer together. Cleaire tightened her stomach muscles, hoping it would lessen the sound.

"Why would they *want* to harm you," she wanted to know, in a confidential voice. "You're new but everybody likes you. Are you sure that they aren't just playing a little game? These gang kids can think up some pretty terrible games."

"No," Tim shook his head. "It's not a game." Cleaire's stomach snarled, and this time even Tim noticed.

"Good heavens, Cleaire," said Evelyn. "Eat something, for God's sake." Cleaire looked hopefully at Tim, who was mortified by his rudeness to the only one who had even tried to listen.

"Do you mind?" She wanted to know. "Just a little fruit and yoghurt."

"Of course not, Cleaire. I'm sorry." With a strange sense of detachment, Tim watched the sharply colored, artifi-

cially bright woman as she opened the refrigerator and
pulled out a neatly wrapped package of grapes and an apple, with a small container of strawberry yoghurt. There
suddenly seemed nothing more to say as she arranged the
items on her lap. Tim decided he would have to wait for
Marge, who would take less than an hour to get to Ross, unless she got caught in some kind of traffic. He had asked
her to meet him right at the faculty lounge number three.
Every time the door opened to admit a teacher, Tim
thought it might be her.

"Hello." Jimmy Janis had come in quietly, and Cleaire
immediately stopped fussing with her lunch.

"Hello, Jimmy," she said, following him with her eyes as
he went to his secret hiding place in the cupboard for his
pipe tobacco.

"You going to smoke that foul thing?" rasped Evelyn
Raintree, without looking up from her book.

"You bet, old dear," he said amiably, coming over to
the window with a faint smile. He addressed Cleaire. "I
just bumped into Roger—" Tim could not help interrupting him.

"Jim, would you mind listening to a crazy story for a few
minutes? It won't take long, and maybe you can make
something of it." Nervously, Tim looked at his watch, as
Jimmy studied Cleaire, her hopeful, impossibly bright
face, and thought of those damp girls in their ill-fitting
gym shorts. He smiled at them both. "Sure, Tim. After a
morning with those kids, I'm ready to hear anything." He
saw the expression on Tim's face, and laughed like a short
burst of machine gun fire. "Just kidding you, Tim. Come

on down to the cafeteria. Cleaire, why don't you bring, um, whatever that is and have a glass of milk with us."

"I have to wait here for someone," said Tim. There was a silence, which embarrassed them all.

"Well, Roger and Dave went on ahead, and they're waiting for me. I'd be glad to listen, though."

"It's all right, never mind."

"You coming?"

"No, I'll have to wait—" Tim glanced at his watch, which said quarter past noon. What had happened to Marge?

"Suit yourself, Tim. Coming, Cleaire?"

"Oh, I just hate to take my lunch down there—it's such a slap in the face of the dietitian, but I swear, I can't—" Even as she was talking, she was gathering her lunch.

As Jimmy and Cleaire walked out the door together, Tim caught a glimpse of Jesus-Maria Ortiz in the hall, and supposed that the boy was watching him. Jesus-Maria was one of Tim's best students, and if he could talk to him, perhaps—

On the chance that it might do some good, he went to the door and found the boy gone. He took a deep breath, figuring he had been wrong on that one. Perhaps he was wrong on all counts. Then he looked toward the principal's office, and saw Jesus-Maria jump back as the door opened suddenly. He froze in place by the water fountain as the substitute secretary came out, too closely followed by Mr. Conrad. She seemed to be avoiding him as he tried to talk to her, and they were both much too preoccupied as they headed for the stairs to pay attention to Jesus-Maria.

Almost before Tim realized what was happening, the boy had sauntered into the office and closed the door, so casually that no one in the hall had given him a second's notice. Theoretically, Miss Twigg was supposed to be in Miss Peter's office, but on a hunch Tim decided to make sure.

He was walking faster than usual as he headed for the office door. Ismael looked at him curiously. As a Reporter with nothing at the moment to report, Ismael decided to check out.

A moment later when Tim opened the door, sure enough the secretary's desk was unoccupied. The same could not be said for Jesus-Maria, who had cut all three phones in a matter of seconds. How could he be so quick, Tim marvelled, as they looked at each other with equal surprise. For a moment the boy's expression clouded with fear, and then he remembered what Angel had told him the last time he was nearly caught. Just play it cool, and before they can do anything, it will be Zero Hour.

"Hello, Mr. Nielsen," he said, the wirecutters dangling loose over his knee. There was no point in trying to hide them.

"Come with me," said Tim, feeling that this would do it. Surely, the wirecutters, and the brazenness . . . "We're going to see Mr. Conrad." The boy shrugged and gave up the wire-cutters as Tim took him by the shoulder and propelled him through the doors, and into the hall. Ismael watched without expression, following a little behind as the teacher moved his captive at double-time. Several students stopped eating to watch.

It was not too late. As Tim came down the back steps of

the administration building, holding Jesus-Maria firmly even though he was not struggling, he saw the principal. Mr. Conrad was standing forlornly near the parking lot where the substitute secretary had gotten into her car and closed the door. It was only a moment before her car started, snorting up a cloud of dust from her misdirected exhaust.

"Mr. Conrad," Tim called, still holding the boy by the shoulder. Ismael stood near the wall of the lunch yard.

● ● ●

Marge had managed to get onto Western Avenue before the car started to cough. She looked at her gas gauge, and it read half-empty, so she could not understand it as the car jerked several times, and then rolled to a stop in the middle of the street. One rude lady honked, but most of the drivers behind her simply signalled, and waited for a light to go around her. For a full minute Marge waited for some gentleman to offer her a push to the gas station that was less than half a block away.

No one did offer help, but a policeman was there five minutes later with the information that she was blocking traffic and would have to get off to the side of the street.

"I'd love to," Marge said sweetly, "but the car's a little heavy for me by myself."

The policeman walked around the car, while she turned the ignition and received a slight whining noise for her pains. Any chance she might have had to get a push ended as the motorcycle officer came full circle and asked to see her driver's license. At least that was good, she thought, as she reached for her purse, only to discover that she had left it at school in her locker.

• • •

To say that the principal was unpleasantly surprised to be loudly addressed would be an understatement, but when he saw who it was that had interrupted his scene with Miss Goetz he felt as though his entire throat had turned to lye. Several hundred yards away students were sitting in the lunch yard, eating and studying the scene, wondering what had happened to Jesus-Maria Ortiz. Mr. Conrad had only one thing on his mind, and that was how to put the best possible light on the substitute secretary's sudden departure, feigning a mysterious malady.

"What is it, Nelson?" said the principal, looking at Jesus-Maria distrustfully. He recognized the boy who had reported the Bart Arthur mishap to Miss Peters and the nurse, and the repercussions of that were not over yet, not by a long shot. Tim glared at the boy, who remembered what Angel had told him. He was not worried.

"Tell him, Jesus-Maria." Silence. Tim turned to Mr. Conrad, holding up the wire-cutters right under his nose. The principal looked as though he had never seen such things in his life. "He cut the lines to the telephones in your office and the front office, sir, with these, right after you and the young lady left. Miss Twigg was not at her desk." Tim left the words in the air as a reproach. Mr. Conrad did not care for the intonation of *you and the young lady* either. He studied the boy, who, despite his painful position and the tightness of the young teacher's grip, was preserving a studiously blank expression.

"Is that true?" he asked. For a moment the boy did not answer, but as Tim tightened his grip even more he nodded. The principal looked grim, but not at the truth of the accusation. He should have locked the door to the office as he left, since Miss Twigg had been sent away for the lunch hour. Normally he would have, but the tense conversation with Miss Goetz, which had ended as a farrago of deals and counteroffers, accusations and threats, had unnerved him. He turned to Tim with a frown.

"You know, of course, that you should have taken him at once to Mr. Sousa. I am involved in an emergent situation with an ill substitute, Mr. Nelson, and we are understaffed and all of us at the end of the week are overtired. It is the only explanation for your increasingly bizarre behavior. You might have read in the Faculty Handbook—if you have read the Faculty Handbook—that teachers do not physically handle students." A grin crossed the boy's face, and Mr. Conrad turned on him quickly. "You are to report to Mr. Sousa's office and wait for him, do you understand?" Jesus-Maria nodded, amazed and delighted. "You are in serious trouble, son," the principal continued, "and no more trouble from you will be tolerated. All right, you can go." There was a moment of hesitation. "Release him, Mr. Nelson. And bring the wire-cutters with you to Mr. Sousa's office for a conference, after school."

Shocked, Tim loosened his grip, and Jesus-Maria ambled away in the general direction of the administration building, his head held high with the awareness that the others were watching him from the lunch yard.

"Mr. Conrad." Tim tried to keep his outrage and humiliation from making him mute. "Your phone is cut, so are your secretaries' phones, and the public phone in the first floor booth, and the only one I've checked in the faculty rooms. I would bet that there is not a single operative phone in the—"

"Report the matter to Miss Twigg before your sixth period, Mr. Nelson, and don't forget the conference after school." Mr. Conrad looked at Tim, knowing that he should not have spoken so harshly in front of a student. He tried to soften his tone. "There isn't much time—it's nearly twelve-thirty. But I haven't eaten yet. Perhaps you'd like to have lunch with me, as I suggested earlier, so that we can get back onto the right foot, so to speak. I was afraid you were going to suggest that the boy's vicious vandalism was not just taking advantage of Miss Peter's unfortunate bereavement and the resultant disorder, but a part of some great conspiracy to get *you!* You weren't going to suggest that, were you, Nelson?"

"My name is Nielsen, sir." Tim swallowed furiously. "I'm waiting for my fiancee—"

"We'll have that lunch some other time then," said Conrad. "Don't lose those wire-cutters, son. They're city property."

Before Tim could say anything, he was gone.

● ● ●

Angel was sitting in the meeting room with Rico when the door swung open and Ismael came in, out of breath from running up the three flights of stairs three at a time. Angel looked at him, his heart suddenly in his throat.

"Report?"

"Mr. Nielsen catch Jesus-Maria with the cutters, in Rat's

office. He took him to Rat, out near the cars." Angel thought a moment, as Ismael remembered something else. "Also the new secretary went out the gate."

"Lucky girl," said Angel, frowning, deep in thought. "What Rat doin' outside?" According to his calculations— Hm.

"Beats me, Angel."

The three of them reacted as Gil Lieber came in.

"Report?"

"Margadonna let out a yell while Craner was taking his turn guarding. One of Old Jack's guys nearly caught us in the head. It would've been up." Gil licked his lips.

Angel considered this, but Rico got slowly to his feet.

"They still in the head?" Lieber nodded. Rico addressed Angel. "Be back in ten minutes. It won't take no longer than that."

Angel knew better than to say anything, except "Go ahead, Rico. Ten minutes." He looked at his watch. Thirty-five minutes to Zero.

"I left the new dude standin' there," said Ismael, faintly worried. "You think he'd cut out?" Angel shrugged.

"I don't know, man. He ain't supposed to leave the grounds."

"What if he do anyhow?" Angel knew the answer to that.

"We go ahead. He can't prove nothing."

"What about Jesus-Maria? He got caught with the cutters."

Angel shook his head. "If Nielsen gets out and blows this because of Jesus-Maria, I feel sorry for him." Angel reached for a cigarette, opened his book of matches and found it empty. He studied the cigarette, and tossed it on the floor. Tio, who was waiting for his next assignment, retrieved it and straightened it out for himself. Angel turned to Ismael. "Check out Coop and the blood-sponges, and get back fast."

Ismael nodded, wondering if something was up between Angel and Rico. They did not seem tight like they usually were, but putting it down to nerves, he went out the door.

"Come on, Gil, move around," said Angel tautly. "You supposed to be reporting." With Rico gone to the auditorium, he suddenly did not feel easy.

• • •

Police brutality, Marge was thinking as she accepted the citation for driving without a license, but she put on the meekest possible face, and thanked the officer profusely. He could have ticketed her as well for no registration, technically, although she was only three weeks late. Only the goodness of his heart prevented him from doing so. She thanked him separately for that, thinking all the while that power was an ugly thing in a mediocre man, such as this policeman. He had not cracked a smile as he searched for violations, to the point of asking her to try her brake lights. She tried to explain that she was in a hurry, but that just seemed to put him in an even uglier mood.

The topper was that one of the brake lights must have just burned out. With trepidation, she demonstrated her high and low beams for him, and although he said nothing she sensed they were probably cross-eyed, or worse.

"Well, Miss," he informed her, "you could be ticketed for no evidence of registration, driving without a license, right brake light not working, and double parking for starters. You have fourteen days to answer this complaint, and bring your license with you when you go to court." His tone clearly implied, if you have one.

"Thank you again, officer," said Marge, wondering what Tim must be thinking. He must be climbing the walls, poor lamb. "Do you think you could help me get this rattletrap up to the gas station?" she asked sweetly. "I'd like to make a call and have somebody look at the motor."

"If you have Auto Club they'll tow you."

She took a deep breath.

"I do have Auto Club, but it's in my purse and if I had my purse I wouldn't have this ticket."

He was unperturbed. "You'd have it for one of the other violations, Miss. Do you want me to call a tow truck?"

"Yes," said Marge, although she had no money or identification, or anything. The next problem was that she did not have a dime to call the school. Marge the panhandler, she said to herself, that's me. As soon as the officer had roared off, after calling for a tow truck, she positioned herself on the sidewalk, in front of a lovely little cabaret called BEER. Someday she and Tim would laugh about all this.

FIFTEEN

Maria Estragon sat quietly on a circular cement bench in the lunch yard, under the only tree on the grounds, a blowsy Chinese elm that was toppling in front like a pregnant woman. She had made up her mind several times already today, changed her mind, and changed it again. After two semesters of never sitting by herself, it was a funny feeling to be alone, making up her mind about Mr. Nielsen one last time by pulling leaves, hard little plasticky leaves, off of a branch that had scratched her face when she had accidentally walked into it. Her mind had been on preserving the distance between her and her former friends, rather than on where she was walking. And so she had gotten scratched, and serve her right. Maria LeSanto had laughed. Owl had sneered right back.

Nobody in the lunch yard was eating much, except for Lizard, who had discovered to his hand-clapping delight that he could get anything he wanted by merely pointing. I want *that* apple, he got a small spotted apple. *That* peanut butter sandwich. It was his. Nobody was hungry, nobody was talking much. Certain boys, always the same, seemed to be all over the place, watching first this one, and

312

then that. Maria Estragon knew that she had to be very careful, but she had learned to be patient. She came in at the part where the principal was walking away from Mr. Nielsen, although loud-mouthed Jennifer Baily was quick to fill her in on what had happened before with Jesus-Maria. Some kids, including Jennifer, thank goodness, had taken it in their heads to run all the way around and cut through the building to ask Jesus-Maria what the two men had said to each other. Big deal.

Now she was watching Mr. Nielsen, and waiting for the exact second to approach. She knew his contact was Ismael, and he had taken off at a great rate and was nowhere to be seen. Soon as Mr. Nielsen gave up and came back to the administration building she would drop her paper bag for Lizard to find, and go right up to him. But she had to be patient. Mr. Nielsen could stand there a long time, it was easy to see, thinking about something a long time. Maria opened her paper bag and studied her jelly sandwich she made herself. She took very small bites, just to kill time, as she kept an eye out for wandering Gatemen.

She was humming the same song at that moment as was Clark Cooper, humming and taking small bites of her sandwich to kill time. That man certainly could stand a long time without moving.

The Gate Men ready?
Ready. Checked off.
Observers all ready?
Observers ready. Checked off.
Weapons in hall?
Weapons in hall. Checked off.

Telephones cut?
Telephones cut. Checked off.
Bell Man Ready?
Bell man ready. Checked off.
Time check?
Five minutes to one o'clock.

In the arsenal, squatting in front of two huge piles of pocketknives and switchblades, Clark Cooper was humming cheerfully to himself, repeating his tedious job with all the rhythm of a dance and the joy in repetition of a church rite, again and again and again. The knives, delivered by the Turner boys, had the fingerprints of every kid at Betsy Ross, so Clark was handling them like precious jewels, his long black hands turned a funny purple by the skintight stretch of surgeon's gloves that he was wearing. The Turners watched, fascinated, as Clark went faster to show off a little. Open the knife, wipe both sides of the blade on a blood-dampened sponge, close the blade carefully, without disturbing the fingerprints, drop the knife on the finished pile, pick up another, and start again. Over and over.

The whole operation took only ten seconds, to be repeated more than four hundred times. Clark kept humming, his blurred black hands keeping time with the expertise of a woman knitting. He smiled, knowing he would be through in plenty of time to distribute the knives for Zero.

"*Ouch,*" he said, as he looked up and nicked himself.

"Somebody comin'," said Bill Turner, his eyes wide.

Clark Cooper regained the rhythm of his movements

as Ismael poked his head in, and watched for a moment.

"Report?"

"A-OK, baby."

"A little extra blood won't hurt none," said Clark Cooper, his teeth flashing like the blades of the knives.

● ● ●

Tim looked at his watch, and saw that the bell for sixth period would be ringing any minute. Even if Marge came he would have no time to speak to her. Furthermore, he did not have any idea how he could make her understand what he was feeling. Marge would say to him, you control your own destiny; things only happen to you that you allow to happen, if you are a man. You master your environment, you modify it to conform to a symbolic idea that you have formed in a unique and nearly infinitely powerful intellect. Etcetera. Etcetera. Etcetra. It was true, he was sure it was. Why then did he feel so thoroughly mastered?

"Mr. Nielsen?"

He turned to see Maria Estragon, looking over her shoulder as she held something in a grey hanky. "I just wanted to give you a present, Mr. Nielsen. Here."

Swiftly, she pressed the hanky and its solid contents into his hand, with a quick look around to see if anyone was watching. Tim started to look inside, but Maria nearly had a fit. "Put it away," she whispered. "Put it away."

Tim could feel it was a pocketknife, as he slipped it into his pocket, and pulled out the dirty square of cloth.

"Could I have that?" she asked. "It's my only one."

Hastily, disguising his distaste at its appearance, Tim returned the hanky, which the girl promptly stuffed down the front of her print dress with a huge sigh of relief.

"Maria, why did you give that to me?" She looked at him scoldingly.

"Lotta good it did to call you."

"It was you, then." Tim followed her nervous look around the yard. The bell rang, and with a last look at the auto gate Tim abandoned Marge for the moment, and concentrated on the girl. "Can't you get into trouble for this, Maria?" She stared at him. "With Angel?" It was a guess, but her look and shrug told him it was the right one.

"Don't worry, your contact went to class already, I think. Nobody saw."

"My contact," said Tim, faintly understanding. Maria nodded, with great dignity.

"You shouldn't have no chance. I still like you and I'm sorry what I said before. I gotta go. I got three tardies already with Mr. Melnick. I sorta like him too but I only got one knife." They started for the administration building, and Maria's expression changed suddenly. "Oh-oh, there's your contact." She was looking at Ismael, who was standing by the stair way. "Goodbye, Mr. Nielsen. I hope I made it up to you." Ismael saw he had been spotted, and made no effort to turn away.

"Goodbye, Maria." Tim watched her run off, legs and elbows flying, a jiggling, cavorting hop and skip that covered the distance surprisingly fast. She raced Lizard up the stairs, but he quit halfway, holding his stomach. Tim was late, but he kept his stride measured as he approached Ismael. His wallet was pressing the knife against his hip so that he was aware of it with every step. It was uncomfort-

able, but he did not dare reach down to adjust it as he got
to the stairs.

"Hello, Mr. Nielsen." The yard was empty now, as
Ismael stood and looked up at him. He seemed to be wait-
ing for some particular move from Tim. "Hello, Ismael.
Aren't you coming to class?" The boy grinned.

"Sure, but you ain't there yourself."

"Walk with me then." Tim was stabbingly aware for a
moment of how doll-like the boy really was, beardless,
saffron pale, with big black eyes the color and shape of wet
water melon seeds. His hair was absolutely straight, as
glossy as lacquer. It took so long for these children to become individuals, he told himself. At that moment he felt
that he knew Ismael, and had really looked at him, for the
first time as they walked together, not talking, up the
stairs.

Thank you, Maria, Tim was thinking, as he listened to
classroom doors being shut all up and down the corridor.
He might need that present.

Across the yard at the gym, the door opened to the boy's
locker room, and Contreras poked his head out to check
the Gate Men. They were at their posts as all over the
school the calling of roll began, and window blinds were
being adjusted to the new angle of the sun.

• • •

Tim walked into class, and everything seemed normal.
Ismael walked in front of him, past the Great Architect
display, to take his seat beside a preoccupied, unsmiling
Provencia Perez. The writing on the board was still there
from the previous class, a correctly parsed French sentence

in Miss Del Valle's large, elaborate script. Tim had no briefcase with him, no papers at all, which stirred some momentary unease. It seemed to him that there was much antsy shifting in seats by everyone except the one boy he was most interested in observing. Angel was staring straight ahead, as Tim indicated the writing on the board to Maria Valdes. She looked blank. "Erase the board, please, Maria," he said. She nodded and got oh-so-painfully to her feet, with a sidelong glance at her brother.

Sitting in his usual seat was Angel, still brooding over what Rico had said to him about Louis Margadonna. *Well man*, Rico had said, just before the tardy bell, *I guess Zero hour here. I just took care of Louis.* Tim saw that Angel was surrounded by his tightest buddies, who ranged around him like a magic circle. There was Jesus Contreras, who looked seventeen, with a duskiness on his long upper lip that was threatening to become a mustache; Ismael Sato, his own contact, with a disarming smile that never left his face unless he was surprised. Ismael directed his immediate grin at the nervous exchanges between John Valdes and Maria, who was erasing the board, with painful slowness. Directly to Angel's right was Rico Moreno, compact, self-contained to an unnatural degree. Usually he was as tightly strung as a violin, but today for some reason he was relaxed, almost slumped, oblivious to the attention that Tim was clearly focusing on Angel and his boys.

Behind Tim, Maria Valdes was making ever slower swooping shapes with the chalk-imbedded eraser. She was now smearing the words more than she was obliterating them, and every few seconds she paused to look at the teacher.

"There will be no roll call," said Tim, leaning on the front of the desk as casually as he was able. "It's clear that you are all here." He paused, and then dropped the bomb. "Angel, please stand up." It was the first time he had ever asked a student to do that.

There was an electrifying moment, when it seemed that Angel might not obey. His eyes, broken from their thoughts of Rico, held Tim's through several anxious beats of the teacher's heart. Then, as though he were going to stretch, Angel stood up, and shifted his weight so he could lean comfortably against his desk. He admired Tim for having the nerve to give him a command, after all he had surmised. He admired style.

Looking over at the window, Angel estimated that it would take five more minutes for all the entrances to the school to be sealed off, and the doors to the buildings themselves closed and locked. Another minute for the Gate Men to get to their home rooms, and another minute for Tio to relay the message to Jesus-Maria, the Bell Man. Seven minutes in all.

"Angel, today is going to be a very special class."

"Yes, sir," said Angel, without irony. It was Tim's turn to admire the boy's coolness.

"We're not going to talk about ceramics, or the history of pots, or anything at all like that. We're going to talk about something else." He watched Angel shift his weight to the other foot, as effortlessly as a thoroughbred changing leads into the stretch. The yard outside the window seemed ominously quiet, and occupied the boy's attention so that he was only half listening to what Tim was saying. Rico was paying better attention, thinking that there was something new in Mr. Nielsen's eye and even voice; whatever it was just might make him hard to kill.

"As a matter of fact, Angel, I don't want to do much talking today at all. I want you to talk, and it might as well be about what you really think. Maria, stop erasing now and go to your seat." Maria put the eraser down, and a puff of chalk dust bounced into the still air, where it hung for a long time before settling. Wiping her hands distractedly on her dress, she was unsuccessful in catching her brother's eye. He was now watching Angel and the teacher with fascination. "Angel, you know Provencia Perez, don't you?" Angel glanced at Provencia without interest. What was Nielsen getting at, he wondered, sneaking a quick look at his watch. He had an urge to shake it.

"Yeah, I know her."

"What do you think of her, Angel?" Angel snorted, and then he laughed. In the respectful hush, his laughter seemed especially loud. Tim persisted, talking as he walked to the window, adjusted the venetian blinds, and looked out.

"What do you think Provencia will be when she grows up?"

Angel thought a moment, and shrugged. "Cleaning woman."

"Why?" Tim looked over towards the parking gate, and saw with a jolt of shock that two boys were calmly looping chains around the metal poles. He tried not to reveal on his face what he was seeing. "Why did you say that, Angel?"

"Because her old lady is."

Click! went the oversized spring lock, securing the

chain. The two boys moved out of Tim's line of sight, on their way to the north gate. They seemed unhurried. Several passersby walked within twenty yards of them without noticing what they were doing. A car stopped across the street at the hamburger stand, and for a moment it looked like Marge's Pontiac.

Turning back to the class, Tim saw that Provencia Perez had lowered her head onto the desk, and was crying silently. She had always done good for Mr. Nielsen. Why was he doing this to her? Tim felt sorry, but he had to continue, or lose Angel. He pressed harder.

"And yet Provencia could do something else, don't you think, Angel. Something more interesting?"

Angel shrugged, a little embarrassed by the girl's tears. "What did you think of the sculpture that Provencia did, the one we put in the display case last week? Angel?"

"It was all right, I guess." Angel looked toward the window. If everything was timing right, the Gatemen who had been at Elm Street Gate at ten minutes past one were now finished and had started their walk to sixth period class, easy, calm, normal walks.

"But Angel, don't you think if Provencia gets a chance to study, she might be able to get a better job than her mother when she gets out of school?" This was too much for Angel.

"Yeah, man, I think the Owl's gonna be an artist." He glanced at his watch. *Six minutes to go.*

● ● ●

In the principal's office, Mr. Conrad was dictating thank you letters to the various educational dignitaries that had attended the Human Relations Conference at the Ambassador Hotel. Miss Twigg was valiantly trying to keep up with him, but her shorthand was rusty and she was afraid to tell him. She was not sure what had happened that the substitute should have taken so suddenly and violently ill, but from Mr. Conrad's vile mood she thought she could guess.

Next door Jesus-Maria Ortiz was standing with as much patience as his character would allow beside the cabinet that contained the mechanisms for the school bells. The locked door had been jimmied, and he had fooled around with it enough without the current on to feel confident he could make Zero as noisy as the inside of a rollerskating rink. He had completely forgotten the note in his pocket from Mr. Sousa, that his father would have to sign before he could come back to school. He was engrossed with the last of his assigned tasks, and the easiest. He was ready to set off the bell, immediately upon word from Angel, or, in case of Angel's death, Rico.

As Mr. Conrad tried to think of a new turn of phrase for the same tedious paragraph, he stood at the window in his characteristic Napoleon at Elba pose. Miss Twigg's pencil poised over the shorthand pad, but Miss Twigg herself was relieved by the momentary mental block of the principal. He turned away from the window as Jack's panel truck pulled up at the closed gate, and discharged a grumbling, gaseous, stomach-rumbling hung-over Jack, who immediately knew when he saw the chain and lock that none of his keys were made for it. Instead of waiting around to puzzle it through, he got back in the truck and nearly backed into a Pacific Telephone repair truck. Something had just started to make sense.

● ● ●

The perspiration was standing on Tim's upper lip now like miniature blisters, as he tried to keep the pressure on. Angel started to sit down. He wanted to turn away.

"Ask somebody else—" he started to say, but Tim's sudden angry "No!" brought him back to his feet, and made Rico's head snap up from its nodding.

"Keep standing, Angel. I want your comments on what the others say. You are the leader, aren't you?" There was a suggestion of a smile on Angel's face as he realized that the teacher had cleverly arranged it so he had to stay on his feet, answering questions. What did he hope to do? Stall forever?

"I am leader," Angel admitted, with a sidelong glance at Rico. But Rico was thinking of Angie, dimly wondering what would happen to them after this was over. He was not sure who had changed, Angie or himself. The teacher had just asked Willis Zardas what he wanted out of life. Willis looked at Angel, as much as to say, is it all right to answer? There was the slightest shrug from Angel, so Willis said, "I want to be a doctor."

"Angel?"

"I guess he can be a doctor. There's black doctors."

"Will he be able to, Angel, after today?" Tim was trying to look out the window, but it was hard to turn his back on Angel. There were footsteps in the hallway; a Gate man, probably, getting to class late, carrying his pre-stamped pass. He went past the Bell Man, past the principal's office, past the water fountain. Then too faint to hear. The Weapons Committee was coming up the stairs from the arsenal, carrying the blood-knives. Five minutes, no, four. Tim had begun to speak a little faster, as he saw Angel checking the time again.

"Provencia wants to be an art teacher, Maria wants to be a nurse, Willis wants to be a doctor; I guess if we asked any-body what they wanted to be, there would be something, wouldn't there?"

Angel smiled, and nodded. "I guess you right, Mr. Niel-sen. A lot of people wants things, but not too many gets 'em."

"What about you, Angel?" I don't have to want to be anything, Angel was thinking; I already am. Being is bet-ter than wanting.

"Or you, Rico?" Rico looked up from his revery, and frowned. Tim saw that he had not heard the question, and turned immediately to Angel again. Something he had said was right, because for the first time Tim saw that Angel was shaken.

"What, man?" said Rico, shaking his head to clear it. "What?" What time was it? It must be practically time.

"Tell me what you want, Angel," Tim repeated desper-ately. He was not sure, but he thought he heard a siren. Was it an ambulance? Had someone discovered the locked gates? He went to the window and looked out, as Angel looked blankly straight ahead. The gate was still locked, but nobody was paying any attention. They walked by. Tim wanted to scream out to them, but he was sure if he did he would be as ignored as the mute locks, or the poor

Chinese elm in the lunch yard. There were never any birds in that elm, he had noticed, on lunch-yard duty. What kind of tree would hurt or insult or bore them so that they could not stand to rest on one of its branches for even a moment?

Tim turned away from the window suddenly, to a room of utter silence. "What do you want, Angel?"

It was as though he had made an offer. Angel returned his look evenly, and shook his head.

"All right then, what do you expect to get?"

"Better, Mr. Nielsen. That's all. Just better." He looked at his watch, and wondered where Tio was. It was time to finish it, to ring the bell—but no, they were slightly late. Until Tio got there, it meant the Turners had not finished locking all the doors. Until the entrances were locked, the Executions could not begin.

"It's sad for anybody to lose the chance to be as big as he can be, but it's especially sad for you, Angel."

Angel forced himself to meet Mr. Nielsen's look, without dropping his eyes. This was what it meant to be leader, to be expected to know what you could be, as well as what you were. He could feel Rico's eyes on him, and he wanted to shout to him, I'm going to give it to you, all of this. Don't love me, Rico! I'm not really better than you. But he would shout nothing. He stood firm.

"You're good, Angel," said Tim, moving from the window to a position only a few feet away from him. "You set the whole thing up yourself, didn't you?" There was a murmur of surprise from several girls as Tim moved still closer to Angel, very much aware of the extra weight in his back pocket caused by Maria's knife.

"Back off, man," said Angel softly. "You're getting too close." But the teacher did not move. He was listening for something outside, and for a moment Angel caught himself listening, too. At that exact instant the Turner brothers had sent a perspiring Tio up the stairs to tell Angel that everything was ready.

"Call it off, Angel." Tim was so close that only those closest to where Angel was standing could hear. "It's not too late now to call it off, and you'll still have proved that you could have done it *if you wanted*." Angel said nothing, as Rico turned in his seat, and was facing him. "They'll all lose something if you go ahead, but you are the one who will lose the most." Angel shook his head, refusing to accept what the teacher was suggesting. He forced himself to remember that he was giving up the leadership to Rico, and he would have nothing to lose that he cared about at all. If he knew anything, he knew that you had to care about something to lose it.

"You know all about it, man," said Angel, his voice weighted with sarcasm that was missed by everyone in the room except Tim. There was an immediate murmur of fear, and then a babble of voices. "It's time." "What's happening?" "I hear somebody in the hall . . ." John Valdes rushed to the window as an ambulance shrieked by on the nearby freeway.

• • •

There was more than the usual confusion in Miss Devereaux' class, as the gangly, nervous-fingered Negro boy unfolded unexpectedly to his full height and said "I heard it!" in an unnaturally high, thin voice.

"What are you doing, Mr. Cooper?" said the teacher with great sharpness once she caught her breath. "I heard it," Coop said again, in the nature of a general pronouncement. He tried to look very sure, but the ambulance wail was fading now to nothing, and someone said "Hell, no," and "That ain't it," and even "Sheeeyit!" before Miss Devereaux could get her bearings. She signalled the recovery of her voice by saying, *"Please,"* but anything she was about to add was buried in an avalanche of garbled comment, "It was the ice-cream man." "An ambulance, man." "It wasn't nothin'!" "You're hearin' things, man." "Yes!" "No." "Yes!"

"Shut up!" said Miss Devereaux, at the top of her lungs, and for an astonished instant, the room was quiet. The more composed took the opportunity to listen closely for sounds of riot in the other rooms, and to Clark Cooper's disgust, there was nothing. "What is the meaning of this outburst?" she went on, trying to control the shaking in her voice. "Mr. Cooper, you seem to have been suddenly taken with an idea. Perhaps you'd like to write it out on the board for all of us. Mr. Cooper?"

The boy was still standing, and looked at the teacher with perfect poise. "That was the bell, Miss Devereaux," he insisted. He signalled Bill Turner to grab her. Instead Bill crossed his arms and frowned in disgust.

"No it ain't, man. Jesus! You deaf?"

• • •

A handful of boys had left their seats, forming a pattern behind Angel within easy striking distance of Tim. Maria Valdes turned her face away and began to cry painfully, to her brother's intense annoyance. John Valdes noticed Angel's signal for them all to sit down, but he hesitated. Neither the teacher nor Rico had moved, until Angel said, "What are you guys doing? *Sit down*." A few obeyed, but the majority hovered suspiciously behind Angel, glaring at the teacher as though he were some dangerous new creature. Charley Lees was the first to speak, in an anxious whisper.

"Hey, man, what d'y mean, he knows all about it?"

"Why ain't he told?" Juan Laurindo wanted to know.

"Could be he did, man," said Willis Zardis ironically. "Could be he told and they just waitin' for us to start up. Just waitin'."

"He spill his guts and nobody buying," insisted Rico, with a wink at Angel, "Ain't that so?" but there was still another muttering. A second, then a third girl started crying. Then a general uproar.

"Shut up all of you," said Angel, having to raise his voice. There was a silence, but it was plainly conditional. Tim turned away and went back to his desk, feeling an elated hope that he had broken them up. When he turned around again, half the class was out of its seat, with Charley Lees at the window. Tim decided not to give Angel any help by adding the weight of his own authority, whatever might be left.

"There's nobody out there, Angel," said Charley.

"I haven't given the signal," said Angel harshly. "Don't forget I'm the one who says go ahead. As for the teacher, he knows but he don't know. And nobody'll believe him anyway."

Tim made no move to confirm or deny what Angel said.

"Hey, man, maybe somebody started already, without the bell." Johnny Valdes considered a new problem, and turned his furrowed brow to Angel. "What happens if they started?"

Angel brushed the question away with an "It's OK now." It *has* started, he was thinking. It started when Rico took care of Bart Arthur, and then Louis Margadonna. Angel looked at Rico, and knew that they were both thinking the same thing. If he had to say why he could not call it off now, he would say, simply, it was too late. There was a sound of running footsteps outside the door, and then Tio Valdes poked his head in.

"Doors locked," he gasped to Angel, who nodded. Johnny Valdes looked in the hall, and saw that the blood-knives were outside each door, right on time.

"Weapons ready," he said to Angel.

"Don't give any signal, Angel," said Tim, "unless you want to end the futures of every student in the school."

Tio looked at Angel expectantly, impatient for the go-ahead. Tim was backing slowly to the blackboard, aware of the shape and weight of the knife in his own pocket.

"I'm gonna tell you something, Mr. Nielsen," said Angel, moving across the front row of seats to the window. He reached up and pushed the warped wood shut with a fierce effort that took all his weight and strength. When the other windows were closed, the street noises were muffled. "You're not a bad head, so I don't want you to think it's anything personal. It's your tough luck that you came in just now. I'm sorry." Angel looked thoughtful. "Chances are you'd've been just like the others pretty quick though. Tio, signal the Bell Man." The boy nodded

eagerly, avoiding his sister's reddened eyes. As the door
closed behind him, and the sound of his running feet faded
to nothing, Contreras was at the lock and turning it with a
heavy final click.

• • •

The bell had rung.

As bells rang in Big Ben, muffled wooden Easter egg
bells in Olvera Street, temple bells at Angelus and church
bells two blocks away, as telephone bells in the station
house rang, an accompaniment to complaint, nasal, so-
prano, and gruff, of nameless fears and those named all-too-
easily, of shakes and shakedowns, lechery and theft so signalled, station bells, as the tall tower bells of church answered the trilling school bells everywhere, the switch-
boards, oven bells, and wind-chimes at the jade merchant
answering the fire clang, and the dinner bell the salesman's
rings and the beggar's bell, the calls from surveys, the ding
of secretaries' million carriages, in the carillon of office
buildings, as the bell rings by the ear in sleep, announcing
death or need, inheritance, warning or deliverance, so did
the single unexpected change bell of Betsy Ross bewilder,
warn, dampen and whet.

In his office Mr. Conrad looked at his expensive watch,
saw that it said thirteen past one, and assumed that it was
wrong. He shook it and listened, but could not hear it tick
because of the bell. The endless bell. As it continued to
ring, long past reason, Cleaire Devereaux was looking at
Clark Cooper in disbelief as he stalked her. It was her
nightmare come true, that she would scream for help and

everyone would come, not to help but to add gleefully to the hurt, that the biggest boys in class would grab her hard and throw her hard like a straw-stuffed scarecrow against the hard blackboard, the bruising slate, just as bruisecolored Clark Cooper now was reaching out to grab her arm with his delicate, mother-of-pearl palms. Of course it could not happen, but it happened anyway, as Cleaire tried desperately to wrench away and call out. "Elena, Carmen" —what a ludicrous warble was her voice—"Run for help. Run!" The girls look elsewhere, embarrassed, just as in the nightmares, as Cleaire Devereaux screamed and jerked her head away from the pink and black hand that was reaching for her hair. She felt a blood vessel explode agonizingly in her neck. The pain blossomed wildly in all directions from that fractured, focussed pinprick of blood, just as she had her final shout in mind her mouth snapped shut in midcry, and her left ear caught on the edge of her wig.

Civil Defense drill? Air raid? World War III? William Conrad called for Miss Twigg, and dropped his glasses immediately in front of his own foot. He cursed as he stepped on the frames at almost the same place in time, stumbling awkwardly on the way to the office where he found Miss Twigg listening in stupefaction to a blank phone with an equally blank face.

"Sir," she started to say, but in a fury William Conrad pushed past, "sir, the phones are—"

"I know about the phones, Miss Twigg. Why aren't they fixed?" The classroom door were opening as he went into the hall. To his right the office door was ajar, and he saw a slight boy standing proudly by the open bell box. Mr.

Sousa, sneezing from allergy, came out of his office with a
puzzled expression on his gentle face and was immediately
felled with the brass nozzle of a fire extinguisher, in mid-
sneeze by a boy larger than himself. Opened! The principal's mind returned to the bell box, vandalized, wide
open, as indeed were all the doors that he could see from
his vantage point in the corner. Students were pouring out
of the rooms, fleeing as though from natural disaster, most
panicky, some cool, some clinging together for companion-
ship, a few crying and sobbing. What was it? What could it
become? Mr. Conrad felt like screaming a questionnaire at
them as they rushed past. He fumbled with his emergency
pair of glasses, and cried into a wind: What disaster? What
was driving all of them into the halls in shock?

Upstairs, he could hear the second floor in the same con-
dition, therefore general, not localized, and called upon
himself to take the proper steps, and assured himself he
would. The whole building had begun to tremble. Whatever had taken place, he must prove up to the responsibility. He was where he was for just those rare occasions when
a gentleman like him was—He spun around, arms out for
balance, and landed back where he started, with a rush
coming toward him. He would get them lined up—where
were the trained, experienced teachers?—and march them
shaken but whole out of the trembling building before all
was disaster. He found his voice, and used his elbows to
keep from being spun around again like a weathervane.
Rasping, no longer drawling but full of fresh, unexpected
strength, William Conrad started bawling for the stragglers to get lined up. And then he noticed the boy's vice-
principal lying by the vandalized extinguisher, blood

streaming from a mouth that never uttered the mildest of oaths for fear of dying out of grace with an exacting God.

With a wild yelp, Clark Cooper held it up. His own scream was so shattering that Cleaire could only gape in surprised silence. She peered into that screaming, wet, pink mouth only inches from her face with a sort of dreamy amazement—the cords in his throat were throbbing, swollen, long and black, his particolored mouth's breath astonishingly sweet—The room itself began to crawl as she looked up like an El Greco through the kaleidoscopic blur of her own tears and saw her precious wig, shaking like a half-dead but crazy animal at the end of its spear. "Awww Haw!" said Clark Cooper, like a cowboy.

The bell continued, but the noise in the halls was more than competition now, and the ringing had become a background, a funerary keening for the not yet dead. What was the matter with them? The crazed imbeciles would not line up as the principal rushed past, looking for leaders. They watched him half in fear, and half in anticipation.

"Mr. Conrad." A changing voice pierced louder than the rest, for it addressed him directly. The principal peered doubtfully around for several moments, then saw a thin rashy boy who was unknown to him. It was Harold Craner, the blood beating wildly in his throat as he walked toward the principal, holding in one hand the unrepudiated badge of his office, in the other the knife that had been carefully wiped clean of blood by Rico, and presented to Harold. Rico had handed him that knife, after pulling it out of the body of Louis Margadonna, who moments before had been making periodic feeble struggles in Harold's arms trying to escape. Margadonna's body was still lying like a pagan sacrifice across the urinal of the auditorium Boy's Room, his choirboy eyes looking in dull wonder, a single nearly invisible stab wound just below the heart. And Harold had been there to watch it.

Now, Executioner Craner's voice cracked once, cleanly, and dropped in register as he addressed his puzzled victim. All of a sudden, his voice had changed. "Mr. Conrad, sir, get in your office at once. I am your executioner. If you don't follow my orders, you will be dispatched here in the hall."

Dispatch? The dull eyes of Lizard watched the thin boy with the blade and wondered when someone would give him his own knife. He knew that they were killing the teachers, but he did not recall why. He wanted at the Surfers. Like a flatfaced reptile Lizard watched the principal puff up, and blow.

"Put that away at once and report to the vice-principal's office. What is your name?" He looked around, and saw a familiar face. "Staples, grab him."

Larry Staples was pale, but he did not move. It had gone too far. He could neither stop it, nor participate. As he looked at the outraged principal's face, he thought of another kind of outrage in the face of Bart Arthur. Nothing had happened to the ones who killed Bart. Perhaps they would get away with this as well. Many seemed to know what they wanted to do, even more knew what they wanted to see. The remainder, like himself, were immobile. They watched Harold Craner, one of the quietest boys in the school, knowing what he wanted to do.

"Staples?" The principal's voice was less confident.

Larry tried to say he was sorry, but nothing would come out at all. There was so much yelling and running that he had trouble knowing where the sound was coming from. He looked around for a place to hide, and remembered the maintenance supply closet on the second floor.

"Hell, man, everybody high on something. Look at them pigeons. They high on blood." The girls were huddling together, some, like Jennifer Baily, thrilled by what was happening, others hysterical with terror they had been suppressing for weeks, or months. Maria LeSanto had taken the opportunity to pull Juan Laurindo out of the stampede of kids and into the empty homemaking classroom. At the last minute he had backed out, and not forced Charley Lees to take Mr. Watson. Now he felt in danger as Maria put his hand on her breast, and tried not to breathe out too much in case her breath was not good. Juan was thinking of what he had done in the gym, running away in disgrace. He was too panicky to get excited over Maria. Still, he did not dare go back in the hall, for fear of meeting one of the other Generals. He tried to kiss her, but all he could think of was somebody coming through the door to get him.

Two boys, both stocky, one with a faint mustache over eternally puckered lips, the other younger and more anxious, started simultaneously after a girl who was leaning against a wall, holding her blouse together where the buttons had been ripped off. She was listening warily to the sounds of boys fighting around the corner, and then she saw the two fat boys coming at her. She could not think of any place to run where there would not be somebody waiting.

Tim was riveted to the floor, his back against the black-board. He had heard the bell, and known at once what it meant. The sudden rush of students in the hall, the sound of doors cracking like rifle shots, the shrill cries, and the beginning of the evacuation of his own home room, with too many trying to get out at once. Apparently his was not a popular execution. The thought gave a grim if brief satisfaction. He looked at Angel.

Next door in the supplies closet, a couple was feverishly making love through their clothing until the door opened and Larry Staples peered in. They stopped a moment, looked at him, and then went on. Without bothering to close the door, Larry stumbled away down the hall, avoid-ing the others who were also looking for a place to hide. Contreras came around the corner, after finishing the evacuation of Nielsen's room. He was on his way to see if anyone needed help with the faculty rooms, or the B-7s. He saw Larry and held up his black handkerchief with a superb white smile. His boys were performing beautifully.

"Man," he croaked, hoarse from shouting, "This the greatest ever. I dunno why I was scared. Fuck'm all!"

Larry Staples tried to nod with enthusiasm and failed. Luckily, Contreras was much too busy to notice.

Angel shook his head without looking at Tim. He was sorry for any teacher who came in for less than a month and got killed for his trouble, but there was no way to stop it now.

"Anybody left alive and we all dead, Mr. Nielsen," said Angel, motioning for Rico to keep his knife ready. Rico was Angel's support, and although he had come near killing a couple of guys in gang fights, he had never had to know the person, and like him a little, and do it anyway. It would be a good test of the idea of the common good, he thought, because he was trading this one teacher for a lot of lives. There was a certain distasteful fascination for Angel in the idea of killing someone, but he knew he would not like it. He was not like Rico.

"You could make some of them stop," said Tim, wondering why Angel had not already tried to kill him. He saw that there was something in the boy that abhorred action, even when he knew it was inevitable. He was an intellectualizer. He liked to turn a thing every which way, and know what it was made of, even if he was going to smash it. Tim decided to give him something to turn over in himself, and perhaps he could keep from getting smashed.

Tim kept a nervous eye on Rico as he got up from his desk, as though he were awakening from a light sleep that had not refreshed him. There was the sweatiness of bad dreams on the knife that Rico turned over in his palm, a different knife from the one he had used on Margadonna.

There was a terrific racket everywhere now, and Angel knew that if the cops were not already on their way, they soon would be. There was noise everywhere, great shouts from various parts of the hall, and it seemed to Angel that most of the teachers were probably lying in their own simple blood, in a pool of noise and mounting wildness. Angel wished he could be in several places at once, watching what was happening when people thought they were getting away with murder. Tim looked at Angel without rancor.

"You're going to fail, Angel," said Tim. "Will it make a

difference to you, or is this all just an experiment?"

"Fail, man? It sound like a failure?" Angel was listening to the noises now, which had become riotous. Windows were being broken, he could hear a systematic splintering, and decided that someone had thought to grab the fire axe.

"It's a failure for you, Angel, if you don't succeed in killing me. And you might not. The Nielsens have a strong sense of self-preservation."

Tim felt the knife in his pocket, trying to position it higher. He was not pleading consciously, but he knew he had to get Angel to accept the inevitability of the police coming with his emotions, and not just with his brain. Then he might hesitate, and save himself.

"We ain't gonna fail, man." Angel had suddenly stopped listening to the rampage, as Ismael came skidding through the door, face flushed, and saw that the teacher was very much alive. Angel told him to close the door and lock it like it was supposed to be. Ismael looked from Angel to Rico, uncertainly. Then he locked the door, as Angel seemed to come out of a daydream, shaking off his secret thoughts like a dog might shake off water after a swim. Rico moved a step closer.

"No failures," said Angel, talking dangerously from his heart now. "I'll tell you why. Every dude in this place got his prints all over a bloody knife. Every one will swear to God he didn't do nothing. What you big deals gonna do? Electrocute us? Shoot us?" The last words were spoken with a degree of passion that made Tim distinctly uneasy.

"Hey, Angel." It was Rico, starting to sweat. "Let's go, man. You gonna do it?" Ismael looked at Rico, the only one he knew for sure had put a knife into anybody. He had come to tell Angel that things were going wrong with the other executions. They had a bunch of teachers trapped in corners, and somebody said they saw Old Jack's car parked outside the closed gate, empty—Ismael had a lot of things to tell Angel, if he wanted to listen.

Tim kept the corner of his eye on Rico, who was standing closer now, his own knife in instant readiness. Angel still was unarmed, reluctant to open the handkerchief and add his own fingerprints to the ones on the knife handle. The weapons were clear on the other side of the room from Angel, near the door.

"Go on, Angel," said Rico, "Get your knife. I'll cover him from here. You gotta do it, Angel."

Tim edged slightly away from Rico, who was shining from a sweat that seemed to bother his eyes. He kept shaking his head backwards, as though to clear a nonexistent forelock from in front of his face. The knife in his hand was being held so tight that Tim could see the fingers lose color at the edges.

"Go on!" said Rico. "Get a knife." There was the loud sound of something large being dragged along the hall outside.

"Even if you kill everybody, Angel," Tim said, softly, trying to keep him rooted. "Even so they'll find out who the leader was. It'll be obvious. And no matter what, they'll send more teachers, and school will start again, just like it was before."

"Not just like," said Angel passionately. "We ain't bloods, Mr. Nielsen. They got their gig and we got ours. You know that hospital in Watts that's going up? You guys voted against it, baby, even though you scared. It going up just because the bloods are gonna start killing some nice white folks if they don't get theirs. And the bloods got it better than we do."

"Angel!" Ismael's voice was anguished as there came a definite sound of activity outside. He went to the window, as the second floor hall grew briefly quiet, and then came the crash of broken glass. Somebody outside called up, "We got a bonfire."

"Angel, get a knife." Rico moved into a position near Tim where he could hit him with a single fast stroke. There was another loud crash as a window was kicked out and the glass hit the blacktop below. In the basement at that moment Jesus-Maria was patiently tending a bonfire, throwing the student body log on, and watching it start to curl at the edges. All the notebooks, papers, the dossiers on the teachers were burning, along with a few articles of clothing, books, and a red wig that was charring and prickling until it resembled a scorched hedgehog. Angel had entrusted Jesus-Maria with his own black notebook, and as he heard the fire siren, he was just about to throw it on the fire.

Tim glanced nervously at Rico, who had offered his own knife to Angel. "Take it, man. You the Executioner! *Take it!*"

"No." Angel backed off. "I was gonna give it to you anyway afterward. I might as well do it now. You the leader, Rico."

Rico looked stunned. The knife was still in his hand, being offered handle first to Angel. He shook his head.

"Angel, you wanta tell me to kill him? You want to

make me Executioner again? I'll kill him for you, man."
For an instant he turned his eyes on Tim. "I'll cut him to
ribbons, Angel, for you. *Tell* me!"

Angel had lost all the color in his face as he looked at
Rico's reaction to what he had offered.

"Jesus, Angel, there's cops at the gate." Ismael looked as
though he couldn't believe his eyes. "They sawing the
chains."

Tim thought of the knife in his pocket, wondering if he
would be able to get to it fast enough. He was not sure how
it worked. The look on Rico's face was the most tragic he
had even seen, and he was sure the boy would do anything
to try to return to his former relationship with Angel.

"Angel! There's cops and firemen! All the teachers ain't
dead!" Ismael left the window, but Angel would not even
hear him. Angel tried to explain.

"I can't do it, man. I can tell how, I can make the Plan,
but I can't really do it. I was gonna let you be leader after,
Rico, I really was."

Tim felt the knife press against him as he leaned against
the blackboard. While Rico and Angel were not looking,
he got his hand into his pocket, and brought out a long,
curved switchblade. He could feel the button on the side
with his thumb, and caressed the button gently, behind his
back.

Rico was shaking his head in disbelief.

"Rico, I'm sorry," said Angel. "I'll still be leader if you
want. Nobody'll know I gave it to you and you didn't want
it."

Rico's eyes blazed. "I did want it, man. But I wanted to
take it."

There were sirens all around the school now, as Rico brushed past Ismael to look out the window. The gate was open, and two more squad cars had pulled up. A bonfire was burning in the lunch yard, but nobody was tending it. Rico watched the flaming debris start to scatter, as some of it caught up against the cement around the Chinese elm. He turned to Angel with a strange, glittering look. His voice was hoarse, almost amused.

"All right, leader. What do we do?"

At the door Ismael unlocked it and slipped out as Angel looked at Tim for a moment, considered something, and smiled bitterly. "Nothin'. We wait and see what happens."

"You crazy, man? Margadonna's dead. I don't know how many teachers—" He turned his dazed look on Tim. "I don't know if any of 'em are dead. The only ones I know about are the ones I killed myself."

"We can't do nothin', Rico."

Suddenly the bell stopped ringing, leaving its shadow in the air and making the sound of riot louder even though it had diminished. After a couple of taps the public address system came on, just as Ismael raced out the door, leaving Angel and Rico with the teacher. A man's loud voice broke through in the middle of a word, "—ention, attention, everyone. Do not move. Stay where you are and you will be safe. Do not try to leave the building. We will be entering, fully armed. I repeat—"

Angel looked at Tim, a slight smile crossing his long, dark-honey face. He looked vindicated, and even a little relieved, but Rico was looking at the window as though he might consider trying to jump. Angel addressed Tim.

"You win. I guess they gonna shoot us after all."

Tim did not know what to say, and then he saw Rico staggering toward him, his knife ready to thrust.

"Nobody killed but me!" Rico said, moving toward Tim bitterly. "You the only teacher who know, and I'm gonna get you. And Angel, he the Executioner, so he gonna get the blame." With a look of desperation Rico lunged at Tim, who stepped back easily, putting the desk between them.

The knife stabbed forward, but Rico cut air, inches from Tim's face. As Rico got ready to attack again, Angel stepped in front of him. "Don't, Rico, they're in the building now. Listen, there's nobody doin' nothing. Nobody can prove nothing against you."

Rico would not take his eyes off Tim. "But he knows."

He lunged again, forcing Angel to step back. This time Tim lost his balance and nearly fell against the first row of drafting tables. A stack of drawings started riffling like cards, slipping from the table to the floor in front of Rico's feet. He kicked at them. "Get out of the way, man," he said to Angel, "or I'll take you, too."

"Rico, we didn't lose. They can't do nothin' to us."

"You did it!" said Rico, to Angel, allowing Tim to move to a safer position behind a desk. A quick glance out the window told him the building was surrounded now.

"You said we was gonna kill them all. All of them!"

"Rico—"

"You gave me Angie, and then you made me do things that made her hate me. Why'd you give me Leader, Angel? So you could make me the pigeon for a bunch of stabbings while you walked off?"

"Rico, I didn't—" said Angel, but he was very pale, and a new thought had come to him.

"Get out of the way, man."

"No."

Tim watched fascinated as the two boys started circling each other, Angel unarmed, but Rico with a knife that he held not in offering but in supplication. Angel might have been able to reach one of the weapons on the desk in the corner, Tim realized, but he made no move to do it.

Rico was concentrating on Angel now, trying to keep the image from getting fuzzy so he could slash at it. Angel realized that Rico's moves were slow from the way he lunged at Mr. Nielsen, and he had decided to keep away until the cops came. There were heavier sounds of running in the hall now, and a few loud grown-up voices shouting something that he could not understand. All of a sudden the door was pushed open and Jimmy Janis stepped in. There was a cut on his cheek, and his jacket sleeve was slashed elbow to wrist, but he had an exhilarated, intense look that changed to sudden caution as he saw Rico with the knife, and assumed that Angel had a knife as well.

You all right, Tim?" he said, but before Tim could answer Rico had made another lunge, and barely missed Angel's throat. Jimmy stepped forward cautiously, but Rico was too far away to grab. Noticing nothing now but Angel, his face distorted with a suffering that made him wish to die at the same time as he was fighting to live, Rico whispered, like a litany, "Come closer, Angel, come closer—"

Then he stopped. He had worked Angel into a corner, and had only to keep Angel in focus to step in, and push the blade into his unprotected chest. Just before he lunged, he was distracted by Tim's cry, "Here! Angel!"

A thin black object made an arc toward Angel, who looked toward it with surprise. He reached out to grab it, but it missed his fingers and clattered to the floor, releasing the blade with a snap. Angel crouched, ready to make a grab for it, when Rico screamed and drove blindly forward, bowling Angel toward Tim. His knife was straight out in front, like a lance.

"Nielsen!" Janis jumped forward as the two boys collided, and both fell momentarily to their knees.

"Angel, pick up the knife," said Tim. The boy reached for the knife as he tried to grapple Rico sideways to the ground. Rico was the stronger, and Angel could not force him down, even though he tried. With a last effort he got his hand on the knife. Then he seemed to freeze.

Tim watched in horror as Rico's hand broke free and lifted his own blade, just above Angel's heart. Janis stepped forward to aim a kick at the glitter of blade, but missed.

Tim watched in speechless horror as Rico struck Angel right through the ribs, so deep that try as he might he could not pull out the blade to strike again. A policeman came through the door, gun drawn, before Tim could move forward to pull the now immobilized boy off Angel. It took a second policeman to pry them apart, so tight was Angel's grip. Rico made no resistance as his arms were whipped up behind his back and he was slammed face first against the wall to be searched.

"There's an ambulance outside," one of the officers said to his partner. "Get the stretcher for the other kid."

Grabbing Rico by his wrists and holding them behind him the younger policeman pushed him out the door while Tim tried very gingerly to get Angel's shirt open so he could see the wound. His own heart was pounding harder now than it had when he had been in danger, for he thought that perhaps he had not been in danger at all. Angel had not moved, and his eyes were closed, but when he moved slightly there was a groan.

"Don't move, Angel," said Tim, holding the boy's hand away from the protruding knife handle.

"So . . . you . . . had . . . a knife," Angel whispered, as Janis signalled to Tim that he was going to see how Cleaire was. Tim nodded, as several more sirens were heard out in the school yard, sliding to stops on the blacktop as close to the administration building as they could get.

"Get the stretcher," Tim started to say, but Janis was gone.

"I even . . . thought . . . about letting . . . you go, Mr. Nielsen," said Angel. "That was . . . mistake. I should . . . have . . . killed you." Tim waited, thinking the boy was going to say something else, but although his lips stayed open, and his eyes looked at Tim, he never moved again while he was alive. Tim watched the ambulance attendants as they wrapped him up. They jostled him a good deal as they took him downstairs, past the shocked teachers, five of whom were injured. Only two stiffs, said one of the policemen as he surveyed the wreckage. He proclaimed that pretty good, considering.

Tim went to the hamburger stand to make a call to Marge's place to see what had happened to her. He felt totally defeated. In the hysterical melange of sensation, color, sound and terror that had been his natural environment for the past hour, he tried to think of anything he had managed. All he could think of was Angel's evaluation of him—*after a while you would be like all the rest*—and his final judgment. *I should have killed you.* He ignored the lady outside the telephone booth who was looking at her watch and muttering.

Tim tried to think what that would have changed, as he let the phone ring.